I0563816

Hollow Pointe

By Adam Cornell

Jade, Hudson & Steele Publishing
Watertown, New York

All characters appearing in this work are fictitious. Any resemblance to real persons, living or dead is purely coincidental and not intended by the author.

No portion of this publication may be reproduced, stored in a retrieval system, or transmitted in any form or by any means, mechanical, electronic, photocopying, recording, or otherwise without written permission of the publisher. For information regarding permission, write to Jade, Hudson & Steele Publishing, Attention: Permissions Dept. 218 Flower Ave E, Suite 4, Watertown, NY 13601

ISBN: 978-0-9853165-8-7

Copyright © 2016 by Adam Cornell

All rights reserved.
Published by Jade, Hudson and Steele Publishing

Book layout and design by Adam Cornell

For Belinda.
It wouldn't be possible without you.

Hollow Pointe

By Adam Cornell

Jade, Hudson & Steele Publishing
Watertown, New York

Dread and the hollow and the trap are upon you, you inhabitant of the land. And it must occur that anyone fleeing from the sound of the dreaded thing will fall into the hollow, and anyone coming up from inside the hollow will be caught in the trap. For the very floodgates on high will actually be opened, and the foundations of the land will rock.

- Isaiah 1:17-18

NWT Reference

Prologue • Autumn 1947

He hurt all over. The doctors had never been able to dig out some of the bullets that were lodged in his body. His left leg throbbed most of the time. He had trouble sleeping. Walking for any distance brought out sweat on his brow from the pain. Even sitting in his favorite wooden swivel chair, the one he'd found so comfortable for so many years, now made his back ache after just a short time. For a few weeks, during the summer, the dull aches would let up, but summer didn't last very long in Coopers Hollow, New York. Even if it had been a rough number of years, and even if those years were taking their toll on him, he couldn't let something like pain stop him from doing his job. He was the chief of police, after all.

He began his personal war with the mob almost a decade and a half earlier. The particular faction of organized crime, that he crossed, did not care that he had just been trying to protect his friend, Isaac Jacobson. Mafia bosses didn't see things the way other people might. They didn't look at the situation from all sides, didn't weigh the justice of it. There was only their side. They saw things in terms of what was theirs and what was taken from them, and therefore, what was owed to them. They had long memories about debts. Especially when it concerned the killing of one of their favorite trigger men.

In the fall of 1934 a lone gunman shot at him while he sat in his patrol car, sipping his coffee. It was in front of the hardware store on the corner of Main and Railroad. Two bullets struck him in his side, one destroyed his plaid Thermos bottle. He was able to return fire, shooting the mob thug dead in the middle of the street. He was stuck recovering in the hospital for five weeks, after undergoing emergency surgery to remove the bullets. And he had to buy a new Thermos bottle. That made him a little angry.

In 1935 it was an all out war. Four mobsters were sent to Coopers Hollow to put an end to him for good. They caught him in his office, which, at that time, was in a shared building with the fire department. It had been a quiet morning, until he heard the commotion of the volunteer firemen raising protest over mobsters storming into the station, with guns drawn. Two fireman, husbands and fathers, both of them, lost their lives for their bravery. Two others were seriously injured and took months to recover.

Chief McIntyre was a deadeye shot, and put down two of the bad guys before he had to reload his .38 revolver. The other two thugs took the better part of an hour to fight it out with him. They lost, he won. It was a bloody battle. Messy. The fire station looked like Swiss cheese and he ended up with six bullet wounds of varying detriment. Three were just grazes, the others somehow managed to miss anything vital, but still spilled his blood all over the concrete truck bays and his office, as he called for help. He was in the hospital for three months that time, nearly dying of pneumonia during his recovery. He was fortunate to have a very skilled surgeon from New York City offer his services to dig out the bullets and somehow stitch him back together. The doctor just happened to own a vacation home in Coopers Hollow, and just happened to be visiting when the shooting happened.

Then it was quiet for half a decade. He hoped that it meant the grudge against him had burned down and extinguished. There were other pressing issues facing Coopers Hollow during that time. The small town lost many tourist-related businesses, due to a shift in habits of people from the big city. Fewer individuals rode the train up from New York City for their summer vacations. Instead, they drove their new family automobiles all across the country. Everyone wanted to see Niagara Falls or the Thousand Islands. Coopers Hollow was no longer so exotic a destination, even if it was still a lush mountainous region with pleasant summertime weather. There were still vacationers, of course. Still some seasonal farm workers who rode the trains up from New York City during apple picking season or strawberry season. But it wasn't like it used to be. The numbers of visitors dwindled each year.

The Lexmore Hotel wasn't the same since Jacobson had been killed. His poor widow tried to keep it running, but she needed help to make the repairs that were necessary each year. It was too much for her, by herself. She never really stopped grieving, so she never really had the will to work hard and make the place a success. Each year, more and more was left undone, and it slowly lost its luster. McIntyre tried to help where he could, but he had his own house and family to look after. Plus, it was growing more difficult for him to get around, with all the lead that had passed through his body.

Money in the town was simply drying up, as well. Farms were shutting down. The banks were foreclosing on families. It wasn't just Coopers Hollow, the whole country had it tough. They weren't calling it the Great Depression for nothing. The Catskill communities were taking a beating and McIntyre didn't know if they'd ever recover.

Before it had gotten this bad, there were happier times. In 1934, six months after he was first shot and lost his Thermos bottle, he'd married Ellen Brobach, a local farmer's daughter. She bought him a new Thermos as a wedding gift. She was a hard worker and pretty enough for his tastes, but a bit daft at times. She was forgetful and clumsy. But she was also loving and supportive.

Their first child arrived the following year. McIntyre was in the hospital recovering from the firehouse shootout when his son was born. They'd named him Thomas James McIntyre, but the kids in town took to calling him TJ by the time he'd started school. He was a weak child, he didn't have his father's size or countenance. He was constantly sick. His nose was always running, and he would stay home from school as much as he could. His mother would always dote on him when he was sick. McIntyre believed he was faking it half the time, just for the attention.

Chief McIntyre tried to teach TJ how to be a man in the only way he knew how, in the same way his own father had taught him.

Hunting and fishing, building things around the house, working on the car; whatever he could think of to try to shape TJ into a man. It was an uphill struggle. TJ was disinterested in most of it, and downright contrarian for the rest. McIntyre would try to wrestle with him, but TJ would always get hurt, or feign injury, and go crying to his mother. It made the chief fume, on more than one occasion.

McIntyre was a disciplinarian as well. If the boy didn't do well in his classes, he'd get the belt. If he got report that he and his friends were dragging sticks along the fences in town, he'd use the belt on him. He'd left big red welts across the boy's backside dozens of times. It was how you grew a boy into a man.

McIntyre took the boy deer hunting on opening day, when TJ had turned eight years old. His mother had forbidden it prior. For weeks, the chief and his son had gone target practicing to get ready for the season. He felt like maybe he was growing up a bit. Maybe all his work would pay off.

They bundled up on opening day, with shotguns and sandwiches and the Thermos bottle full of coffee. They only had to drive a few miles out of town to get to a spot that McIntyre had scoped out.

There was frost on the ground, and they could see their breath as the morning sun peeked over the horizon. TJ tried to keep up with his father, but he was much smaller. Finally they settled into their spot and waited. It didn't take long.

A four point buck came wandering out from the trees, to the edge of the field. They were maybe thirty yards away, behind a big fallen oak tree on the adjacent edge of the field. TJ had his gun raised and aimed at the deer. He stared down the barrel at it. He put his finger on the trigger, but he didn't pull it. He just stayed there, motionless. McIntyre took the shot with his own gun before it got away. It meant venison for the winter, and bragging rights at the bar. As he began to field dress the felled deer, TJ began to cry. Great, heaving sobs. Finally, he sent TJ to the car.

After dragging the carcass back to the vehicle and draping it over the fender, they drove home. TJ didn't say a word for nearly two days, and refused to eat any of the venison all winter. He never told his father he'd wet himself as he tried to pull the trigger. McIntyre knew, though, he just hadn't said anything. He was too ashamed of his boy.

Three weeks after the deer incident, the mob came calling, once again. Chief McIntyre was struck by a bullet in the back and left for dead. They couldn't remove it this time, as it was too close to his spine. It functionally destroyed one of his kidneys. Every once in awhile, especially after he'd been sitting for too long, he would lose all sensation in his left leg, from hip to toes.

It was the fact that the leg had gone numb and had no strength in it, which left him unable to leap clear of a speeding 1939 Ford, eighteen months later. It didn't help that the '39 Ford was aiming for him, with another mobster behind the wheel. He put a bullet in the driver's head, and then tried to move himself to safety before being struck. He'd been standing behind his patrol car, just off the curb, in front of the station house. His leg betrayed him. It didn't work when he needed it to. For that, it was crushed between the bumpers of the colliding vehicles. This injury landed him in the hospital again. He was laid up for two months with a huge cast on his leg. Just about everybody in town came to sign it. His son refused.

He walked with a cane for five months as he built the strength back in the leg. With the surgery and the cast, it had atrophied, and would never be strong again. He was getting too old and he'd put his body through too much. He was a stubborn man, though. After the five months of recovery, he threw the cane away. Even if the knee locked up on him every now and again, he wasn't going to hobble about with a cane, he was the chief of police. He couldn't show weakness.

When the violence in the small town finally subsided, around the time of the Second World War, it was due to the federal government cracking down on organized crime. Revenge on a small town cop in the northern Catskill Mountains no longer merited attention, not when there were federal agents sniffing around, closer to home. There were bigger fish to fry.

In all, Chief James McIntyre put seven mobsters in the ground. Legend persisted that he was responsible for another half dozen, but according to his count, it was seven. Watching seven men die by his own hand was plenty. He was tired of the killing.

1944 began with joy for the McIntyres, even as the rest of the world was still embroiled in war. Their second child, a baby girl they named Elizabeth Jane, came into the world in January of that year. She was a healthy and happy baby, and James and his wife Ellen were pleased, even if TJ was upset that it wasn't a baby brother. It was a brutal year for the war, Coopers Hollow lost two of its sons on the European front.

Despite the war, there was a general sense of contentment, if not happiness in the McIntyre home. It had been two years since there had been an attempt on the Chief's life, the war was nearing an end, and baby Lizzie was an absolute joy.

Then, in autumn of 1946, it came crashing down. Elizabeth fell down the steps descending from the second floor of the house. She never woke up after the fall. It took two days before she died. Two horrific days of praying by her bedside, of holding out hope for a miracle. It broke their hearts.

TJ claimed to have seen the accident, and he said that one of their cats had tripped his little sister as she started down the steps. TJ said it just ran under her feet and she just fell and fell. James and Ellen McIntyre mourned their loss, and TJ became even more sullen. Chief McIntyre couldn't stand to look at the cat anymore, so a week after his daughter's funeral, he took the cat into the woods and shot it. TJ asked him several times about what had happened to it, but he never told him the truth. The boy wouldn't have been able to take it.

By the time they were burying their daughter in Coopers Hollow Cemetery, most of the boys who had gone off to war had returned home. Some came back to families they'd left behind, others didn't come back at all. They'd poured out their blood on the battlefields of Europe or at sea in the Pacific, their parents or wives received their medals and triangularly folded flags in return.

With the soldiers coming home, Chief McIntyre was forced to deal with a new problem. Some of the returning boys had young wives, and many of the children that they'd fathered before they left were now school aged. The rigors of war and the stresses of family life led some of the former soldiers to the bottle. The bottle led them to violence. All too often, that violence was aimed at wife and child.

Paul "Buck" Everett had served in Europe. He'd rushed up the beaches on the first wave of attacks to recapture France from the Nazis. When he came home, he liked to brag to the boys in the tavern about how many Nazis he'd killed, and how he'd done it. The more he drank, the more graphic he'd become. He once beat a man who'd called him a liar. It took five men to pull Buck off the guy. McIntyre threw him in jail for the night and let him sober up. Nothing more came of it. He was a war hero, after all.

He didn't just get into barroom brawls, though. He'd drink at home as well. He'd shoot his gun off at night, making a nuisance of himself. He'd also smack his wife, Maggie. She would come over and cry with Ellen, from time to time, in the McIntyre's kitchen. She'd bring her son, Billy, and he'd play with TJ, while the women would talk softly in the other room.

Billy didn't escape the cruelty of Buck. He'd have black eyes and bruises on his arms on a regular basis. Like McIntyre's own son, Billy was a soft spoken, more tender-hearted boy, even if he did exhibit his father's mean streak every now and again. Chief McIntyre had seen that meanness for himself.

He once caught the boy drowning kittens in the brook. It was a common way to get rid of a litter in those days, but Billy was handling the task with his father's cruelty. He would hold the struggling kitten underwater and then bring it back up, letting it gasp and choke for air. The screeching and mewing of the cats was awful, but Billy was taking glee from it all. He'd dunk, hold under water and then pull them out. Then he'd repeat the plunge for longer and longer periods until the kitten was finally drowned. Chief McIntyre just happened to be walking across town and over the bridge that crossed the creek, when he caught sight of what the boy was doing. He put a stop to it and then retrieved his .22 pistol to finish off the three remaining kittens. McIntyre didn't like cats, but there were humane ways to deal with them. He promised not to tell Buck about the episode and sent Billy on home. He knew the boy would have been beaten to within an inch of his life.

Though Billy was three years older than TJ, they were the only friends each other had. When Maggie came to talk, she'd bring along Billy. The boys would go off into the woods and play until dark. Billy would say they couldn't talk at school, because TJ was so much younger. But after school, and all summer long, they were best friends. As they grew older, they both became more secretive in their games and adventures.

Coopers Hollow had a theater at the time and spy films were all the rage. The theater rarely ran the newest movies, but the boys did get to see Casablanca, when it came out. From that point on, the two boys were French and American spies, dodging Nazis at every corner. They were always carrying on secretly, passing encrypted codes to each other, which only they could decipher and so on. Chief McIntyre thought maybe having a friend who was older would help his boy grow up a bit. He was thankful that at least his son had a friend. Even if he thought the games they played were a bit immature, especially as Billy was older, he just let them be. He had his baby girl and that made him happy. After she was gone, he didn't care much about anything, really. So the boys were constantly off doing who knew what.

The Northern Catskills had a drier than usual year in 1947. It certainly wasn't as bad as the drought of '34, but it was dry enough for the forest rangers to declare a moratorium on open burning in the area and to enlist the help of the local police departments to enforce the no-burn rules.

People still burned their leaves in their backyards, still had fire pits at their cabins but they were instructed not to have campfires without a ring of stones. Protecting the woods meant protecting their homes, so the locals had more than a vested interest in not burning down the forest. It was mostly the visitors and vacationers that worried the rangers. They were from the city and were used to just tossing aside a cigarette butt on the sidewalk. Sidewalks didn't catch fire like dry leaves or pine needles. So, the rangers were kept a keen lookout for any campers cooking without a proper ring. They posted signs around town warning of the danger.

Smokey Bear was declaring on posters: "Remember . . . Only YOU can prevent forest fires." The ad resonated with people, and it very well may have prevented a fire that year in the Catskills.

Though limited, the rangers did what they could with their resources. Those resources included a fire tower and ranger station at the peak of Mount Pratt. Though it was a large area to survey, the fire tower aided in spotting any smoke above the trees for nearly twenty miles in all directions.

In October of 1947, with his leg and back hurting from his old wounds, Chief McIntyre sat in his wooden swivel chair. The clock on the wall ticked away the minutes. The temperatures were dropping outside. There would be a frost. He knew this because his knee told him.

He was due to head home, as the sun was already behind the western horizon. But he resisted the urge to move out of his chair. There was nothing for him at home any longer. His wife was becoming more and more unhinged. Since the loss of Lizzie, it was ten times worse. He looked at his revolver on his desk. He'd just finished cleaning the weapon. It called to him. It was trustworthy, loyal, dependable. He thought about letting it do one last job. He slid one cartridge into the revolver's cylinder, but left it open. One bullet.

He felt a twinge of relief when the phone rang. It might mean he didn't have to head home just yet. It was Timothy Garrison, the forest ranger currently assigned as lookout on the peak of Mount Pratt.

"Hey, Chief. Sorry to bother you," Garrison said. "I spotted a small fire over on Hollow Pointe. Can't leave my post, just me here tonight. Was wondering if you could go have a look-see."

"Are you sure?"

"Yeah, I can see it with my field glasses."

"Okay, I'll drive over and take a look," McIntyre said reluctantly. "You owe me one, Garrison." McIntyre cradled the phone. He slid his notebook from his pocket and scribbled with the small pencil, then slid five more cartridges into the cylinder and rolled it closed. The revolver slid comfortably into his holster, which he snapped secure. He pulled himself to his feet and willed his left leg to unkink and function the way he needed it to. He limped the first few steps towards the door, but by the time he pulled on his fleece-lined patrol jacket, his knee had loosened up enough for him to take the front steps with relative ease.

The way the peaks were situated, Mount Pratt was the tallest of all the surrounding mountains. It stood at roughly 3,200 feet above sea level. It sloped from its peak to the southeast to what was called "the saddle" and then the ridge climbed again to 2,900 feet to Hollow Pointe. The two mountains formed a spectacular backdrop to the small town of Coopers Hollow, and were featured in just about every picture or post card of the town. To the east of the ridge was the rest of the Catskill Mountains. To the west were foothills that didn't measure up to the stature of mountains. Thus Coopers Hollow was known as the western gateway to the Catskills. An oil and gravel road, called Saddle Brook, climbed from the town up to the saddle, where dirt access roads split off to each of the peaks.

Whereas Mount Pratt held a small rangers cabin and a fire tower that could oversee the surrounding terrain in all directions, Hollow Pointe was where many of the locals went for picnics and relaxation. Hollow Pointe caught all of the afternoon sun and provided gorgeous sunset views. Also, it was not nearly as windy as the taller peak of Mount Pratt. A large, bare rock outcropping, just to the east of Hollow Pointe's peak, provided an eighty foot drop to the trees and forest growth below. Many a couple had spoken their nuptials at this rocky protrusion, and several depressed souls had taken their lives by diving off the natural platform. It was alternatively known as "Wedding Rock" or "The Last Step."

Chief McIntyre steered his 1941 Plymouth off the relative smoothness of Saddle Brook Road and onto the bumpy dirt path of Hollow Pointe's access road. The car's springs moaned and squeaked with protest, so he slowed. There was no money for a new patrol car. This one had to last a few more years.

He peered through the darkness ahead, the headlights failing to illuminate anything with distinction, as fog had settled onto the peak. The clouds descended with the cooling of night. The yellow headlights reflected off the fog, making McIntyre slow more and focus on the few feet of dirt path he could see over the bulbous nose of the Plymouth. There were plenty of tire tracks in the dry dirt, as many people had come and gone that day. It had been a warm October day, and the fall foliage was still quite spectacular. Usually by this time of year, a strong rain storm would have already swept in and taken all the leaves down. But this year, pleasant weather had stayed with them longer and the leaves still clung tightly to the trees. It was simply a nice autumn season in the area for that year. Hopefully it meant that a gentle winter was ahead. Tonight, however was going to be colder, maybe below freezing. There would definitely be frost up here on the peak, maybe in the valley as well. The fog would clear up soon, and would settle into the valley. He'd see the stars in the sky, in no time.

At this elevation, McIntyre wondered if he could catch the World Series game on his radio. He turned the silver knob on the dash-mounted radio, tuning in for one of the stations out of Binghamton or Oneonta. He found a station carrying the game, surprised at how clear and crisp the signal came in. It made sense why Garrison didn't want to leave the tower, he was more than likely enjoying the game, himself.

The Yankees were up to bat, and they were putting in a pinch hitter. Yogi Berra stepped to the plate to face Ralph Branca on the mound. The pitch was made and Yogi put it out of the park. Just like that. Crack, homerun! McIntyre made a fist in the air in silent victory. Even though he was from Boston, the Yankees were his team. Heck, they were most of America's team that year.

Through the trees, up ahead, McIntyre made out the flicker of a fire burning, sending out an orange glow in the fog. The road ended in a dusty parking area just large enough for about three cars, with room between the trees to turn around. The parking area gave way to a walking trail that would take him the rest of the way. He put the Plymouth in park, and eased out from behind the wheel. He took his flashlight with him and started through the pines, towards the flames. It took a moment for his legs to get warmed up to the action. He could hear voices near the fire. Giggles. It was probably just a couple of teenagers necking, he thought to himself.

There was a campfire in the clearing near Wedding Rock. He stepped from the shadows of the walking path and stopped short. In the light of the flames he recognized one of the faces. A chill went down his spine as he saw the other face. He felt sick to his stomach. Once his brain registered what his eyes were telling him, he flew into a rage.

He burst forth from the trees and grabbed Billy Everett by the hair, pulling him to his feet. The boy was naked except for his stocking feet. McIntyre reeled back and put the back of his hand across the boy's face, knocking him to the ground. Next he turned to his son, TJ.

"Put your clothes back on and get in the car," he barked at him.

"Dad, we weren't doin' nuthin'. We were just wrestlin' around, like in gym class," TJ said in his defense. He too, only wore his white gym socks. The back talk sent McIntyre into a rage. He slapped his boy to the ground, then rained down open handed slaps on his bare back and buttocks. He connected hard with the slaps, TJ let out a yelp with each blow. Glowing, bright red palm prints formed on TJ's flesh, illuminated by firelight. McIntyre grabbed his boy by the hair and pulled him to his feet. He slapped him across his face, bloodying the boy's nose. TJ cowered on the ground covering his head with his arms, his backside in the air. McIntyre kicked it, hard.

Chief McIntyre turned towards Billy, when suddenly he felt that familiar stabbing pain. He felt the bite of the bullet before he heard the report of the gun shot. It was an instantaneous flash of light from the muzzle and a stab of pain in his chest. Billy held his father's Army service pistol, hands trembling. Smoke was still rolling out of the barrel.

"Billy, no!" TJ cried. Billy didn't listen. He pulled the trigger again and again, each bullet tearing into Chief McIntyre's chest.

The big chief of police stumbled backwards, but remained on his feet. He fumbled for his own revolver, but his hand couldn't manage the snap of the holster. He felt weak, cold and confused. The adrenaline pumping through his body during his raging attack of the boys, now left him thoroughly exhausted. Another shot hit him in the shoulder, knocking him to the ground.

He laid on his back, looking up at the stars peaking out through the fog. He thought they'd come out tonight. His breathing grew more labored with each gasp. The steam from his mouth mingled with the steam from the blood seeping from his chest. It was caught up away from him, illuminated in the light of the campfire. The stars and clouds blurred, and he had a strange vision.

It was as if he was standing over his own body. He could see himself clearly, from above, his shirt bloodied from his wounds. The firelight illuminated his panicked eyes. In his mind he saw it all as a crime scene, but oddly, he was both the victim and the investigator. He was standing above his own body, looking down at himself, sprawled out on the bare sandstone of Hollow Pointe. He was staring into his own lifeless face, taking notes in his little notebook. The orange, dancing firelight, changed, shifted hue, darkened to a sicky-green.

His perspective jumped back and forth. He was the investigator; he was the corpse. He knelt beside his own body; he saw the shadow of the investigator leaning in to look at his face. He opened the dead body's jacket; he felt his wallet sliding out from his jacket pocket. He checked his own identification, it was stained with his own blood. He drew a blanket over the body; the shadow of a blanket was drawn over his head.

"Am I dead?" he sputtered. They were the last words he would ever say.

The boys stood in shock, frozen in place. TJ felt weak in the legs and queasy, like he was going to vomit. He had just witnessed his father getting murdered and his brain couldn't comprehend the scene. Billy was awestruck by it. He'd brought the gun along just in case there was a bear or coyote. He never planned to shoot anyone. He'd brought it to show off to TJ a little, as well. He'd certainly done that.

"What did you do?" TJ cried. He was sobbing. Billy hated it when the younger boy cried.

"I-I didn't mean to."

"Billy, what did you do?" TJ repeated, face wet with tears.

"I didn't do it on purpose. He was going to kill you. I just wanted to scare him!"

"You killed him!"

"Calm down. TJ, we just need to calm down," Billy said. He stepped closer towards the body of the big man, gun hanging loosely at his side. The hot barrel touched his leg and gave him a jump.

TJ finally unfroze from his shock and ran to his father, shaking him, telling him to wake up, that he was sorry.

"Listen, nobody knows it was us. It was just an accident," Billy said, quietly. He was hatching a plan. He was using his spy voice.

"You kept shooting him," TJ wailed.

"I was scared, my finger slipped," Billy countered, himself again.

"But he's dead. You killed him!"

"Nobody else knows that, TJ," Billy said, pleading with his

friend. He wanted to undo it, make it better. But that was impossible now. He was quiet for a moment, he needed to think.

"What would Humphrey Bogart do?" Billy asked, after a moment.

"What?"

"Bogey would have a plan, right? We can have one too," Billy said, hopefully. He wanted to put his arm around his friend, but he didn't want to take another step closer to the body. "Listen, if we take off and take all of our stuff, people will think it was a mobster. They've been trying to kill him for years, right? If we just keep our mouths shut, nobody will ever know."

"I don't know if I can do that," TJ said, still sobbing.

"Here." Billy retrieved a flask from his pile of blankets and handed it to TJ. The whiskey was sharp in TJ's throat, and it warmed his stomach. "Take another drink," Billy ordered.

TJ immediately felt warmer, and started to believe that Billy's plan could really work. Billy put his arm around TJ and gave him a squeeze.

"Like Bogart, in Casablanca?" TJ asked.

"Yeah. We just have to think like him. What would Bogey do if he just shot a guy they'd been trying to kill for a long time?" Billy asked.

"He'd probably push him over the edge," TJ said, indicating the rocky outcropping. The alcohol was working fast on his twelve year old body. He'd had a few drinks already before the shooting, so his head was starting to swim.

"You're right, good idea," Billy said. "You push him over the edge, and I'll sweep up our tracks with a branch. That way nobody will know it was us. Then we'll swear to secrecy, never to tell. Forever."

"I want to get dressed," TJ said.

"No, you'll get blood on them," Billy ordered.

TJ handed the flask back to Billy and slowly stepped over to the body of his father. He didn't hate the man, but he didn't really love him like some boys loved their fathers. He just felt like he never really measured up to the man's standards, to his ideals. Whereas James McIntyre was a larger than life man, TJ was small and thin, taking more after his mother. TJ always felt that he was somehow a disappointment. Especially after Elizabeth died.

The cat hadn't done it. TJ was angry at Elizabeth for taking one of his toy soldiers and chewing off its head. It was his favorite, a general leading the charge. He'd pushed his baby sister expecting her to fall immediately. But she just kept stumbling and stumbling, trying to catch her balance. He watched as she tottered closer to the stairs and then went over the edge, tumbling all the way to the bottom. He could still hear the awful sound in his mind, the way she hit her head on just about every step. How she cried at first, and then went silent.

This was like that time. It wasn't really his fault, it was an accident. And if he kept to the story, no one would blame him.

TJ bent low and put all of his strength into it. The big man was so heavy. Sweat was pouring out of his naked body, and going up as steam, as he struggled to roll his father towards the edge. First onto his stomach, then onto his back again. There was no momentum at all. It was harder than moving all those bales of hay over the summer. He used all of his strength, all of his energy. TJ had the strange thought that if his father could see him now, he might be impressed.

Finally, he got his father's body to the edge of The Last Step. With one final heave, the Chief of Police tumbled off into the blackness. There was a loud impact below, that gave TJ a shiver.

Then it was quiet. Deathly quiet.

Chapter 1 • Present Day

"So what have you got for me?" His cigarette burned down dangerously close to his fingers. He'd been waiting for a long time for his contact to arrive. A face to face. He didn't do many of these anymore. Below his pay grade. A drizzle began to fall from the gray sky, and this dampened his spirits even more. This time of year always made him melancholy. The trees were bare of leaves, the wind was full of chill, and the days were shorter and shorter. Though he was a man who liked to travel in shadows, he hated the gloom of autumn and winter. It didn't help that he was trying to piece together details of an operation that was officially under his control, but had involved just a single operative and a single technician as back up, namely the chubby man who sat next to him on the park bench.

"Well you're not going to like it," the man said. The contact's name was Howard Dimmler and he was middle aged, balding, wore thick glasses and a thick middle, as well as a rumpled trench coat. He looked like an unpolished salesman or a government bureaucrat who had climbed about as high as he was going to climb and was now finding his way back down the ladder. Dimmler wasn't government, however. He was a freelancer who had been useful in the past. If he continued to prove his usefulness, his bank account would continue to grow. As he was the only other individual assigned to this particular project, his usefulness was now in question. His value balanced on a razor's edge.

Dimmler handed him a manila envelope. Within was a tablet computer which contained all of the photographs, reports and dossiers on Operation: Tiger Trap.

"Why am I not going to like it?" He was a man of particulars.

Details. He was excellent at reviewing data and picking out the aberrations, the anomalies, the inconsistencies.

"Well, it's all been blown up. The whole thing. All of the contacts, all the inroads, even the tiger cub himself. Gone," Dimmler said. He brought his fat hands together into a ball and then exploded them out, wiggling his fingers as he brought his hands down. He made an exploding noise with his plump cheeks, just for the right effect. He always found a certain amount of joy in being the bearer of bad news. All these smarty-pants federal investigators with their perfectly orchestrated stings, their iron-clad convictions and their well tailored and pressed suits; they were humans just like everybody else. They had to be brought back to reality every now and again, and Dimmler was more than happy to be the one to do it.

"So it's a total loss, then." He stated. "And our man?"

Dimmler shook his head.

He took another pull on his cigarette. Some called him Mr. Shadow, others called him the Shadow Man. He'd had dozens of names over the years. One of them was actually real. He'd received the moniker of Shadow during his days in East Berlin, spying on the Stasi. It started with a joke. With tensions so high back then, they were always pulling pranks on each other, to lighten the mood. One of the jokesters on his team, thought a little laxative in his drink would be funny. It had caused a reaction, that was for sure. After the his embarrassing episode, they took to calling him *der schatten*, the German word for shadow, but used because of its proximity to the English language vulgarity. The nickname had confused the Stasi and in turn, made him more important to them than he ever really was. He found out later they had obsessed over his identity.

"Wer ist der schatten?!"

Of his team, he was the only one to get out of East Berlin alive. Sometimes one need only survive to be considered valuable.

When he was home, his children called him daddy and his wife called him dear. They didn't understand what daddy dearest did for a living. He infiltrated the organizations of the bad guys. He played by his own rules, and worked outside of the major government agencies. His was a small team, just nine regular players with a few freelancers like Dimmler. They would sometimes spend years infiltrating an organization so as to attain a small snippet of information that would bring down the whole house of cards.

In the 1990s they had all of the information on one Osama Bin Laden. They were close. They knew the players, they knew a plot was in the works. By 2001, they even knew the month. But it was a different time then. The men he reported to didn't take the threats seriously. They were drunk on the profits of their stock portfolios and didn't want to upset the apple cart. When the apple cart exploded, they were quick to point the fingers and allocate the blame. Mr. Shadow simply closed the case and filed his information away. He would never be called in front of a congressional inquiry or have a news microphone shoved in his face. Then again, he wouldn't be assigned to international matters again. They didn't blame him per se, but he got a little black mark next to his name. He had one military general tell him he should have been more forceful with his recommendations. That general had been one of the key people to dismiss the findings of Mr. Shadow and his team. In the general's words, Mr. Shadow was no longer Mr. Fix-It. He was out of the terrorist game for awhile. If he was going to work, it would be at home, in the good old U. S. of A.

Fortunately or unfortunately, depending on your viewpoint, there was plenty of work to be had at home. The war on drugs was faltering. The moral high ground had been lost. The enemy had gained an initial advantage by utilizing the newest technology, which was readily available in the form of hand-held devices or internet connectivity. The NSA played catchup by harvesting as much as it could, without spilling the beans that it was doing it at all. The bad guys weren't oblivious. Some were quite savvy. Some had been trained by the United States government to be that way and had just opted to use their skills to enrich themselves, rather than Uncle Sam. This meant there was still a call for good old-fashioned investigation and even some undercover work.

Mr. Shadow had several members of his team currently working undercover. Deep undercover. They were cleared to cooperate with and or participate in any manner of law breaking in order to keep their cover concealed. The assignment was more important than adhering to laws. If you wanted to catch the dirtiest of the dirty, you had to expect to get a little dirty yourself. It was recently decided that it was bad business to let the drug war continue south of the border. Legalization and regulation was about to be on the table in the US. But before that could happen, you had to remove the major players. Government sanctioned players had to be installed, so the drug trade could be taxed and regulated. That meant clearing the playing field, both home and abroad.

"Is the information complete, have we got the full story here?" Mr. Shadow took one last puff on his cigarette and then flicked it into the drizzle of rainfall.

"Not exactly. The reports encompass what could be gleaned from the state police and sheriff's reports. Those were all kept on their network drives. Very easy to punch into. The bulk of the investigation went through the local police chief, though. All of his files are still hard copies and locked away in steel filing cabinets in his office," Dimmler said.

"And?"

"And what? I don't do B and E. I hack. These are my lock picks," Dimmler said, wiggling his fat fingers again. "You pay me to get into their systems, grab the good stuff and forget everything I see. Done and done."

"Then I guess our business is done," Mr. Shadow said with a level of finality. He reached into his jacket, causing Dimmler to stand quickly and flinch. Mr. Shadow began to laugh with his throaty voice. He held a new cigarette between his fingers.

"Nervous?"

He put the cigarette up to his lips and fished a lighter from his pocket. Click. Light. Puff.

"Did you think I was going to shoot you?" Mr. Shadow asked with a chuckle.

"I didn't - I mean, of course not. I just have to go is all," Dimmler said quickly. "I guess the payment will show up like usual?"

He nodded. "And Dimmler -"

The chubby computer tech flinched at his name being used. He looked around guardedly, as if people were going to leap out of the bushes and take him down now that his real name had passed the lips of the man he only knew as Mr. Shadow.

"Never bring up payment again."

Dimmler nodded. He turned and walked briskly back towards the sounds of traffic at the edge of the park.

Mr. Shadow enjoyed his cigarette for several more minutes. This whole operation had gone bad. There was a chance they would lose their footing in the organization they had infiltrated. He had to be cautious about his approach. Give it some time to breathe. Moving too fast on an operation like this, trying to sweep it under the rug too quickly, could throw up major red flags for the target. It would require a deft touch. Caution. One thing was certain, it looked like his team needed to pay a visit to the town of Coopers Hollow, New York and call on one Police Chief Jack McMurphy Jr.

Chapter 2

In the dreams he remembered, he was still high school age; before college, before marriage, before the children. When he woke from his time in a younger body, in those early hours before reaching over to turn off his alarm five minutes before it sounded, he lay quietly next to his wife and wondered why his subconscious took him back to high school. Did he leave something unfinished back there in Coopers Hollow? Was he happier in the provincial town?

The dreams would come to him out of nowhere, usually in times of anxiety and stress. They weren't of any particular event, nor did he remember specific people from them. He just had that feeling like he was home. Nestled in the mountains of upstate New York, safe, secure, home.

It had been another night of dreams. This time he was up on the mountain, he and a bunch of the guys. They were drinking beers and telling stories about the girls they had made out with. Lies, all of them. But he was happy. He felt contentment in his very core looking out over the valley below, over the small village of Coopers Hollow. They were all competing to see who could launch a bottle cap the farthest. It was absolute bliss.

When he awoke and took a moment to remember where he was, he was filled with sadness. His reality was anything but lush valleys and mountain hikes. He had to deal with budget overruns and missed deadlines, inadequate cooperation from city officials and unsatisfactory building materials. And a sad wife.

She stirred in the bed beside him. At least they were sharing a bed again. She could sleep for another two hours, it was only five a.m. He had to look over the plans for the bridge one more time.

The meeting involved the DOT, the Mayor's office, the city police and multiple city council members. It took nearly three weeks just to schedule the thing. It was a necessity. Ramifications of Bridge Project 103 on Local Traffic Patterns, the title read at the top of the agenda he'd completed the night before.

It was a wonder that the antique hadn't collapsed and killed somebody yet. It was a decade past due for replacement and could fail any day, not that the public was aware of the danger. But yet another meeting was necessary. Such was bureaucracy. He and the project foreman had a pre-meeting meeting, and they'd probably have a post-meeting meeting as well. He would never understand why some people believed that having meetings and working were the same thing, when they were anything but.

There were three options on the table. Close it entirely and reroute traffic to the other bridges over the expressway, which were roughly eight blocks away in each direction. This would require adjusting traffic signals, narrowing lanes to allow for turning lanes, as well as restricting commercial vehicles. The second option was to reduce the flow to one-way traffic and replace the bridge one side at a time. A one-lane bridge with a traffic signal to allow traffic to alternate flows was simply not an option. Lastly, and most expensively, was the option of building a temporary bridge alongside the permanent bridge, flowing a lane of traffic across the new structure during construction, then disassembling it once the construction was complete. Though more expensive, it would immediately aid in stabilizing the current structure besides allowing for two way traffic to continue during all phases of construction.

Each of the participating members of the meeting scheduled for that day favored a different plan. The DOT wanted full shut down because of the safety hazard of the bridge, the Mayor's office wanted one lane open and didn't want to spend the money on the temporary bridge, despite state and federal funding, and city police wanted the temporary bridge because reflow would cause gridlock. The city council members each had their favorite plan as well

Back in the dusty recesses of his mind was a better solution, he was sure of it. As if locked in a crate, at the bottom of a stack of crates, waiting to be discovered, was the right answer. He was a problem solver, always had been, ever since he was a kid on the playground finding a way to split up teams evenly so the football game would be fair. Maybe that's why he kept having those dreams. Maybe there was some problem he never solved. Or maybe that was a time when there weren't any problems that needed solving. Psycho-analyzing himself was a new pastime. One, at which, he was growing quite adept. It was his way of trying to figure out what made his wife depressed all the time. If he could just figure out his own issues and hangups, maybe he could help solve hers.

With all the problems his family had been facing lately, it could just be his subconscious telling him he needed a break; a vacation. This project had consumed him for nearly two years now. The planning stage, the budget stage, the awarding of the contract stage, only to go into the halting stage and the back to planning again stage. Three options, and they just had to get everyone to agree. There was a fix to it, a way that everyone would be happy. It just hadn't come to the surface yet.

The map was already up on the computer screen, just as he'd left it only hours before when he'd finally crawled into bed. The aroma of the coffee he'd made for himself was already having an effect. Several sips and he was on his way. With a mug in one hand and the computer mouse in the other, he tried to clear his mind and will a solution into existence.

His team took the time to create a three dimensional environment of the surrounding structures of the site so he could fly around the bridge and see it from all angles in virtual space. He overlaid the proposed temporary bridge and looked at how the traffic patterns would flow. He started to zoom out, tapping on the arrow key. The view on the screen took him right through one of the buildings and was then suddenly obstructed by a wall. He hit the arrow key forward, and the wall disappeared. He sipped at his coffee and tapped the arrow key again: obstruction.

Then the solution struck him.

"Honey," he called out, as he came in the door. "I did it!" It was the closest thing he'd come to absolute success since he'd become a project engineer for the DOT bridge and tunnels division. With the quagmire-like bureaucracy, he had just performed the closest thing to walking on water in his entire career.

He was floating ten feet off the ground. The solution was so easy! The buildings on both sides of the proposed bridge site were derelict. They should have been torn down years ago. It was one of those sections of town that had just never recovered from the economic downturn of the 1980's. The only reason people drove through that area was because of the bridge. On the north side of the overpass, a block-long warehouse, empty and falling in on itself. On the south side of the bridge, an apartment building with boarded up store fronts on the street level with two additional empty homes filling out the block. Tear down the buildings, move the entire street over by forty feet, put in a new bridge and tear out the old one. No need for a temporary structure, no need to reroute traffic at all. Everyone is happy. Including the landowners who get a nice check from the city for their properties which now become a street.

It wasn't just a viable solution, it was the ultimate fix. The purchase and demolition of the properties in question were going to be a fraction of the price of any of the others. It wasn't even a particularly brilliant fix. It was how they handled bridges for thousands of years previously. Build the new bridge right next to the old one and then tear down the old upon completion of the new. River banks across the country still carried the remnants of the anchors of old bridges decades and even centuries old. It was as if all involved had gotten so tied up in the project with their own biases and agendas that no one was able to clearly see just how easy the solution actually was. Even the normally cantankerous city council loved it, because they could coop part of the funds from the beautification grant that had been approved by the state. They could create a nice little park where the former street was. All within budget, all a major improvement the mayor could hang his hat on. It was like he'd performed a magic act, and it was such an easy solution. So easy no one else had seen it.

"Honey?" He tossed his briefcase onto the couch and loosened, then removed his tie. He was in the mood to celebrate.

The house was very quiet. He suddenly realized that he'd left his phone silenced because of the meeting. Checking it, he saw there were eight missed calls and six messages.

He thumbed the voicemail icon and held the phone to his ear.

"Eric. Yasmine, she- she tried to- she hurt herself. On purpose. We're going to West Memorial Hospital." He was out the door and in the car before the message from his wife finished playing.

Why would a thirteen year old girl try to kill herself? Yasmine was beautiful, smart, talented; she had her whole life ahead of her.

"Why would she do this?" He weaved through traffic, breaking just about every speed limit and, at least partially, ignoring just about every stop sign on his way to the hospital. He parked mostly between the lines, probably in a restricted spot.

"Yasmine Owens," he asked at the emergency room desk. He had to show his ID, but they let him back to see her.

The first thing he noticed was how pale she was. Both of her arms were bandaged with gauze, from hand to elbow.

He kissed his little girl on the head, trying to will his eyes to stay dry. He had to be the one to keep it together. He had to be strong for everybody.

She was going to pull through. The doctors were ninety-nine percent sure. She'd lost a lot of blood, but fortunately, they got her to the hospital in time, got her stabilized. If it hadn't been for her little brother, six-year-old Riker, she would be dead right now. His baby girl tried to kill herself!

She was awake, with tubes and wires running from her to an IV bag and heart monitor. She was crying to her mother, and she wanted to hug Riker, but he was scared that he would make her wrists hurt again. Over the course of the next two hours, she confessed to what had led her to attempt suicide.

It started the first week of school with a boy. He'd been nice to her between classes, talked to her so sweetly. He was a grade ahead of her, but two years older, as he'd been held back a year when he was eight. The flirting escalated to texting, which escalated to her lifting her shirt and flashing him on her computer webcam after he'd flashed his privates at her. She knew it was wrong, but it seemed harmless. What she didn't realize was that he was recording the video feed. He emailed it to his friends, bragging about the whole thing. And they emailed it to their friends. Someone then posted it to a website notorious for hosting revenge videos of ex-girlfriends and spouses along with their contact info. Hot teen flashes cam. Before the night was over, she was being called every vulgar and foul name imaginable, propositioned by boys for sex, and ridiculed by the growing number of girls whose boyfriends had seen it. Men twice and even three times her age were sending her suggestive emails, some even with pictures that were so filthy they made her cry. She didn't dare tell her parents because she was embarrassed and she felt like it was her own fault. She endured three weeks of it.

Finally, another guy at school, a senior, cornered her while she was at practice for cross-country track. The cross-country course went through the woods, and he was there waiting for her. He pulled out his privates and tried to force her to perform a sex act on him. She was able to run away, but she was afraid to tell anyone, as he was a popular senior. She didn't want even more blow back from the kids at school for getting him in trouble. She just wanted it to end.

Shaken by the attack, she found no comfort from her friends. Her girlfriends banded together against her, they called her a slut and shunned her, completely excommunicating her from their group. When her best friend wouldn't even talk to her in the hall, that's when she decided to. . .

It hurt so much, and she was so scared. As soon as she'd done it, she regretted it. Then when Riker had found her, she tried to tell him it was okay, but she was losing consciousness. She didn't remember anything after that.

As she told the story, a rage built up inside of him. He had visions in his mind's eye of when she was a newborn, sleeping in her crib. The thoughts grabbed him by the throat and he couldn't keep the tears in anymore. It was like a slideshow of her life playing through his mind. He saw her learning to walk, then learning to ride her bike. Playing with her dolls, riding on his shoulders at Disney World. Those things seemed like they just happened yesterday. Now she was laying in the emergency room, her sliced up wrists stitched and bandaged, her heart broken, her trust in humanity completely betrayed. The raw anger flared his nostrils. He felt himself clenching and releasing his fists. He wanted names and he wanted to make them hurt in the same way his baby girl was hurting. He wanted to destroy them.

He looked across his daughter's hospital bed and into his wife's eyes. She was staring right through him. He recognized that empty, hollow gaze. They had worked so hard to bring her back from the edge, and now this. It was as if he could see his wife withdrawing again, before his very eyes, back into her world of depression, desperation, and hopelessness. The rage drained from him even as his stomach began to knot.

"Sylvia, we'll get through this," Eric Owens said to his wife. She didn't reply.

It shouldn't have come as a surprise that Yasmine would attempt suicide when the stress became too much. It ran in the family. Sylvia was prone to depression. Debilitating depression. The depression started postpartum a few weeks after Riker was born, and it had never really gone away. There was one scary night when Riker was two. She swallowed a bottle of sleeping pills and washed it down with a bottle of Merlot. Eric arrived home in time to induce vomiting and get her to the hospital. Yasmine was eight.

The emergency room workers saw sleeping pill-alcohol cocktails more often than any of them wished to admit. Sylvia was hydrated, given some drugs to counteract the sleeping pills, and kept under observation for three days. After that scare, they tried all forms of therapy, both pharmacological and psychological. Therapy brought some relief, and the last year or two were somewhat normal. With this new tragedy, however, he was afraid she would slip right back into it.

He reached over to take his wife's hand. He took Yasmine's fingers with his other hand.

"We'll just have to be strong together," he said. Yasmine shook her head in acknowledgment. Eric turned to his son. Riker had fallen asleep in the chair.

They took Yasmine out of school for the rest of the year. Eric made enough money to afford a home-schooling tutor, and Sylvia wasn't working anymore, so she could help out. By the second week of October, Yasmine's wrists were healing. The stitches came out, and she was feeling better. Sylvia was struggling, however.

It was a Saturday morning, Sylvia was still sleeping in bed, Yasmine was snuggled on the couch with Riker watching cartoons. Eric was making breakfast when the phone rang. They were on the no-call registry for telemarketers, so more than likely it was his mom and dad.

"Hello? Oh, hey mom," Eric said, cradling the phone against his shoulder as he poured batter onto the waffle iron. "What are you talking about?"

Riker sat up when the tone of his father's voice changed.

"When?" Eric was no longer cradling the phone, trying to multitask. The phone had his full attention.

"Dad, what's wrong?" Riker asked.

"I don't understand," Eric continued. "Why was dad hunting a cougar?"

The waffle iron began to burn through the batter, smoke seeping out from the edges.

Riker was off the couch and into the kitchen.

"Dad, the waffles!" Riker yelled.

The smoke alarm sounded with a shrill beeping.

"Dad!" Yasmine called. "You're smoking up the house!"

Eric tried to open the waffle iron, but the batter was burned on, and the smoke continued.

"It's just the smoke alarm," Eric continued on the phone. "I burned breakfast. Just walk me through it from the beginning."

"Dad!" Yasmine called. The smoke alarm beeped on.

"Riker, open the sliding doors," Eric said, indicating the glass doors that exited from the kitchen out onto the large deck.

Yasmine grabbed a chair and climbed up to pull the battery out from the smoke detector. Eric pulled the plug from the wall and tossed the whole waffle iron out the back door onto the deck, even as he tried to listen to every detail his mother was giving him.

"Okay, Mom. Okay. We'll get packed up and be up there in a few hours. Mom, I love you," Eric said. "Okay, see you soon."

"Dad, what happened?" Yasmine asked.

Eric didn't say anything for a few moments. He just hung his head. Sylvia came into the kitchen, bleary eyed and still groggy from the prescription sleep aids she had taken the night before.

"What's going on?" Sylvia asked.

"It's dad," Eric said, his voice cracking. He took a deep breath and looked up at his family. "Dad was killed this morning in a hunting accident."

"I really wish we could change your mind," Irvin Dietrich said to Eric as he watched him complete the task of cleaning out his desk. "But everybody understands. It's been a tough year for you."

"It's been a couple of rough years right in a row," Eric said. "We just need a break."

"Moving brings on its own stresses, though. You're leaving one set of known anxieties behind in exchange for a whole set of new, unknown anxieties."

"Which is the definition of 'fear of change' I believe. Listen, I grew up in Coopers Hollow. It's a slower pace, everybody knows each other. It's what we need right now," Eric said. "We need it, mom needs it. It's the right move."

"What about that whole shootout thing up there?" Dietrich asked.

"What about it?" Eric hoisted the box in his arms. "I have to come back for the plant."

"I'll get that and walk with you," Dietrich said. "First the cougar attack, then the shootout. It's like the wild west up there."

"I read that it was some kid getting mixed up with drug dealers," Eric said. "Like that doesn't happen here."

Eric Owens said his goodbyes to the rest of the team in his office. He was the head engineer and lead project coordinator for the bridge and tunnel division, had been for just two years. For six years prior to taking over the team, he was the assistant coordinator. It wasn't easy leaving after so long a time with the same people, but he knew it was right. He had to set the box down several times to give and receive hugs on his way out. Dietrich followed him right to his car.

"Well, if you change your mind, give me a call," Dietrich said, handing the potted plant to Eric as he loaded the Ford Expedition.

"Thanks, Irv. I really appreciate it. You and the wife are always welcome to come up for a weekend visit," Eric said.

"We just might. We'll probably let you get settled first. Maybe in the spring," Dietrich said.

"I'll hold you to that," Eric said. He shook his friend's hand and climbed into the truck. There was a lot of packing left to do at the house.

The next few days were a blur of activity at the Owens' New Jersey home. Packing and cleaning involved everyone, and everyone pitched in. Almost everyone. On day three, Eric found his wife sitting on their bed looking through a photo album that should have been in a box, stacked and waiting for the moving crew.

"We worked so hard to protect them, to give them everything," she said, her fingers tracing the edges of the photos held in place behind the clear acetate sheets. "But we can't do anything, really."

"That's not true," Eric said. "We can remove ourselves from the situation. Give them a different environment. Listen, my friend Perry, you remember Perry and his wife Dee. He's the airline pilot. Perry says that in any air traffic accident, there's a string of at least seven events where a catastrophic accident can be stopped dead in its tracks. At any time along that string of events, if you implement a corrective measure like a safety check, you can prevent the accident. So that's what we're doing. Don't you see?"

"All I see is introducing a whole bunch of new problems, ones we don't even know exist. Like the shootings up there," Sylvia replied. Eric wondered if she had been speaking to Irv Dietrich's wife.

"Should I go online and pull up the data on the number of shootings here or in the city as compared to Coopers Hollow? It's not even close. I grew up there, it hasn't changed at all. It's like getting to go back forty years in time before life got so crazy."

"I just want them to be safe," Sylvia said. "Tell me we'll be safe."

"We'll be safe there," Eric replied. He gave her a hug, burying her head in his chest. "I promise."

Chapter 3

Snow was coming. When you grew up with it, you could tell just by the flavor of the air. He would tell people, who didn't know about such things, that he could actually smell the snow coming, before it started. Of course had he been a white man instead of Mahican Indian, people would have scoffed. Instead, people would look at him with awe, as if he held some secret, ancient Native American power. The simple fact was, you could indeed smell the snow before it arrived. And you didn't have to be a Native American Indian.

The Mahicans were part of the Algonquin Nation of tribes, and had called the Hudson River Valley their home before the white man had come. His particular extension of the tribe settled near the headwaters of the Delaware River, along the western branch. They called that section of the river the Mohawks Branch, as that was the main water avenue used by the Mohawk tribes trying to reach the Delaware for trading purposes.

Prior to the Revolutionary War, much of the tribe had moved to Connecticut. Years later they would fold in with other tribes and settle on reservation land in Massachusetts. His family ancestors didn't move, but sought to integrate with the white people in the area that eventually became the village of Coopers Hollow.

For generations they did well, accepted by the local white settlers as equals, at least at first. His grandfather raised the family there, and was known to the locals as Chief Jimmy. He sold crafts in the summer season from a small shelter, built at the top of Mount Pratt near the fire tower. Chief Jimmy was known by locals and visitors alike, and regarded as a wise if not slightly eccentric character who belonged to Mount Pratt. Chief Jimmy's son Sam didn't take to the family business, thinking it foolish and demeaning. He found a job at the woodworking factory in town, making crates and then wooden furniture until the day he died. At the time of his death, he was the longest working employee they ever had, punching a clock for nearly sixty years. Sam married a daughter from the tribe out of Massachusetts when he was thirty five, and they had three children. They lived well, but more like their white neighbors than their patriarch, Chief Jimmy, up on the mountain.

John was the only boy. Because of the shared heritage of his parents, he and his sisters were part of the few Mahican Indians left in the world who could be considered full-blooded. Both of his sisters married white men and moved away from the area, one to Arizona, the other to St. Louis, Missouri.

When he was a boy in grade school, he wished that he had been born white and had a name like Smith or Jones. When he received a full scholarship to SUNY Binghamton, partially because of his heritage, mostly because of his grades, he was proud to be John Anakausuen. His last name was an Algonquin word meaning "worker," and had been bestowed upon his family generations earlier. His father had embraced the name his entire life.

"We are workers, son," his father told him on more than one occasion. "It's the only way a red man will ever earn the respect of the white man; hard work."

He was named John after John the Baptist, as his father and mother had joined the local church and were baptized as Christians.

Until this moment, John hadn't set foot in Coopers Hollow for nearly twelve years. He had attended the funeral service for his father then. Shook the hands of all the men he remembered working with his father when he was just a boy.

"Your father," they each said. "He didn't say much. But the one thing he would tell people was how proud he was of you."

He was a man who rarely let his emotions show, but with each person that told him how proud his father was of him, he found it more and more difficult to keep the tears in.

John Anakausuen was a larger than average man; over six feet tall, wide shouldered, but with a short torso and long legs. Finding business suits was nearly impossible. Once he began making real money, he had all of his suits custom tailored in a small shop in Chinatown in New York City. He never cut his hair, and wore it in a tight, rope-like braid of ebony. There wasn't a touch of gray in it, as he had yet to even reach forty years of age.

He drove a new Mercedes-Benz S-class s550, and the trip from his financial office in New York City took him nearly three hours. He nosed the Mercedes into a spot in front of the Stewart's Shop convenience store and put it in park. The sky was a dull and depressing gray and there was slushy snow all about the parking lot.

He stepped from the vehicle, cringing as the slush rose over the tops of his Brooks Brothers wingtips, soaking his feet. As he entered the convenience store, a chime rang, and the girl behind the counter gave him a pleasant hello. Men in suits like his, in cars like his, with hair like his, didn't frequent her store often, so she tried to not stare. She wasn't terribly successful at the attempt.

He poured a cup of coffee. Black, nothing added. The bitter taste was part of what woke up his senses. He needed to be sharp to complete his task.

A glance outside and he saw the snow coming down. The thick, heavy, wet flakes that immediately stuck to the already cold ground. It was the snow he'd smelled as soon as he'd stepped into the slush of the parking lot and gotten a whiff of his old hometown. As he sipped at the piping hot caffeinated beverage, he watched as the snow became so thick it was difficult to see across the street.

"Really, coming down out there," the girl said, from behind the counter. Her name tag said "Brenduh." It made him chuckle. The purple streaks in her hair and the pierced nose went along with the sarcastic tag.

"Yes it is," Billy said. "They say we're going to get a few feet up here today into tonight. I picked a great time to visit, huh?"

"Yup," she said, as she rang up his coffee. "We're running a special on the coffee, get a donut for fifty-cents more."

"Okay, sold." She handed him the change and he used plastic tongs to retrieve a chocolate donut out of the plastic cabinet.

"At least you get to leave," the girl said, several beats after he believed the conversation to be completed.

"You don't like Coopers Hollow?"

"Ugh. It's like a black hole that sucks in and destroys anything fun or interesting," she said. "I can't wait to get out of this place." As she said it, there was a wistfulness in her voice. It was like she just unplugged from reality right then, and her mind was a million miles away.

The door chimed, and a uniformed police officer walked in. He was about six feet tall, probably in his late fifties, with silver hair.

"Morning, Brenda," Chief Jack McMurphy Sr. said. He gave a nod to John, then stopped.

"Well, it's been awhile since I've seen you around," Chief McMurphy extended his hand. "Johnny, right?"

"Yes, sir."

"Well, picked a heck of a day to visit your old hometown."

"Yeah, but really, as soon as it hits October, you're rolling the dice up here, right?" John said.

"That's the truth." McMurphy Sr. filled his stainless steel mug with coffee. "So what brings you up here? Do you still have family in the area? Your daddy passed away years ago."

"No, sir. I'm doing some research, digging around in old records, looking for old contracts and agreements," John said. "I work in finance now in the big city. New York City," he clarified. Some people in this small town considered Oneonta the big city.

"Really, that's interesting. There are some old records in the basement at the police station. Both the bank and the old newspaper in town stored some boxes down there. Boxes and boxes of microfilm. I don't even know how you'd look at that stuff. I don't think the library has a microfilm reader anymore. I should probably throw it all out one of these days. But you know how it is, the day after you throw it out, somebody will need it," Chief McMurphy said.

"That's how it always is," John said.

"Well, good luck to you. Be careful out there. I have a feeling I'm going to be busy today," Chief McMurphy said. "Brenda, thanks for the coffee."

"My pleasure," Brenda said in a voice devoid of any sincerity. McMurphy Sr. headed out into the snow and climbed back into his idling patrol car.

"Thanks," John called to Brenda, as he exited the convenience store as well. Between the front door and his vehicle, snow fell from the sky in such a heavy fashion, his head and shoulders were nearly covered. The locals would manage the driving just fine, but any visitors could be in trouble. Auto accidents due to snow covered roads took more lives every year on average than hurricanes and tornados combined. Interesting statistic one of his insurance buddies had fed him, over lunch one day.

His first stop was the law offices of Palmatier and Rosscoe. They inherited files from Attorney Donald Swangler when he retired. Swangler was the attorney for Colleen Ingersoll Woodworth, who passed away in 1978. She was the last descendant of Zadock Pratt, founder of the neighboring town of Prattsville, Congressman for New York State, and the reason why Mount Pratt was named as such. It was John's hope that within the files of Palmatier and Rosscoe, resided a copy of Colleen's will, or, if he was lucky, a copy of Zadock's final testament.

The Mercedes handled the snow without issue. All-wheel drive, traction control and good tires made a big difference. It only took a few moments to reach the law offices. He directed the Mercedes up the driveway and into a rear parking lot. It was a large, two story house, built in the 1800s and converted into law offices years ago. Four tall pillars accented the front of the red brick building. The front door hadn't been used in ages, however, as there wasn't easy handicap access. A wooden ramp, already covered with an inch of snow, led to a rear door. He gathered his laptop case and his coffee and headed towards the door.

"Mister, uh Ana, um,"

"Anakausuen," John said.

"Sorry," the young receptionist said, genuinely embarrassed. "Is that Swedish?"

John had never been mistaken for a Swede before. He did a double take to see if she was serious. Her young face betrayed no hint of sarcasm.

"Uh, no. Not Swedish, Native American. Mahican Tribe," John said.

"Oh. Sorry, I'm not very good with names," she said. He guessed she was maybe nineteen. Very pretty, but obviously inexperienced and naive. "You can have a seat over there, my grandfather is expecting you. He has your name down on the calendar here."

"Thank you," John said. He didn't have to wait, amongst the outdated magazines and wall-framed newspaper clippings of successfully litigated, previous cases, for very long.

"Mr. Anakausuen, thank you for waiting. Can I get you something to drink? Coffee, water?" Albert Rosscoe extended a hand to shake.

"No, sir. I have coffee already."

"Let's go in here and chat a bit, shall we?"

It was a plush conference room, with deep crimson carpeting, dark, mahogany woodwork, and matching mahogany table and chairs. Rosscoe took a seat at the head of the table as John took a chair on the side.

"So, how can I help you?" Albert began. He was well into his seventies now. He'd lived in Coopers Hollow his entire life, except for the years away at university. He had some hair left, but not much. His face was full of wrinkles, and thick glasses rode atop a short, upturned nose. It was difficult to imagine how the pretty girl from the front desk could possibly have shared any of the same genetics as the stooped, shriveled man sitting at the enormous table.

"Well, probably the best thing to do is let you read the letter," John said. He opened up his laptop, and after a few moments, turned it towards Rosscoe. The elderly man adjusted his glasses, and read what was on the screen through his bifocals. After a few moments, he sat up and rubbed his chin.

"And this is authentic?"

"I believe it is, yes," John replied.

"Well, I have to say I don't think we have any of the records that would help. Anything from the Woodworth estate would have gone over to the museum," Rosscoe said.

"The museum?"

"Pratt House Museum over in Prattsville. They have a huge archive of everything relating to the family. I know we sent the Woodworth boxes over when we acquired Mr. Swangler's firm. I'm sorry. If you had told me over the phone what this was regarding, I probably could have saved you the trip over," Albert Rosscoe said.

"It's not really something I want to discuss too openly," John said as he closed down his computer and returned it to his bag. "And I'd appreciate it if you used discretion as well."

"I can certainly see why. I now understand the non-disclosure you had me sign and why you sent the check along with it."

"Playing this one close to the vest," John said as he stood. "No need to cause any trouble if it's all just rumors.

"I understand."

"Thank you for your time."

"My pleasure," Rosscoe said. "Let me know if I can be of any further help."

John shook hands again and stepped out of the conference room heading towards the rear exit.

Albert Rosscoe watched the Mercedes pull back onto Main Street and head east, towards Prattsville. He then walked back to his office and pulled out a legal pad. He scribbled a few notes and then picked up the phone. He had to check to see just how ironclad the non-disclosure was.

By the time John arrived at the Pratt House Museum, the curator was already well informed that he was coming, but Albert Roscoe hadn't told her why. She was an elderly woman who had overseen The House, as she called it, for nearly fifty years. Her age had not diminished the fire in her belly.

"And what do you want, sir," she met John at the door with arms crossed and teeth set.

"I'm hoping you can steer me in the direction of some old legal papers belonging to the Pratt estate. Specifically, I'm looking for Zadock's will, and perhaps any documents relating to Colleen Woodworth's will as well," John said. He could sense that she was spoiling for a fight, the five-foot-nothing, curator. The corners of her mouth seemed to curve even further into a frown.

"I don't think we have those," she said. Her name tag read: Velga Curator. Curator being her title, not her last name, though John had heard of stranger coincidences. Her hair was short and dusty gray, her face weathered and wrinkled, but her eyes were bright and full of vigor.

"Would you mind if I looked?" John asked. "Maybe I could step in and explain why I'm looking for those documents."

She let a pregnant silence grow even more so as she contemplated the man with jet black hair and braided ponytail, dressed in an expensive Brooks Brothers suit and driving and even pricier Mercedes. She looked at the falling snow which was already coating John's shoulders and head.

"Alright, come in and talk," she relented. "I'll give you five minutes."

"It will only take three," John said.

Two hours later, John left with that for which he'd been searching for a year. It was amazing what a checkbook and pen could do to change an individual's attitude. The drive back to Manhattan seemed to take but moments, though it was longer than three hours with the weather. The next few months seemed like days, and two years mere weeks. It had taken his family decades to gain the advantage over the white man. Now, if he took his time and avoided mistakes, his descendants, if he ever had any, would never have to worry again.

Chapter 4

They sat on his desk, aligned as brass soldiers with hollow heads. These were .38 Special +P loads. Unjacketed, soft lead, hollow tips. They were also known as FBI loads. They would spread better than a traditional bullet, when hitting unprotected flesh. They'd stop whatever he needed to stop.

Next to the cartridges was his father's revolver. A Smith & Wesson .38 Special, well oiled and black with a wooden grip. He carried a speed loader on his belt just in case. It's the type of weapon that one would expect an old, small town cop to have. He'd taken to wearing the belt and the gun, replacing his old 9mm. He still carried that Glock in the glove box of the police cruiser, but his duty weapon was his dad's trusty Smith & Wesson.

"Never misfired, never will," his dad used to say about the gun.

Removing the hollow point cartridges was a necessity when cleaning and oiling the weapon. They stood there, waiting patiently to return to their home as he worked. The procedure was almost done. He finished by polishing the gun with his cleaning cloth. The metallic, oily fragrance of a clean and ready gun was relaxing.

Deep breath.

He delicately plucked a cartridge from the desk and slid it into the cylinder. He repeated the motion five more times until the .38 was fully loaded.

The gun felt comfortable and familiar. Jack McMurphy Sr. had carried it for the entirety of his career. It was strapped to his hip the day he took a sucker punch to the jaw, cracking his skull when he fell to the sidewalk. It happened just a few blocks away, outside The Peachy Keen. They'd handed the gun to Jack Jr., along with the rest of his father's effects, after he'd passed away in Albany.

Jack Jr. had thought about burying the gun with him, but when it came to that final moment when he needed to make the decision, he opted to keep it for himself. He couldn't part with it. It *was* his dad. He wore it now as homage to his old man. The guy everybody, including Jack Jr., called the silver fox.

He sat there with his dad's gun, contemplating it like a revered, religious icon. He liked to believe he was above superstitions, and he didn't believe in an afterlife, even if both of his parents had. His belief system was an amalgam of evolution learned in science class, classic Christianity learned in the few visits to church when he was younger, and a heaping helping of skepticism ingested from binge-watching the History Channel. Tubby had been working on him in recent months to believe in a creator. The guy was going headlong into the religion thing. If the big man, who had changed so dramatically over the last six months, kept it up, he might actually win him over.

Jack lifted the .38 in his right hand, hefted its weight in his grip. He looked it over, eventually turning it toward himself, so he could stare into the abyss of the barrel. A voice inside him begged him to slide the cold steel between his lips and thumb the trigger. The hammer wasn't cocked, so it would take more pressure with his thumb on the trigger, but with his teeth holding the barrel, it wasn't like he was going to miss. Just twelve pounds trigger-pull-weight. Only a bit of pressure to relieve the pressure.

"Permanent solution to a temporary problem," Jack said aloud, shaking out of his reverie.

"What, honey?" Paula asked, as she came through the door. "What are you doing?"

"Just cleaning dad's revolver," Jack said quietly. It wasn't in his mouth, it was still in resting in his hands on the desk. He stood and holstered the weapon. He then took the oil and rag from the desk and returned them to his top desk drawer.

"Were you talking to him?"

"No, just repeating something he used to say, is all."

"Well, it's done," Paula said, gleam in her eye and a smile from ear to ear. She and Jack were now a couple, had been since October. She'd nearly lost her life at the hands of a band of drug dealers, bent on revenge against someone she barely knew. She was collateral damage. Almost. If it hadn't been for Tubby McIntyre and Jack McMurphy, she would have died that night. She was indebted to them both, and in love with Jack.

"Where is it?" he asked.

She fished in her purse for a moment, pulled out a small black chip, and held it up between thumb and forefinger.

"Ta-da."

"Kind of anticlimactic. I was expecting a ream of paper or at least a thick binder," Jack replied.

"Well, you'll just have to be excited about it this way," Paula said.

"How do I read it, do I have to print it out?"

"I'll put it on the Kindle I bought for you," she said. "This is just a back-up. You can put it on your computer if you want, too. It's in PDF format."

"Okay," Jack said, taking the small memory card from her. He slid it into the slot on the side of his laptop, and a window popped up. He clicked to open the folder, and there was the file.

"When can I start it?"

"Whenever you want. I'm sending it off to the publisher this afternoon. My agent is very excited. She thinks it could be a big hit," Paula said. She slid into the chair opposite Jack and slouched down in it, crossing her legs. "What do you think of your girl now?"

"I'll let you know when I'm done with it," Jack said, a twinkle in his eye.

"Oh, you are going to get it." She leapt from her chair and ran around the desk, jumping on him. He let out an "oof," but cradled her on his lap.

They made for a good looking couple. Jack, with his square jaw and steel-blue eyes, his tall and muscular build, and Paula, half-a-foot shorter with dark hair and dark eyes and a trim, athletic frame. They looked like the perfect couple to the casual observer, like they were meant for each other.

They heard the door open to the police department. Paula quickly slid off his lap, adjusting her skirt which had ridden up.

"Hello?"

"In here, Hank," Jack called out.

"Hope I'm not interrupting," Patrolman Ballard said, as he entered.

"Not in the least," Jack replied. Paula returned to her seat. "Paula was just telling me she finished her book."

"Really? That's great!" Ballard said. "Can't wait to read it. When does it come out?"

"Well, I'm just sending it off to the publisher today," Paula replied. "It will probably take six months to a year before it actually hits the shelves."

"Well, let me know and I'll buy it," Ballard said. "Chief, you got a second? I need to talk to you about something."

"Sure," Jack said, he cast a glance at Paula, who got the message.

"Well, I'm off," Paula said. "I need to get the book emailed off. See you later, hon."

"Bye, baby," Jack replied. He waited until the door closed, before he picked up the conversation with Ballard.

"So, what's up?"

Ballard took a seat. He had pretty much been a full member of the McMurphy family, since he'd come aboard the department several years earlier. He watched football and NASCAR every Sunday with Jack Sr. and Jr., and had been a pallbearer for both Jack's mother and father. Henry "Hank" Ballard, the skinny kid from Coopers Hollow High who just wanted to be a cop. He took the courses Jack Sr. had told him about, and he passed the competency test to become a patrolman. He had just had his twenty-fifth birthday.

"Jack, I don't know how to do this. You and your family have done so much for me. I mean, when nobody else was looking out for me, you and your dad showed me the way, you know," Ballard was looking at his shoes.

"You're leaving," Jack said, rather than asked.

"Yeah, I'm leaving. I got an offer to work with the police department down in Deposit. Jules lives down there, and, well, we're going to move in together," Ballard said. "I'm putting in my two weeks, Jack."

The police station was silent, except for the radio chirping dispatch calls from the county sheriff's department.

"I hate to see you go, Hank. You're a good cop, you know," Jack said. "But I'm not going to stand in the way of you moving up in the world. You'll get more money in Deposit, right?"

"Yeah."

"And you'll get to be with your girl."

"Yeah."

"Then it's the right move, right?"

"I think so. I hope so. I just feel like, after everything that's gone down up here, I'm abandoning you. I mean, who are you going to get to come in and help?" Ballard said.

"Well, I won't be able to replace you right away, but I'll survive," Jack said.

"I'm sorry."

"Me too."

He knew this was coming. It was pretty clear that Ballard was head over heals for his girl, Jules. It was also clear that she didn't want to move away from her family. "Listen, finish out your two weeks for me, and don't worry about it. You've got to live your life."

"Thanks, Jack. I really appreciate everything you've done," Ballard said. He stood, as did McMurphy. Jack extended his hand, but Ballard reached forward and gave him a big hug.

"I gotta get back out there," Ballard said, turning away quickly. If there were tears in their eyes, neither man was going to acknowledge them. Ballard escaped through the front door and down to his patrol car.

Jack sat back in his chair and swore under his breath. With his dad passing not a few months prior, the department was already understaffed. Losing Ballard as well was going to cause all kinds of problems. There was just too much for one person to handle, despite the relatively small size of Coopers Hollow. Every traffic stop came with paperwork and sometimes a court date. Each domestic dispute even more so. He'd had to call the New York State Troopers twice in the last year to get assistance with a call. Kind of embarrassing.

He opened a file on his laptop in Microsoft Word and read it over. It was a recruitment advertisement for the position of patrol officer for the Coopers Hollow Police Department. Paula had helped him write it up several weeks previously, and they had posted it in several newspapers around the state. They had received exactly one call from an actual, potential candidate. All the other calls were from employment websites pushing their special offers.

He had initially allocated a budget of three hundred dollars for the search, but that was exhausted with only a few ads in the Albany, Binghamton and Oneonta newspapers. It was going to cost a bit more.

The simple website that provided information about the department had a link at the top which boldly proclaimed: "Now Hiring!" The link jumped to a basic page featuring the info from the very Word document which he now had open.

He was going to reach out to larger cities in upstate New York: Syracuse, Rochester and even Buffalo. The hope was to attract a young recruit from those cities, who wanted a more peaceful existence. The trouble was, the salary couldn't match those big city payrolls, even if the cost of living was lower.

He spent the next half an hour going to various websites of the newspapers in the metropolitan areas he was targeting and purchasing classified ads to run for the upcoming week. Additionally, he posted to Craigslist and a few other free job boards. As he hit "post" on the last ad, he let out a sigh and leaned back in his chair.

The sun was shining, and it looked like the temperature might rise to about fifty degrees for the first time in months. That meant that the remnants of the snow might finally melt away and yield to Spring.

McMurphy checked his watch and then ran his hands through his reddish-brown hair, brushing it slightly to the side. It was a bit early for lunch, but his stomach was telling him to ignore the clock.

Jack grabbed his keys from the hook by his desk and headed for the front door, retrieving his jacket on the way. The walk over to the Peachy Keen diner took only a few moments, and was almost pleasant in the bright sunshine. The jacket was still required, however. The breeze demanded it.

The familiar chime of the door filled his ears, as Jack entered the small diner. At the counter, a fixture for years, was Tubby McIntyre. Thaddeus McIntyre, Jack reminded himself. He wasn't calling himself Tubby these days.

The man was enormous, probably close to six feet, eight inches tall, if anyone had actually ever bothered to measure him. He was built like a Sasquatch. The big man used to wear flannel and sport an unruly nest of hair and mountain man beard. These days, Thaddeus dressed in khaki pants with a white shirt and tie, and had the wild-man looked tamed down with a good shave and a haircut. He'd found a home with an elderly couple after his mother had been sent away to a mental hospital. It would take awhile for him to shake off all the mental and emotional damage his mother had inflicted on him. So far, he was off to a good start. Thaddeus sat at the counter, perched upon a swivel stool, like a hulking Goliath, eating Frosted Flakes with a tablespoon.

Everyone knew the owner of the Peachy Keen as "Seemo", which was short for Simonopolis. He'd left Greece nearly four decades earlier, and found his way up to the Catskills to open his own diner. He stood behind the counter, watching the news on the small flat-screen television, above the milkshake machine. A few other patrons were eating and chatting at the tables, they looked up and waved as he took a seat at the counter.

"Morning, Thaddeus. Seemo," Jack said. Seemo broke away from the television to come over to Jack. His apron was already quite splattered, meaning it had been a busy breakfast day. Though Jack never remembered a perfectly clean apron on the man, during all the decades he'd been slinging food at the diner.

"Morning, Chief," Seemo said with a smile.

"Don't call me that," Jack said. "I've told you, my father was the Chief, I'm just..." His voice trailed off.

"You are just the Chief," Seemo said. "But I won't call you that if you don't like. I don't call Tubby Tubby no more, right, Tubby?"

"That's right," Tubby replied with a mouthful of breakfast cereal. "Seemo is good like that."

"Why are you so dressed up today?" Jack asked.

"Going out preaching," Tubby said, before stuffing another spoonful in his mouth.

"Preaching, really?" Jack asked. "Taking after your mama, with all the Jesus stuff, I guess."

Tubby put his spoon down and looked directly at McMurphy.

"No, nothing like mama."

"Okay," Jack said after a pause. "Well, good luck with your preaching."

"So, what's new?" Seemo asked. "Get you a burger?"

"Yeah, burger and chips with a water."

"Okay, coming right up." Seemo went to get things started in the kitchen. He was back in a moment and set a plastic cup on the counter.

"So, you were telling me what is new."

"Oh, well, Ballard quit today," Jack said sipping at the water.

"Really? Because of the girl you think."

"Yes, the girl. He's going to move in with her down in Deposit. You know where that leaves me?"

"Very underhanded."

"Short handed."

"Right," Seemo said with a half smile.

"Why not hire Mr. Cooke," Tubby said. "You know, until you find somebody."

"That's not a bad idea, Thaddeus," Jack said. "But I don't think he wants to work anymore. When you retire, you don't want to go back to work again."

"You could ask him. Nobody ever gets what they don't ask for," Seemo said.

"What are you Confucius now? I'll ask him, but I already know the answer." His cellphone rang in his breast pocket. He had it out and answered before the second ring.

"Chief McMurphy," he answered. He listened to the voice on the other side. "Okay, I'll be right there."

Jack closed down the connection and hopped to his feet.

"Sorry, I'll be back for the burger," he called out to Seemo. "Something's going on at Hollow Pointe."

Chapter 5

Spring was definitely in the air. The bite of cold was gone, though a fleece pullover was still needed for his morning cup of coffee. Eric Owens closed his eyes, letting the warm embrace of sunlight envelope him. A light fog was over the valley beneath Mount Pratt. The back porch of the old home opened out to the magnificent view of the wooded peak. Twin peaks, actually, Mount Pratt, and the lower, Hollow Pointe.

It was Friday, and his work was done for the week. He'd completed a few freelance architectural drawings for a firm out of Baltimore, sending them via FedEx the night before. According to his calculations, the discs would be arriving at their destination any moment. Some companies still required large format prints and computer CD's with the files, rather than emails. Most had switched over to all digital. The particular firm in Baltimore, Englund & Raftery Architects and Builders were run by two partners who weren't exactly computer literate, but were very good at greasing the wheels of the local planning boards and getting structures up, under cost. Eric was more than happy to be their freelance architect and engineer as long as they didn't mind paying his freelance rates. He was due for a road trip to Baltimore for a face-to-face meeting in the near future, but he could put it off for a few more weeks until the threat of a late winter storm was gone.

"Hey, dad," Yasmine said as she padded out onto the porch, still in her pajamas. "I don't want to go to school today, I don't feel good."

"Come here." He felt her forehead with his hand and then put a soft kiss there. "You don't feel warm, sweetie."

"I know, I just don't want to go."

"Are you having any trouble? Anything you want to talk about?"

"No, it's nothing like that. Don't worry, it's nothing like before. I just don't want to deal with it today."

"Well, you've got to learn to deal with getting up and going, even when you don't feel like it," Eric said. "It's part of learning how to grow up." She leaned in and wrapped her arms around his waist, her head nestling into his shoulder.

"I don't want to grow up anymore," she said. "I want it to be like before."

"Well," Eric thought out loud. "I'd sure like to climb the trails up on Mount Pratt today. Do you think Riker and Mom would be up for it?"

"I know Riker would, but Mom's still in bed."

"She's still dealing with things," Eric said, kissing his daughter on her head. "Maybe we can just make it a daddy day out, then."

"Yeah! We haven't had one of those in a long time. I'm going to tell Riker."

He let her run back inside, and continued to sip his drink. He felt a bit guilty about letting his kids skip school just because they didn't feel like going. His parents would never have given him a day off just because he didn't feel like it. They were old school like that. Of course, they never had to deal with a bipolar wife or a daughter who'd attempted suicide either. You tend to adjust your scale of what's important and what isn't, when dealing with trauma like their family had, over the last eighteen months.

"Are we going hiking?" Riker ran out onto the porch in his bare feet.

"Do you want to skip school and go on a hike?"

"Totally! I'll get ready!" Riker shot back into the house. "Thanks dad!" he called over his shoulder. Eric sipped from his coffee and just smiled in the sunlight.

When they left the house to climb into the Expedition SUV,

his wife was still asleep in bed. She'd taken her prescribed dose of Ambien, but she'd taken it much too late. Rather than take it just before bedtime, she'd waited until she'd tossed and turned for several hours, finally taking the pill around 2am. The effects were different for everyone, but taking it at that time meant that, if she was awoken before ten o'clock, she'd be groggy and grumpy. Eric just let her sleep.

Mount Pratt was unique in that it had a drivable road all the way to the peak. A pure beauty of a mountain, with an even mix of deciduous and coniferous trees covering its slopes. In some areas bare rock could be seen from the surrounding valleys, but usually only in the winter months, when leaves were off the trees. For most of the summer, the mountain was lush and green.

Some of the taller mountains within the Catskill Mountain Region had walking trails across their faces and even to their peaks, like Hollow Pointe, the sister peak just across the connecting ridge called the saddle. But those required hikers to park at the base and hike the trails. Mount Pratt required no hiking. Though not as popular with die-hard hikers, those with limited mobility found it to be a delightful excursion. Most recently, an article in the *New York Times* heralded Mount Pratt as the King of the Catskills, sitting at the most northwestern tip of, what could be considered, the Catskill Mountains. Providing amazing views, a pleasant picnic area, and all within a day's drive from New York City, it had read. It meant more vacationers were taking in the small town of Coopers Hollow and its majestic peak of Mount Pratt.

Atop the mountain, an old fire tower stood, as it had for over a hundred years. It once offered the forest rangers of yesteryear a full three-hundred-sixty degree view for miles. Now visitors would climb the tower and take selfies with cellphones, the vast countryside behind and below in the photos. Along with the tower, there was an old structure where the Native Indians once ran a gift shop in the summer. They'd ceased doing that years before Eric had even been born. Now, it was locked and boarded up. A few time it had been defaced with graffiti from some of the local kids, but each time the town would come together and repaint the building.

Mount Pratt was once an attractive location for hang gliders from all around the world. A thirty-foot-long, wooden pier once stood on the northwestern side of the peak. It descended at an angle and the dropped precipitously just above a twenty foot natural cliff. The pier provided an amazing runway for the gliders to launch into the airspace above the valley. The regular winds of the area and the way they rushed up the northwestern face, provided the natural lift that the single-winged gliders required. As it grew in popularity in the late seventies and early eighties, Coopers Hollow became a noteworthy east coast destination to participate in the sport. All it took was a single death of one thrill-seeker for the town to pass an ordinance making the sport illegal on the mountain. Eric was fifteen when that had happened. Sadly, no more did the colorful single-wings fly above the valley of Coopers Hollow.

Whereas, many hiking mountains had parking at the base with trails up to the peak, Mount Pratt had parking at the top, with walking and hiking trails that looped down the slopes and then back up to the peak. Many hikers would climb the trails on on both Mount Pratt and Hollow Pointe, making a day of the adventure.

Eric Owens had spent his childhood and teen years criss-crossing the two mountains, hiking, camping, and later, drinking there with his friends. He wanted to show the kids all he could. Whenever they'd visited his folks previously, it would be around the holidays, and they never had the time to go hiking. Or, later, when they'd ventured up in the summertime, Sylvia never wanted to do it. The children were too small for Eric to manage by himself, so they had never seen the beautiful view from atop the mountains.

Eric steered the SUV along the dirt path, nosing the big vehicle up Mount Pratt, thankful for the four-wheel-drive. About halfway up the mountain, they started to see snow on the ground, still melting after the long winer. Granted, in the valley, many of the huge parking lot piles were still around, but most lawns were now clear of "Winter's Dandruff," as Yasmine had called it once. Here on the mountain, there were still areas where there was feet of the stuff, shaded from the sun by the various evergreen trees, and kept cool by the prevailing winds coming down from the north.

The twin tire grooves of gravel were wet with the runoff of the snow, causing a muddy mess, through which the Expeditions tires forged valiantly. To the left there was a steep bank, to the right, a sheer drop off. Then a tight switchback turn, and the drop-off was on the left and the steep bank on the right. If the SUV veered off the road, they wouldn't have tumbled far. Thick tree trunks lined the road, creating an almost impenetrable fence for such a large vehicle. The trail hair-pinned back again, and Eric carefully steered the four-wheel-drive monster around the turn, making sure he wasn't going to hit the trees at the road's edge.

Cell phone towers had been erected since the last time Eric had been there. Additionally, well engineered picnic tables were cemented into the ground by large steel posts. The town had turned it into a very quaint scenic area. Gone was the graffiti on the rocks, and the empty beer cans. Now it was like a mini state park atop the mountain. There was even an area for parking up to four vehicles. Eric nosed the Expedition into one of the spots and put it in park.

"Well, we're here," he said, exiting the vehicle and closing his door behind him, keys still in the ignition. The kids jumped out as well, taking it all in.

From the peak of Mount Pratt, one could look in every direction and see to the horizon. It was the tallest peak for hundreds of miles. The town of Coopers Hollow looked like a play model from their vantage point, like one of those miniature towns that accessorized a toy train set.

"Who wants to climb the fire tower?"

"Me!" Riker ran over to the steps which led up, nearly a hundred feet, to the look out point.

"I'm good," Yasmine said. "I'll just look around down here."

"Are you sure? The view is like nothing you've ever seen."

"Yeah, I'll be fine down here," she said. A breeze kicked up, with icy fingers due to the heightened elevation. Yasmine pulled her fleece jacket closed and zipped it up to her nose. She then pulled her hands inside the sleeves and went towards a group of rocks that looked out over the valley.

"Be careful of that edge," Eric called, as he started up the second flight of stairs on the tower. "People have been blown right off those rocks. Winds can be tricky up here."

"I'll be careful," Yasmine called back. She strolled lazily across the open area, towards the rocks, as Riker and her father climbed higher and higher.

Eric was winded and his thighs were burning as he made it to the final flight of steps, leading up to the look-out perch. The heavy-grade work boots he'd decided to wear weren't making the climb any easier. The last flight up to the tower's roofed upper deck was more of a ladder than stairs. He climbed them slowly, legs burning even more. Riker was already looking out the windows, elbows on the sill, hands to his chin.

"Wouldn't it be cool if we could fly like an eagle right off this tower," Riker said, with a sense of wonder in his voice. Eric neared the window, and the height made his stomach drop slightly. He wasn't afraid of heights, but there was that natural nervousness of being very, very high up, that caught him just as he was about to speak. It came out as a kind of squawk in his throat.

"What was that?" Riker asked, laughing.

"Nothing," Eric answered, chuckling as well. "I think it was my stomach telling me not to get near the edge."

"It sounded like you were stepping on a duck," Riker said, catching the giggles and not being able to stop. Eric just mussed the boy's hair and gazed out over the scenery.

"On a clear night, you can see all the way to Oneonta from here," Eric said. "That's like thirty miles away."

"Whoa. What did they use this thing for?"

"Well, it's called a fire tower for a reason. Back in the day, during the dry part of the summer, they'd station a ranger up here to scout out the area and warn the other rangers and firefighters if there was a forest fire. Of course, back then, everyone heated or cooked with wood fires, so a spark up in the air could catch something dry, fairly easily." The wind picked up, and rattled the windows of the small room atop the tower.

"What do you think, want to head back down and find your sister?"

"I could stay up here forever," Riker said. "How about just a few more minutes."

"Okay," Eric didn't mind giving his legs a rest for just a bit longer. He lost himself in thought, thinking back to the guys he used to run with, and how many times they'd come up to this very spot. In fact. . .

"Look at this," Eric said. He pointed to an area on one of the posts. It was about five feet above the floor, so he lifted Riker up to see it.

"What is it?"

"Those are my initials. I carved them here when I was about fourteen, I think. Me and the guys I used to hang out with, came up here all the time," he said.

"Cool." Riker ran his fingers over the carved initials. "But you really shouldn't have done that. You're not supposed to write on things like that."

"I know. Sometimes we make mistakes," Eric said.

They spent a few more minutes looking out at the scenery, before they descended to join Yasmine, who had climbed back into the truck due to the cold. By the time the boys reached the vehicle, she had it running, with the heat on.

"Do you want to see the other mountain?" Eric asked.

"Yes!" Riker said.

"Sure," Yasmine said.

Eric reversed and then steered the large vehicle back down the twisting access road. When they came out onto Saddle Brook

Road, rather than turn right and head further down the ridge and back into Coopers Hollow, they drove straight across the road and into a parking area.

"It's not too far of a hike, but it's worth it," Eric said.

The kids followed him out of the vehicle. He took the keys with him this time. They stopped at the trail head and looked at the map. It was posted under the roof's edge of a large gazebo that was also used for picnics. Eric indicated the line on the map they would take. It wasn't a very far distance at all. They got started along the path, gravel crunching under their shoes. It only took a few minutes before Riker started walking funny.

"What's wrong?"

"I have to pee," he said.

"Okay, well, we can just step off the path and go in the woods," Eric said.

"What about-" Riker indicated his sister.

"Do you have to go to?" Eric asked.

"No!" Yasmine said with disgust.

"I meant, I don't want her to see," Riker said.

"Okay, Yasmine walk on ahead. We'll catch up."

She shook her head and walked along the path, on her own. Riker wouldn't unzip and relieve himself until she was out of sight.

After the two minute pitstop, which included retying Riker's shoes, the boys got back on the path. Eric thought he heard something, like a person yelling, but he dismissed it as a bird's call.

As they got closer to the peak, he heard it again, but louder.

"I think that's your sister," Eric said, a sudden panic jolting him. "Come on, let's run." They started with a jog. He wanted to run faster, but he also didn't want to leave Riker behind. As they came out into the clearing at the peak, he heard his daughter scream again. It was definitely Yasmine, and she was near hysterics.

"I'm coming," he yelled. "Riker, wait here." He ran as fast as his tired legs could take him. There was a path that led away to the west from the clearing, to a rock outcropping. Another scream. It sounded like she was being murdered, the fear and anxiety powering her full-throated shriek.

He rounded a small wooded bend and saw her, standing near the edge of the rocky outcropping of Hollow Pointe. She was staring down at something, screaming and screaming. Eric reached her and pulled her back from the edge, hugging her tightly to him.

"It's okay baby, I've got you," he said. He repeated it several times, and she changed from screaming to whimpering. She buried her head in his chest and hugged him, shaking with each sob.

"What's wrong baby, did you almost fall?"

"There's a," she heaved with each breath. She couldn't get the words out. She had just about hyper-ventilated from screaming.

"Just calm down," he said. "Tell me what happened."

"There's a dead body." Just then, Riker came out of the trees, having ignored his father's direction to stay put.

"What happened?"

"I told you to wait" Eric said.

"I wanted to help."

"Okay. Listen, take your sister by the hand and take her back down to the truck." Riker did as he was told. Yasmine walked slowly off the rocky precipice and, once she was within the safety of the trees, started sprinting back to the vehicle.

"Hey! Wait up," Riker called after her.

Eric edged his booted feet closer and closer to the sheer drop off, trying to peer over. Finally he saw it. Fumbling for his phone, he stepped back from the edge. Managing to get the stubborn piece of technology out of his pocket without dropping it from his shaking hands, he called 911, and they patched him through to Chief McMurphy.

Chapter 6

"Show me exactly where you found it," McMurphy said after listening to Eric's story. He followed Eric up the Hollow Pointe hiking trail for nearly a mile, through the trees, across the clearing at the peak and finally to the rocky edge. Jack peered over, and saw the naked body, partially covered in the snow, nearly a hundred feet below.

It was quite obvious that he was dead. His legs were bent at horrific angles, the foot of his right leg almost completely severed from the rest of the appendage. Blood had soaked into the snow from his head, abdomen and leg wounds. The body had dark brown hair, and looked like a teenager, as he had very little body hair.

"Jeez," Jack breathed out as he stepped back and walked with Eric away from the edge and back into the clearing. He muttered it several times, as he ran his hand over his face. It took about ten minutes to get back to the vehicles. Jack was more winded than he anticipated from the hike. He made a mental note to do some jogging to get his endurance back up.

"Wait here," Jack said as he opened his police SUV door and reached for his radio. He put the call in to county dispatch and requested the fire-rescue team. In moments, his phone rang.

"Hey, Goldie," Jack said into the phone. "Yeah, we have a body up here - I don't know, looks like a kid, I'll check missing persons when I get back to the office - no, you'll have to get him from below Hollow Pointe, you'll have to go through the woods. Okay, Goldie, thanks." Jack walked back to Eric, who was hugging his daughter.

"Can I get a quick statement from you?"

"I can make the statement," Eric said.

"Okay, we'll just need you to tell me everything again, but I'll record it on my handset and type it up later, okay?" Paula was trying to get him to embrace technology, but it wasn't easy to do. A year ago he would have taken down notes on a pad with a pencil. Now he was pushing a button on a little digital recorder and holding it out for Eric to speak into.

By the time he was done taking Eric's statement, Goldie Bristol drove up in her 4x4 pickup truck. She was the new fire chief in Coopers Hollow. From what he heard, everyone liked her and she was doing a pretty good job so far. This was a good thing, as she was taking over for something of a town legend, when she stepped into old Copper's position. She'd been a volunteer from the time she was eighteen, joining her two older brothers on the squad as soon as she could pass the test. All of them had served under Chief Copper Owens' tenure. Copper Owens, Eric's father.

Both of Goldie's brothers had moved away, but she stayed in Coopers Hollow, enrolling at SUNY Cobleskill, just a twenty mile drive away, to the north. Along with school and firefighting, she also worked part-time as an assistant manager at the Grand American grocery store in the center of town. She was blond, and rugged, standing nearly six feet tall. As much a tomboy as one could be. She was a snowboarder, rock climber, horse rider and snowmobiler. Now, even at age thirty-three, she could whip just about all the guys in the department in any sport. She was one of the first responders on the scene when Copper had bled out in the woods, back in the fall.

"Chief, where's the body?" she asked as she strode up to the men.

"Up the path, through the clearing. Off the edge of Wedding Rock," Jack indicated. "Eric, I have what I need from you. You guys can take off."

"Okay, thanks." It only took a few minutes for Eric to get everyone situated in the vehicle and get it out onto the road and back into town.

"Come on, I'll show you," Jack said to Goldie. They hiked up the path, Jack leading, but Goldie right on his heels.

"So, how are things?" she asked.

"Good. You know, over-worked."

"And under-sexed?"

"Easy, Goldie," Jack answered with a bit of a laugh.

"What? If I was a guy, we'd laugh about it," Goldie said. "I'm not hitting on you, Jack."

"Yeah, well. . ."

"You know, you're not God's gift to women, the way you think you are."

"I don't think I'm that," Jack answered. "What are you talking about?"

"Nevermind," she snorted. "Just messing with ya. Don't get your panties in a twist." She knocked him against the arm with her elbow and walked out onto the rock outcropping, right to the edge, not hesitating a bit.

She stared down at the corpse below for several moments, eventually letting out a low whistle. She turned back to McMurphy.

"You're right, we'll have to hike through the woods from below. Trees are too tight to use a snow mobile. It's going to be a beast getting him out of there."

"Okay," Jack said. "We hike in together to take a look. Not sure if we're dealing with an accident, suicide or homicide yet. I'll call the doctor, see if he can come over and at least give us a body temp. Depending on what this is, I may have to call in the sheriff's boys."

"What for, we can handle this," Goldie said. "Probably a suicide. It's not the first time up here you know."

"I know. Dad came up here a few times for jumpers. Of course that was back when this side of the mountain was logged, and you could practically drive in. Listen, can you get some of your guys to block off the trail head?" He paused for a beat. "Please, and thank you."

"Already on it. Get your tall boots, partner," she said, as she slid past him along the trail back to the vehicles. "We're going to hike down there."

"Yeah, I know."

He was thankful, when they got back to the cars, that he was able to sit down for a bit to change into his boots. It was just over a two mile march up and back from the peak, and he'd just done it twice. He was ready for some water and a rest. He grabbed a water bottle from under the seat, he alway kept one there. A few gulps and he felt somewhat refreshed.

McMurphy placed a call to the county dispatch and requested an ambulance as well as the county coroner's office to send out their photographer. He knew it would take at least an hour for them to show up, he might as well get the ball rolling now. It hadn't been six months since the last time he'd had to make a similar call. There were a few more bodies that time. It was a rough rodeo back in October. He didn't want to think about it right now, so he focused on the boots.

From October until the end of April, Jack kept a pair of knee high winter boots in the trunk of his car. He could slip off his regular, department-issue, black steel-toes and get into the deep boots in just a few moments. By the time he was ready to hike the path that would take them down and around the cliff face of the mountain, to the body, Goldie was standing impatiently with her arms crossed.

"Let's get a move on," she said, as she waited for him to pull the drawstring secure on the top of each boot. "What, are you tired? Come on, old man."

There was no telling how deep some of the snow would be. More than likely, he was going to get soaked. He'd thought about calling Ballard to have him hitch up the trailer with the department's four wheeler on it. But frankly, the only thing worse than not having a four-wheeler to ride through the woods, was getting a four-wheeler stuck in the woods, that you then had to somehow get unstuck. With the snow the way it was, he decided to just man-up and hike it.

By this time of the year, the remaining snow on the ground could more accurately be described as icy ball bearings. The color was still white, but the consistency was more like that of a snow cone, without the syrup. In places, it would yet be frozen solid, and a grown man could walk on it. But in most places, especially during the increasing warmth of the day, the icy crust would give way, and you would sink down. Not just through the snow, either. As the ground beneath the snow also thawed, the snow-covered, rotting leaves and spongy earth could turn into a terrible muck.

As they left the parking area along the lower hiking path, Jack's phone rang. It was the sheriff this time. Kenneth Kerr was elected as the Sheriff of Delaware County for his fourth term last election. He ran unopposed. Jack Sr. Had always spoken well of the man, but he had less to say about a few of the deputies on the county payroll.

"What have you got up there, Jack?"

"I think it's a suicide off Hollow Pointe. Kid is naked. Looks like a teenager. Still covered by snow, partially. You got any missing persons?" McMurphy said. He stifled a grunt, as a branch smacked against his face.

"Sorry," Goldie said without looking back.

"Not a teenager. We have a seventy-two year old with dementia who walked out of her house earlier this morning. Can't seem to find her. What's the kid look like?"

"Haven't actually gotten to him yet. He's at the bottom of a cliff. We have to hike around to get to him. I'll give you a call back when we get a chance to examine the body. Give me a few minutes."

"Okay."

"You know if Oscar is coming out with his camera? I had

dispatch put in a call, but I didn't hear anything back." Oscar was a freelance photographer who lived in Delhi, NY, the county seat. Most of the county departments tapped him to handle their picture taking. The sheriff's department even used him for some forensic photos, including a murder a year back. He'd taken the photos at Gloria Graves' house in October, and of the Lexmere Hotel after it burned down. Since everything had moved to digital, though, there were rumblings that they really didn't need him anymore. They could just shoot all the pics themselves. Jack didn't care either way. He knew enough about digital cameras to point and shoot, but beyond that, he had no clue what an f-stop was or what speed was best. There weren't too many occasions when he needed the photographer. In the last two months, Paula had actually subbed in as the photog, snapping pictures of two intersection accidents during the winter.

"Nope. Oscar is out of pocket. There's some car show down in Daytona. He'll be gone for another three or four days. I can send Deputy Patterson up with the camera if you'd like."

"Naw, I've got a camera. Just wanted to spread the wealth and get a professional to do the dirty work," Jack replied. "I'll manage without him."

"Okay. Let me know if you need anything from me," Sheriff Kerr said. His tone implied 'call if you screw up and need to be bailed out.' Jack's relationship with the sheriff's department had improved somewhat since the shootout back in October. Cops tend to put aside their differences and have each others' backs once the bullets start flying. It wasn't Kerr that had McMurphy concerned. It was his deputy, Patterson, brother to Coopers Hollow Mayor Patterson. If Jack slipped up, the deputy would be right there to swoop in and replace him, with his mayor-brother's backing.

"I will, thanks, Sheriff." Jack closed down the connection and then dialed Paula's number.

"What's up, buttercup?" she answered with a cheerful giggle.

"Hiking around to the face of Hollow Pointe to look at a body.

Why are you so giddy?"

"I'm not giddy. I just like to get a call from my boyfriend. Is that wrong?"

"I guess not. Listen, can you grab your camera and come up here? Looks like a suicide jumper, and I need to take pictures. Oscar is at some car show in Florida." Though he had been walking in Goldie's footsteps, he out-weighed her by fifty pounds, give or take. So in a few places, where the snow held her, it did not support him. He fell crotch-deep into the snow pack and dropped the phone. He cursed, and this grabbed Goldie's attention.

"Easy there," she said. "Here, give me your hand."

"I got it," Jack replied. He retrieved the phone and pulled himself out of the snow. He crawled a few feet until he was away from the break, and got back to his feet.

"Sorry," he said into the phone.

"Is that Goldie Bristol with you?"

"Yeah, fire and rescue will have to pull the body out," Jack said. "We'll need a sled. Snow is still crotch deep in places."

"I got the camera, I'm coming up."

"You can just give it to one of the fire guys, and they can bring it over," Jack said.

"No, I'll bring it and be your photographer."

"You don't have to do that," Jack said. "I can manage the camera."

"I want to help. See ya!" He closed the phone and slid it into his breast pocket. Paula wasn't a big fan of Goldie's, thinking her a tomboy, trying to prove she was as good as the guys. Goldie didn't much like her in return, thinking Paula was a flirt who used her looks to get what she wanted. In a small town, when something is said over a beer, it gets repeated. In Goldie's case, she had a few too many drinks with the boys at the Christmas party and decided to start tearing down all of their girlfriends or wives. Paula wasn't spared. Goldie made a few enemies that night.

"So, how's the ball and chain?" Goldie asked.

Jack let it slide as they walked on in silence. It was only another fifty paces until they were on the scene of the deceased.

There was more damage than they had been able to discern from atop the rock bluff. Jack pulled out his recorder and pressed the button.

"Deceased is male, caucasian. Uh, probably between eighteen and twenty-five. Brown hair. A bit on the long side. No discernible tattoos or piercings. Body is completely unclothed." He stopped the recording and kneeled next to the corpse. He lifted an eyelid and then recorded "blue eyes" before depressing the button again.

"Gash on the forehead. Compound fracture to left tibia and fibula. Probable broken pelvis and dislocated right femur. Chest and head contusions. Additional contusions on the rest of the body: Chest, abdomen, right shoulder."

"Jack," Goldie was looking up at the rock cliff above them.

"What?"

"Look how far away the body is from the cliff face. He's a good twenty-five, thirty feet away," she said.

"He landed in the snow there, not much cushioning against the rocks," Jack indicated just a few feet away from the body. "And he rolled down the incline to here."

"He didn't just jump, Jack. He ran full speed off the cliff up there," Goldie said.

"Which means he either really wanted to die, or was running at full speed and didn't know the cliff was there," Jack replied, catching the line of reasoning. "If it was the latter, more than likely it happened at night. Interesting."

"Yeah. Just interesting."

Jack bent closer to the body, looking at his face. His head was on top of his left arm, and his right arm was beneath his torso.

Jack pulled on a pair of latex gloves and moved the head, to get a clearer view of his face. As he did, he revealed the left arm.

"Look at this," Jack said. Goldie knelt next to the body and looked at the wrist area where Jack was indicating.

"Bruising on the wrists," Goldie agreed. "I'm no CSI, but I think he was bound. Handcuffed or tied up. Whatever it was, it rubbed the skin raw. Maybe he didn't jump. Maybe he was thrown off."

Jack rolled the body slightly to get a look at the other arm. Similar markings were on the right wrist as well.

"Okay, that is definitely suspicious. I'm calling this a suspicious death now. I've got to turn this over to County. Don't touch anything else. We need to make sure no one else gets up here," Jack said. He swore under his breath.

Goldie immediately called down to the volunteer guys she had stationed at the trail head. Jack was dialing Sheriff Kerr.

"Sheriff. Jack McMurphy. I got a feeling we're looking at something more than a suicide here. Not sure if it's a homicide, but definitely suspicious. Sorry to ruin your day, but you better send up your investigators. I think I have to turn this one over to you guys."

"Suspicious, huh? What makes you think that?"

"Well, young male, eighteen to twenty-five. My guess is closer to eighteen. Naked. Bruises on his wrists," Jack looked at the mangled feet and legs. There were signs of bruising around the ankles as well, though it was tougher to decipher with the all the damage from the impact of the fall. "And bruises on the ankles. Looks like maybe he had been tied up. Also, based on a quick guess-timate of his trajectory, he was running full speed when he came off the cliff. Or maybe tossed off by somebody else. Something just isn't right about it, for it to be a suicide."

The sheriff was quiet on the other end. Jack wasn't sure if he was thinking, writing down what he was just told, or silently cursing a small town cop trying to play big city investigator.

"Okay. I'll grab Isaac and come on up. It will take us forty minutes or so. Don't touch anything," Kerr said.

"I won't."

"And make sure nobody else drives in or out of there. If there's any evidence, we don't want it run over or trampled down. Lock it down," Kerr said.

"Okay. See you guys when you get here." The connection closed down.

Jack and Goldie stood quietly looking at the nameless body, which was grotesquely mangled from the fall.

"Gonna be a long day," Goldie said.

Chapter 7

Riker was quiet throughout the entire ride back down the mountain and to the Owens' residence. He stared out the window and watched the sun flashing between the gray tree branches. Back in New Jersey trees were already budding. Up here, everything was still gray.

Yasmine had earphones in, and she was riding in the front, with her eyes closed. When Eric pulled into the driveway, he barely had the SUV in park before she bolted out the door, slamming it hard behind her. She was up the front steps and into the house before Eric had even unbuckled his safety belt.

Riker was still sitting in the back, staring into oblivion.

"You okay, partner?" Eric asked.

"I guess," came the reply, accompanied by a sigh.

"It's a tragedy, and very sad. If you want to talk about it, we can," Eric said.

"Do you think he's in heaven?" Riker asked.

"Probably."

"When he got to heaven, did they give him a robe to cover up?"

"Definitely, and wings and a harp and his halo," Eric replied.

"What do you think he's doing in heaven?"

"I don't know. I guess we'll have to wait to find out."

"I don't want to go to heaven. I want to live here. I want to be with you and mom," Riker started inhaling deeply, gasping a bit. "I don't want to die, dad." That was it, he was over the threshold of control, and the levy gave way. Tears and heavy sobbing erupted.

"Buddy, it's okay," Eric said, trying to soothe his son. He climbed out of the front seat and opened Riker's door. His boy, reached up for a big embrace. Eric kissed his head and held him tight, rocking him back and forth gently. In his arms, it was tough to accept how big he'd gotten. It seemed like he was just a baby not long ago. Then he started school, now he was getting long and thin, losing his baby fat. His little boy was growing up so fast. Riker didn't need this whole scene. Not with what he'd already faced with his sister before, and the on-going challenge of his mother and her issues.

"It's okay," Eric said again. "Let it out. You'll feel better."

"We didn't even know his name," Riker sobbed. "His mom and dad probably don't know where he is."

"Shhh. Shh. Shh," Eric carried him up the stairs to the front porch and in through the door, which Yasmine had left wide open.

"What's wrong?" Sylvia was still in a bathrobe, but had managed to find the Keurig to make herself some coffee. "What happened? Is he hurt?"

"No, nothing like that," Eric said. He sat Riker down on the couch, and Sylvia sat as well, taking him onto her lap. "Up on Hollow Pointe, Yasmine found a dead body."

"Of a person?"

"Yeah. He looked like a teenager. It was off the cliff that looks out over town. The kid must have jumped. Anyway, the kids are a little shaken up by it," Eric said. "I'm going to make some coffee, do you need a refill?"

"No I'm okay," Sylvia called after him. Then to Riker, she spoke softly. "My poor little monkey. It's okay, baby. It was probably just an accident."

"Is he still out there, I mean, did they take him away?" Riker asked.

"I'm sure they've taken him to the hospital," Sylvia said. "Don't you worry about it anymore. Let's think of something else. Let's watch a movie, to get our minds off things. What would you like to watch?"

"*Captain America*."

"Oh, I don't know," Sylvia said. "We haven't let you see that one yet."

"Can I, please? I'm not scared," Riker said, wiping his eyes. "See?"

"Honey, that's PG-13," Eric called from the kitchen, as he prepared his coffee.

"Okay, we can watch something else," Sylvia said.

"No, I want to watch *Captain America*," Riker insisted. "Dad, please? It will help me get my mind off everything."

Eric came back into the living room, with his coffee mug. He shot a scowl at Sylvia, but she wasn't paying attention. She had taken to hugging on Riker again.

"Okay, but I'm skipping a couple scenes," Eric said. He pulled the disc off the shelf and slid it into the player. With the remote he skipped through the previews and got to the play menu. When Eric had replaced their old television with the new sixty-inch flat screen, Sylvia had just about blown her top. She complained that it was too big and ugly to have on the wall. Eric had reasoned that since the closest movie theater was forty-five minutes away, they'd be watching a lot more movies at home. It only made sense to install a surround sound system as well.

As the movie roared to life, Eric's cell phone buzzed in his pocket. It was Jack McMurphy.

"I have to take this," Eric said, handing the remote off to his wife. He took the phone and his coffee back to the kitchen and gazed out the sliding glass windows.

"This is Eric."

"Chief McMurphy here. Sorry to bother you again. You didn't happen to see anybody else around while you were up here, or at Mount Pratt, did you? Any vehicles coming out of the access roads or anything?"

"No. I didn't see anything up there," Eric replied. "Why?"

"What about on your way up Saddle Brook Road, on your way to the access road. I know it may be tough, but do you remember any vehicles coming from this direction?"

"I don't know. I can't really remember if we passed anything or not. I don't think so, though. Why? What's going on?"

"Okay," McMurphy said. " Just trying to narrow down a timeline. I really appreciate it."

"Jack, what is going on, was the kid murdered?" Eric asked a bit under his breath. He didn't want Riker to hear him.

"Eric, I can't. We're still investigating," Jack said. "Thanks again. And sorry the kids had to see it."

"They'll be okay. Thanks."

The connection went dead, and Eric slid the phone back into his pocket as he looked out the back windows. A big gray squirrel was sneaking onto the deck, with aims at absconding with a slice of stale bread, which Sylvia must have just tossed out. The squirrel grabbed the bread and looked right at Eric.

"You're welcome," Eric said, raising his mug to the squirrel. He spent a few more moments looking at the wooded peaks of Mount Pratt and Hollow Pointe. They had a picture-perfect view of the mountains. It was one of the reasons they bought the house. Setting his mug on the counter, he sprinted up the stairs to his office, where he knew he had binoculars in one of the drawers. It took a few minutes of searching, but he eventually found them. They had been pushed way to the back of his bottom drawer, still in their zippered case.

The best view of the mountain was out Riker's window on the second floor. Eric left the case on his desk, and took the field glasses to see what he could see.

After a moment of fine tuning the focus, he could clearly make out the police and firemen moving through the leafless trees. It wasn't sharp enough to be able to make out faces, just the recognizable movement of humans.

After a few minutes of zeroing in on the accident scene, Eric began drifting his view over the rest of mountain ridge. There wasn't much to see. Bare trees, with a few evergreens interspersed. The further up the mountain, the more spots of snow he encountered. He was just about to put the glasses away and go back down to watch the movie with Riker and Sylvia, when he saw another person on Mount Pratt. He pulled the glasses away, but couldn't see him with his naked eye. Putting his eyes back to the binoculars, Eric tried to scan the area again, but didn't see anyone.

It had probably just been another policeman or fireman walking through the woods, he thought to himself. But the person he saw wasn't wearing a uniform. It had been a brown jacket, like a long canvas jacket, the kind with all the pockets on the front. Eric had a similar green one in the front closet. The man had been carrying something as well. It looked like a rifle.

He brought the field glasses down again and cursed quietly to himself. He snuck a glance back at the door to see if either of the kids had suddenly materialized and overheard him. He was alone. He cursed again.

He spent another twenty minutes looking for the man he'd spied, but never saw him again. During that time, Eric debated with himself about calling Chief McMurphy back and reporting what he saw. Or more accurately, what he thought he saw. Finally he relented, and took out his phone. He pressed the call back feature, and the phone dialed out to Jack.

"Hey, uh, Chief?"

"Yeah, what's up? Remember something?"

"No, not exactly. It's probably nothing, but I was looking out my back window with my binoculars, and I thought I saw a man in a brown coat walking through the woods with a rifle or shotgun on Mount Pratt. He had a yellow case, like a rifle case. I can't really be sure, though."

"When?"

"Just now. Like ten, maybe fifteen minutes ago."

"Did you get a good look at him?"

"No, I was just scanning the mountain with the binoculars, and caught a glimpse. It was way over on the," Eric paused for a moment, trying to get his compass bearings so as to provide Jack with at least something tangible. "Eastern side of Mount Pratt. Almost all the way over. It was probably nothing. Or a hunter or something," Eric said. "I probably shouldn't have even called."

"No. It's good that you called. There's no hunting seasons going on right now. Are you still looking, can you see him now?" Jack asked. Eric could hear him talking to someone else in the background.

"No. I can't spot him again. It was a darker brown coat. The kind with all the cargo pockets down the front. He was white, I think. No hat. It was just a glimpse. I'm sorry."

"It's okay. Keep looking and give me a call if you spot him again," Jack said.

"Okay."

"Thanks."

"You bet," Eric said. "Bye."

"Bye now."

Eric spent the next twenty minutes scanning the mountain, but he didn't see the man again. He saw plenty of firemen and he even managed to spot Jack, his badge reflecting the sun. He probably would have stayed there for another hour if he wasn't pulled away by a sudden scream from the living room.

He tossed the binoculars onto Riker's bed and sprinted down the stairs to see what was wrong. The television was no longer playing the movie, but rather on the Blu-ray's menu screen. Riker had buried his head into Sylvia and was sobbing uncontrollably.

"What happened?" Eric asked, heart racing.

"Bucky fell off the cliff," Sylvia said with a sigh, as if to say, 'Of course he did.' She looked up at her husband with pursed lips and furrowed brow. "I forgot about that part. I'm sorry, monkey." She rocked her seven-year-old and ran her fingers through his hair. Eric rubbed his son on the back for a few minutes. He went to the kitchen to get more coffee, after his boy had calmed down. He found himself gazing out the sliding glass windows again, wondering about the mystery man on the mountain.

Chapter 8

"I think you're right." Sheriff Kerr was squatting next to the body, looking at the bruises to the boy's wrists. "If you look around the mouth as well, there's abrasions consistent with being gagged." Jack bent in for a closer look. There was unmistakable redness on both sides of the mouth, and the lips were swollen.

"Bound and gagged, escaped and ran off the Pointe?" Jack conjectured out loud. Isaac Phelps was the lead investigator for the county's homicide department. It was a department of two, Isaac and his assistant Shelly Northman. There simply weren't many homicides in Delaware County. Each year only one or none. The majority of the investigations, on which Phelps was called out, had more to do with him reviewing the scene and or paperwork and determining if he agreed with a coroner's view that foul play was, in fact, not involved. There were thirty or more of those types of calls a year. They usually had to do with elderly individuals found dead in their homes.

"If I had a guess, it would be a college prank gone bad. I'll start with the SUNY Delhi campus. I'll also give a call out to the schools in Oneonta and Cobleskill. There's probably four or five kids that are scared to death and ready to talk about this whole thing," Phelps said.

"Well, I've seen enough here," Kerr said. "Get the pictures then bag him up and get him down to the morgue. We'll see if an autopsy turns up anything else."

"Let's go up top and see if there's any clues to what happened," Phelps said.

"Do you mind taking the photos? Does it bother you?" Jack asked quietly of Paula, as the two other cops started walking away, along the path back to the parking area.

"No, it's really not that bad. Just sad, really. He looks so young," Paula said.

"Try to get everything you can, including orientation of the body to the cliff and the like."

"I got this, Jack. Run along with your cop buddies and play Sherlock Holmes," she turned with the camera and began taking shots of the corpse. "Love you."

"Okay," he said. "I love you."

Jack caught up with Kerr and Phelps after just a few minutes. They stopped to look at the gravel parking lot, but there were just too many overlapping tracks to get anything.

"Maybe some better tracks along the path. Right here, everything's been compromised all to hell."

"My initial investigation along the path didn't find any drag marks or anything like that," Jack said.

"Well, let's get three pairs of eyes on it," Phelps said. For the third time that day, Jack followed the gravel path through the trees to the peak of Hollow Pointe. They took their time as they walked, eyes panning across the ground. They also stopped to look out between the trees, to see if there were any tracks through the snow. None of them came up with anything of substance.

"Anything else you think we should look at?" Kerr asked of Jack as they stood on the rock outcropping, looking down on the fire and rescue guys, who were now securing the bagged body to a sled that they would drag out of the woods.

"Not that I saw, but I wouldn't mind doing a slow walk back to see if anything pops up," McMurphy said. "Also, got a call back from Eric Owens, the guy who found the body. He said he was looking over at Mount Pratt with binoculars and swears he saw somebody walking through the woods, maybe carrying a rifle. But he couldn't spot the guy again. Could have just been his imagination, but I can check on it, see if there's anything over there."

"Okay. Well, I've got appointments," Kerr said. "I'll leave it to you and Phelps to dig up evidence."

"Thanks for coming up so quickly," Jack said extending his hand.

"That's what I'm here for. You know, your old man and I never always saw eye to eye on a lot of things. It doesn't mean I didn't respect the hell out of him. Looks like he raised a good kid, too," Kerr said as he shook McMurphy's hand. "And just so there's no misunderstandings, this is a sheriff's department case now. We'll let you know if we need your help. Don't go screwing anything up."

Kerr turned and walked down the pathway back to his car. It was going to take him fifteen minutes to get to it, if he walked slow and scanned the ground again, as Jack knew he would.

"I don't see anything else up here. No additional tracks, no beer cans, no nothing," Phelps said as he walked over to McMurphy.

"Yeah, I didn't see anything either," Jack said quietly.

"Hey, don't let him get to you. With Kerr, it's always a pissing contest. You should see how he talks to the state troopers. He was elected to that position, he didn't earn it with good police work. It's a political position, you know. He has to look like the big guy in charge," Phelps said. "I actually thinks he likes you. That thing back in October? Yeah, people are still talking about that. You shot a freaking tiger, man. I guarantee you, Kerr ain't never shot a tiger."

"I didn't actually shoot the tiger, that was Michael Cooke," Jack said. "I did take out one of the guys, though. The driver."

"Well, see that?" Phelps said, slapping McMurphy on the shoulder. "Ninety-nine percent of the cops in this country will never fire in the line of duty. You're a one-percenter, Jack."

"What? Are you trying to get me to like you or something?" Jack asked with a half smile.

"I'll be calling you a lot more than you think on this," Phelps said. "You'll see."

"I'm going to meet the fire and rescue at the parking lot, make sure they've got everything they need. Then I'm going to hike a bit on Mount Pratt, see if I can see any trace of the guy Eric Owens thought he saw," Jack said. "Thanks."

"For what?"

"I don't know, the pep talk, taking this case off my desk, not being a jackass."

"Don't judge too quickly," Phelps said with a laugh.

They walked back down the path, still scanning, but less so than the first pass. The team that was extracting the body was bringing it through the trees on a sled. An ambulance was waiting in the parking area.

Phelps gave a curt wave to Jack and continued past the ambulance and on over to his squad car. McMurphy stood by and let the ambulance and fire-rescue guys do their thing and get the body bag into the back of the ambulance. Paula came over and gave Jack a tug on his coat.

"Oh, hey. How did you do?"

"Want to see?" Paula held out the camera and let Jack toggle through the pictures on the LCD screen.

"Looks good. Very thorough."

"I need coffee," Paula said. "Can we go?"

"Yeah, there isn't anything else for me to see here. I do have to do some checking over on Mount Pratt though. Somebody thought they might have seen a guy over there. Probably nothing. How about I meet you at the Peachy Keen in ten minutes? We'll get the coffee then I can come out and trek through the woods."

"It's a date," Paula said. She reached up and kissed him on the lips and headed across Saddle Brook Road, to where her car was parked on the Mount Pratt access road. She was followed by four volunteer firemen who had just finished with the retrieval. One of them was dragging the empty sled.

"Want a ride?" Jack heard one of them say to Paula, as the others laughed.

Jack turned to walk towards his truck. When he did, he almost ran over Goldie.

"Looks like it's all wrapped up here," she said. "Want to grab a coffee?"

"I'm already meeting Paula, sorry."

"Right. The girlfriend."

"She's a bit more than just a girlfriend."

"Really? I didn't see a ring. Didn't know it was that serious," Goldie said as they walked. She wasn't content walking beside him. She had to be at least a half step ahead.

"Well, I haven't given it to her yet," Jack replied with a scowl.

"So there is a ring?"

"Maybe."

"I agree, string her along for long as you can," Goldie said. "A girl like that won't be content living up here, married to a cop. You get married and she'll be nagging you to move to Florida or something."

"How would you know?" Jack asked.

"I went to school with forty of them just like her," Goldie said. "All they ever talked about was getting out of Coopers Hollow. Going to New York City, or the west coast or, of course, Florida. Girls don't want to stay here. Not girls like her."

"What about you," Jack countered. "You stayed."

"Yeah," Goldie looked at him, with a smile. "I stayed. Catch you later, cowboy." She climbed into her 4x4, and Jack shook his head.

"Maybe next time, Jack," she called to him. "Maybe next time

I'll let you buy me a drink." She started the big Ford pickup and revved the engine.

Jack watched her drive away, then got into his own SUV and headed towards the welcoming arms of coffee in the warm diner.

He thought about what Goldie had said regarding Paula and girls like her. Jack admitted that they had talked about leaving it all behind more than once. They had the money. The loot that they had found, in the basement of the burned out Lexmere Hotel, was enough to allow them to live comfortably for the rest of their lives. If they so chose, it could be a life of beaches and umbrella drinks, cruises around the world and villas by the bay.

He thought about the ring. It was still in the top drawer of his desk at the station, in a plain box, just in case Paula went snooping. He wanted to ask her, but he didn't know the right time. Since October, since they had started dating seriously, they had both been so busy. Paula with the writing of her book and Jack with everything that goes along with being a small town police chief. He wanted it to be special, to be memorable, maybe even romantic. He wasn't much of a romancer, but he could stand it for such an occasion.

He drove out to the road, and two volunteer guys were still there. Jack rolled down his window.

"You want us to tape off the entrance, or leave it for people to get in?" the tall one, Jasper Oxbow, asked.

"Put up the tape," Jack said. "We might want to take another look tomorrow after everything settles down a bit."

"Sure thing," Jasper said to Jack. He stood and called out to the other first responder. "Tape her up!"

Jack drove, as if on autopilot, to the Peachy Keen. He had to park almost a block away, but the sun was warm and there wasn't a cloud in the sky. It was a beautiful early April day.

The door jingled as he entered, and he saw the group of usual suspects sitting around the tables and at the lunch counter. Tubby was in front of the TV, dressed in a slightly rumpled suit, eating, what looked like a tuna sandwich and chips.

"Hey, Thaddeus," Jack said as he scanned the diner for Paula. He didn't see her, so he sat at the stool next to Tubby. "No Frosted Flakes?"

"Not now. It's lunch." He took an enormous bite of the tuna salad sandwich so that mayo smudged onto both cheeks. It was strange seeing the mountain of a man without his trademark beard. That old Ukrainian, Anton Oleksandr and his wife, had gotten the big man cleaned up, and flying right. Word was he was even going to the library every day and reading.

"So, how'd the preaching go?" Jack asked. Seemo came out from the kitchen and gave a quick nod to Jack. He was carrying plates of food over to one of the tables.

"Good," Tubby said, as if that was all to be said about it. He finished his sandwich with one massive bite. He raised his arm to wipe away the mayo on his mouth, then stopped mid motion. He reached over to the napkin dispenser and pulled out a handful, wiping his face with those.

"Well that's good," Jack said. "It means you're staying out of trouble."

"Yeah," Tubby replied. He then turned to Jack and got a very serious look on his face. "Can I ask you something?"

"Sure, what is it?"

"Well," Tubby rubbed his massive hand on his neck and looked down, as if he was embarrassed. "I have this thing coming up on Thursday. I was wondering if you and Miss Paula would come."

"What kind of thing, Thaddeus?"

"Well, it's my first Bible reading," Tubby said. "I been practicing for four weeks now. It's just, with mama at the hospital, and Rusty moved down to Florida, I don't have nobody else to ask to come."

"This Thursday night?" Jack asked.

"Yeah. You don't have to stay for the whole thing. I just thought you might like to see it, is all," Tubby said.

"Well, jeez, Thaddeus. I'm honored you'd ask me. I'll tell you what, I'll talk with Paula and see if we can come," Jack said.

"Come to what?"

"Oh, hey honey. Thaddeus here is having his very first Bible reading at the church on Thursday night, and he invited us," Jack said. He really didn't want to go. Baseball had started up, and there was a game on ESPN, Mets versus the Phillies.

"What time?" Paula asked.

"Seven."

"Sure, we can go," Paula said. "Which church?" There were several in town, Catholic, Baptist, Methodist, a non-denominational one that was in an old storefront on Main street.

"It's not a church, it's called the Kingdom Hall," Tubby said.

"Oh, I know where that is," Jack said. "Off Railroad. They tore down the old one and built the new one a few years back."

"Okay, Thaddeus," Paula said. "We'll be there at seven." The big man smiled, then reached over and pulled Paula in for an unexpected hug. She hugged him back, not able to get her arms all the way around.

Thaddeus McIntyre released Paula and then looked at Jack.

"Sorry, pal. Not a hugger," Jack said.

"Let's go get a table," Paula said. "See you Thaddeus."

"Bye, Miss Paula!"

Once they got to their seats, Seemo came over with menus.

"You need these or you know what you want?" he asked.

"First up, I think we both need coffee. The sun may be out, but we've been outside all morning," Jack said. "Still a little brisk."

"Okay, I get the coffees, then take your order," Seemo said.

"So, where you been?" Jack asked.

"What do you mean?"

"I just expected you to be here before me, is all."

"I said we'd meet here. I didn't say I was coming right here. I dropped the camera off at the station," Paula said. "What, are you worried I was off with one of those big, sexy firemen?" Those first-responder, volunteer firemen were not of the sexy variety. Big, perhaps, but really the antithesis of sexy on almost every count.

"No, I was just curious is all," Jack replied. The coffee arrived and he took a sip of it right away. He closed his eyes and let out a contented sigh.

"I've been thinking about this since about ten this morning," Jack said to Seemo. "I'll have a burger and fries."

"Um, are you sure?" Paula asked. "Chicken would be better. You've already had red meat three times this week." Jack looked at her, then back at the menu. He really didn't care, and he didn't want to get into a discussion about his eating habits right now.

"Yeah, sure. Make it a grilled chicken breast," Jack said.

"Still want the fries?" Seemo asked, looking at Paula instead of Jack. She shook her head.

"Do you have mixed veggies?" Jack asked.

"Coming right up. And you?"

"I'll have one of your delicious gyro wraps, with feta," Paula said. "And chips."

"Okay. Be just five minutes," Seemo said.

Jack took a sip of his coffee and chuckled to himself.

"What?"

"Look at us," Jack said. "We're acting like a couple of old, married farts."

"Yeah, kind of." She smiled and sipped her coffee, after having diluted it down with cream and four sugar-substitutes.

"Just got me thinking," Jack said. "Well, I've been thinking a lot lately."

"About?"

"I was thinking about maybe taking a weekend trip."

"To where?" she asked.

"I don't know, someplace I've never been before," Jack said. "Someplace neither one of us has been to before."

"Well that narrows it down," she said. "My friend Aimee in Oneonta, she's a travel agent. We could go see her and see what she suggests."

"Is that the one who's always changing her hair color and spells her name with way too many letter?" Jack asked.

"Yup. What were you thinking, like a cruise, or what?"

"I don't know. Not a long trip, just like two or three days."

"That isn't very long. It's not like we're on a budget," Paula said.

"No. I just can't be away for long. I need more help at work. I put another ad out online," he said. "Hopefully we get somebody in quickly and it eases up a bit."

"What about Michael?" Paula asked.

"You know, you're the second person to mention him to me."

"Maybe it's a sign."

"Maybe." Jack sipped at his coffee. He had almost drained the cup already. "Next time I see him, I'll ask."

Tubby got up off his stool and paid for his lunch. He waved to Jack and Paula and left through the front door. It hadn't even closed, when none other than Michael Cooke came in.

"Speak of the devil," Jack said to Paula. She turned to see Cooke, and gave him a smile and a wave. He walked over quickly without hesitation, his knee showing no weakness from the injury the previous fall.

Michael Cooke was taller than Jack, and at least two decades older. His hair was graying, but his eyes were bright. He was thin, muscular, and carried himself with assured confidence. He still wore his hog's tooth necklace, from his time in the Marine Corps. The empty rifle cartridge attached to the neck chain was peaking out from his button down shirt and it reminded Jack of all that the middle-aged man, who stood before him, was capable.

"Hey, thought I might find you here," Michael said.

"Pull up a chair, we were just talking about you," Paula said.

"Well, I don't think you'll have time. Jack, I just walked past the station, and there were two guys at your door. Suits and ties. They looked like feds. They were screwing around with the door. I asked them if they were looking for somebody, and they told me to get lost," Cooke said.

"Feds?" Jack was already on his feet. "Paula, get that to go for me, will you?"

Michael followed him out the door and down the steps to the sidewalk. Jack turned and looked at him.

"What are you doing?"

"I thought you might like some backup," Michael said, with a half smile.

"Just like old times, huh?"

"God, I hope not," Cooke said.

Chapter 9

They definitely looked like federal agents. With which letters of the government alphabet soup they were labeled, that was yet to be seen. Black suits, white shirts, dark glasses, close cropped hair, bulges under the suit coats indicating sidearms; they were the clichéd picture of federal agents. One of them was looking out into the street with his hands clasped in front, while the other was up by the door, facing the street, hands behind his back.

"Can I help you gentleman?" Jack asked. The one near the door brought his hands around front and slid something into his inner breast pocket.

"We're looking for Chief McMurphy. I'm Agent Summers, this is Agent Haas," the one on the sidewalk said. He looked to be in his thirties, maybe Jack's age, with a hint of gray to his short hair. His face was well tanned, as was his partner's.

"Yes, I'm the Chief, what can I do for you?"

"We need to speak with you," said Agent Haas, stepping down the to the sidewalk level. Neither agent extended a hand to shake.

"Can I see some ID?" Jack asked. The agents exchanged glances, and slowly retrieved their badges from jacket pockets.

"Who's this?" Agent Summers asked.

"A friend," McMurphy said, as he looked at the badges. They said Federal Department of Criminal Investigation. There was little doubt in Jack's mind that this was about the shooting incident from six months ago. But who was FDCI?

"I've never heard of the Federal Department of Criminal Investigation," Jack said, handing back the badges and identification.

"It's part of a joint venture between Homeland Security and the FBI," Agent Haas said. He didn't offer any additional information.

"Okay, so what's up, fellas?" Jack asked.

"Let's step inside," Agent Summers said. McMurphy unlocked the door, noticing a few scrape marks around the lock. It appeared to Jack that Agent Haas was trying to break in when he and Michael had walked up. Something unusual was going on. Federal agents, from an agency he'd never heard of before, breaking and entering a police station in broad daylight?

"After you, gentlemen."

"Please, Chief McMurphy. We'll follow you." Agent Haas said.

"We won't need you," Agent Summers said to Michael.

"Jack?" Michael looked at his friend and back at the two agents.

"I'll be okay. I'll give you a call in a bit, I've been meaning to talk to you about something anyway," Jack said. He went into the station house followed by the agents.

Cooke stood on the sidewalk for a moment, shifting his weight between his feet. He finally turned and walked back towards the Peachy Keen.

Once inside, Jack made his way to his office, which was really just several framed glass dividers that sectioned off the rest of the desks in the small station house. There wasn't even a ceiling to his office. It was the old bank manager's office back when the building housed the Coopers Hollow Savings Bank. Decades ago, it had been converted. The vault was transformed into a very small holding cell, and the basement received two additional cells. The rest of the basement was dedicated to the storage of old case files and anything else that got left there over the course of time.

"Come on back," Jack said. He pushed open his door and got around his desk. He indicated two chairs that were against the wall for the agents.

"We'll stand," Agent Haas said.

"Well, I'm sitting. I've been on my feet all morning. We have a murder investigation. So I'm very busy. I have fifteen minutes," Jack said.

"It shouldn't take that long," Agent Summers said. "We need all of your files on the shooting incident from last October. We need all of the files and all of the evidence as well. Just a standard transfer is all. We'll be right out of your hair in no time."

"Um, okay. And you'll be returning it when?" Jack asked.

"The FDCI is officially taking over this investigation, so you'll need to cooperate fully," Agent Haas said.

"Yeah, well I'd be happy to help out. Do you have evidence transfer request forms and an official request to take the files? I'll need to have something on my books with a signature so I can track where all of it went, you know. If someone ever comes back and wants info, I have to give them a name," Jack said. The agents exchanged glances. Agent Summers stepped forward and slid out a large smartphone. He started poking at it with his index finger.

"This is a special case," Agent Summers said. "The normal protocols aren't in play here."

"If I didn't know any better, I'd say that trashing the normal protocols was akin to making evidence disappear, now why would you want to do that?" Jack asked. Glances exchanged again.

"I think you need to realize, that as long as you hang on to all of that, your career is in jeopardy," Agent Haas said.

"And now the threats. Not normal protocols, huh?"

"Not threats. You don't realize the identity of one of the men you gunned down," Agent Summers said. "Let me show you." He poked at his phone a few more times and then showed a picture to Jack. It was the drug dealer, El Tigre, the man who eventually lost his life to the escaped Siberian Tiger. What a mess.

"Yeah. He's dead," Jack said. "El Tigre became el luncho." Summers poked and swiped the phone again. He held it up for Jack again. This face was not as familiar. The man in the picture was clean shaven, and outfitted in a suit and tie.

"Who's this?" Jack asked.

"One of El Tigre's guys," Summers said.

"And one of our guys too," Haas said.

Jack cursed.

"He was undercover?"

"Deep."

"And I shot him."

"Yes."

"And your team is doing clean up."

"Correct."

He cursed again. He thought back to that night in the mountains north of town. All hell was breaking loose. He had almost lost Paula, and if it hadn't been for Michael Cooke, everything would have been a whole lot worse. Gloria Graves, her daughter and her daughter's punk boyfriend would have all been killed. Maybe. Maybe the agent would have stepped in and stopped it before it went too far. Maybe not.

Jack reached over and took the phone from Agent Summers and looked closer at the picture. He knew the man. He was the driver of the SUV which tried to escape. Jack was the one that pulled the trigger that killed him. Shotgun blasts through the windshield and the driver's door. It tore him to pieces. It wasn't a surprise he didn't recognize his agency photo. There wasn't much left to the man's face after Jack had shot him.

He suddenly felt ill, like he was going to vomit. He reached for the bottle of water on his desk and fumbled with the cap as he brought it to his lips.

"So now you understand," Agent Summers said.

"The investigation into El Tigre's network went far beyond his little drug running business. He was a low man on the totem pole," Agent Haas said. "We had a man who was poised to take over his business and get closer to the top guys. And now we have nothing."

"Thanks to you," Agent Summers said.

"Okay, enough," Jack barked back. "Your agent, your man was killed while perpetrating a crime with known criminals. It was viewed as a matter of life and death. You guys put him there, you guys hold the bag for this."

"This isn't a blame game, Jack," Agent Haas said.

"We just need this stuff to go away. We're inserting another agent who will be playing the cousin of Agent Spaulding," Summers said.

"That was his name? Spaulding?"

"Yes."

"All of your documentation needs to be unavailable to any free-dom of information requests," Agent Haas said, quietly, as if there might be someone listening. "These dealers, they're sophisticated. They have their own group of people investigating us right back. So here's how it goes: you handed everything off to us, and forgot to get the proper forms. You don't remember to whom you gave the evidence. You boxed it up and agents came to get it. Got it?"

Jack was quiet for a few moments. He understood the reasoning behind what they were doing, but it certainly wasn't legal. Maybe the government had gotten to the point where bending the rules and breaking a few laws didn't mean much to them, but it didn't mean he had to be a part of it.

"Well, I appreciate you coming all the way out here, Agent Haas and Agent Summers," Jack said. "But I'm not going to transfer anything without the paperwork. If you guys want to lose it in your system, that's fine. But I'm not going to be a part of purposefully destroying evidence. So if there's nothing else, I can show you to the door." Jack stood, his thighs burning from the mountain hiking from earlier. He felt a bit weak, knowing he had skipped breakfast and hadn't gotten lunch yet. When he got hungry, he got grumpy. He was about to get a lot grumpier if the agents didn't leave.

"You're making a mistake," Agent Summers said, putting his phone away.

"If you play hardball, it won't go well for you," Haas said.

"Okay, I've had enough. You two get the hell out of my station right now, before I arrest you for obstruction of justice and attempted evidence tampering," Jack barked. He felt his face become flush.

"We'll go," Summers said. "For now."

"Enjoy this office while you can," Haas said. He knocked on Jack's desk with his knuckles, as he turned to walk out of the office. They left Jack standing behind his desk, clenching and unclenching his fists. He heard the front door close with a rattle, and he closed his eyes. The rage inside of him had built up quickly, and he was trying to let it die down. Then he heard the front door open again. He instinctively drew his .38 revolver.

"You okay?" Michael's voice called out.

"Jeez," Jack breathed out. "Yeah, come on back," he called out. He holstered his revolver just as Michael came in to his office.

"Everything okay?"

"Not really, no."

"What did they want? More grilling on the incident?"

"Not exactly," Jack flopped down into his chair. "One of the guys we – I shot that night, he was a federal agent. Undercover."

Michael swore, and took a seat in one of the chairs Jack had offered the agents.

"Which one?"

"Driver of the SUV."

"The one guy you got," Michael said pursing his lips.

"Yeah, the only guy I got," Jack repeated.

"I didn't mean it that way, I just meant," Michael stammered for his words. "I just meant I'd rather take this on me, you know? I'm done with my police work. They can't do anything to me. But they can make your life a living hell here."

"I know."

"What did they want besides dropping that bombshell?"

"They wanted me to disappear the evidence," Jack said. "They want it to go away so they can slide in another agent and pick up where they left off. They're worried the bad guys will dig up the info and everything will fall apart."

"Oh, that's BS," Michael said.

"No kidding."

"Leave you twisting in the wind when someone else comes looking for the files. You told them no, right?"

"Of course I told them no," Jack said.

"They didn't look happy when they left."

"Good. Think there will be blow back?"

"Not officially, but who knows what they'll do. They might get the IRS to audit you, they might just harass you until you can't take it anymore. They might do nothing and actually send through the proper paperwork and then make it go away themselves," Michael said.

"See, that's what I don't get," Jack countered. "Why not just leave me out of it and make the stuff disappear internally at the FDCI, or whatever they call themselves."

"FDCI?"

"Federal Department of Criminal Investigation," Jack said.

"Never heard of it."

"Me either."

"Computers," Michael continued. "And RFID tags."

"RFID? What?"

"Radio Frequency Identification Tags. The reason they can't just lose it internally. Nothing gets lost anymore. Once it's scanned in and tagged with a radio tracker, it never goes away. They had to try to get to it before it got into their system."

"But the sheriff's department and even the state police, heck, the state forest rangers all had reports on this. It was a cross-agency thing. I didn't even do the preliminary investigation, that was all the sheriff. I just wrote my reports and submitted them. I only have a few files here and a few boxes of evidence down in the basement," Jack said.

"Well, then maybe it's not what they're saying. Maybe it's something else. Maybe you've got something in the evidence that none of the other departments have," Michael said. "Might be worth looking through again, just for curiosity's sake."

"Yeah," Jack replied, thinking about the four boxes in the basement vault. They contained some of the clothing from all the deceased individuals, anything that was on their person when they were taken to the medical examiner. The SUV's were towed to Delhi and were still sitting in lockup behind the sheriff's office. The only reason he still had the boxes of clothing was because Dr. Fuller lived in Coopers Hollow, not Delhi, and he had it at his office there in town, after doing a thorough review. That wasn't exactly by the book, but everything had a paper trail with appropriate chain of custody. Anybody from the sheriff's department, the state troopers or even the feds could have put in an evidence transfer request and he would have packed it up and sent it on its way, happily. He just never received a request.

"Listen," Jack said. "I need lunch. Walk with me."

"Okay."

Jack locked up the office door again, making sure he also turned the deadbolt lock, further up on the door. It was the first time he had bothered with that since he'd taken over for his deceased father.

"Ballard's leaving," Jack said as they started up the sidewalk towards the diner.

"No kidding. What are you going to do?"

"I already placed an ad in the papers, Paula's going to help drop it onto a few police forums too. But in two weeks, it's going to be just me," Jack said.

"That's not good," Michael replied.

"Can I ask a favor of you?"

"I'm retired."

"I know, that's why it's a favor. Favors are things that you do for a friend even when you don't really want to," Jack said.

"You're a bastard."

"It will be just for a few weeks until I get somebody or somebodies in to help. Pull the shifts you want. I'll pay for the uniform and get you a new pistol. I just need the manpower right now," Jack said. "Short term, promise."

"Jack, you know you can count on me. Remember, though, I'm an old man. I'm not going to be chasing down criminals for you."

"It's more like writing tickets for blowing through the red light, or just coming out with me when we get a domestic call," Jack said. "Light duty."

"Okay, I'll do it," Cooke replied, quietly. "Of course I'll do it. Gloria will probably be happy to get me out of the house, I think." He smiled, and clamped a hand down on the younger man's shoulder. There was a lot resting on those shoulders. Being the number one guy, even in a small town like this, wasn't an easy task.

"Thanks, bro."

The door chimes at the Peachy Keen didn't catch Paula's attention. Her plate was all but empty, and she had a to-go box ready for Jack. It was sitting on the table in front of her, but she was two-thumbing her phone, preoccupied. He walked over and kissed her on the head.

"Oh, hey. Everything okay? I was just about to come over," she said.

"Yeah, a couple of federal agents just wanted to talk about October again," he told her. He sat down and snatched the Styrofoam box.

"Drink?" Seemo called from behind the counter.

"Coke," Jack said.

"Make that a water, Seemo. He doesn't know what he's saying. Very hungry man. Delusional," Paula said. Jack snorted a smile. Other guys might have been annoyed by it, but he kind of liked having someone take care of him. Michael pulled up a chair next to them.

"You don't mind, do you?"

"Not at all," Paula said.

"Paula, meet the new Deputy Chief of Coopers Hollow," Jack said between bites of his lukewarm chicken sandwich.

"Temporary," Michael added.

"Oh, that's great. I was worried. With Ballard flying the coup, we didn't know what was going to happen. Thanks, Michael," Paula said, reaching over and patting his hand.

"You're welcome," Michael said. "You know, we never discussed salary or benefits."

"Details, details," Jack replied, almost done with his sandwich and starting in on the veggies.

"I'll type up a press release," Paula said.

"No," Cooke replied. "No press release. I don't want a big thing made out of this. It's just for a little while, right? I worked a long time to get to retirement."

"Just a little while," Jack said. "It will be over before you know it, and you'll be missing it."

Michael laughed out loud as Seemo brought over Jack's water with a lemon.

"We'll see how much I miss it."

Chapter 10

The creaking startled her awake. She lay there quietly, listening to the old house, too scared to move. She heard the wind outside, as it rattled the old wooden doors of the barn. Then she heard the sound that had awoken her. Footsteps in the hallway, a telltale floor board creaking. A voice. A man's voice. Saying something just out of earshot. Words without meanings.

"Eric," she whispered as loudly as she dared. The words barely made a sound. They were choked up in her throat from fear. She knew what was in the hallway. "Eric, wake up. Somebody is in the house."

Her husband didn't stir. He was so fast asleep that she knew waking him would take too much work. She heard the footsteps again, they were going away from their room and towards the back of the house, towards Riker's room. Was it laughter, as well?

She mustered as much courage as she could and slipped out from the covers. She tiptoed across their floor, praying that the floorboards wouldn't creak and give her away. The house was pitch black. Clouds had moved in to fill the night sky, the moon was covered, there was no light coming through the windows from outside. She slowly opened their bedroom door, and the footsteps stopped. They had put a nightlight in the hallway outlet, so the kids could find their way to the bathroom at night, without fear or stubbing of toes. The nightlight was out.

"Eric," she tried to whisper, but the word failed to make it past her tongue. There was a big knife on the dresser, a hunting knife. She didn't remember seeing it before, but Eric must have bought it since they moved up to the mountains and away from the city.

She took the knife in her hand, it was cool and heavy. With it held in front of her, she slipped into the hallway.

Up ahead, entering Riker's room, was a shadow of a man. She could barely make it out. She was stricken with fear. Her feet wouldn't move. The shadow slipped completely into her son's room.

Suddenly her fear gave way to rage, and she ran down the hall, knife raised above her head.

"Get out of his room! I'm going to kill you if you touch him!" She screamed at the top of her lungs. She burst into Riker's room and turned on the light. She didn't see anyone but Riker, who was stirring from his sleep.

"Mom?" Riker said with eyes still closed against the sudden burst of light. She frantically ripped open his closet. Nothing. She was on the floor, looking under his bed. There was no one. Sylvia looked over at his back window, and realized that the man must have escaped through it. She pushed it open all the way and looked out. There he was, standing in the yard, looking up at her. He'd tripped the motion detector light. She could see he was stark naked and had gashes on his body. He'd tried to hurt her little boy! The rage boiled up into her throat and she let out a animalistic howl, like a banshee, hanging halfway out of the window.

She turned and flew through the hallway and down the steps. She was into the kitchen and then through the sliding glass doors, out into the yard. She still held the knife, and she was ready to use it. The naked pervert moved away from the light and ran out into the trees behind the house. He had a sneer on his mud-streaked face. She tried to follow, but the trees had grown thick, and the branches caught at her nightgown and hair.

She finally burst through into another back yard, and then around the house out to the street. She looked up and down the street, but didn't see him. She was on Main Street, and the red light at the corner was blinking red, as it did every night after 11pm. There was a light fog in town. As the light blinked on, it bathed the entire street in a hellish red.

"Where are you? You pervert!" She screamed profanities into the air, calling out the sick, pedophile who'd just tried to hurt her little boy. Lights started to come on in the houses that faced Main Street.

"Come out and face me you coward!" She screamed. "I will cut it off and make you choke on it!"

A few of the neighbors came out of their homes, more than one had a phone to their ear. She screamed and screamed until her voice gave out.

Flashing lights and the screeching of tires came from behind her. She whirled around to see the police SUV hurtling down Main Street towards her. She didn't realize she had been standing on the double yellow lines. The police vehicle slammed on the brakes, and out hopped the chief in his undershirt and bare feet.

"Are you hurt? Are you okay, ma'am?" He called to her. She was bathed in the bright spotlight attached to the door post of the SUV.

"No! Somebody broke into the house! Somebody tried to take Riker!" She tried to scream, but her voice was scratchy now. It made her cough. She went into a coughing spasm. This made her head hurt terribly, like a massive migraine swooping in and tap-dancing in football cleats on her brain.

"Sylvia!" Eric Owens came bursting onto the street in just his boxer briefs. When he saw her, now doubled over, with hands on her temples, he rushed to her. "Sylvia, what happened?"

"Eric, you wouldn't wake up! Somebody tried to hurt Riker!" She started sobbing. "Oh God, it hurts. It's a bad one."

"It's okay," Eric said. He hugged her. Her skin was freezing, cold to the touch. "It was just a dream. Nobody tried to hurt Riker, honey. It was a bad dream from the migraine."

Chief McMurphy walked up to the Owens and bent over with his hands on his knees.

"Is she okay?" McMurphy asked. "I mean, has this happened before?"

"I think she's okay. I think she's having one of her headaches," Eric said. "No, this has never happened before. She's had headaches, but nothing like this."

"I saw him outside," she sobbed. Her voice croaking with each syllable. "He was in the house, going into Riker's room, then I saw him out the window. He was naked. He jumped out the window and tried to run away. He's here somewhere. You need to find him! He looked right at me and was laughing."

"No sweetie. Nobody was in the house," Eric held her close. He took the small, crystal flower vase out of her hand. When he did, she looked at it with a puzzled expression.

"I was going to kill him. With the knife," Sylvia said.

"What knife, honey? This is a vase. I got it for you last week," Eric said. He looked around and saw his neighbors start to go inside and shut down their lights again.

"It was a knife. A big hunting knife," Sylvia said. "I don't understand."

"It was a bad dream. It was all in your head, baby," Eric said.

"You want to hop into the truck and I'll give you a ride back to your house?" Jack asked. "I just need to get down some notes on this."

"Okay," Eric said. Sylvia was now shivering. The overnight temperatures had dropped down to below freezing again. She was ice cold in his arms. He had to practically carry her to the truck, as her legs buckled, with lack of strength.

"Do you want me to call an ambulance?" Jack asked.

"Honey, do you need to go to the hospital?"

"No, I just need my headache medicine and to go to sleep. It's not really happening," she said.

Jack made sure they were secure in the back seat and then

followed Eric's directions to their house. It only took a few moments to get there, practically just around the block. All the lights were on. Riker and Yasmine were in blankets standing at the door when Eric helped Sylvia inside. Jack followed, having pulled on his overcoat and boots from the trunk.

"This won't take very much time," Jack said.

"Okay."

"Do you believe anyone was in the house?" Jack asked.

"I swear I saw him" Sylvia said. "But I don't know now. It seems like a dream. God, my head. Eric, get me my meds!" She cursed at him. Eric looked at his wife and then at Jack.

"I don't think so," Eric said. "Let me take her up to bed and I'll be right back down. Kids, get back to bed. Mom just had a bad dream."

The Owens kids dutifully headed back up the stairs to their rooms, while Eric helped Sylvia up the steps. He was gone for a moment, leaving Jack in the living room.

After about five minutes, Eric returned. He had pulled on a pair of khakis, but was still barefoot.

"I didn't see any evidence of anyone in the house. I heard Sylvia screaming and heard her run down the hall and out the back door. I tried to follow her, but I didn't know which way she went. I didn't see or hear anyone else," Eric said.

"She's on medication?" Jack asked.

"Yeah. She's suffering from some issues."

"Do you believe she's a threat to herself or anyone else? Do you think she would hurt the kids?"

"No. No way. I think she was just confused. I think she woke up with a migraine and was in the middle of a bad dream. Maybe she was sleep walking. She takes a sleep aid," Eric said.

Jack nodded as he took notes.

"It's for insomnia, and also for stress and depression," Eric continued. "We'll go to the doctor and see if maybe the medications are getting crossed up. I'm really sorry."

"It's okay. It happens," Jack said. "I just need some details and I'll let you get some sleep."

He asked the standard name, age and residence questions. He then asked if they needed any medical attention again, just to be sure. Eric declined an ambulance, once again. Sylvia called out for him from upstairs. Yasmine ran down the hallway and into the master bedroom.

"Mom, it's okay. Do you want some water?" Yasmine said.

"We've been through a lot," Eric said. "She's been battling depression for awhile now. Last fall, with dad dying and other family stuff, well, it's been a challenge, you know?"

"I understand," Jack replied quietly. "Let me know if you need anything else. I'm just going to file this as a medical issue. If you need a copy for the doctor, just let me know. It will be ready in a day or two, okay?"

"Okay," Eric said. "Thanks."

"No problem. Mind if I just look around a bit. See if maybe there's anything to her story? I mean, stranger things have happened."

"No, go ahead. I'll turn on the outside lights. The barn lights too," Eric said.

"Thanks."

"Jack," Eric said, before McMurphy went out the door. "I never thanked you for trying to save dad. None of us blame you for what happened."

The comment caught McMurphy off guard. His head was a million miles away from that Saturday morning in October. It took him a moment to form a response.

"He was a good man," Jack said. "A real good man. I miss him."

"Me too. Goodnight."

"Goodnight."

Outside Jack shone his light on the grass. There was frost on it. As far as he could tell, there were only two sets of tracks leading from the house, and they both came out the back door and off the deck. He shined his flashlight beam up on the rear of the house and then down to the flower bed below Riker's window. The dirt was undisturbed. There were no prints.

He made a note in his notebook. He'd left his digital recorder at home. Heck, he'd left half of his clothes at home.

He had received an urgent call from Dennis Ponder, the town pharmacist, owner of Ponder's Pharmacy on Main Street. He lived in the apartment above the pharmacy, looking right out onto the street. He said that Jack had better hurry, someone was being murdered on Main Street. The short drive had taken mere seconds, as Jack pushed his vehicle to over one-hundred miles-per-hour on the state route into town.

He finished looking around the Owens' house and then climbed back behind the wheel of his department SUV, and retraced his path back home.

Adrenaline was still pumping through his veins when he pulled into the driveway. He didn't bother climbing back into bed, he wouldn't have gotten any sleep. Instead, he slid into his over-stuffed recliner and switched on the television. Sportscenter had the highlights from the west coast baseball games. He was finally able to fall back to sleep an hour later. The clock on the wall read ten minutes after three in the morning.

Chapter 11

He awoke with a start at just before five in the morning. After the visit from the federal agents and a middle of the night call out for the Owens' family, Jack was exhausted. But his body wouldn't let him sleep. His internal clock told him it was time to get up. Paula had stayed at her apartment that night. She had been staying over more and more, but she still liked having her own place. He'd thought about inviting her to stay with him more, after the Lexmere Hotel, the place where she'd had an apartment and her office, had burned down. That was a pretty big commitment, however. Not to mention, the small town still had very traditional views, and he didn't want to give them anything else to talk about.

He was thinking about Paula. He went to the bathroom and then padded, barefoot, to the kitchen.

Had they been together long enough to fall in love? He'd dated his first wife for years before getting married. Not that that relationship was a paradigm from which to take a lesson. She had been his high school sweetheart, and they both went to the same college and dated all during. After that, after joining the force with his dad, it just made sense to get married. It was the next logical step. With Paula it was different.

She was not some country girl. She was brash and bold and no-nonsense. She would make a good cop, Jack had always thought. But she was also very feminine. She knew how to use her sensuality to her benefit. At first, it had been annoying, even a bit of a turn off. But she wore him down. And then there was October. She was there for him when his dad died. She was genuinely concerned for him. It was like the whole ordering-a-water-instead-of-a-Coke-for-him thing. A year ago he would have thought she was just being bossy. Now he knew that it was a case of her being genuinely concerned for him. And he loved that. He loved her. It's why he bought the ring.

Sportscenter was repeating the overnight broadcast. There was nothing new. There wouldn't be for another hour or so. He was wide awake. He decided to drink his cup of coffee and go out to the garage. It took only a few moments to get the coffee brewing. In the meantime, he cranked on the area heater in the garage. It would knock the chill off by the time the coffee was ready.

The 1969 Chevelle SuperSport was a hobby for which he had nowhere near enough time. It sat in unfinished condition, up on floor jacks, in the furthest bay of his two-stall garage. He hadn't lifted a wrench on it since October. His dad had helped get the engine installed the previous summer. The numbers wouldn't match, so they put in the 427 cubic inch V8 rather than the smaller 350 V8. When it was all done, with the improved Edelbrock carburetor, it would pump out over four hundred horsepower. He'd toyed with the idea of going with an even bigger engine block, but he didn't want a scoop on the hood. The original, numbers-matching color was champagne, but he was going to get it painted Daytona Yellow with black rally stripes.

The vehicle itself had been in relatively good condition when he bought it three years prior. The engine compartment could more than accommodate the beastly V8. All that was really left was getting everything put back together and getting the new paint job, and of course, the interior; the last element completed on any hot rod or restoration job. The chrome wheels he'd ordered had come in and were stacked in the corner. The tires he'd ordered had arrived four months ago and were down at Emilio's garage, waiting for him. They were paid for, so Emilio wasn't giving him trouble abut picking them up.

The coffee was ready, so he slipped on his jacket and went out to work for an hour or two, mug in hand. It was still a little chilly in the garage, but not bad. The carburetor was still in the box on the fender. He had placed it there months ago, and it hadn't moved.

Jack spent an hour puttering around, locating the tools he needed and then bolting in the new carburetor and fitting the air filter housing back into place. It would have taken a pro less than fifteen minutes, but Jack wasn't really focused, and dropped his tools down into the engine compartment a few times.

For the most part, the vehicle was ready to be fired up. But it was approaching six-thirty. He needed to get his hands cleaned up and then shower before heading into the office.

He had to plan a swearing in ceremony for Michael Cooke. He also had to finalize the Owens' report. Then he owed a call to Detective Phelps to see if he needed anything on the John Doe investigation. Not to mention anything else that might roll in. Something always rolled in.

He walked back into the kitchen and got out the degreaser hand cleaner. He spent ten minutes washing his hands, getting all the junk out from under his fingernails. Even though he wore gloves, he always managed to get his hands dirty when he worked on the car. Next he started the coffee again and headed for a shower.

It was a peaceful, foggy morning. Warmer air was supposed to be moving into the area today. The weatherman said it was going to be partly cloudy with a high in the upper forties or lower fifties. Weather like that, after the long winter, felt like summer to him. The beginning of the following week didn't look so good, though. Lots of rain coming through, with a chance for flash flooding. That was a few days out, so lots could change between now and then.

He pulled his SUV around to the back of the station house. He locked the vehicle, something he wouldn't have done the day before, and went in through the rear entrance. The station was equipped with an alarm system, but his father hadn't paid for the subscription service in several years. It seemed to be an impractical expense on an already strapped budget. Jack contemplated calling the company and getting the service switched back on. He didn't like people trying to break into his building, federal agents or no.

He started the coffee maker, switched on the lights, and settled into his chair. He had his notebook from the previous night, but he didn't really feel like typing up a report right away. What he was really curious about resided in four boxes sitting in the vault in the basement. He thought about what Michael had said, that maybe there was something else in the evidence. Something everybody had missed. He clenched his jaw and drummed his fingers on his desk in deliberation.

It only took a few moments for him to locate the boxes. They weren't that heavy, as they only contained personal items from the deceased. He carried them up to his office, two at a time. One box went on his desk, while the others were stacked on the floor next to it. He pulled the cardboard lid off the box and started through the contents. This one belonged to El Tigre. The clothing was bloodstained and ripped. There was an envelope with a cellphone, watch, gold necklace, gold bracelet, a ring, a money clip with a sizable fold of cash, and a folding knife. There wasn't much to it. Maybe there was something on the cellphone. He tried to power it on, but the battery was long dead, and he didn't have a charger for it. He looked over everything else for a few minutes, and then boxed it back up.

What he wanted was Agent Spaulding's box. He opened the next one and knew he found what he was looking for.

The black shirt still had small glass shards embedded in it from where his bullet had destroyed the windshield and showered the undercover agent with glass. Jack remembered that night vividly. The shotgun blasts, the SUV steering into the ditch and flipping. The already dead agent slamming into the ceiling and then against a side window. Bones had been fractured, but it was decided by Dr. Fuller that those occurred post mortem. Spaulding was dead before the vehicle had landed on its roof.

During the autopsy, his black jeans had been cut away from his body, and placed into a plastic bag. They were stiff with blood saturation. A paper envelope contained a watch, cash, a cellphone, which had been destroyed by the shotgun blast, a necklace with a pendant, and a money clip that had been separated from the cash.

There wasn't much at all. Again, maybe it was the cellphone. Jack held it in his hand. Bent and thoroughly smashed from the shot. He set it down on his desk. The FDCI probably had a team that could recover something from the broken piece of electronics, but to Jack it looked like a total loss.

He took out each item and looked them over carefully, before lining them up on the desk next to the previous item. If he were an undercover agent, he wouldn't have carried anything that could give him away. He took the necklace in his hand and held it up to get a closer look.

The pendant was the type that opened to reveal a picture. Jack looked for a release with his thumbnail, and finally found it. The pendant opened to reveal a picture of a child, perhaps two years old. A smiling little girl with pierced ears. The sight made Jack sick to his stomach. He reached for the bottle of water he'd left there from the previous day. There was only a swallow left, so he went to get another bottle out of the mini fridge, in the corner of his office. Opening the door, he saw that he was out. Nothing but an old bottle of ketchup and a salad dressing packet. He could hop in the SUV and head down to the Stewart's Shop on the corner, which would already be open for business. Or he could go to the Peachy Keen and see if Seemo was up and serving yet. Some mornings the diner opened at five, sometimes at six. Sometimes someplace in between. He opted for the diner and the full breakfast.

Making sure that the station house was locked up and secure, Jack walked the short block and a half distance to the diner. The lights were on and the open sign was illuminated. McMurphy wasn't surprised to see Tubby sitting at his normal perch at the counter. He was wearing jeans and a big flannel shirt today.

"No preaching today?" Jack asked. He thought Tubby's church always had people preaching on Saturdays. In fact, there was a time when the police station would receive complaint calls about solicitors in town. It would turn out to be just the people knocking on doors with Bibles and tracts. Jack Sr. usually took those calls. He'd go out and talk with the evangelizers, then go to the home or homes of the citizens who called it in and let them know he checked it out. There hadn't been a complaint like that in years.

"Not today," Tubby said. "There's a 'sembly. Everybody is there. I couldn't go, because I don't drive. Mr. Anton didn't feel up to driving either."

"'Sembly? What's that, like a revival?"

"It's a big meeting at a big 'sembly hall in Newburgh," Tubby said. He was bringing a spoonful of Frosted Flakes up to his mouth. "I'll go to the summer one."

"Interesting," Jack said, quietly. Seemo came out of the kitchen, wiping his hands on his towel.

"So, what you have permission for today," Seemo laughed. Jack just shook his head. "Only kidding. She's good for you. A little bossy, but what woman isn't, hey?"

"Can I just get an orange juice and a toasted bagel with cream cheese?"

"Coming right up, bean sprouts and tap water!" Seemo laughed again, as he headed back to the kitchen.

Jack watched the news quietly. Seemo returned with the orange juice, then returned to the kitchen for the bagel.

A story on the television caught his attention. Something about finding a hidden chamber in the old Post Office building in Oneonta. Apparently it had been walled off under a stairwell in the basement. It was something of a bomb shelter, with provisions, blankets and even gas masks all dating back to the World War Two era.

His mind drifted back to the evidence boxes, and specifically Agent Spaulding's locket with the picture.

"Hey, Seemo," Jack called to him in the kitchen. He came through the swinging doors a moment later with a toasted bagel with cream cheese.

"What's up Chief?"

"Anybody still work on jewelry in town? You know, like intricate repairs?" A thought was percolating in Jack's mind.

"No, all them jewelers packed their bags. You have to go to the city," Seemo said. By 'the city' he meant Oneonta. Seemo didn't leave Coopers Hollow but maybe twice a year, so a trip to the small city of Oneonta, thirty miles to the west, was considered a big deal.

"Mr. Anton works on watches," Tubby said. "I seen him do it."

"Do you think he'd look at a locket for me, from a necklace? I want to see if there's a hidden compartment in it."

"Mr. Anton would do it. He's nice like that," Tubby said.

"How about after breakfast, you and I walk back to your place and see if he can take a look," Jack said, taking a bite of his bagel.

"Okay," came the reply.

Fifteen minutes and two more bowls of Frosted Flakes later, the two of them were walking back to the station house, to retrieve the locket. Jack grabbed the watch for good measure.

"Why do you think there's something hidden in the locket?" Tubby asked.

"It's just a hunch."

"Mmm." Tubby was quiet for a second. "What's a hunch?"

"It's an educated guess."

"Oh."

From the police station, it was only a walk of a few blocks to the small house owned by Anton Oleksander and his wife. Tubby stayed in the back bedroom, now that his mother had been institutionalized.

"Ah, Chief!" Mr. Anton said as Tubby brought him in the back door into the kitchen. "Sit! Have breakfast!"

"Thank you, but I just ate," Jack replied. "Thaddeus here was telling me that you tinker with jewelry and watches, is that true?"

"Yes. I do this for long time now," Mr. Anton said. "Nobody bothered by it before."

"No, it's no bother. I was wondering if you could look at something for me? These two items were taken off a shooting victim. I was just wondering if there was a hidden chamber or something on the locket or maybe an inscription on the inside of the watch back or something."

"I can take a look," Mr. Anton said. "Let me get my tools."

Jack's phone rang, and he fished it out of his pocket.

"Hello?"

"Hey, hon. I just woke up. You want anything for breakfast?"

"Just had a bagel and cream cheese. Seemo gave me crap about whether I had gotten permission from you," Jack said. This elicited a laugh from Paula.

"Next time I see him, I'll make sure to give him grief about it," she said. "I might drive down to Oneonta and see Aimee at the travel agency. Not sure yet."

"I thought we were going to do that together."

"We have girl stuff to catch up on. She just dumped her boyfriend, so I need to get all the dirt. I'll bring back all the booklets, and we can look at them this afternoon."

"Okay," Jack relented. He was actually relieved that he didn't have to pretend to be interested in all the soap opera drama of Paula's girlfriends.

"I'm pretty excited about this," Paula said. "We've never gone anyplace together."

Jack's phone buzzed again, indicating another call was coming in.

"Hey, I got another call. Gotta go. See you this afternoon. Pick out some good places."

"I will. Love you."

"Love you, too." He pressed the button to pick up the other call. "This is Chief McMurphy."

"Chief. It's Phelps down at county homicide. Just wanted to let you know that I checked all the schools within a fifty mile radius. No missing students. I'm going to post his info as a found John Doe on the wire to see if it connects with anyone out there. Just a head's up. You got anything?"

"I haven't had a thing change on my end, but if it does, you'll be the first person I call," McMurphy said.

"Appreciated. Have a good one."

No sooner had he closed down the phone, when it rang again. He didn't recognize the number.

"This is Chief McMurphy, Coopers Hollow Police Department." His voice didn't completely mask his annoyance.

"Chief. My name is Duane Norbson with the National Brotherhood of Law Enforcement Professionals. The reason I'm calling, and I apologize for calling on a Saturday, but the reason I'm calling, is because you've been selected as an Honorary Officer of the Law for your bravery and service. This stems from an incident, uh, six months ago. I'm sure I don't have to remind you," Norbson said.

"Okay," Jack didn't know how to reply to such a call.

"Okay, well, um NaBLEP has an annual convention every April, and we always invite the honorary officers that are selected from the previous calendar year to join us and give a small speech. It's all expenses paid. We put you up in a nice hotel, furnish you with food vouchers, provide you with entertainment as well. This year the convention takes place on April fifteenth in Las Vegas, at the Hilton. As an honorary officer, do you think you would be able to attend?"

"Wow, the fifteenth is this weekend. Not much notice," Jack replied.

"Well, we had another recipient for the award in your place, but he is, uh, having some legal issues at the moment. So, we wanted to extend the invitation to you," Norbson explained.

"I see. Can I think it over and call you back?"

"Certainly. Do you think you'll make a decision today? The reason I ask is I've taken the liberty of reserving a room for you at the Hilton for three nights, thirteenth through the fifteenth. If you won't be able to attend, I'll let the hotel know to release the room. It's really a very nice room."

"There's no cost to me?" Jack asked, skeptical to say the least.

"None at all. We'll book your flight, we already have the room reserved, and like I said, we'll take care of the food and entertainment. Of course, none of this is possible without our sponsors. You'll be asked to meet with some of the executives. You know, shake some hands and smile for the camera," Norbson said. "We wouldn't be able to do this without them."

"Okay, I have your number in my phone, I'll give you a call back today."

"Promise?"

"I'll do my best, Mr. Norbson."

"That's all I can ask. Thank you, and congratulations, Chief McMurphy."

Jack closed down the phone and shook his head. He held the phone in his hand for a moment, anticipating it to ring at any moment. It remained silent.

Mr. Anton was tinkering with the locket. He'd placed a head-band with magnifying lenses on his head, and studied the piece of jewelry over and over.

Jack stepped out of the kitchen and dialed Paula's number. She picked up on the first ring.

"Hey, babe. You're not going to believe this, but I just won a trip to Vegas for next week," Jack said.

"Won? Really? What's the catch?"

"It's part of some Law Enforcement Brotherhood convention. The guy who called said all I have to do is give a little speech and then pose with some of the sponsors. Probably the usual companies, gun and ammo guys and the vest people," Jack explained. "All expenses paid. Flight, hotel, entertainment, everything. Do you want to do it?"

"Which hotel?"

"He said the Hilton. I have no idea if that's good or bad."

"Las Vegas Hilton is good. One more thing, we're upgrading the flight to first class. I've never flown first class, and we have the money so we are flying first class," she said.

"So it's a yes?"

"Yes, definitely."

"Okay, that means I've got a lot of work between now and then. I've gotta go. Love you."

"Love you, too, Jack."

He went back inside, and Mr. Anton was unscrewing the back of the watch now.

"There was nothing special about the locket. Just a picture. No note, no nothing." He had a special tool that gripped the watch back, allowing him to spin it on the very precisely machined threads.

"Very nice watch," Anton said. He delicately removed the back to reveal miniature clockworks, a small circuit board, and a tablet power cell. As he set the back on the table, a small piece of black plastic fell out. He took a pair of tweezers and picked up the small rectangular plastic object. He held it for Jack to see.

"What is this, I wonder," Anton said. Jack looked closer and saw that on the other side, there were little metal contacts.

"It's a mini memory card, like for a cell phone," Jack said. "Can I see the watch?" Anton handed it over. He looked closely at the inner workings to see if it was just a memory card that belonged in the watch. It wouldn't surprise him if watches started coming with memory chips. It didn't look like it the chip belonged to the watch, but rather, that it had been hidden there.

"Well, this is interesting," McMurphy said.

Chapter 12

Jack walked back towards the station house, with the small piece of technology pinched between his fingers. It was about a half-inch long and not much more than a quarter of an inch wide. Just a little fleck of plastic with copper contacts. On the side opposite the contacts, it read the brand name and 4GB. As he approached his office, he noticed an individual waiting at the door. It was the second time, in as many days, that he had an unannounced visitor, whom he did not recognize, waiting for him at the station house door.

She wasn't very tall, perhaps five feet and five inches. She was dressed in a short sleeved, white button-up shirt with dark pants and shoes. Her hair was pulled tight into a bun. She was the blackest woman he had ever seen in Coopers Hollow.

"Hello," Jack called to her. "Can I help you?"

"I do hope so," she said. Her accent was exotic, perhaps from Zimbabwe or Mozambique. To someone else, it may have sounded Jamaican, but he had met several people from Zimbabwe when he was in college, and the accent was different, crisper, more enunciated. "I am looking for the Chief of Police for Coopers Hollow."

"I'm Chief McMurphy, how can I help you?" he asked.

She smiled brightly with a set of perfect teeth and extended her hand.

"I am Tricia Wallace," she said. "I am applying for the position of police officer. I had planned to just drop off my resume with a secretary, but I see -" she indicated the closed office.

"Yes, well, I'm really understaffed at the moment. Why don't you come in and we can talk a bit," Jack said. He unlocked the door and held it open for her. He flicked on the lights and invited her past the empty desks and back to his office.

"Would you like anything? Water, coffee? I brewed up some coffee earlier. It's still good," Jack said.

"No thank you, Chief," she said, still smiling.

"Well, have a seat, and let me take a look at your resume." She handed it over to him, and took one of the chairs against the wall.

"Oh, I'm sorry, you can bring that a little closer. I don't usually have too many guests," Jack smiled as he looked over her experience. As he reviewed, it seemed impressive: Bachelor's of Science in Criminal Justice from New York Institute of Technology, specializing in forensics and criminal investigation. She had further education with several certificates from the Zone 5 police training facilities in Schenectady, NY. Additionally, she had three years experience as a patrol officer with the City of Albany police force.

"This is quite impressive," McMurphy said as he read on about her typing skills, computer skills and office management experience.

"Um, tell me, why are you leaving Albany PD?"

"Left. Past tense," she said. "I no longer work for the Albany Police. My superior officer and I no longer," she paused. "We couldn't -"

"If you don't want to tell, me, it's okay," Jack replied. "If the matter is private. But I have to admit, I'd kind of like to find out why, exactly, you left your previous place of employment."

"It's okay," she said. "I think it is important to be honest with people. You see, when I joined Albany PD, I was very young, very eager. . . to learn. I fell into a trap with a superior. He wanted one kind of relationship and I wanted another. I had to get out."

"So now you want to find a nice and quiet department to get away from it for awhile? Are you looking for long term or just a few months or years?" Jack asked. He got the picture. She had an affair with her superior. If he had to guess, that superior was married, and it would have been a big mess to try to break it off and still work there. The relationship was strictly against policy, he imagined.

"I wasn't born in this country," Tricia said.

"Mozambique, Zimbabwe?"

"Zimbabwe, yes. You are the first white person I've met who guessed that. Most say Jamaica."

"I had a few friends in college from that area," Jack said. "Do you have other family here?"

"No. My family sent me over when I was thirteen. I lived with a foster family. My father is a dentist in Harare, the capital of Zimbabwe. He is very well known. He wanted me to come to America to learn dentistry, like him. But I grew to love police work. He and my mother are not very pleased. My brother has become a dentist and is back working with my father, but I am the black sheep," she said.

"I see," he replied. "So you're going back eventually?"

"No. America is my home now. I am just looking for a new start after almost wrecking things. I saw your advertisement on the internet. It was only an hour or so to drive down here, and I wanted to see if it was as beautiful as I had heard. I have never been to the Catskill Mountains before," she answered.

"I'm glad you like it here. I think that's really important for the right candidate. It's not like Albany. Everybody knows everybody here. Back in October, we had my father, myself, and another patrolmen here. My father was killed. Then just a few days ago, Ballard turned in his two week notice. I'm really hurting for people. Good people. I have a retired officer from New York City, who has agreed to come on board for the time being, but I imagine he's going to want to re-retire pretty quickly," he said. "I know the salary isn't as good as Albany, but cost of living is lower. Apartments are cheap."

"I see. Well I am interested, Chief," she said smiling. "It seems nice. Quaint."

"You can call me Jack. Everyone calls me Jack. Except Seemo over at the diner. He called me junior, now he calls me chief. He's kind of a pain in the backside sometimes," Jack said. "But you can't beat his cooking."

She laughed, and it seemed genuine. He liked this girl from Albany PD very much. She certainly wasn't what he was expecting when he'd placed the ad. He'd envisioned guys who had taken the college courses, but hadn't landed a job yet and were just looking for a few years experience. He had to admit, in his mind, he'd pictured a man as the perfect candidate. But his mind was changing pretty quickly.

"I like what I see on your resume," Jack said. "Do you have any references I could call?"

"Certainly," Tricia said, sliding another paper out of the petite purse she was carrying. It contained three names with phone numbers and email addresses.

"Well, Tricia," Jack said, standing up. "I really appreciate you coming all the way down here. I think I'll just make a few calls to your references, and then we'll be in touch. Is the number on your resume the best way to reach you?"

"Yes. It is my mobile phone," she said. She extended a hand, and Jack shook. It was a strong, confident grip.

"I think you'll be hearing from me very soon," Jack said. "Let me walk you out."

"Thank you so much for seeing me. I hope it was not inconvenient."

"No, not at all. I hope you weren't waiting for very long," Jack replied.

"Only a moment or two," Tricia said as she exited his office and headed for the front door. "Thank you Chief, um. Jack. Um. Is it okay if I call you Chief? I think I like that better."

"Sure, whatever you'd like. Thanks again. You can expect to hear from me," Jack said as she closed the door. She gave a pleasant wave and smile through the glass, and then headed down the front steps.

He scratched the back of his head and smiled. Again, she wasn't what he was expecting, but if her references checked out, she could fit in just fine. He was weak with the computer skills. Not exactly a novice around a keyboard, but not a pro. He typed with two fingers, and had to check a couple of different pull down menus every time just to get what he wanted.

He went back to his desk and ran his hand over the sheet of paper containing the references. Two were numbers in Albany. The other was a 212 number. New York City. Probably a professor. He wondered if she'd slept with him as well. As soon as he had the thought, he felt bad about it. It wasn't a fair thing to think, about her. He'd made plenty of mistakes himself, some very recently.

It all came flooding back to him, like a tsunami of guilt. His father's death. The dead agent. Jack stopped himseld. He wasn't just *the agent*. He was Agent Spaulding. The man had a name.

There was nothing he could do about it. Any of it. All of it was back there, in the past. What happened, happened. That was it. He had to focus on the right now. The micro memory card was still in his pocket. He'd slid it there absentmindedly when he saw Tricia at the door.

He dug for it in his pocket and then held it up between his thumb and fore-finger. He rotated the small piece of plastic between his fingers when he heard the front door open again.

"Chief? I'm sorry to bother you again." It was Tricia Wallace, calling out from the front door. Jack came out of his chair to see what was wrong. The memory card went back in his pocket.

"I'm really sorry," she said. "But my car won't start. I think the battery is dead. It won't even turn over. Is there someone I can call?"

"I have a charger box around here somewhere," Jack replied. "And an extension cord. We should have you ready to go in no time."

"I'm so embarrassed. Thank you so much," her brows were

furrowed. She looked frustrated, embarrassed and worried.

"It's no trouble, really," Jack replied. The charger was in the basement. He'd laid eyes on it when he'd gone down to get the boxes on the El Tigre case. "I'll be back in just a second."

The charger and cord were right where he'd left them. It was one of the benefits of working almost completely alone, things stayed where you left them.

"See," Jack said as he returned. "No trouble. Where did you park?"

"Right outside."

"Okay. We'll just plug in the extension cord and get your rolling."

Her car was a green Oldsmobile Alero. It had some rust bubbling up the paint around the wheel wells, but looked to be in fairly decent shape. She pulled the lever to the hood, and Jack put the charger into place. Red to red, black to ground.

"Let's give it a minute," Jack said. "You might want to take it over to the auto parts place," Jack indicated the store down the street a few blocks. "They can test to see if it's the battery or your alternator. I'd hate to have it conk out on you on the drive back."

"I think it will be fine, once it's running. I don't have the extra money for it right now," she said. "On a tight budget."

Jack nodded. He didn't have much else to say, as they waited for the car battery to charge. He absent-mindedly turned the micro memory chip over and over, between thumb and fingers, in his pocket.

"Hey, I have a question for you," he said. "How familiar are you with technology?"

"Familiar enough," she replied. "Is there something specific?"

"Yeah," he pulled the memory chip out and showed her. "How would I go about pulling the info off this little guy? It looks like the memory card in the back of my phone."

She reached over and took it in her fingers. She looked at it closely then handed it back."

"They sell adapters that will let you put it into your computer. Most computers these days have a slot for the larger memory cards, like in your camera. You can either order it online, or go to a computer store." She looked around the town. "I don't suppose you have a computer store here."

"No," he laughed. "No computer store. The closest thing is the big office supply place down in Oneonta. They carry that kind of thing."

"That would be my suggestion," Tricia replied. "Is it for a case?"

"Well, not really. Not an open case," Jack replied, not entirely truthfully. "I just found it and wondered what was on it, is all."

The charger, attached to the Alero's battery, emitted a beep and the small display illuminated with OK. Jack gave it another few moments and then told her to try to start it.

On the first turn, it didn't want to catch. She tried it again, and it fired right up. Jack turned off the charger and pulled the cables off the battery terminals. He closed her hood for her and then walked over to her window.

"Thank you so much, Chief. I am really sorry to bother you with this."

"No trouble at all, really. Listen, are you sure you'll be okay? Does your display have a voltage meter to see if the alternator is charging?" She looked at her dial cluster, but shook her head.

"Okay," Jack said. "Listen, just drive on over to the auto parts store. It's right next to the Grand American market about two blocks that way. Right on Main Street. I'll come over with you. If you need a battery, it's on me."

"You don't have to do that," she said. She bit her lip, concern on her face. She was blowing her interview. She was sure of it. "It will be okay. It seems to be running just fine."

"I'd feel better about it," Jack insisted. "Just to get it checked out."

"Okay," she relented. "Just back by the grocery?"

"That's right. I'll put this stuff away and come over in a minute to make sure the guys don't give you a hassle," he said. She nodded and rolled up her window.

Jack coiled the extension cord as he walked, and set the charger down, just inside the door. He had his keys on his belt, so he just had to lock the door and get in his SUV.

The auto parts store was part of a national chain, but was locally owned. Del Hastings was the mustached owner, and if he hadn't started drinking yet, he would be able to figure out what was wrong with her car just by looking at it from behind the counter. He'd grown up in Coopers Hollow, and his dad had once owned a garage in town. Del's favorite line was that he spent more time on his back than a Vegas whore. He tended to be a bit crass.

Del was already outside looking at her car, by the time Jack pulled up in the department SUV.

"And then it wouldn't start again," Tricia was saying.

"And you just charged it up, gave her a jump?" Del asked. "Hey, Jack."

"Hey, yourself, Del. Everything going alright this morning?"

"Oh, it's going," he said. He had a meter in his hand, and he popped the hood to hook it up to the battery. "Looks like more rain on the way."

"Looks like," Jack replied. "It's hitting Ohio right now, I heard. Flooding all over. I hope it's not as bad as they're saying."

"Well, looks like your battery won't hold a charge. I can't test the alternator until we fix the battery problem," Del said. "Sorry."

"How much is a new battery?" Tricia asked.

"Well, that'll run you about seventy-five, less the core charge for your old one. I do believe I have one in stock for this model.

Come on in and we'll check," Del said. Tricia looked stricken.

"I got it," Jack said.

"No, that is okay. I will pay for it," Tricia replied. "I don't want you to think that I cannot pull my own weight."

"It would be my way of paying you for your consulting," Jack said. "On the memory card thing. I would have had to drive to Oneonta to get that question answered, so let me get the battery." She paused for a moment, weighing it over in her head.

"Okay," she said. "But I will pay you back. And, I don't want this to jeopardize what you think of me."

"It won't, I promise."

When they got to the counter, Jack supplied his card. Del took it, somewhat surprised by the gesture. He swiped the card and handed it and a pen to Jack to sign the receipt. Del then took the battery out to Tricia's car to install it. In just a few minutes, she was ready to get on her way, back north.

She thanked him several times, and promised to pay him back as well. She couldn't have known that Jack wasn't exactly hurting for money. Of course it was all Paula's money. They'd found the treasure on her property, and she was rightful owner. All the same, they were a couple, and she had been very open to letting him spend it. At least some of it.

"She was cute," Del said as he gave a wave. "Not from around here. She get lost or something?"

"Actually, I was thinking of hiring her as a patrolman," Jack said. "Maybe deputy chief, if she works out. I need people, you know."

"You don't think it'll be a problem? You know," Del said.

"Because she's black? I don't know, Del. You think anyone will have a problem with her?" Jack turned and looked him in the eyes. Jack was a few inches taller and definitely in better physical shape.

"Jeez, I don't. I love all God's creatures," Del said with an cough. He cleared his throat. "And you know I love all the ladies. I have no problem with an ebony chick. I mean officer. I mean. Uh, if you ask me, she'll be fine."

"Good to hear," Jack replied.

"She just needs to get rid of that beater Olds and get something that actually runs," Del replied. He gave a nod to Jack and walked back inside. "Take it easy chief."

"You too, Del."

A SUV pulled in and gave a honk. It was a new Mercedes-Benz ML350. Silver with tinted windows. Jack didn't recognize it, so he gave a short wave and walked around to the driver's door. His hand rested instinctively on his gun. The tinted driver's window slid down, and he smiled.

"What's this?" he asked, not able to mask his surprise.

"This is my new car," Paula said proudly. "I didn't want to tell you because I wanted to buy it on my own. What do you think?"

"Wow, it's gorgeous," he said. She revved the engine, and smiled from ear to ear. "It's got the big V8 in it. Five hundred-fifty horses under the hood. Come on, I'll take you for a ride."

"Okay," he replied. He really should have been heading back to his office to check on getting an adapter for the memory card, but he wasn't going to rain on her parade. Plus, he'd never ridden in a Mercedes before.

He was barely in the passenger seat, when she gunned it in reverse and then sped out of the parking lot.

"Whoa, take it easy. Don't make me write you up for reckless driving," Jack said, only half kidding.

She took it out of town a bit before she put her foot into the accelerator. It took the corners of the mountain road as if it were riding on rails. The suspension ate up the bumps, and the riding compartment barely let in any road noise. The interior had just about every bell and whistle one could dream of.

"Fully loaded," she said with a grin from ear to ear.

"This wasn't cheap," Jack noted.

"Nope. You should have seen the guy at the dealership when I paid for it in cash, up front," she said. "That's why he drove it out to me this morning all the way from Syracuse. I thought I was going to have to figure out a way to get you to drive over there and surprise you. You're surprised, right?"

"Absolutely," he said. He ran his hands over the leather interior. It smelled new. It smelled fast. "When can I drive it?"

Paula let out a laugh.

"Did you read my book yet?" she asked.

"Well, I - super busy, you know," he said.

"You can drive it when you've read my book. By the way, what were you doing at the parts store?"

"Oh, I think I've found a new officer," Jack said.

"That was fast."

"She came down from Albany to apply in person. Her battery was dead, so I was just making sure Del didn't give her any grief," he said.

"Or an STD," Paula added.

"You're so crude," Jack laughed. Then he grabbed onto the handle above the door as Paula accelerated through a series of s-curves, using all of the traction available from the all-wheel-drive vehicle.

"Going a little fast, aren't you?"

"What, don't you trust my driving?"

"No, no. It's just-"

"Female cop, huh? Think she'll do okay with the rednecks around here," Paula asked. She made a u-turn on Brick House Road and headed back towards town. She mashed the pedal down and left a little rubber on the road.

"I think she'll be fine," Jack said, getting forced back into his seat. "Jeez, Paula. Take it easy."

"Sure thing, chief."

"Five hundred-fifty horses?"

"Yup."

"I'm reading your book tonight," Jack said.

Chapter 13

It was a cloudy day in Washington D.C. The hints of spring were awakening all about the city. Blossoms on trees, more tourists walking at the National Mall, red baseball hats with white Ws being worn by men in suits at noon; all those little things that one notices when one was truly looking.

He stood in his fourth floor office, which had a beautiful view of the parking lot, and if you squinted, the very tip of the Washington monument. His suit was spotless, his shirt crisp and white. A power tie of alternating red and black stripes completed the image he wished to portray. He wore red whenever he could fit it into his outfit, usually in neckties, but occasionally in suspenders or socks. The nine people in his office, mostly aides, assistants and interns, feared him like the devil. Like the one and only Satan. He enjoyed the fear, reveled in it. The boys he had in the field weren't nearly as scared of him as they should have been. Part of the reason they were on the team to begin with was the fact that nothing scared them.

"Mr. Scutter," the intercom chirped on his desk. He waited for a moment before answering. He wanted her to think he was busy and annoyed, despite the fact that he was really dreaming about retirement and sipping an afternoon cocktail.

"Yes, Ms. Weaver?" he said, depressing the button.

"You have a call, he said you were expecting him," she said. "Line two, sir."

He set his drink on his desk and placed both palms on his blotter. He looked at the blinking red light on line two and licked his lips.

"And?" he said as he pressed the button, as if continuing a conversation with the person on the other end.

"He's got it all, but he's being difficult," the man said over the speaker. It was Agent Haas, one of Scutter's best.

"And?"

"We can get everything, but I just need to verify what kind of latitude we have on this."

"Complete."

"Copy that."

"No screw ups this time."

"No, sir. Copy that."

"And you're sure he has everything?" Scutter asked.

"Yes, sir. We'll get everything."

"When can I expect it?"

"Forty-eight hours, barring any unforeseeables."

Scutter was quiet for a moment.

"Sir?"

"We are getting chatter. There may be another team in the arena. Watch your six."

"Copy that," Haas said. Military lingo died hard for the formerly enlisted.

"Maybe," Scutter continued. "Maybe we give it a few days, see if the chatter materializes into something more. Maybe we stand by, see if the cockroaches come out when they think the lights are off."

"A few days kicking back in the mountains, we can do that," Agent Haas said.

"If the chatter is nothing, then it's nothing," Scutter said. "But, if there's something to it, then we might catch a break and recover the operation in some fashion."

"Agreed."

"Be careful," Scutter said. "Stay in touch."

"Yes, sir." The line went dead.

Chatter. It was a way to describe getting one of those little tidbits of information that might just be something. Or nothing at all. Six months of silence on the case. Nobody interested, nobody cared. Spaulding was an undercover agent who was lost in the mix. No family except for an aunt in Jackson, Mississippi. She was merely informed that he was lost in the line of duty. There was a quiet service for him, attended by the agents on the team. That was it. Wrapped up. Done.

He had been patient with this one. Let everything die down, then he sent the boys in, all nonchalant. The direct approach had met with resistance, so they were trying something a bit more subtle. There were reasons for doing the things that they did in this branch of the agency.

He'd been a big fan of illusionists growing up. He loved the slight of hand and misdirection. What he enjoyed most about it was that the tricks were usually so very easy in their explanation. The real trick was in the performance. Misdirection wasn't about steering attention away from the illusion. It was about building up a false foundation of truth on which the audience relied, so that when the final reveal was performed, they had confidence that what they had seen was impossible.

Just like when the Stasi in East Berlin had worn themselves ragged trying to find out who the Shadow was. His agency loved it. Of all of the misdirection they could have manufactured, it didn't work nearly as well as a joke and a nickname which was repeated. While the East German secret police were trying to track him, other agents were infiltrating. So he understood the game. The human need to know, to understand, to have all cards finally revealed.

In his line of work, misdirection was a key element in almost every phase. The work with El Tigre, or the Tiger Cub as he was code-named within the agency, was all about building the cocksure kid into something bigger than he actually was. It was done for a specific reason. When the sting came down on his superiors, they'd have no clue as to how it happened. That had all been severely ruined by the episode in Coopers Hollow. Three years of work, flushed.

Building up another man, like they had with Tiger Cub, was going to take time. It was going to require more rule breaking, more string pulling, more misdirection. But first they had to make any possible info about the operation go away. As much as his team was utilizing technology to the fullest, the bad guys had their own assets. One of which was a tool that had been created to help the good guys keep an eye on their own government. The Freedom of Information Act was that checks-and-balances-tool for the people. All people. With good or bad intentions. All they had to do was file an FOIA for the files on the case and the bad guys might discover that their operation had been infiltrated by an undercover federal agent.

It wasn't just the bad guys he was concerned about. His team had determined that Agent Spaulding was becoming disenchanted with his role. He had misgivings about the rules he was being asked to bend. He viewed it as breaking not bending. He was young and naive. Summers and Haas were good at managing the situation, but they were recommending Spaulding be removed and reassigned. Or just removed. The operation with Tiger Cub was not entirely legal, nor was it entirely on the books. And there were reasons. When a senator's son was involved, things were played differently. According to the last report from Spaulding, it may have been more than a senator's son. It may have netted a few senators as well. There was a new regime in Washington, and many were playing fast and loose with the rules. Or ignoring the rules all together. It was sticky territory. It was also potentially lucrative territory. One good senator in one's pocket could prove to be a highly valuable ace when played at the appropriate time.

Disconcerting to Scutter was whether Spaulding had left some sort of come-to-Jesus message on his person. Did he spill the beans? There would be far more to worry about than a busted operation.

His whole career might be in jeopardy. The government didn't mind his type of operations when they weren't public. As soon as something like this showed up on the six o'clock news, there was wringing of hands and chopping of necks.

Then there was the chatter. An intercepted phone call. Would a certain someone be interested in knowing that some of their misdeeds were about to be made public? If those misdeeds could be kept private, how much would it be worth? Which misdeeds? The ones that ended in the Catskills.

That word had been flagged. As soon as it was spoken, the whole recorded conversation was immediately sent up the chain to Scutter. What did it mean? Was it connected? If so, to whom? He had a clue. How much involvement was there really? That was the million dollar question, as they say.

Right now, Scutter believed he had the winning hand. But the game didn't always go the way it was supposed to. Sometimes winning hands were folded. Sometimes aces were slipped from the deck to be used later. Other times you just had to shoot your opponent and take his money. And yet there were still other occasions when you let your opponent win, only to pick his pocket later that night.

Mr. Shadow, *das schatten*, Llywelyn Scutter, or Lou to his wife and friends, smiled. He swallowed the last of his afternoon cocktail and sat down at his desk to type a few emails to a few important people, who had been nervous for a few too many months. One way or the other, everything was going to be just fine.

Chapter 14

"We're going to be fine," Eric said quietly to his wife.

"Bull piss," she spat.

Eric and Sylvia sat side by side in the drab waiting room of Dr. Fuller's private practice. There were old magazines on the coffee table, and the chairs were of the metal, folding variety, which had been popular in the 1960s; cold and hard, no cushion. It was nearly twenty minutes past time for their appointment, and Eric couldn't sit next to her anymore. She was no longer the person he'd married. She wasn't even the same person who'd moved with him from down state just a few months ago. Her behavior was becoming more erratic and her language was far more foul than he'd ever known it to be.

He looked at his watch for the twentieth time in as many minutes. Eric stood up and began to pace. He looked at the pictures on the walls; old photos of Coopers Hollow back in its heyday. Railroad cars, vacationers, old automobiles, the bank building. It would never be like it was.

"Sit down. You're making me nervous," Sylvia said. Her voice was devoid of emotion. It was tired but louder than it should have been in the quiet of the waiting room.

"I can't sit anymore. I have to move," he replied quietly, stealing a glance at the receptionist behind the glass. She was oblivious to them.

"You're such a pain in the ass," Sylvia said with an exhale that would have seemed more appropriate coming from a teenager who didn't get their way. She crossed her arms and her legs and pumped her foot up and down as if she were as angry as she'd ever been at him.

"Why are you saying these things? You never used to curse, now you're dropping four letter words, and calling me things that I -" he couldn't take it anymore. The exit looked so inviting. He thought about running away, just leaving her there in her misery. It was a passing thought, a cowardly one. He went over and sat down next to her once again, taking her hand in his. "We'll get through this, baby."

She began to cry.

"I don't want to be like this," she whimpered.

Dr. Fuller's nurse opened the door and let an elderly gentleman out. He walked with a cane, and carried a face of annoyance. Stepping to the window, he raised his cane and rapped it against the glass. The receptionist slid it open.

"Mr. Everett, please! Behave yourself," she said.

"I'll do whatever I dang well please, missy. Where's my prescription?" Mr. Everett said, tapping his cane on the floor.

"The doctor just has to bring me his notes and I'll write it up for you," she replied sternly. "Now go sit down and be good."

The old man strode across the waiting room and selected a chair in which to sit. He bent at the waist and lowered himself down. He sat, staring at the receptionist window, both hands on his cane. Eric remembered the old man from when he was a kid. He was old back then. The guy owned half the mountain, overlooking the town, and would threaten to shoot the kids who would sometimes hike there. Parents had told their children to steer clear of the old curmudgeon for decades. At least three generations of Coopers Hollow kids were afraid of Old Man Everett, Eric surmised.

Sylvia let out another sob, and this caught the old man's attention.

"What's her problem," he asked. His voice was filled with annoyance. He had a general cantankerous nature about him. He wore corduroy pants, a button down sweater, a white shirt buttoned all the way up to the top, and a long scarf which hung loosely around his neck down to his waist.

"She's not feeling well," Eric said.

"The whole damned world isn't feeling well. What makes her any different," he snorted. Eric wanted to tell Mr. Everett where he could go, but he was probably suffering from some sort of dementia himself, and couldn't help it. Or he was off his meds. Either way, it wasn't worth an argument.

The nurse opened the door to the waiting room and called for Sylvia. Eric was relieved, and nervous at the same time. He wanted out of that waiting room, but wasn't sure what he was about to discover about his wife.

The nurse took them into room B. She went through all the preliminary examinations; blood pressure normal, pulse normal, temperature normal. Her weight and height matched up with the notes they'd been supplied from their previous family physician. The nurse excused herself and they began their wait for the doctor again.

He didn't make them wait very long.

"Sylvia and Eric, how are you this morning. So nice to meet you both," Dr. Fuller said as he entered the room. He wore a white coat that matched his white horseshoe of hair on his head. He shook both of their hands, and then sat on the black-cushioned rolling stool. He had a laptop with him, and he read quickly through the notes which were forwarded to his office.

"So, I know what you told the nurse over the phone, but why don't you tell me what's going on again," he said. He looked at Sylvia, but quickly realized she wasn't talking.

"Well, um, she's suffered from depression for awhile now. We had her going good for a few years, until Yasmine, our daughter, well, she had an accident," Eric said.

"What type of accident?"

"She tried to commit suicide," Eric said.

"Tried? I take it she didn't succeed. Is she okay?"

"Yes. She hasn't shown any signs of hurting herself since then.

It was a bullying thing from school. It's why we moved up here, to get away from it all. Anyway, since then, Sylvia has sunk deeper and deeper. She hasn't been sleeping, so she started taking a sleep aid. Well, then she had a little episode in the middle of the night. She thought someone was in the house trying to get the kids. She ended up in the middle of Main Street yelling at two in the morning," Eric said. It felt good just to talk to someone about it.

"Is there a history of mental illness in the family?" Dr. Fuller asked.

"Not that I'm aware of," Eric replied.

"And her current medications?"

"Here," Eric said. "I made a list with all the dosages." Dr. Fuller took the list and read it over. He typed a few notes into the computer and then stood to wash his hands.

"You know, the common keyboard has more germs than the average public toilet seat," Dr. Fuller said. He spent a few minutes under the water, then dried them and put on his stethoscope. "Let's have a listen to your heart."

He probed around her chest with the listening end, and then moved to her back. He then took out a light pen and opened her eyes, moving the light back and forth to gauge her pupil dilation.

"Is she talking?" Dr. Fuller asked.

"She talks when she wants too," Eric said. "It's been really bad the last two days. She's barely gotten out of bed. I've never seen her this way. And she's started cursing."

"Like swear words?"

"Yes," Eric replied. The doctor nodded and pressed his thumbs against the sides of her head and around her ears. She winced a bit.

"Does that hurt?" he asked her. She nodded. Dr. Fuller looked gravely concerned.

"I think this may be serious. We need to get you up to Albany for a CT scan and an MRI," he said.

"For what? What's wrong?" Eric asked with worry in his voice.

"It's possible your wife may have a tumor in her brain. I'm leaning in the direction of a physiological explanation as opposed to a mental health one. The depression may have masked the real symptoms as they worsened," he said somberly. "I really need you to get her up there as quickly as possible. Today if at all possible. If it is a tumor, and her behavior is worsening, then it could mean it's putting pressure on her brain and needs to be removed immediately. If it turns out that there is no tumor, then we're back to dealing with a measure of dementia. We'll try to manage it by changing up some of the prescriptions."

"Okay," Eric replied barely making any noise at all.

"Has she had any seizures? Any slurring of words?"

"No. Not that I've noticed."

"Okay, good. Can you take her today? I'll make a call and get you scheduled in," Dr. Fuller said.

"Yes, absolutely. Just give me the address and we'll get going. I have to get my mother over to watch the kids, but it will be okay," Eric said. He stood and helped Sylvia to her feet.

"I'm feeling better, honey," she said to him.

"Sylvia, I'm sending you to Albany to get some tests done. I think something may be putting pressure on your brain, dear," Dr. Fuller said.

"Okay," Sylvia replied and leaned her head against Eric. He walked her out to the receptionists' desk and waited patiently behind the glass. The doctor spoke to the girl behind the computer. The old man was gone, obviously getting his prescription and shuffling off to go make someone else's day miserable.

The glass window slid open and the receptionist typed onto her computer keyboard with machine-like precision. Moments later a sheet of paper rolled off the printer and she handed it to Eric.

"The address is right there, it's very easy to find," she said.

"Just walk in and hand this to them and they'll take you right in. Feel better, Sylvia."

"Thank you, orange," Sylvia said smiling. Then she scowled. Eric walked her toward the front door, retrieving her jacket and putting it over her shoulders.

"Listen, guys," he said to Yasmine and Riker, as they sat on the couch in the living room. "Grandma is coming right over. We're going to the hospital to have mom checked out. The hospital in Albany. We'll probably be gone all afternoon. Maybe overnight."

"What's wrong with her?" Yasmine asked.

"They think she may have a tumor or something in her head that's putting pressure on her brain," Eric replied. He was finishing the task of putting together an overnight bag for his wife. Her normal toiletries and some extra undergarments.

"Is that why she's been acting so -" Riker didn't finish the sentence. He just looked at his mom sitting on the edge of the bed staring at the carpet. He ran over and hugged her, and she responded with a warm, loving embrace. She kissed him on his head.

"I'm not going to let anybody get you," she said. "I'll protect you."

"Okay, sweetie, we have to go," Eric said. "Listen guys, watch TV or something. Grandma's on her way. She was in Oneonta shopping, but she'll be here in just a few minutes. Don't answer the door, don't let anyone know you're here alone."

"Dad, we'll be fine," Yasmine said. She leaned in and kissed her mother, then hugged Eric. "Just make sure they fix her, dad."

"Okay, baby."

It took an hour to get to the hospital, and they brought her into imaging right away. Eric could tell that the few others in the imaging waiting room weren't too pleased to see someone going in ahead of them, but the hospital seemed to be treating this as an emergency. Eric was asked to wait in a secondary room as Sylvia was taken into the MRI room and put onto the table.

Twenty minutes later, the imaging technician came to get Eric.

"I'm Nina," she said, shaking Eric's hand. "I just wanted to show you what I'll be showing the doctor when she comes down." Nina took a seat behind a large monitor and began an animation of Sylvia's brain. It was in three dimensions, and they could take away slices with the click of the mouse. The tech took a pen tool and then pointed to a section of the screen. It expanded, and there, in three dimensions, was a dark object that looked like a walnut.

"That is most definitely a tumor," Nina said. "I know once the doctor sees this, he's going to want to operate immediately, probably tomorrow morning. I'm sorry."

"It's okay," Eric said. "I'm almost relieved we know what it is. How dangerous is it?"

"Well, I really need to leave that to the doctor, but based on its location, I think she has a good chance of coming through just fine. But I need to let the doctor tell you for sure," she said. "I'm just the tech, so I'm talking out of turn here. I just run the machines."

"Okay, when can we see him?"

"He's finishing up another surgery now, so he should be down shortly. We're going to go through the process of getting her admitted, and the doctor will see her in her room upstairs. Okay?"

"Thanks, Nina."

The phone rang and Yasmine raced Riker to get it. She was far quicker and had the cordless to her ear in moments.

"Hello?" she said. She held the phone against her chest and told Riker and her grandmother that it was dad.

"Okay. When will you be home? Okay. Can we come up and see her? Alright. Okay." Yasmine held the phone out to her grandmother. "He wants to talk with you."

Yasmine handed off the phone and took Riker back to the living room.

"What's going on?" Riker asked.

"Mom needs to have surgery. They're going to take out the thing that's making her act so weird. She'll be back to normal in no time," Yasmine said.

"Promise?" Riker asked.

"I promise," she said, hugging him.

Chapter 15

There were a few people gathered in the police station house for the occasion. Gloria sat next to Paula and Goldie, and a few of the firemen were there, as well. The town council were all present, as were a few others from the town. All told, it was less than twenty people on hand for the swearing in ceremony.

They'd pushed the desks up against the walls and arranged the chairs in the center of the station house for the ceremony. Jack sat up front in his full uniform, facing the audience. Beside him were Michael Cooke and Tricia Wallace, both in uniforms as well. Jack had paid the rush charge from the uniform supply company. The name tags would arrive in just a few days. They already had the badges in the bottom drawer of Jack's desk.

The Mayor stood before them all, dressed in a short-sleeve button down shirt, with a poorly knotted tie. He had a few notes in his hand, as there wasn't a podium. Paula had typed up a quick press release and sent it out to all of the local media, but only a TV station from Oneonta was there. Not even her old paper had bothered to send anyone out to take a picture. Paula took notes, then she held up a digital camera of her own once the ceremony began. She'd send out a ready-made story to the press and maybe it would get picked up by a few papers or websites.

After a few words, Mayor Patterson asked both Tricia and Michael to stand and raise their right hands. He then had them recite an oath to serve and protect, thus swearing them into service. It only took a few minutes and then it was over. Everyone who came, enjoyed some refreshments, compliments of the restaurant at the bowling alley. Just some pizza and sodas, but it was a nice gesture, nonetheless.

Jack got his picture taken with both Tricia and Michael together, and then one each by themselves, posed in a mock handshake.

"I really never thought I'd wear a uniform again," Michael said.

"Well, I'm glad you said yes," Paula quipped, as she came up to Jack's side. "We wouldn't be heading to Vegas if we didn't have someone to help out."

"Yeah, well, always ready to help," Michael said. "Congratulations. When do you head out?"

Jack looked at his watch and smiled.

"Our flight leaves at ten-thirty tonight. We'll land in Vegas around midnight or a little after," he said. "Three time zones."

"So, I guess we need a quick briefing on duties," Michael laughed.

"I'll only be gone for a few days. If something big comes in, just pass it on to the sheriff's department. Otherwise, you know what to do probably better than I do," Jack said.

"I'm going to get you back for this, one day," Michael said. "Throwing me right into the fire on the first day."

"You'll be fine," Jack said. "I feel worse for Tricia. She's been in town for one day, and the training wheels are coming off."

He looked over at her, and she was chatting up the mayor quite adeptly. The girl from Channel 7 came over and interrupted them to take their picture. The mayor straightened his tie and put his hand on her shoulder. The Channel 7 girl had a small video camera on a tripod. She aligned the camera and then asked them a few questions. There were smiles all around.

After the refreshments started to thin, so did the crowd. Eventually it was just Paula, Jack, Michael, Gloria and Tricia left in the station house. They spent the rest of the afternoon cleaning up and getting the office in order. Tricia took the desk closest to the front door, while Michael laid ownership to the one nearest the coffee maker. Not that there was any other desks to claim. Jack gave them each a set of keys, and showed them how to operate the holding cell lock. It was a bit tricky. There was a certain way you had to turn the key and pull on the door to get it to unlock.

By five o'clock, everyone except Tricia got ready to head home. She was taking the shift until eleven o'clock. She'd volunteered for it.

Michael shook his head when she did it. He'd learned the lesson a long time ago in the Marine Corps. Never volunteer for anything.

By seven o'clock, they had their bags in Paula's new Mercedes and were doing one last review to make sure they hadn't forgotten anything. Then she gasped.

"What?" Jack asked her.

"Oh my God! We forgot about Tubby's thing!"

"That's tonight? We can't do it," Jack said. "We won't have time."

"No, we can go right now and leave right from there," Paula said. "Jack, we have to. We promised."

"He won't even know we missed it," Jack said. "I don't want to be late for the flight."

"Jack McMurphy," she said sternly. "You are going to church. Don't make me get the wooden spoon." She said, with mock sternness.

"Alright, you win."

"I always win. Don't forget that."

It only took a few minutes to get to the meeting hall from Jack's house. The parking lot was full, so they had to park on the grass. They walked to the front door, and a man in a suit opened it for them.

"Can I help you?" he asked.

"We're here to see Tubby, er, Thaddeus do his reading," Paula said. "He invited us."

"Oh, okay. I'm Ken. The meeting has already started, but I can find you a seat. Thaddeus gives the first talk in the school. Have you ever been to one of our meetings before?"

"No," Paula said, and Jack shook his head no.

"Okay, well tonight is like a Bible school," Ken explained. "Students are members of the congregation. They are given assignments. Thaddeus has a chapter to read from the Bible. It helps us to prepare for the ministry."

"Okay, I get it," said Paula. Ken led them from the foyer into the main auditorium. It was a fairly plain meeting hall. Nicely decorated, but not ornate. A man was standing on the small raised stage at the front of the hall, and about forty or fifty people were sitting in the audience, listening. Ken showed them to seats that were near the back. Thaddeus was near the front. He was impossible to miss, even dressed in a suit and tie. The man on the stage then introduced him as Brother McIntyre, and Tubby got up and walked onto the stage to the podium, which looked tiny compared to the enormous man. Another man came over and adjusted the microphone stand. The mic had to come way up to be close to Tubby's chin. This got a chuckle out of the audience.

Tubby then began to read his scriptures. Ken slid a copy of the Bible into Paula's hands and pointed to where Tubby was reading.

For Jack, it was uncomfortable. Tubby was not a good reader. It seemed like he must have practiced, but it wasn't very smooth reading. It only took about five minutes in its entirety, and then Tubby was done. He let out a deep sigh of relief, and this got another chuckle out of the crowd. The audience applauded, as the first man took the stage again and waited for the microphone stand to come back down to his level. He talked about how good a job Thaddeus had done for his first reading, and how he looked forward to the next one.

"Okay," Jack whispered to Paula. "Let's go."

They quietly got up, and walked back into the foyer. Ken was still standing there, apparently he was an usher. Paula handed the Bible back to him and thanked him.

"Any time you want to come back, we'd love to have you," Ken said. "Hey, aren't you the chief of police?"

"Yes," Jack said. "Not in uniform. We're about to catch a flight to Las Vegas."

"Oh, okay. I'll let Thaddeus know you were here," Ken said. "He'll like that."

"Would you? Thank you so much," Paula said, shaking his hand.

They exited the building and got into Paula's Mercedes. She was driving as Jack hadn't finished her book yet. He planned to read it on the flight, if he couldn't sleep.

"That wasn't so bad, was it?" Paula asked.

"I guess not."

"So what did you think?" she asked.

"He did good, I guess. For Tubby, he did really good."

"I think he did a wonderful job," Paula said. "You know six months ago he could barely read."

"I did not know that."

"And what did you think about the passage he read?" she pressed.

"I, um. I wasn't really paying attention," Jack admitted.

"You went to church and didn't listen? Jack!"

"Well, I was, I mean, he kind of made me nervous," he said.

"Nervous about what?"

"I was just nervous for Tubby. I didn't want anyone to laugh or anything. I don't know. He did good," Jack said. He squirmed slightly in his seat and looked out the window. Paula stole a glance at him and saw he was done talking about it.

"Yes he did."

She drove on through the winding road towards Albany. A bit faster than Jack preferred. There wasn't much on the radio except commercials, so she hit the button for her iPod, and cranked up an old song by Chicago. Even though it was a bit chilly, Jack reached up and hit the button to open the sunroof. The woosh of wind filled the car, so Paula cranked up Chicago a bit more.

He had been listening to the reading, at least a little. And that made him nervous as well. He caught something about a man leaving his father and mother and sticking to his wife. Six months ago he couldn't comprehend getting married again. The first marriage hadn't gone so well. He didn't think he was the marrying type. But now, he was finding it hard to imagine a life without Paula. All the excuses he used to delude himself, as to why he shouldn't get married, didn't seem to matter anymore. She had been pressing him on moving in together. He wanted to, but he also didn't want to. He was a man of duty and honor. Just moving in together, without the commitment, it just seemed out of line. Just because.

He hadn't really thought about the God angle. He didn't like thinking that God was judging him, but he supposed God was judging everyone, everyday. Most people got by not thinking about Him on a daily basis. Jack was one of those people. Just easier that way. In fact, Jack couldn't remember the last time he'd prayed or tried to be spiritual in any way.

That changed when they began taxiing on the runway at Albany International Airport and a cross wind rocked the plane enough to make one of the overstuffed, overhead compartments pop open. A flight attendant hopped up and snapped it closed again and then returned to her backwards facing seat, at the front of the plane. Jack stiffened in his seat and closed his eyes. He had heard that most accidents occurred in the first few minutes of take off. He couldn't remember where he'd heard it, but it made sense.

The aircraft accelerated down the runway, buffeting from side to side. A storm front was moving in, and they were getting out of town just before the rain was about to start. Jack found himself holding onto the armrests tightly, and wondering if God was getting back at him for not paying attention in church.

The aircraft bucked and buffeted, as it accelerated along the runway. The plane finally took flight, with a shudder, and it sent a chill down his spine. Paula looked over at him, and put her hand on his. She seemed cool as a cucumber, as she liked to say. Sweat was beading on Jack's forehead.

After a few minutes, the plane climbed above the clouds and above the worst of the wind. The flight smoothed out substantially, and he was able to relax.

"Have you ever flown before?" Paula asked, quietly as she gripped his hand.

"No. Never. You?" He exhaled. Had he been holding his breath the whole time?

"I used to fly all the time with mom, before she - passed away," Paula said. "But it's been several years. Not much has changed. Security is a bit friskier."

"Yeah, I think your girl was getting a little too friendly," Jack said, beginning to relax.

"I feel safer, don't you?" she asked sarcastically. "Just sit back and relax, we'll be there before you know it."

Time during the flight did seem to elapse quickly. Jack nodded off several times, which was easy to do in first class. The seats were wide and comfortable, and the free drinks helped as well. There was also meal service in first class, as it was a five hour, direct flight. They ate and talked in hushed tones, so as not to bother the other passengers, some of whom were sleeping.

Jack tried to read Paula's book, but suddenly found his eyelids had anchors attached to them. He set the Kindle tablet down and closed his eyes.

He awoke when the cabin lights were switched on to prepare for landing. The flight attendants collected all the trash and then the cabin lights were dimmed once again.

When the jet touched down at McCarran International Airport
in Las Vegas, his watch said three fifteen in the morning. He wound
it back to local time, twelve fifteen.

"The night is still young," he said to Paula who was coming
out of a much deeper sleep. She stretched, took a sip from her
water, and started getting ready to deplane.

A direct flight meant no changing planes, no hassle of connecting flights. Jack was oblivious to just how convenient this
was. Paula knew better. She'd spent more than one night in an
airport terminal after missing a connecting flight, back when she
was a teenager. That was before her mother's death. She still had
trouble calling it a suicide.

They retrieved their bags from the carousel twenty minutes
later, and were out on the sidewalk waiting in the taxi line within
a half hour of landing.

The driver took them right to their hotel, with a slight detour
along the strip. All Vegas taxi drivers knew the game. Driving
down the strip made the tourists happy and raised the cost of the
fare as well. The bright, blinking lights of Las Vegas were on full
display. Both Jack and Paula peered out of the taxi windows at
the huge video screens advertising the different attractions at each
casino. It took nearly twenty minutes to reach their hotel. Traffic
was still surprisingly heavy along the strip for this time of night.

Check-in went smoothly at the hotel. A king-sized bed with a
view of the strip, paid for and waiting. A bellhop took their bags
and showed them to their room. Jack tipped him well. The door
closed and they were alone. Despite the activity still going on
outside the window, it was quiet in the room. Peaceful.

"So, what now?" Paula asked, as she put her arms around
Jack's neck and kissed him.

"Want to go hit the casino or get some sleep? It's really nearly
four in the morning," he said.

"Oh, don't tell me you're going to do that the whole trip,"
she whined.

"What?"

"The whole 'it's really this time' thing," she said. "You do it after daylight savings time too."

"I do?"

"Yes, you do. For like a week." She kissed him again.

"There you go, sounding like an old, nagging wife again," Jack said.

"Yeah, maybe I want to be," she replied softly.

"Do you?"

"Are you asking?"

"Well, I have thought about it," Jack said.

"So, you're not asking," Paula said, leaning away from him so she could study his face. "Thought is past tense."

"Well, I mean -" he was at a loss for words. This wasn't what he had in mind as a romantic way to ask her. But she seemed like she wanted him to. He had the ring in his pocket. His heart was racing. He was suddenly very cold.

"You mean, what?" She pressed him on it. He slid his left hand into his pocket, and felt the ring. He'd done this once before. His first wife had been his high school sweetheart. He'd planned an elaborate dinner with her parents at the big restaurant on the hill in Oneonta, Schaffer's Restaurant. The best restaurant in Oneonta, which wasn't saying much. He'd practiced the speech, then gotten down on one knee. Her mother was taking pictures the whole time. It seemed like it was supposed to be romantic, but felt anything but to him. To Jack it was more like signing up for college or becoming a cop. You went through the procedure, but there wasn't much emotion to it.

This was different. Standing here with Paula, the bright lights blinking in from the strip below, having her basically beg him to propose. It felt so spontaneous, and right.

"Let's go for a walk," Jack said. "I've always wanted to see the big fountains at the Bellagio."

"I think they stop at midnight," Paula said.

"Well let's go for a walk anyway."

"Okay."

They walked out the front of their hotel, into the comfortable night air. The temperatures were in the lower sixties, so Paula had a sweater. It felt like a summer night would feel, back in Coopers Hollow, yet it was just April. The sidewalks were wide and made it easy to stroll along without bumping into anyone. They were littered with small, business-card-sized ads for strip clubs and massage parlors. They walked all the way to the Bellagio, but the fountains were dark. A sign on the railing gave the schedule, and Paula had been right. The last show was at midnight.

"We can come back tomorrow night to see the fountains," Jack said.

"Sure."

"It's funny, but I don't really want to go," Jack said. "It's kind of nice here."

"It is."

He slid a hand into his pocket and felt the ring. Before he knew it, he was down on one knee.

"Jack?"

"I don't think I want to wait for tomorrow night," he said. He held the ring up to her. "Will you marry me?"

Chapter 16

"What are they doing?"

His kids were playing in the pool. Their mother was close by, but the nanny was the one really paying attention to them. Two weeks in Hawaii seemed like a great idea until all the movement began. It was like being in the middle of a chess game and suddenly having a third party come and rearrange the pieces on the board. It had started with chatter. A simple phone intercept. Then there was news that boys were being rounded up. Former military, former agency, all current mercenaries. The real money was overseas right now. So whoever was calling guys in for "a little job in the Catskills," had plenty of money and was plenty motivated.

He could see his kids splashing and laughing from the vantage point of a comfortable chair in the hotel suite. Even though he was near retirement, the kids were still very young. That's what happens when you divorce at forty and get remarried to a woman half your age. He held the phone to his head, his mind miles away from the hotel pool.

"They're in a hotel room in Las Vegas," the voice said on the other end of the call. "What do you think they're doing? They didn't get in until late, and they haven't come out yet. Oh, wait. There they are."

"Keep an eye on them," Mr. Shadow said. "We may have movement on this thing from another source. Lots of chatter out there. I think the cat's out of the bag," He wasn't happy at all. His men, Haas and Summers, had initiated contact with McMurphy. They were poised to step in, get what they wanted and close the whole thing down. Nice and neat. Then this thing with the Benevolent Police Brotherhood or whatever it was, screwed things up. The timing was too perfect. He was suspicious. Was somebody just trying to get McMurphy out of town for a few days? He had an agent tracking down whether it was legit. As of right now, it seemed so. The organization had a cancellation, and McMurphy's name was next on the list. Scutter didn't like it. It meant splitting up his already meager assets. He sent Haas to Vegas and kept Summers in Coopers Hollow.

"Really?" Haas asked. "Another team in play?

"I don't say things I don't mean, and I'm not sure yet."

"Okay. You want tight or loose on them?"

Der Schatten thought for a moment. There was a report. It was vague, with paragraphs of ifs, mights and coulds. There was something he and his team were missing about this whole thing. Yes there was a son of a powerful US senator involved with the group in New York City. Yes it was understood that he and El Tigre not only knew each other, but were, perhaps, in business with each other. That news wasn't really news at all. The three years they'd spent gently propping up El Tigre where they could, then inserting their undercover agent, Spaulding, into the mix, wasn't just about snagging a senator's son. It was about bringing the whole enterprise down. It was possible that there was a second investigation going on, unbeknownst to his team. Any number of government agencies could have stumbled into their game; DEA, FBI, heck, even ATF. But he would have seen something along the way. For three years, nothing. Then Coopers Hollow blew up. Things calm down as he and his team tidied up, and now, suddenly, there's a little report, merely a note, mentioning tying up loose ends in the Catskills. Maybe they were related, maybe they weren't. What other loose ends were there floating around in the Catskills? Then there were expensive men, on their way back to US soil. And it all seemed related.

"Tighten up if they leave the casino. Otherwise be the wall-paper, not the waiter," Mr. Shadow said. "But you know how to do your job."

"Roger that," came the reply.

Mr. Shadow ended the call. No goodbyes, no pleasantries. Just 'cease transmission.'

He looked at the phone and punched a number into the keypad from memory. The line engaged after one ring.

"Yeah?"

"What's the situation?" Scutter asked.

"Nothing right now," the man replied. "It's four in the morning. Mayberry rolls up the sidewalks after seven." Summers wasn't really the asset he wanted to have sitting in a car in a podunk, nowhere town, in the middle of the night. Summers was much better with a big gun hanging out the side of a helicopter picking off Afghan poppy smugglers or Columbian coke exporters.

"There's been movement," Mr. Shadow said. "This can't be another Baton Rouge."

"Roger that. We're on it," Summers said. It was as if he'd perked up a bit with the news that there might be action.

Mr. Shadow closed out the call and paused in silent contemplation. Baton Rouge was bad. A congressman and his family wiped out over something so trivial as formulas for a liquid-plastic display for televisions, which had been stolen from a Korean lab and sold to a Mexican businessman. Even though it wasn't his team that led that particular slip up, he did have eyes on the Mexican businessman as part of another investigation and he didn't warn the right people in time. Not that anyone would have listened. They hadn't listened about 9/11. It was his second strike. Another, and there was no doubt in his mind he'd be out.

Desperate times.

He weighed the information he had at hand. Right now there was maybe a thirty percent chance the situation would percolate into something. The thought gave him a chuckle.

"You're getting too old for this game," he said aloud. No one was in the room, and no one was listening with any devices either. The room had been swept before they arrived and the staff had been checked and cleared. So he was, indeed, talking to himself. "Nothing percolates anymore. It heats up and then bursts, suddenly and violently. Like Baton Rouge. We don't want another Baton Rouge."

He sighed. What he really wanted was a cigarette. There was one waiting for him across the room. A whole pack, in fact, smuggled along on this family excursion in his laptop bag. He opted for a drink by the pool. He slid the cellphone into the pocket of his plaid shorts and exited the suite through the sliding glass doors.

The laughter of his children brought a smile to his face.

Chapter 17

Back on the force. An odd development. When he'd planned his retirement, envisioned it in his mind, working hadn't been part of the equation. Not this kind of working, at least. It wasn't that he wanted a life of laziness and irresponsibility, he had just pictured taking walks, maybe traveling a bit. There were to be days filled with fishing and hunting, or chopping wood for a backyard fire. That was work, but it wasn't *work*, work.

At first he'd wanted to just find someplace to hole away to read some books and enjoy nature. But over the last few months he'd found himself getting a little restless. Maybe he'd buy a motor coach and travel across the country to see the sights he'd never had the opportunity to take in while enlisted with the Marine Corp or on the NYPD. Maybe he'd get a passport and set sail on a transatlantic cruise. Whatever form retirement was going to take, he certainly hadn't projected his current situation: serious relationship, position at the local police department, and strangely enough, not living in his own place.

"What are you thinking about, Cooke?" Tricia asked as she read over the report on the John Doe found at Hollow Pointe. As far as she could see, the investigation was by the book. Cooke didn't reply. She looked up from the report. "Come on now, out with it."

"I don't know, I just -" he went quiet.

"Just. What?"

"I just didn't think I'd end up here, in a place like this, doing, well, this again."

"You don't want to be deputy chief?"

"It's not that. I'm happy to be helping Jack out. It's just, when

I gave up the badge, downstate, I really felt like I was giving it up. I could have stayed on, ridden a desk job. Maybe even been a big wig. But when you're done, you're supposed to be done. Now it feels like I'm twenty-two again. Rookie cop learning the ropes," Cooke said. He was thumbing through a copy of *HotRod Magazine* he'd found laying around. It was from the previous year, but with a magazine about fixing up old cars, it really didn't matter. It was new to him.

"I kind of feel the same way," Tricia said. "But on the other hand it's kind of nice to have a place to be. I could see myself belonging here for a long time. I like the Chief."

"You know about all the stuff that went down here?" Cooke asked. "I mean here in Coopers Hollow?"

"Just what I read in the paper and online."

"It got hairy. Jack lost his dad. Almost lost Paula. Hell, I almost lost Gloria." He was quiet for a few moments as he thought about that night of violence, barely six months ago. "You ever fired your weapon in the line of duty?"

"Never," she said. "Never even had to draw it."

"I hope you never have to," Cooke said. He reached for his coffee and took a sip. It was cold. "I need a refresh, how 'bout you?"

"I'm good," Tricia said. "One more cup and I won't sleep for days."

It was a completely uneventful first day without the chief. Not a phone call and nobody through the door except the postman. It was already late into the afternoon. Michael was going to stay on until eight o'clock, but he was sending Tricia home at five. She was going to open the office at seven the next morning. The office would be closed overnight, but both Tricia and Michael had their phones and their scanners at home.

Tricia had found an apartment above the hardware store, not two blocks away. She didn't even move her car in the morning. She walked to the office, and could take either the chief's SUV or the other patrol car if she had to go out on a call. Ballard still had the third patrol car, but had the day off. He would be in, working his regular shift for the rest of the week. He was just a kid, but he was the senior officer of the group.

"Why don't you head out a bit early. It will give you a chance to get some groceries and get settled in your new place," Cooke said.

"I'm on the clock until five," Tricia answered. "I've got exactly twelve minutes."

"Oh, so you're one of those kind," Cooke said.

"And what kind is that?"

"A rule follower."

"I try."

Cooke was standing at the coffee pot when they walked in. The way they spread out as they entered made the hair on the back of his neck stand straight up. These guys moved with power and professional, military precision. Though they were wearing suits, Cooke could picture them in fatigues or body armor. These guys were serious news.

He thought back to the guys who had tried to kill Gloria. These guys made those guys look like amateurs. He suddenly had a sick feeling in his stomach. There was going to be violence tonight.

They each had a glass of champagne to celebrate the engagement with their late breakfast/early lunch. Then it was down to the big ballroom where the conference was going on. He checked in, got a badge for himself and Paula. Since he was going to be speaking, he had to check in a second time with the organizers. He was directed over to another room off the main ballroom, where the conference organizers were apparently busy organizing.

After just a few moments a perky, young woman came toward them with a broad smile. She was carrying a packet and a welcome bag.

"Hi! I'm Dana, one of the organizers here. Thank you so much for attending!" she gushed. She spoke rapid-fire, like she was on five cups of coffee with numerous espresso shots.

"Hi, Dana. Jack McMurphy. This is my fiancé, Paula Schumann."

Paula absolutely beamed when he introduced her.

"Pleased to meet you both. This packet has all of your information for tomorrow. You'll be interviewed about your particular incident in room D. That's just down the hall from where we are now. Please arrive about ten minutes early, so we can get the mic attached. The speaker is just going to ask you a few questions about your ordeal. Feel free to explain it the best way possible. If you could too, I always feel funny about asking this, but if you could, please take a look at this list of sponsors before hand. If you can remember to mention any of their products by name, during your interview, that would be great. They're the ones that make this all possible. And of course, they are huge supporters of law enforcement across the country. Do you have any questions?"

Jack and Paula both shook their heads.

"Okay, well here is my card. It has my personal cell number on it. If you have any questions or problems whatsoever, don't hesitate."

"Thank you, Dana," Jack said, shaking her hand.

"Just remember, plug, plug, plug," Dana said, with a laugh. "Then we'll just have a few minutes of Q and A. Oh, and a photo-op for any sponsors. You know. Pose, smile. Snap, snap. That's it. You'll do great."

"Okay," Jack said. Dana said goodbye and good luck.

They wandered in and out of the different rooms that were active. Some of the presentations were straight sales pitches from manufacturers of law enforcement products. There were a few talks in the conference that he thought he might like to attend. One on utilizing new technology sounded interesting. They found themselves listening to a presentation on non-lethal weapons for crowd control, until Paula couldn't sit still any longer.

"Can we go?" she whispered to him.

"Go where?"

"Just go walk around for a bit," she said. "I need to move."

"Okay."

They walked and talked, until they got to the casino floor. A vague scent of liquor graced the air. It all felt very exciting. As they moved onto the gaming floor the dinging, ringing, clicking and clanking of the slot machines produced a sweet cacophony that made it tough to converse without raising their voices.

"We should just do it," she said.

"What?"

"Get married. Right here, in Vegas."

"Really? Now?"

"Yes. Absolutely. Then we can go back down to the front desk and change our registration to mister and missus McMurphy."

"Where would we go? Justice of the peace?"

"There's chapels. I'll check," she said.

She had her smartphone out and was thumbing at it with precision. In just moments she found what they were looking for, and only a few blocks away, too. They took a cab. Just to see, they'd said to each other. Just recon.

They stood in the parking lot in front of the chapel.

"It's so tacky," Paula said, laughing.

"We don't have to."

"Oh, no. It's perfect!" Paula said, kissing him on the cheek. "I can't think of anything better, can you?"

"Let's do it," Jack said, kissing her.

They walked, hand-in-hand, towards the 'Open 24hrs' sign blazing in glorious neon on the side of the white stucco building. It was designed like a full sized chapel, but was actually miniature in most ways. Including the tiny bells atop the tiny tower. The website had promised no wait for weddings.

"Are you sure about this? Not too cheesy?"

"No, it's romantic. Spontaneous, right?" Paula said.

"Very spontaneous. Don't you want your friends here? What's her name from Oneonta?"

"We live in a tiny town where everybody knows everybody. My mom is dead. Your parents are gone. Who else would be here? Aimee is not what I'd call a close friend. We have drinks together and I listen to her complain about men."

"What about Michael and Gloria?"

"Are you getting cold feet?"

"No," Jack said. "Hell no. That's not it at all. I just don't want you to look back on this and regret it. To wish we'd done something different. I just don't want to cheat you out of it."

"I will never regret this, Jack McMurphy Junior." She threw her arms around his neck and kissed him on the mouth. She still tasted like champagne.

Mr. Shadow, Lwelyn Scutter, had to excuse himself from breakfast. It was a beach breakfast, with fruit and cereal for the kids. They had a gazebo all to themselves, just a few yards from the rolling surf. He stepped down into the sand and walked along the beach so as to be out of earshot of the wife and kids.

"Better be good," he said into the phone. "I'm missing breakfast with the kids."

"They're in the Chapel O' Love," Haas said. "Getting, frickin' hitched."

"You called me for this?"

"Um, no. There are a few boys here who are sniffing around. I picked them up in the casino last night. They tailed our happy couple to the conference this morning. Now they've followed them to the chapel. Not sure what they're up to yet, but I just thought you should know. Anybody else you know of working this? DEA, FBI?"

"Not that I have been informed. Doesn't mean it's not happening."

The phone beeped in his ear. Another call coming in.

"Stay on them," Scutter said.

He punched the touchscreen and took the other call.

"Yes?"

"We've got guys in the office. Three of them. They look armed and dangerous. Cooke and the new lady cop are in there. Should I intercept?" It was Summers in Coopers Hollow.

Scutter was silent for a moment. He breathed in slowly through his nose. The thirty percent chance had turned into a hundred percent.

"Boss?"

"Any idea who they are?"

"If I had to gamble on it, I'd say they were former military working for a private entity. They are in suits, trying to look like FBI, but they move more like military. Maybe ex-special forces," Summers said. "Professional opinion? They aren't agency boys." He was to be trusted on such things, being former special forces himself. Sometimes it took one to spot one.

Scutter swore.

"Call the sheriff or state police. Don't go in alone. You're too important to lose," Scutter said.

"Aw, gee. I love you too, boss," Summers said. "Anything else?"

"Call me at regular intervals. I want those boxes of evidence," Scutter said.

He closed the call with Summers and dialed Haas again.

"Yeah?"

"Things are heating up in Cooper Hollow. This sounds co-ordinated. Intercept if things get dicey."

"Roger that," Haas said.

Scutter closed the connection again and held the phone to his lips. He stared at the surf for a few moments, then walked back through the sand to his breakfast with the kids.

Chapter 18

"I now pronounce you husband and wife. You may kiss the bride."

Jack slid his arm around his wife and kissed her on the mouth. Though it was just for a few seconds, it seemed like an eternity. There was a group of other couples sitting in the pews behind them, patiently waiting for their turn. They applauded the McMurphys, as Jack led his bride towards the back of the ornately designed, faux-chapel.

They had paperwork to fill out. It had taken twenty minutes for the blood test, and then another fifteen to wait for two additional weddings. It was an amazing little outfit, very efficient. Jack signed his name and Paula signed hers. It was official, they were married.

They bought a picture from the photographer. There was also a small catalog of announcements and other wedding extras from which they could choose, but they opted only for the picture and a nice frame.

"Be careful," the woman said, as she slid the print out of the photo into the back of the frame. "This is real glass. I'd suggest carrying it on when you fly home. TSA will smash it in your bag, guaranteed. Also, should you ever need any additional copies, you can order them online. Just use this number," she indicated the number on the back of the photo, as she closed up the back of the frame. She wrapped it into a gift box and then took Jack's credit card to settle up the whole affair.

"Let's go celebrate," Paula said.

"What do you want to do?"

"Let's go back to the hotel and make love. Then go out and see a show," Paula said. "I'm so happy!"

"Sounds good to me, Mrs. McMurphy. Lead the way," he said. His smile was stretched ear to ear.

They exited the Chapel O' Love into bright sunshine and warm temperatures. The cab driver had left, but where they were wasn't but a few blocks from the hotel.

"Want to walk back?" Jack asked.

"Sure."

It was starting to get hot, but it wasn't too bad yet. It was the dry heat everyone talked about as not being so bad. It felt hot to Jack, but he'd spent his life in the mountains. Anything above room temperature felt hot to him.

As they crossed the parking lot, hand-in-hand, heading for the sidewalk, two doors opened on a full-sized sedan. Two men, both in dark suits and sunglasses stepped out, leaving the doors open. Jack stopped walking, and gave a tug at Paula's hand.

"What's wrong," Paula asked.

"Not sure," Jack said quietly. "These guys look like they want something."

The men walked at an even pace, scanning the area as they approached.

"Who are they?"

"FBI maybe," Jack replied, quietly. "Or maybe FDCI boys, again."

"Jack McMurphy?" the one on the right asked. He was the driver and was slightly larger than the other man. Both were bigger than Jack, in height and weight.

"Maybe," Jack replied. "Who wants to know."

"We're federal agents. We need you to come with us," the other man said.

"Which agency, boys?"

"We can talk in the car," the driver said. Paula clutched at Jack's arm.

"Yeah, not a good time for us," Jack said. "We just got married. We're going to hit the town for a bit. Come back tomorrow."

The men were now only a few paces away. Jack took half a step back and eased Paula back behind him.

"Make it easy on yourself and your lady," the driver said.

"I've never taken the easy road," Jack replied. "If you boys did your homework, you'd know that. So how about some ID?"

The men stopped about five feet away. Their hands were at their sides, hanging not far away from their holstered sidearms.

"You don't need to see our identification," the driver said. "We just want to talk."

"No dice," Jack replied. "Not talking without seeing your IDs."

The two suit-clad men exchanged glances, then started walking towards the couple. There was a bit more menace in their gait now. The driver was pursing his lips and clenching his jaw. It looked like things were about to get physical. That made Jack think that they weren't federal agents at all. That's not how normal agents would operate.

"Don't take another step," Jack said. "I'm warning you."

"You're warning us?" the driver smirked. "We'll give you to the count of three to start walking toward the car." They continued towards Jack and Paula, but their pace slowed a bit.

"One -"

Jack bolted forward towards the driver before he could say the next number. Coach had drilled it into him for four years in high school. Hit low, come up hard, de-cleat your opponent. It didn't matter if the guy was bigger than you. A solid hit would knock him on his can and take him out of the play. Coach would have been proud. The driver certainly wasn't expecting such a blow and was sent off he feet and into the air.

His partner to the left was stunned for a beat, then reached for his 9mm pistol. Jack spun and brought his left hand down on the pistol hand, trapping the gun in the holster. He brought his right fist in for a crushing blow to the man's jaw.

It was over in just moments. Two dark suited men who claimed to be federal agents were on the ground and Jack was standing over them with one of their own guns.

"You touch that weapon and I'm going to regret it," Jack said.

"You're going to regret it?" the driver questioned in a gasp. The blow and subsequent impact on the flat of his back, against concrete, had knocked the wind from him.

"Yeah, killing a man always comes with a lot of paperwork," Jack replied. "I hate paperwork. Roll over onto your stomach and lock your fingers behind your head."

"What if I don't?"

Jack stepped forward as if he was going to pull the trigger and end the guy right there in the parking lot of the Chapel O' Love.

"I get something extra to remind me of my anniversary," Jack said.

Suddenly there was a rev of an engine and squealing tires from their left. A car that had been sitting at the far end of the parking lot raced towards them. Jack pushed Paula further back as the car aimed directly for the two suits, and brought the gun up to aim at the car. It slid to a stop, just a few feet from running over the prone figures that Jack had knocked to the ground.

A man stepped out of the car with his weapon drawn.

"Put the gun down, Jack," the man said. McMurphy recognized him.

"Summers, right? Or was it Haas?"

"Agent Haas. Summers is babysitting back in Coopers Hollow. Please set the weapon on the ground," Agent Haas commanded.

"What. The. Hell?" Paula asked. "What's going on?"

"I'm sorry, ma'am. Not at liberty to say."

McMurphy did as he was instructed and set the black 9mm pistol onto the concrete and took several steps back.

"They wanted us to go with them, but they wouldn't show any ID. They said they were federal agents," Jack said. "But I don't believe them."

"They would," Haas replied. "How ya doin, Brinkman? I think the last time I saw you, you were sitting on your ass. Haven't changed a bit."

"Who are these guys?" Paula asked.

"Brinkman here was FBI. Was. No longer. Fail a drug test and you usually aren't asked to stick around," Haas said. "Isn't that right, Brinkman? Who's your girlfriend?"

The driver, who was apparently former agent Brinkman, didn't say anything.

"Come on, who's your pal?" Haas asked again.

"I want a lawyer," he said.

"Roll over and put your hands on your head before my finger slips and I shoot you," Haas replied. Brinkman reluctantly complied, lying face down on the hot concrete. Haas stepped forward, pulled the sidearm out of its holster and tossed it next to the other gun. He then took handcuffs from Brinkman's own belt and slapped one loop over Brinkman's wrist. He forced his knee into the small of his back, eliciting a grunt from the prone man. Haas made quick work of getting the other arm behind his back and locking up the handcuffs. He fished through the man's pockets and retrieved his keys. He left Brinkman there, face down, and focused on the still unconscious partner.

"You don't mess around," Haas said to Jack, as he toed the knocked out man to see if he'd stir. He didn't. Jack just shrugged as he watched the agent roll the man onto his front and pull his arms back to be cinched up with another set of cuffs, pulled from his own belt. He went through the unconscious man's pockets and came up with a wallet.

"Fake badge, fake ID," Haas said. "Pretty good fakes, but still fake. That's a felony, Brinkman. You're going away for a bit."

He handed the wallet to Jack to look at.

"So, who are you working for these days, Brinkman?"

"I want my lawyer."

"Chief, help me get them into my car, will you?"

"Aren't you going to read them their rights?" Paula asked.

"Maybe," Haas said.

McMurphy and Haas grabbed Brinkman's arms and stood the big man up. They pushed him towards Haas' brown Crown Victoria. Once he was stuffed into the back seat, Haas opened the passenger door and used the power seat to push back into the man, effectively trapping his knees and legs in place.

As they were dragging the unconscious accomplice toward the car, a Las Vegas Police cruiser pulled up and flashed their lights and keyed a whoop from the siren.

"Drop him," Haas instructed. The man hit the pavement with an audible impact.

"Hands up, everyone," the cop yelled.

"Take it easy," Haas said. "I'm Agent Haas. I'm a federal agent, working this investigation out of the New York office. ID is right here in this pocket. I'm carrying a firearm, officer. Just thought you might like to know."

"Take out your ID and toss it this way," the cop said. "Slowly." He had his hand on his gun, but hadn't drawn it. The cop leaned down and grabbed the wallet and looked at it. His tension eased a bit.

"What are you doing with this guy?"

"He was in the process of impersonating a federal officer and attempting to kidnap this newlywed couple here. I've been trailing these two jokers for a month now. Same scam. Flash some fake badges, then dump their bodies in the desert and head back to the hotel to clean them out," Haas said.

"Well, we're going to get this all checked out, so nobody move," the cop said. He radioed for back up, thus postponing the walk back to the hotel for the McMurphys.

"You better never forget our anniversary after this," Paula said.

In all, it took forty minutes for backup to arrive, phone calls to be made, IDs to be recorded from everyone, and finally for the police to let Jack and Paula walk back to their hotel. The walk itself took less than fifteen minutes.

Walking into the casino, they were met with a refreshing blast of cool air, tinged with the scent of alcohol and tobacco. They didn't even have to say a word to each other, as they both headed right for the nearest bar.

"Well that will make for an interesting story to tell the grand-kids," Jack said.

"Add it to the list."

Chapter 19

Michael Cooke was setting his half-full coffee cup down on the table right about the same time Jack and Paula were reciting their vows 2,500 miles and three time zones away.

"Can I help you gentlemen?" Cooke asked, turning to the three men who were now standing in the police department. His instincts told him to rest his hand on the handgun hanging on his belt. He could have it out and shooting in a split second. In such close range, he'd take at least two of the guys before the third could get a shot off at him. It was worth the risk. If he was alone.

When it comes to engagements of violence, there are always variables that greatly affect who it is that walks away and who it is that is carried away.

Cooke looked over at Tricia. She was sitting behind the desk, her hand was indeed resting on her gun belt. Her sixth sense had been piqued as well. She wasn't going to be a burden or liability, she was going to be an asset if this thing went sour.

"You Jack?" The man who asked, had identified himself as the leader of the group, without declaring it outright. He was front and center, he was the one talking. He was the alpha dog. They were dressed to look alike, but their roles would become clear, the more he could get them talking.

"Chief McMurphy is currently unavailable," Cooke said. "Would you like some coffee? Still a little bite to the air out there."

The alpha dog gave a quick glance to his two sidekicks.

"No coffee," he said. "We need to pick up a few boxes. Jack told our office to send somebody by. So here we are." His face went from deadpan and emotionless to a fake toothy smile.

"Yeah? Which boxes would those be? Jack left a bunch of notes for us, and I have to tell you the truth, I haven't read half of them," Cooke said. He was trying to size up each of the guys, while being nonchalant. The more time he had, the more likely he'd be able to go through all the variables in play.

These boys were definitely former military. They were the guys who joined up, got a taste of the action, and then couldn't kick the habit. They loved the violence. Cooke had seen the type when he was enlisted with the Marine Corp. He saw a batch of them again when he was with the NYPD. There were only a few of those types in the ESU, but on the regular force, they were plentiful.

The archetype worked out at the gym more than necessary, and enjoyed flexing in the mirrors. He also liked big, powerful guns. Cooke guessed that each one of them carried a .40 or .45 under his jacket. If they were smart, they'd be wearing waist holsters. If they thought they were Mike Hammer or Arnold Schwarzenegger, they'd have shoulder holsters - not because they were more effective, but because they looked cool and they thought it concealed the gun better. A shoulder holster slowed the draw of a weapon substantially, especially for a big gun. The likelihood that two of the three wouldn't even have their guns drawn by the time Cooke put a bullet in them was very high. He tried to calm himself, breathing with a smooth rhythm.

"Just some old boxes on an old case. We're consolidating all the files. Didn't he tell you about it?" Alpha dog asked. It didn't look like the other two were trained to speak. Cooke could probably teach them to play dead.

"Like I said," Cooke replied. "Lots of notes I haven't read yet."

"Well, I have a list of the boxes right here," Alpha dog started to slide his hand under his jacket as he walked toward Michael.

Michael had his gun out and pointed it at Alpha dog's chest.

"Don't do that," Michael said.

"Kind of jumpy, aren't we? We're just errand boys."

"When three guys roll into my office with forty-fives in shoulder holsters, I don't really buy that they're FBI. I don't know who you guys are, but I'm going to find out," Cooke said. "Tricia, search them."

She had drawn down on the men as soon as Michael had pulled his gun. They'd gotten the jump on the three of them.

"Stay cool," Alpha dog said. "This is just a misunderstanding."

"That's fine. We'll get it cleared up, then."

Tricia started with the guy on the right. She opened his jacket, and sure enough pulled a black pistol from his shoulder holster. It looked like a Glock 17, black plastic, chambering forty-five caliber rounds. One for three, Cooke thought to himself.

Tricia set the gun down on her desk, eight feet away from the guy. She then patted him down thoroughly, removing a cellphone and wallet. She opened the wallet, flashed the FBI identification at Cooke, and set it and the cell phone down on the desk next to the Glock. She repeated the procedure for the other two men. Cooke could see that Alpha dog was trying to stifle the rage. A reddish hue was climbing up his neck and into his cheeks. In a moment, Alpha dog was going to be completely flush.

When she was through with the searches, she handed the wallets to Cooke, and then took up his position covering the men as Michael looked at the IDs. Each of them had big blue letters spelling out FBI, with a picture, a name, and the words Special Agent at the bottom. They looked real enough.

"Got somebody I can call to confirm?" Cooke asked.

"Sure, my boss. Director of the field office in New York," Alpha dog said. Cooke dialed as he gave him the number.

"Hello, this is Deputy Chief Cooke up in Coopers Hollow, how are you? Good. I have a couple of guys here," he said as he looked at their IDs. "A Special Agent Parks, Eaton and Parsons. Do they belong to you? Sure, I'll hold."

It took only a few minutes for the voice to return and confirm the identities.

"Okay, have a nice evening. Thank you," Cooke said.

It still didn't feel right to him. They didn't have the special agent look. They seemed more like mercenaries, like some of the tough guys he'd seen working with private firms with CIA contracts, back in Iraq. If they weren't legit, then it was quite a scam they were running. If they were the real deal, he'd just drawn on a federal agent and was going to live to talk about it. He made his decision.

"Okay, fellas. Sorry for the games. I'm sure you heard about the stuff that happened here a few months back. We're all a little jumpy since then. I apologize," he said. Tricia looked at Cooke, then lowered her weapon and reholstered it on her hip. "No hard feelings?"

"Just being careful, officer. I can appreciate that," Alpha dog said. His ID said his real name was Special Agent Ross Parks. The guy on the right was Eaton, and on the left, Parsons.

"So, seriously, would you like some coffee?" Cooke asked. He returned to his half-filled cup and finished the task of filling it all the way.

"No coffee," Parks said. "Just the boxes on this list." He smiled as he reached back into his jacket to retrieve a slip of paper.

"You know," Cooke said. "I can't let those boxes out of here without the proper transfer paperwork. If you give us a few minutes, we can pull the right forms, get them filled out and with a few signatures and badge numbers, get you guys on your way."

"We don't have the time for that," Parks said. "I need you to get these boxes for me now."

Agent Summers got out of his car when he saw Cooke draw his weapon. Summers hastily hit redial on his phone and drew his own 9mm pistol.

"What's happened?"

"Local cops have the three guys at gunpoint. Should I intercede? Call the cavalry?"

The long pause unnerved him. It felt like an eternity.

"You think they're after the evidence?"

"I don't know, I'm not in the room," Summers said.

"Who is in the room, is it Cooke, the sniper?"

"Yes sir. And the new girl. Wallace is her name. She was Albany PD. She's still wet behind the ears."

Another pregnant pause.

"Did you call anyone? Sheriff, state troopers?"

"Negative, not yet."

A long silence.

"Stand down. If the shooting starts, get in there and finish it. Otherwise, stay out of sight. If these guys get the boxes, you follow them. Find out who they are. Get names. I can back-trace them, find out where this puts us. If it's completely unrelated and they aren't after the boxes, it's not our problem."

"Confirmed," Agent Summers reholstered his gun and pocketed his phone. He watched as the black police woman searched the guys and then gave the wallets to Cooke. He had their names. Even if they left with the boxes, it wouldn't matter. He could find out who this other team was and report back to Mr. Shadow.

Cooke looked at the list. He knew immediately what boxes they were and that they just happened to be sitting next to Chief McMurphy's desk, not twenty feet away. As far as he was concerned, letting the boxes walk wasn't the worst thing in the world that could happen. Knowing that one of the perps that was gunned down was an undercover agent meant that either these guys were here to bury the evidence, or dig it up. One way or the other, it wasn't going to affect him, Tricia or Jack. They were just some boondocks police department in the middle of the Catskills. It would be an easily defensible position. Jack might be pissed, though.

"We were just trying to help out the FBI," he would say. Even if

Jack was angry at him, he'd buy him a beer and apologize. Maybe it would get him fired. He could live with that.

"Okay," Cooke said. "I guess you guys pull rank on me, so I'll get the boxes for you. Tricia, grab a photocopy of their IDs so I can throw them in the file."

"Go with him," Parks said to Parsons and Eaton. The two silent partners jumped to action and followed Michael into Jack's office. They each grabbed a box and exited as quickly as they'd come in.

Michael set the box down on his desk. He saw that Parks had his gun out and was pointing it under Tricia's arm, directly at her heart.

"It's just one of those things you should never do," Parks said.

"What's that?"

"Question your instincts. You had the jump on us. I was getting really nervous there for a second. Too bad you weren't smart enough. Now take two fingers and slowly remove your gun and place it gently on the floor," Parks said.

Cooke swore under his breath. As he followed the order, he saw Tricia's gun already on the floor, kicked under her desk.

"Now kick it over this way," Parks said. Cooke complied.

"Take the boxes out to the car and get it started. Wait for me," Parks said this to Parsons and Eaton, who jumped into action. Eaton loaded up two boxes and followed Parsons out the front door.

"Back into the lock up," Parks barked.

Cooke led the way, while Parks muscled Tricia after him, gun still jammed against her ribs, where her protective vest didn't cover her. Cooke opened the cell door and stepped in. Tricia was pushed in behind him. Parks pulled the door closed and made sure it was locked.

"Nobody points a gun at me," he said through clenched teeth. He slid his gun hand between the bars and fired off six shots.

Chapter 20

Several moments before deafening shots rang out within the confines of the Coopers Hollow police department, Eric waited in the hospital in Albany, sixty miles away. The procedure was scheduled to take four hours. It was now nearing six hours. He'd been to the snack machine several times, but didn't feel like eating anything. He drank coffee, read the old magazines in the waiting room, visited the toilet three times, and spent the rest of the time watching CNN on the television, mounted in the corner. It was an old cathode ray tube version, so the widescreen aspect of the news created black bars at the top and bottom of the screen. The resulting image was almost indecipherable.

It was just entering the sixth hour when a nurse came out to speak with him.

"How did it go? Where's the doctor?" Eric asked.

"He's still with her," the nurse said quietly. "There have been some complications."

He heard the words, but they didn't quite register. His stomach twisted into a knot.

"What do you mean?"

"We removed the tumor, but your wife suffered a seizure and then stopped breathing. We were able to restart her heart, but her pulse is very weak right now."

Eric didn't say anything. All he could think of was the children. Riker specifically.

"Is she going to be okay?"

"The doctor is doing everything he can. He wanted me to

tell you so you would know. He asked that you pray, if you're a religious man." The nurse, her name said Dewey on the tag, looked grieved. The expression she wore was one of lost hope.

"Can I see her? Can I hold her hand?"

"I'm sorry. Not yet. The doctor is closing the operation now. Once he's secured the incisions, we will need to try to wake her up if her pulse can handle it. It may be wiser to leave her in a medically induced coma to allow her to heal with the aid of the life support systems. As soon as I know more, I will let you know." She turned and exited quickly through the doors marked "authorized personnel only".

Eric wasn't a religious man. College had just about squeezed every last drop of faith out of him. At this point, praying felt like hypocrisy.

"Never an atheist in a fox hole," his father, Copper, used to say. Eric had always understood that comment to be a little derisive dig at those who ignored God until they were desperate. He was indeed desperate now. He didn't even know where to start. He remembered the Lord's Prayer from his childhood. At least some of it. He fished his cellphone out of his pocket and searched for "Lord's Prayer". Google provided a litany of results. The first click was on the King James Version he'd remembered. He read it. It was nice, but didn't seem to apply to what he was going through. He put his phone away and folded his hands. He began to pray for the first time in at least thirty years.

He was still in prayerful meditation thirty minutes later when the doctor came out to speak with him. Eric didn't even notice him until the doctor sat down in the chair beside him and rested his hand on Eric's shoulder.

"Is she okay?" Eric asked, barely choking out the words. His eyes were red and tears were flowing down his cheeks. "Doc, please." His voice faltered.

"I'm so sorry," the doctor said. "We did everything we could. I believe my nurse explained what happened. While removing the tumor she had a seizure. It was severe enough to cause her heart to stop. We were able to get her back for a time, but she faded and we lost her. I'm so very sorry."

Eric sobbed in his hands. There were so many things left for them to do together. And the kids. Oh God the kids.

The doctor left his hand on Eric's shoulder, patting him consolingly.

"Mr. Owens," the doctor said. He was perhaps Eric's age. He was clean shaven and wore green scrubs. Eric looked at him, and saw his mouth moving and heard the sounds, but they didn't register.

"I said, do you have someone who can drive you home?" the doctor repeated.

"Can I see her?"

The doctor was quiet for a moment, and then sighed heavily.

"She won't look like you remember her. We shaved her head for the procedure," the doctor said. "But if you'd like, I can take you in to see her."

The doctor stood, holding Eric by the arm to steady him. They walked through the "Authorized Personnel Only" doors and traveled along several yards of hallway. There were quiet voices all about him, with beeps of medical machinery adding to the soft din of unintelligible noise. Finally the doctor pushed through a door. There was a wash station and a place for soiled scrubs. He pushed through another door, and Eric saw his wife lying on the table.

The surgery lights had been extinguished. All that was left on were the fairly dim fluorescents in the ceiling. Nurses were cleaning up tools, and wheeling equipment out of the room.

"Folks, let's give Mr. Owens a few moments," the doctor said. The nurses and other personnel nodded and filed out of the room.

There was still tape holding the breathing tube in place. The doctor delicately peeled away the tape and removed the tube. He then stepped out of the room.

With her mouth open as it was, she looked like she was just sleeping. Her head was covered by some sort of shower cap, but there was a drip of blood on her forehead. Eric wiped it away with his thumb, and bent down to kiss his wife. She wasn't cold, but she didn't have the warmth of life either. Her skin felt waxy to his lips. He took her hand, and found himself pressing his fingers against her wrist where a pulse would be. There was nothing. She was gone.

"I love you," he said. He heaved with sobs. "I promise you I will take care of the children. They both love you too. I'm so sorry these last few years have been so difficult for you. I tried my best. I tried -"

He broke into sobs again. His legs weakened, and he found himself on the floor, in an awkward sitting position, still holding her hand. The nurses had apparently been watching somehow, as they came through the door with a wheel chair. They had him up into the chair and were wheeling him away from his wife. A strong hand squeezed his shoulder. It felt like the entire world was falling apart.

The phone rang and Riker was the first to get it.

"Hello?"

"Put grandma on," Eric said.

"When are you coming home?"

"Tonight. But it will be late. You'll already be in bed."

"Is mom okay?"

Riker heard the sound of his father either gasping or coughing. He sounded sick.

"Just put grandma on, buddy," Eric said after a moment. He sounded like he did when he had a sore throat. Like a croaking frog. Riker did as he was told and handed off the phone.

"Hey, honey. Is it over? How is she?"

Riker didn't hear the answer, but he saw his grandmother's

face turn ashen. She sat down at the kitchen table and put her hand to her mouth. She took of her glasses and and wiped away the tears in her reddening eyes.

Riker ran from the kitchen to his room and locked the door.

Chapter 21

Agent Summers was leaning against his car when the two men came out of the police department, carrying boxes. They were big guys. They moved like trained military. They stood upright, no slouching, with an air of self-assurance.

"Well, that was easy," he said to himself, as he straightened to his feet and rested his hand on his holstered pistol. "But those are my boxes."

He watched them as they scanned the street, walking down the steps towards the big SUV. The second one spotted him and said something to the first. They both watched him as they continued to walk over to the waiting Chevy Suburban. The one with the single box led the procession, opening the tailgate door and sliding his box into the far back of the vehicle. The other guy put his boxes in, unstacking them. Both kept their eyes on Summers.

Summers pulled out his cell phone and watched the reaction of the two guys. They stiffened slightly. They exchanged comments to each other, moving their lips only slightly, so Summers couldn't make out what they said. They were trying to stare him down, intimidate him, but their hands stayed away from the guns in the shoulder holsters. If they were pros, then they would recognize a pro. They were playing it cool.

He had his phone in hand, it was ringing. Then shots rang out from inside the station. Summers counted six. He dropped the phone and drew his pistol. Weapon out, he sprinted across the street. The shots had apparently surprised them as well, as they both spun to look back at the police station.

"Hands where I can see them! Federal agent!" Summers yelled. They spun to face him.

"Hey, hey! We're on the same team," one of the guys said. He reached for his jacket.

"Do it and you'll be breathing out of that shirt pocket," Summers barked. "Hands up where I can see them. No sudden movements!"

A third man came out of the police department, almost at a run. He stopped short when he saw Summers.

"Federal agent! Get down on the ground," Summers yelled. The man didn't move. He was maybe fifteen yards away. It was that time of early evening where everything seemed perfectly crisp in detail. The sun had passed over the horizon, but the sky still reflected enough light to give everything a sharpness and clarity, along with a pinkish orange hue. It was cool and damp, and a chill ran down Summer's spine. For several moments nobody moved.

Time stood still for a heartbeat, and then proceeded at a crawl. Summers saw everything in slow motion. The man who'd just exited the building drew his weapon and crouched low, even as he started running for the nose of the Suburban. As Summers swiveled his gun onto the new target, the two guys with the boxes reached for their weapons.

Summers fired. He saw the puff of concrete as the bullet slammed into the front of the police station building, missing his target. The next shot was on target, clipping the gunman in the shoulder.

Summers was backing away from the Suburban now, conscious of the curb, so as not to stumble. He re-aimed at the former box-carriers, and fired a burst of two shots at the right hand man. The perp was bringing his pistol up, but never got the chance to take aim. The bullets ripped into his chest and exited through his back into the interior of the Suburban. The other former box-carrier was still in the motion of pulling his weapon, even as he was trying to duck around the open tailgate door of the Suburban. Summers fired two more bursts, shattering the rear window with the first shot and hitting the man in the back with his second.

Agent Summers heard two more shots, but was confused. They were close, but not from his gun.

He stumbled, his legs acting like the weak, powerless legs of a marionette. He tried to get them back under him, but they simply weren't moving properly. The pain rushed up on him, stealing away his breath. He realized he'd been shot. He tried to force himself to stay calm, but panic gripped him.

Two more bursts of thunder, and he fell to the sidewalk, his world spinning uncontrollably. Everything was muffled now, and it was like he was trying to move underwater, against the current. He tried to reach for the gun that had clattered out of his hand, but he couldn't get his body to respond. It felt like he was choking. He tried to cough, but convulsed instead, spitting up blood. The pain was intense. Until it wasn't.

He felt warm and comfortable, as if nothing in the world could hurt him any longer. Agent Summers closed his eyes and died on the sidewalk, in front of the Coopers Hollow Police Department.

"Summers! Agent Summers! What's going on?!" Mr. Shadow's voice called out from the cell phone, that had been dropped to the surface of the road. The connection was still open, as the call had rung through just as the shooting had started.

Scutter, Mr. Shadow, heard the gunshots, heard the tires screeching as the SUV sped away from the scene and didn't hear the voice of his agent.

Scutter was still in Hawaii. It was just after breakfast. He knew his family was going to have to continue the vacation without him. He had to catch the next flight back to D.C.

This was going to be a bad one.

Chapter 22

They watched, as Jack McMurphy and his new bride stepped out from the bank of elevators, on the ground floor. They wound their way through the casino, arm in arm, smiling and talking. Their voices didn't carry across the din of gaming machines and human noise in the casino, so the goons were forced to guess what they were talking about.

The men watching the McMurphys were the backup team. The backups to the backups, to be completely accurate. They were the redundancy asset for the secondary team that was tasked with killing the McMurphys in Las Vegas.

"This is stupid," one of the men said. The others in the group only knew him as Denver. He was tall and lean and still wore the beard he'd grown when he'd worked in Iraq. The desert air of Las Vegas reminded him of his time there. He'd spent twenty-one months on a private security team that was contracting with the CIA. Until he'd decided to have his way with that girl. The CIA didn't like that. So, it was back to the good ol' US of A to find other work. It didn't take long. There's always work for a man who doesn't mind pulling the trigger.

"Who is this guy anyway?" the other replied. Unlike Denver, he had never set foot outside of the country. He'd grown up in the Bronx and was recruited into a life of crime when he was thirteen. That was eight, long years ago. The others called him Rook. Short for rookie. Though he was anything but. He probably had more kills than Denver.

"I don't know, some hick cop from outside of New York. If I had a conscience, I'd feel guilty about taking their money for this one," Denver said.

"Okay let's get it done," Rook said.

"Not so fast, hot shot," Denver said. He pushed the toothpick in his mouth so it was standing straight up, next to his nose. He nodded his head up, slightly, and indicated the ceiling with his eyes. Rook nodded.

In the casino, there were literally thousands of cameras and microphones. They kept track of the gambling patrons and staff, making sure everything was on the up and up. To attempt to take the McMurphys down in such an environment, was to court sure police entanglement. Their faces would be all over the ten o'clock news. Their employer certainly didn't want that.

"Bide our time, kid."

"I've never been to Vegas. How 'bout you?"

"Couple of times," Denver said. His cell phone rang. He slipped it from his pocket. "Pro tip: put a jacket on it." He winked and put the phone to his ear.

"Go," he said quietly. The music and the electronic cacophony of the gaming machines made it difficult to hear. Only one person had the number to this phone. Once the job was done, it would get tossed into a trash bin somewhere on the strip.

"Full lights out?" he asked. When he heard the answer, he swore. This got the attention of his partner.

"Okay, we'll stay alert." He ended the call without another word.

"What happened?" his partner asked.

"The lift in New York went sour. We lost Holley, but they got the packages," he said.

"When?"

"Four hours ago."

"And we're just finding out now?"

"The others took shots too. But they're not dead. Not yet. They had to lay low and fix themselves up."

Rook whistled.

"We still on for the cop and his girl?" he asked.

"Yeah. We're to finish the job and drive to LA."

"Alright," there was a level of glee in Rook's voice. "Let's do this."

Both of them had drinks in their hands to blend in a bit more. The suits they wore, now had loosened ties and unbuttoned collars. They'd swiped some trade show badges from the trash, so they could look like a couple of conventioneers, slowly getting drunk on the casino floor. Rook was black and clean shaved and wore a gold watch. Denver had his beard and big, black rimmed glasses with fake lenses in them. His vision was twenty-twenty. He just wanted to look the part of "hipster-business-guy." Just a couple of conventioneers, nothing to see here.

They casually strolled across the casino, staying focused on the McMurphys, who were maybe twenty yards ahead. They followed them to the ticket office, bought tickets themselves, and then followed through the open doors of the theater.

"What kind of show is this?" Rook asked.

"Looks like some singer or something."

"I have a can on my H&K. If it's dark enough, we can take them during the applause. Nobody will hear it."

"Hit the head, go in a stall and get it ready. When the lights go down, so do the McMurphys," Denver said.

"Roger that."

They split up.

"What do you think of all this?" Paula asked.

"I think this singer better be good for the price we paid for the tickets," Jack replied.

"I've seen him before. He's the best. I was out here two years ago for a journalist convention," she said. She looked at her newly minted husband and laughed.

"What?" Jack scowled. "What did I do?"

"You look like a fish out of water," Paula said. "You seem so uptight. Relax a little."

"I can't," Jack said. "How can you?"

"I just put it away," Paula said. "Lock it away. I learned to do it a long time ago. With mom and all, I had to."

"Well, I'm trying to make sense of it. Fake FBI guys. And Haas, why is he following us? You know how I know him? A week ago he and his partner came in to see me. They told me that one of the guys who got shot that night in October was working undercover," Jack said. "I shot him. I killed him. My fault."

"Oh, no," Paula gasped. She was quiet for a few moments.

"I mean, he was undercover, in the act of committing a crime. But still, I pulled the trigger," Jack said.

"You couldn't have known."

Jack was quiet for a moment. The shooting, the violence of that night, it wouldn't go away. It was in his head, ready to pop up at any moment. It wasn't like in the movies where the hero left a trail of bodies and walked away without emotional scars. There were some nights when he didn't sleep at all.

"And I don't know what those two guys wanted with us," Jack said. "I don't know if it's revenge, or if I'm now a loose end somehow or what."

"Why do you think Haas followed us out here? Protection?"

"Protection? I'm a cop, I don't need protection."

"Maybe he's watching us. Looking for something. Maybe he's trying to see if you're involved in something else. Pin something on you."

"Naw, that doesn't make any sense," Jack was quiet. "Unless they got the boxes and they know."

"Know what?"

"Something."

"What? What is it?"

"A chip. A computer chip. Or disc or memory card. Like what you gave me with your novel on it," Jack said.

"A memory card?"

"Yeah, but a really little one. A mini, a micro memory card. I need to get an adapter for it."

"Where did it come from?" Paula asked.

"It was hidden in the back of the undercover cop's watch. The one I shot."

"And you haven't looked at it yet?" Paula asked, with incredulity and wide eyes. "It's been over six months!"

"I told you I have to get an adapter," he replied. "And I just found it. Like two days ago."

"Jack. Baby, those adapters are in any store that sells cell phones or cameras or computers. Why didn't you just ask me?" Paula asked.

"It's been kind of crazy. The body, then the new hire, then the ceremony, then this convention," Jack said. "And getting married."

"Afraid of what might be on there?"

"Maybe a little."

"Jeez, Jack. Maybe you should just let it go. Turn it over to the FBI," she said. "Sometimes it's just not worth getting wrapped up in it."

"This from the intrepid reporter?"

"Well, I don't know. None of my stories have ever come after me," she said.

As they walked into the theater, a well dressed usher asked for their tickets, and then escorted them to their table. It was right up front, next to the stage. He informed them that a waiter would be by to take their drink orders and that the show would start in twenty minutes.

The lights were dim, and a lamp adorned the center of the black tablecloth. Paula reached across to take Jack's hand. He didn't say anything, just squeezed. She squeezed back.

"You know," she said, looking into his eyes. "I never thought I'd end up with you."

"Really?"

"I always thought you'd find some down-home, farm girl who was nice and comfortable, and you'd settle into your life," she continued. "I figured I'd never get married. I had this, I don't know, perception of myself, I guess, that I'd always be married to my work."

Jack was quiet for a moment. His first wife had accused him of that very thing. He'd been told he was married to his work and that she was just an accessory. She said it in a note. She'd left it on a magnet on their refrigerator. He didn't notice it for two days. He cleared the thought from his head and focused on Paula.

"Well, I guess we'll both have to get used to being married to each other and not our jobs," he said.

"You know what else?" she asked.

"What?"

"Watching you take out those two guys today, that was hot."

"Yeah?"

"Oh, yeah," she said, dragging her nails across his palm.

The server arrived, took their drink order and scooted off. Soft music played in the background, when a booming voice announced that there was just five minutes until showtime, and that everyone should please find their seats and turn off their cell phones and other electronic devices.

Jack fished his phone out of his pocket, to put it on silent. He looked at the phone and realized he'd had it set to "do not disturb" for most of the day. He played with the settings for a bit, so it would buzz, but not ring, should a call come through.

"I left mine in the room," Paula said with a smile. "No pockets."

She was wearing a tight, black dress that seemed to sparkle, even in the dim lights of the theater. Jack was wearing a simple charcoal gray suit. Two-button, single breasted, with pleated pants. It was really the only one in his closet that had any semblance of style. Probably five or six years behind the times.

"We should take you shopping," Paula said. "Get you a few nice outfits, like from Brooks Brothers."

"I wouldn't wear them enough," Jack said. "When I'm not in my uniform I'm in jeans and a sweatshirt."

"Okay, then at least one suit, so you can take me out to dinner in Albany or New York. So we look stylish," she said.

"What, this isn't stylish enough?" Jack asked.

"It's fine," she said, but unconvincingly enough that Jack felt a little self-conscious.

"You look very handsome," she continued. She leaned across the table and kissed him, lingering in the moment, even as the waitress tried to place their drinks on the table.

Up on the mezzanine level, Denver and Rook watched the McMurphys, while sipping on their Cokes. They waited for the lights to go down. Waited for the applause. The silencer would suppress the muzzle flash and greatly diminish the noise of the powder discharge. High angle, easy shot. Rook would take the shot.

Agent Haas was behind and to the right of the two goons dressed as conventioneers. He'd spotted them, as soon as he'd hit the casino floor, taking up his stakeout position for the McMurphys. Two guys in the casino, not drinking their drinks, not gambling, watching the elevators. Nobody else paid them any mind, but they might as well have posted a big neon sign above their heads that read "bad guys."

He'd dumped Brinkman and his unconscious cohort with the local FBI office. Actually, LVPD had been kind enough to transport them for him. An old friend from Quantico worked at the local FBI office. Haas had kept up with a few of the guys with whom he'd trained and entered the agency. One just happened to land here, in Vegas. If he had more time, he would have bought him a drink. Maybe a few drinks. Instead, he dumped two ex-FBI agents on him. They were now being questioned about why they were impersonating federal officers. More than likely they wouldn't breathe a word about what they were up to. They were sure to have some contrived story. They'd probably only get a few months in jail and fined a thousand dollars or something soft. Some judge might treat them a bit harsher, as they were former agents and should have known better.

Title 18 of the U.S. Code, chapter forty-three, section 912. Impersonating a federal agent. He knew it and he knew they knew it. Then again, depending on the judge, they might walk without anything at all. Haas shook that thought from his mind and focused on the two new guys who were stalking the McMurphys.

These guys were not former agents. The tall guy with the beard moved like trained military. The black guy just looked like some guy. Had the black guy been working alone, Haas would have had trouble zeroing in on him. He was shorter, slim, but not skinny. Probably all muscle under that suit. The guy simply looked like a regular guy.

The way the mezzanine level arched around the enormous room, Haas could still see the McMurphys down at the stage level, while keeping an eye on the two thugs up on the mezzanine. The McMurphys were oblivious to the danger.

He felt the vibration of his phone in his pocket. He thumbed the screen and saw the text message from Mr. Shadow.

"Agent Summers is dead."

Without reacting he slid the phone back into his pocket. Whoever these boys were, they weren't playing without restraint.

Whatever this was all about, it was important enough to kill over.

He'd gotten the call from Shadow that Summers wasn't responding. FBI was heading to the scene after there were police reports of a shootout in the small town. He'd been waiting to find out what had happened to his partner. Now he knew.

The house music went down and the house lights dimmed. The room was bathed in almost complete darkness. Haas saw movement at the goons' table.

Haas left his seat and circled back away from his table, towards the back wall. He rounded the outside wall, well obscured by darkness. There wasn't much light coming from the stage at all, but there was enough to see the goons in silhouette.

He moved silently between full tables of the audience who were all transfixed on the stage, where the sound of a piano began playing behind the curtain. The footlights were slowly starting to come up. He was about thirty feet away from the thugs now. He could easily put a bullet in both of them, even in the dim light. Not a problem.

Suddenly the curtain on the stage dropped, revealing the ten-piece band and the lead singer, dressed in a dapper suit with an open collared shirt, banging on the keys behind his grand piano. Haas had only glimpsed the name on the ticket he had purchased, as he trailed the goons, who were trailing the McMurphys. Frankie Moreno was the singer's name. Haas had never heard of him, but then again, he wasn't much into music. He couldn't remember the last album he'd bought. The poster for the burlesque show, the following night, looked much more interesting to him.

The crowd obviously knew all about Frankie Moreno, as they were on their feet with roaring applause at the sound of the first note.

Jack's phone buzzed in his pocket. He squeezed at it through his pants to stop the vibration. The music had just begun, and it really was a spectacular show. The blast of music was almost overwhelming. Frankie Moreno was up on stage, playing the piano like a madman, belting out a song Jack didn't recognize, but found that he liked. He'd have to grab one of his albums from the gift shop.

His phone buzzed again. He squeezed it again. The song on the stage came to an end and the crowd went crazy. Jack stole a glimpse at his phone, and saw it had been Goldie Bristol, the new fire chief. As he was looking at his phone, it buzzed again. It was Goldie again. He knew that the repeated calls meant one thing: something bad had happened.

"I gotta take this," Jack whispered as he stood and headed for the back of the room. "Hang on a second, Goldie," he said into the phone. He thought he heard Paula say "Are you kidding me, right now?" but he wasn't sure.

He skirted past the annoyed glances of other audience members. After only a moment he was into the lobby, with the phone to his ear.

"Sorry, this is Jack."

"Jack, where have you been? I've been calling you for the last four hours!" Goldie was practically screaming into the phone.

"What's happened, what's going on?"

"Somebody came and shot up the station house, Jack," she said. His stomach twisted into a knot and the room started to spin slightly.

"Michael and Trisha?"

"They've been taken to Albany. Michael's in a bad way. Trisha was at least conscious," Goldie said. "Where are you?"

"I'm in Las Vegas. There was a police convention. I got invited last minute. Didn't I tell you? I thought I told you."

"You need to get back here, Jack. There's FBI guys all over. They've practically shut down the town," Goldie said. "Jesus, we thought you were dead too. Nobody else knew where you were."

"Okay. Let everybody know I'm okay. I'm getting on a plane and heading right back."

"Where's he going?" Denver asked, as they watched Jack McMurphy stand suddenly and head for the back of the auditorium.

"Phone call?"

"Why didn't you shoot him during the applause?"

"I wanted to hear the song," Rook said. "Sue me."

Denver scoffed and turned towards the stairs to intercept McMurphy. He walked within four feet of Haas but didn't notice him. Rook was hot on his heels. Haas waited a beat, then followed. All three saw Jack in the lobby at about the same time.

Haas fell back, watching and waiting. Denver removed something from his jacket and walked right up to McMurphy and jabbed it into his ribs. McMurphy didn't crumple to the ground, so it wasn't a knife. Denver muscled McMurphy towards the bathroom.

"Take it easy," Denver said as he pushed the small Glock against Jack's right kidney.

"I'm a cop," Jack said.

"Oh, I know who you are. Make for the bathroom over there," Denver replied.

"What do you want?"

"For you to keep your mouth shut, before I put a bullet in you."

Jack was suddenly in fight mode. His heart raced, while his adrenal glands pumped pure lightning.

An overhead sign indicated the hallway for the restrooms. Jack allowed himself to be steered towards it. Without turning, he knew there were two guys, not just one. Multiple sets of footsteps. He cursed himself for leaving his gun back in the hotel room safe. If he had it now, there was a chance he could spin away and draw and fire. Maybe get lucky. But without his weapon, there wasn't much of a chance at all.

The women's restroom was the first door, the men's the next. Both were on the right. The hallway itself was dimly lit and featured large, framed decorations of past musicians who had played the theater. Posters with tickets and gold or platinum records of acts who were huge in the seventies and eighties, and were now playing far smaller venues than the arenas they once filled. Jack thought about pulling one of the frames off the wall onto his abductor, but dismissed the idea. There was a good chance they were very securely fastened and wouldn't budge.

Ahead, there was an exit sign, and a steel fire door. As they approached the men's room door, the gun in his ribs prodded him forward.

"Change of plans," the abductor said. "Straight ahead to the exit."

Jack had no idea what was behind the door. Probably a corridor that led outside. Or perhaps he'd find himself outside in an alley behind the casino.

"Where are we going?"

"Shut up."

"What do you want," Jack asked again. "Does it have to do with El Tigre?"

"Who?"

He was either playing dumb, or it had nothing to do with what happened in the autumn in Coopers Hollow. Or maybe it totally did and the hired gun just wasn't privy to the "why" behind doing what he was tasked to do.

"Through the door."

"Okay, okay," Jack said, wincing as the gun was jabbed deeper. It was going to need to be a flawless maneuver.

The door opened outward, with a crash bar at about waist height. It was a heavy, steel door, painted primer gray. It swung to the right, so Jack readied to activate the crash bar with his right hand, while preparing his left hand to swing it back closed.

Jack banged the crash bar loudly, giving the illusion that he was going to throw the door wide open. Instead, he opened it enough to slide through. He pivoted away from the gun and spun around the door. The abductor's gun hand and arm followed the motion and came through the doorway, only to be crushed by the steel door. Jack opened and slammed it against the gunman's arm again.

Several things happened all at once. The abductor yelled in pain as the audible snap of his forearm echoed down the hallway. He managed to pull the trigger at the same instant. The bullet slammed into the concrete blocks of the fire exit hallway. Jack avoided getting hit, but the sound from the small 9mm Glock was deafening in the concrete corridor.

He wasted no time, by grabbing at the gun hand, while keeping his body weight against the door. Tugging the gun away made the abductor's forearm bend at a sickening angle. The guy's scream was loud enough to pierce the ringing in Jack's ears.

With the abductor's gun in his hand now, Jack ripped the door open and jammed the pistol under the guy's chin. On the floor, behind the guy with the broken arm, was the person to whom the second pair of footsteps belonged. Standing over the prone figure was Agent Haas.

"Hiya, Jack," Agent Haas said. "Fancy meeting you here."

Paula wasn't the only one who heard the gunshot from the fire escape corridor. The hallway ran along the right side wall of the theater, with two additional doors emptying into it, from the theater itself. It sounded as if the gunshot had happened right inside the theater, due to the amplifying acoustics of the corridor.

Several people in the audience, those closest to the fire exits, let out cries of fright. The band members on stage reacted by ducking and immediately stopped playing. The piano and other instruments were abandoned as the group left the stage in a hurry. The rest of the audience was left trying to figure out what was going on.

Then there was a man screaming in agony, and that got people moving. They all rushed away from the sound in the fire escape corridor and headed back towards the lobby. There were screams of panic along with the sounds of crashing and breaking, as chairs and tables were knocked out of the way.

Paula had a sick feeling that Jack was involved. She calmly headed for the lobby, letting the frantic crowd push ahead of her. Her throat tightened at the thought of something happening to him.

Security was flooding into the theater as she finally made her way into the lobby. At least a dozen armed, private security personnel, in their black shirts and black cargo pants moved through the hundred or so people still trying to get out. Paula watched as the security funneled towards the restrooms.

"Ma'am, you need to exit through the doors ahead," one of the security guys said, as Paula tried to look down the restroom corridor.

"I can't find my husband," she told him. "He got up to use the restrooms just before the gunshot."

"Wait here a second," the security guy said. He pushed his hand against an earpiece, just like they did in the movies. Paula had the thought that the guy must have really liked being a big, tough, security guy.

"I've got a woman out here who says her husband is missing," he said. He waited a moment. "I don't know, I'll ask."

"What's your name?"

"Paula Schu- um, Paula McMurphy. My husband is Jack. He's a cop from New York," she said.

"Okay," he said to her. "McMurphy." He waited for a response.

It took too long. She was getting nervous.

"Okay, thanks," the security guy said after a few more moments. He turned to Paula. "He's okay. There was some kind of mugging or something near the men's restroom. He's coming out."

No sooner had he said the words, then Jack slid past a security guard, who was blocking access to the restroom corridor.

"Jack!" She ran to him and threw her arms around his neck.

"I'm okay, babe," he said. "I'm okay."

Chapter 23

Gloria Graves was fixing dinner, chicken cordon bleu with string beans and a bottle of wine. Michael would be home in less than a half an hour, and she wanted the meal to be ready. This whole deputy chief of police thing was new for them. Even though their relationship was just a few months old, it felt like they'd been together for far longer. They just clicked. People used to call it chemistry. Who knows what they called it now. It had been nearly twenty years since Gloria had gone on a date. She almost didn't know how to react, when Michael asked her to dinner, shortly after the shootout.

Going through such an emotional and traumatic experience as they did, drew them together quickly. When she thought about it, they'd barely spent a day apart since that awful night in her living room. Now he would be gone for much of the day and, with Jack gone on vacation, maybe some of each night as well. She supposed it depended on the calls that came in.

The cordless phone rang on its cradle, on the kitchen counter. She still had a landline, as cell reception inside the house was spotty. Her cellphone worked fine in the driveway, but depending on the day, it would cut out just by walking from the kitchen to the bedroom.

"Hello?"

"Gloria, it's Goldie with the fire department. Something's happened. Michael's been hurt. He's being airlifted to Albany hospital."

"What?" Gloria could hardly breathe. She'd taken a phone call over a decade previously, from her first husband, on that fateful day in September. He had been one of the unlucky few who had been trapped in the top floors of the World Trade Center, after the planes had hit. For almost three years afterwards, she made her poor daughter, Starlett, answer the phone for her. She'd needed several years of therapy and a few different runs of pharmaceuticals to help her overcome the fear of even picking up the phone to answer.

And now it had happened.

"Gloria, are you okay?" she heard Goldie ask. She thought she answered her, but she wasn't sure.

"I'm- I don't know," she stammered. "What happened?"

"We think he was shot. Tricia Wallace was shot as well. They're both being treated en route to Albany," Goldie said. "Michael is being taken by helicopter."

"Is he," she couldn't say the words. "Will he be okay?"

"I don't know. He was hit more than Tricia. He'd tried to protect her with his body, shield her," Goldie said. "Gloria, he's a hero."

Gloria found the dining room chair and sat down. Her world was spinning. She remembered how she had come apart when Philip, her first husband, had died. She tried to keep it together for their daughter, but looking back, she knew she had really come unglued. She reached deep down inside, and found a flickering flame there. The whirlwind was trying to blow it out. She focused on that flame, and imagined adding wood to the fire, more and more wood, until it was an inferno. She opened her eyes, cheeks wet with tears, and spoke evenly into the phone.

"Which hospital are they taking him to?"

"I'll text you the address," Goldie said.

"Okay. I'm getting in the car and driving up there to meet him," Gloria said.

"Are you you okay, Gloria?"

"I have to be," she said. "For Michael."

The doctor came out to the waiting room to see Gloria around the same time that Paula was running to embrace Jack, a continent and three time zones away. His look was serious, but not somber. The doctor couldn't have been more than forty years old.

"How is he?" she asked.

"He's in rough shape," the doctor said. "Serious condition. He lost a lot of blood. I was able to pull out two of the three bullets. He was hit in the leg, the shoulder and in the lower back. I want to get him stabilized more before we attempt to remove the one in his back. It's lodged near his spine. The surgery to remove it will take more time. I'd like to have him rest and regain some strength before another surgery."

"Is he going to be okay?"

"It's too early to say, with any certainty. But I think he's tough. I think he's going to fight through this," the doctor said. "Marine Corps are the toughest."

"How did you know he was a Marine?" she asked.

"His hogs tooth," the doctor said. He handed over the neck chain with the single, empty sniper cartridge hanging from it. "I was a combat surgeon. I served two tours in Iraq. I think he'll be okay. But prayers aren't going to hurt."

"Thank you doctor," Gloria said. "Thank you."

"I have to get back and check on him. I'll let you know if anything changes."

"When can I see him?"

"Give us a little bit to get him more stabilized and I'll send a nurse out to bring you back," he said, smiling at her.

A wave of relief washed over her. She found her seat again, gripping the neck chain the doctor had given her. The emergency room waiting area was full of people waiting to be called back, or waiting for news about those who were already being treated.

A New York State Trooper entered through the automatic doors and walked over to the check-in window. He spoke to the girl behind the desk, who listened and then pointed at Gloria.

The trooper removed his hat and walked towards Gloria.

"Ma'am, I'm Trooper Cabot. Have they let you know how he is?"

"The doctor just came out and told me they were able to get him stabilized, but he's still in serious condition. He was shot three times," she said. Suddenly, all the emotions she had held back, controlled for the last four and a half hours, let lose like a torrent. Her face contorted and she started weeping. The trooper leaned down and hugged her, firmly.

"It's okay," he said. "We're all here for you now."

Chapter 24

"We don't know who they are or what they want," Agent Haas said.

"But you obviously know they want something," Jack replied. Other than the small bruise to his ribs where his would-be abductor had jammed his pistol, he was unscathed from the encounter.

"All I can tell you is that we've had chatter. Our agency picked up intel that indicated that somebody was interested in something that has to do with you," Haas said.

"Why did they try to kill Michael and Tricia, if they wanted me, then?"

"I don't know."

"Sure you do," Jack said. "It's the same thing you and your partner wanted. What's so important about those boxes of evidence? What do you think is in there?"

"You don't know?"

"If I knew, don't you think I'd tell you?" Jack asked.

"That's not a denial."

"I wasn't even the lead investigator on the case," Jack said, ignoring the reply. "The only reason I had those boxes was because the doctor didn't know what to do with them. They should have gone off to the sheriff's department, or the FBI to begin with!"

"So why didn't you just give them to us," Haas asked.

"Because there's a right way to do things," Jack said. "You do things by the book. You don't cut corners, you don't make evidence disappear. You do the right thing."

"Things aren't always so black and white," Haas replied. He sighed. "I wish they were, but they aren't."

"I need to get back to Coopers Hollow," Jack said. "I need to be with my people. I need to make the town feel safe again."

"I need to get back there too," Haas said.

"Why's that, so you can try to pilfer more evidence and pretend it's not wrong?"

"We're on the same team here," Haas said. "I need to go back to Coopers Hollow to help with the investigation. You see, my partner was killed in your little town."

"Oh, no!" Paula gasped.

"I hadn't heard about that," Jack said quietly. "I'm sorry."

"He tried to intercept the perpetrators at your police station. They killed him for it," Haas said. He was quiet for a moment. "He was a good guy. Didn't deserve to die in the gutter like that."

"I'm sorry," Jack repeated.

"So, if you have any information that can help us find out who else would be interested in those boxes of evidence, you need to tell me so I can go catch the people who shot your officers and killed my partner," Haas said.

"I need to get back to Coopers Hollow," Jack replied.

Jack did not anticipate getting a wink of sleep on the flight from Las Vegas to Chicago. There was no first class on the flight he booked. One flight in first class, and he was already spoiled. There were three, rather loud, businessmen who had finished a week of trade-showing and apparently drinking, as they had to be asked several times to keep it down by the flight attendant. Then a mother, who looked like an exotic dancer, had a baby that simply wouldn't settle down. She took the little guy to the back of the plane, but for Jack, a crying baby was like nails on a chalkboard. Even muffled by the engine noise, he found it impossible to relax.

He tried to get comfortable in his seat, but it was no use. His mind was racing over the events of the last six months. He thought back to the night of the shoot out in October; the trek through the woods, trying desperately to get to Gloria Graves' house to stop a torture and execution.

There were gunshots, as he ran. His lungs were burning. Then, he saw the SUV fly down the driveway backwards, swing out onto the snow covered road, heading straight for him. He saw the driver's shocked expression as the shotgun came up to aim directly at him. Bang! Bang!

He awoke with a start.

The overhead compartments were getting slammed closed, as the flight attendants were readying the plane for landing in Chicago. He'd fallen asleep after all, though it was anything but restful.

The connection flight was at Chicago Midway International Airport, which was a much smaller airport than the famed O'hare International of Chicago. There were no restaurants open; only a bank of snack machines from which he could grab a soda and some chips. It was 2 a.m. local time, and his flight to Albany didn't depart until 5 a.m. A layover of three hours. He hunkered down in a seat, in an area that seemed out of the way, and tried to get some more rest; a fruitless endeavor. There is no comfort to be found in an airport chair. By the time his flight was boarding at 4:30 a.m., he felt like he'd been hit by a truck.

Chicago to Albany was not a long flight. It was as if they had just gotten into the air, when the announcement came over the speaker that they were preparing to land. The morning light was already creeping over the horizon, as the plane descended into the Capital District of New York State.

The landing and taxi back to the gate dragged on, but they finally opened the cabin doors and people filed out.

Jack had no checked bags, not even a carry-on, so he made a line for his car, which he hadn't expected to see for another two days. He got to drive the Mercedes after all. He had a twinge of guilt about not having read Paula's story and still getting to driver her new vehicle. He promised himself he'd get on it.

Coopers Hollow was a fifty minute drive from the airport, if there was no traffic and he was really pushing it. The Albany hospital was a ten minute drive.

As he drove down Interstate 87, toward the I-90 interchange, he opted to drive east toward the hospital. He wanted to see for himself what had happened to the people he'd left behind.

The last time he was at this hospital, he had come with the funeral home people to claim his father's body. The time before that, he had been much younger, and it was his mother who was dying in a hospital bed there. Jack didn't like hospitals very much.

He parked the silver SUV and took a deep breath. It was still too early to call Paula, so he decided to call Goldie in Coopers Hollow. He punched her number and let it ring three times before it went to voice mail. He didn't leave a message.

Jack got out of the car and felt naked without his uniform. He always had a back up in the trunk of his car, ever since he'd spent an afternoon with a blood soaked shirt, trying to make sense of his father's death. But he wasn't driving his car, he was in Paula's new Mercedes. He did have his sidearm, though. Not completely naked.

The doors slid open to the hospital entrance, and Jack headed straight towards to the information desk.

"Can you direct me to where I can find Michael Cooke and Tricia Wallace? They were brought in here last night with gunshot wounds," Jack said.

The woman behind the desk was in her fifties, and she looked skeptically at Jack. She typed on a keyboard with her two index fingers. Her typing teacher would not have been proud.

"I'm sorry sir, who are you? I'm only able to provide information about our patients to family," she said.

"They're my deputies. I'm Chief Jack McMurphy from Coopers Hollow. They're my officers. They were shot in the line of duty,"

Jack said, voice almost cracking, almost giving in to the emotion. He choked it back, clenched his jaw and showed his badge. "Where can I find Deputy Cooke and Deputy Wallace?"

"They're both in the ICU. Follow the hallway to your left. Then follow the signs for Intensive Care," the woman said, her demeanor softening substantially. "There are a few of the Albany Police and State Police there already."

Jack followed her directions, and started down the corridor when his cellphone rang. He thought it was Paula, but Goldie's name came up.

"Hello?"

"Sorry, I was in the shower," she said.

"I'm back in New York. I'm in Albany at the hospital checking on my people. What's the story at home?"

"There are FBI all over town," Goldie said. "I guess the guy who was shot in the street was one of theirs. There must be, like, thirty agents in town right now. They are not taking this lightly, Jack."

"Good. Maybe they can find out who put two of my people in ICU," he said. "I'm going to check on Trish and Michael and then come down. Are you around today?"

"Always."

"Okay, I'll swing by to talk in an hour or so," Jack said.

"Okay. Jack?"

"Yeah?"

"Cooke looked pretty bad."

"Okay, thanks for the warning. Talk to you soon." He ended the call and continued down the corridor. The Intensive Care Unit, ICU, was truly a state-of-the-art facility. The nurses' station was in the center of the floor, just outside the entry doors. The rooms were all glass enclosed, but most had curtains drawn. Though the temperature was a bit on the chilly side, showing that there was good air circulation in the building, there was that uncomfortable smell in the air that always made Jack want to do an about-face and head for the doors. Despite all of the cleaning and disinfection that occurred, those who had resided for their short time in the rooms of ICU had left a whisper of death in the air.

He approached the nurses' station, but already saw the five officers down the hall, hanging around outside the rooms.

"Michael Cooke and Tricia Wallace?"

"You are?"

"Chief McMurphy. They're my deputies," Jack said. The nurse pursed her lips and nodded gravely. She pointed down the hall to the group of officers.

Jack walked towards them, at about half the speed he'd normally walk. They were there to show their support to the two wounded cops. Two cops who were gunned down in their own station house, in the late afternoon, without provocation. The cops in the hall would be a bit jumpy.

"What's up?" one of the cops asked. His shoulder said Albany City Police, and his name tag said Hargrove.

"I'm Jack McMurphy, Chief of Police of Coopers Hollow. These are my people."

"Where have you been?" The accusatory tone was unmistakable.

"I was in Las Vegas for a police convention. I flew home as soon as I heard the news."

"Cooke is in this room. His wife is in there with him. Wallace is over here. She's conscious. Maybe you'll want to see her first," Hargrove said. The other cops, two from the State Troopers, one Sheriff's deputy from Albany County and another Albany city policeman acknowledged Jack with pursed lips, brave frowns, encouraging nods; no words. What could they say?

Jack lightly rapped his knuckle against the door of Tricia Wallace's door.

"Tricia?"

"Hi," she said weakly.

"It's Jack, how are you feeling?"

"Like somebody shot me twice."

"I'm so sorry."

"It's not your fault, Chief," she said quietly.

"Who were they, what did they want?"

"They wanted boxes. Evidence boxes."

Jack swore.

"These guys, they were bad news. Michael sniffed them out, but I think he decided to try to let them walk out. I think he did it because of me. If I wasn't there, I think he would have put them all in the morgue. Risked taking the shot. I was a liability." She started to cry.

"Nonsense. Sometimes stuff just happens. We can't control it," McMurphy said, taking her hand.

"Cooke. He saved me. He saw what was happening before I did and he put his body between us. He took my bullets," she said, still sobbing.

"He's a good man," Jack said softly. They were both quiet for a moment. Jack was trying to think of something to say that would be comforting, but words escaped him.

Tricia had a bandage around her head, but there was no signs of blood like in the movies. She had been patched up. She also had a bandage around her left arm.

"You still got hit?"

"In the arm, through and through, and then grazed on the head. I could leave, I'm not too hurt. But they want to keep me for a few days to make sure there aren't any complications," she said quietly. "I want to get back to work. You're going to need help."

"Let me worry about that. Just get better."

"Thanks, Chief."

"Do you need anything? Can I get you anything?"

"No. I'm good. Just need to rest. Need to get back to work."

"There's plenty of time for that. Rest up, okay. Don't rush it."

"Okay, Chief."

"I'm going to go check on Cooke," Jack said. "See you in a bit."

"Okay, Chief."

Jack walked out of the room, his heart heavy with guilt. Hargrove was gone. The other officers milling around in the hallway nodded at him again, but kept up with their own conversations.

He knocked on Cooke's door as he entered. The curtain was drawn around the bed, but he could still hear the machines breathing for Cooke.

"Hello?" Jack said quietly as he poked his head around the curtain. He saw Gloria sitting beside Cooke's bed, stroking his hand and talking to him quietly. Cooke was unconscious or asleep. He had all sorts of tubes and wires trailing away from his heavily wrapped body, back to saline drips and breathing machines.

"Gloria, how's our boy?" Jack asked quietly.

She turned and looked at him with reddened eyes. Her jaw was clenched and her nostrils flared.

"No. No sir. I don't want you here," she said.

"I wanted to see-"

"It's your fault he's in here. He retired. He was done. He was mine!" she said. "And you put him in here."

"Aw, jeez, Gloria," Jack said, moving towards her. She was in pain. Her heart was breaking. He reached out to her, but she pulled away.

"You get out of here Jack, before I tell the officers out there to kick you out. We don't need any more of your help. Do you hear me? You stay away," she started sobbing, burying her face into the bed next to Cooke.

Jack shifted uneasily from foot to foot. He looked at his friend who was barely recognizable under the respirator and bandages. What he could see of Cooke looked old and broken. Jack hung his head and stepped quietly into the corridor.

"Everything alright," one of the Albany police officers asked.

"She's pretty broken up," Jack said. "I'll come back another time."

He stepped in and said goodbye to Tricia, promising to come see her again. He felt in a daze as he walked down the hall towards the elevators. He made his way back to Paula's Mercedes on autopilot.

He found himself sitting in the car when the phone rang. He'd lost track of time. He didn't even remember walking out of the hospital.

"Hello?"

"Hey, it's me," Paula said. "How are they?"

"Looks like Tricia is going to do okay. Cooke is out of commission. He threw himself in front of her. Shielded her with his own body," Jack said, his voice cracked. He breathed in. Closed his eyes. Pressed his fingers against his eyes. Willed them to stay dry.

"My God."

"Gloria flipped out on me. Didn't want me there, so I'm back in the car."

"I'm sorry, baby," she said. "I can't imagine what she's going through. She told me not too long ago she was scared of losing him. She hadn't been happy for a long time. The last time she was happy, she told me, it all came crashing down. She was afraid to be happy again."

Jack closed his eyes again and put his head back on the headrest. He breathed in deeply, but found it suddenly difficult in the confines of the car. He hit the button for the window and the cool April air washed over him.

"This is all my fault," Jack said, quietly.

"No it's not. You couldn't have known," Paula said to him. "Babe, we'll get through this. Okay?"

"Yeah. What flight are you on?"

"Well, that's one of the things I wanted to tell you. I can't get a flight any quicker than the one I have tomorrow," she said. "The best they can do for me is fly me to Atlanta and then up to Albany. But not until tomorrow morning. I'd be home like five hours early. It's not worth it."

"Okay," Jack asked. "Just watch yourself. Don't go anywhere alone. Stay in the casino. Don't go anywhere."

"I thought I'd do some shopping or something," Paula said. "Take my mind off things."

"Just be careful," Jack said. "I don't know what's going on. I don't know if it's all over now that they have the boxes or what. I just don't know."

"Okay, okay," she said. "Just relax."

"Trying."

"We'll get through all this," she said.

"I'd really like it if you were home," Jack said quietly.

"Me too. I'll be there tomorrow," she said. "You need to get back to town and settle everybody down. The town is spooked. I've gotten a bunch of phone calls."

Jack was silent.

He had to get back to his people. He had to show them they were safe, that he was there to stand between them and the bad guys.

"I love you," he said.

"I love you too."

"Gotta go."

"Yeah, I know. See you soon."

He closed his phone and started the Mercedes. At least it was a comfortable, luxurious ride back to town.

His phone rang three more times with three different callers on the way back to Coopers Hollow. The first was Goldie, asking where he was and when he would be back in town. The second was Tricia, telling him that Cooke was going back into surgery and that Gloria was still visibly upset. The last was from a man named Scutter.

Chapter 25

"Chief McMurphy? This is Mr. Scutter. I'm the Director of the Federal Department of Criminal Investigation. I believe you've met Agent Haas. I'm his boss. Are you in a position to talk for a few moments?" The voice was calm, probably early to mid fifties. No discernible accent, as far as McMurphy could tell. He was close to the mic of the phone, in a very quiet location. That's all Jack could read about the man on the other end.

"Agent Scutter, you said?"

"Director. I don't usually involve myself at this level. Frankly, I think you've been through enough and could use a helping hand," Scutter said.

"That's sweet of you," Jack replied. "I've got two of my officers in the hospital right now, and you know, I can't help thinking that there's some sort of connection between your agents showing up last week and what happened yesterday. Here and in Vegas. Tell me what's going on."

"I don't know if things would have happened the way they did had you cooperated," Scutter said in an even fashion. There wasn't an accusatory tone to his words, just the words. "But I'm going to be as clear as I can: I've got one of mine in the morgue. You've got two of yours in the hospital. We should probably work together on this thing to put the bad guys where they belong."

"Ok," Jack breathed. "You're right."

"Good," Scutter continued. "I'm going to explain a few things to you, and you need to listen very carefully."

"Ok."

"Last week two of my boys came out to visit with you about the evidence from the shooting in October. I understand that they informed you about Agent Spaulding, our undercover agent."

"They did."

"Well now I need to tell you something else. There is another party that is very much interested in the details of that case. Whoever shot up your officers and killed my agent, they're not FBI, and as far as I can tell, they aren't affiliated with any of El Tigre's former network. To be honest, we don't know who they are. The reason I'm telling you this Chief McMurphy, Jack, is because I want you to understand that whoever these guys are, they don't care about leaving bodies behind. In this day and age, when everything is trackable, traceable and is never forgotten because it's searchable in a computer database, a group who doesn't care about offing a few cops and a federal agent is an entity you would be wise to show a great deal of concern about. And if I am very concerned, then you sure as hell better be concerned."

"Understood."

"So here's my point: whatever you know about the investigation, whatever information, no matter how insignificant you may believe it to be, any evidence, any notes you may have taken, any recollections or even theories you may have, you need to share it all with me. We have the eyes and ears and computers to sort through it all. The more data we feed to the computers, the better chance we have of catching the people responsible. Do you understand?" Scutter asked.

"I do."

"Do you have any questions?"

"Just one," Jack said as he steered his car to the curb in Coopers Hollow, across the street from the police station. "Why was your man following me in Las Vegas?"

There was silence on the line. Jack pushed the selector into Park, and turned off the engine. He waited for a few moments.

"We had a concern. It turns out we were right."

"And no warning about it to me or my wife?"

"It wasn't a solid lead."

"Well it seemed to solidify pretty quickly," Jack countered.

"Chief, I don't apologize often. So when I tell you I'm sorry, that's all you're going to get. We were lucky in Vegas and unlucky in Coopers Hollow. That's just the way it is," Scutter said.

"So you do think this has to do with the El Tigre case?"

"Maybe. But we don't know the angle. We don't know who and we don't know why."

"Would you tell me if you did?"

"Truth?"

"Please."

"Probably not. If I knew who it was, we wouldn't be having this conversation," Scutter said.

"Ok," Jack said. "So I should talk with your agents -"

"This is where it gets interesting. FBI is on site in Coopers Hollow. They are handling the crime scene investigation. Our team has different objectives. And the FBI doesn't always share what they know."

"Ok," Jack said again. "So what do you want from me?"

"I want you to tell me everything," Scutter said.

Jack spent the rest of the ride back to Coopers Hollow explaining everything he knew about El Tigre and the shootout that occurred the previous October.

He left out the bit about the micro memory card he'd found hidden in the back of Agent Spaulding's watch. He still wasn't sure who to trust.

Jack pulled the Mercedes onto Main Street in Coopers Hollow, and saw all the cars parked on the street, in front of the police station. Only one lane of traffic was open, and Goldie had two of her volunteer first responders out there directing the cars through.

The number of State Police, Sheriff's Department and un-marked FBI vehicles must have numbered into the dozens. Jack parked near the Peachy Keen and walked to the station house, just as a light drizzle of rain started. He saw Goldie and waved at her. She rushed over, styrofoam cup of coffee in hand.

"Hey there, Chief," she said. She stood in front of him, uncom-fortably, like she wanted to hug him, but thought better of it. She slapped him gently on the arm, instead. "Hell of a thing, huh?"

"Yeah, no kidding," he replied. "Where's the FBI guys? I need to let them know I'm here."

"Up in the station," Goldie indicated with her styrofoam cup. "I'll walk with you."

Chapter 26

Eric was between them on the couch. Riker was almost completely on his lap, while Yasmine was curled up next to him, her face buried in his chest. They were crying. All three of them.

Eric's mother was in the kitchen. She decided to bake something. Anything. That was how she had always dealt with adversity, even when Eric was young. When he came home from school, and the house was filled with the smell of freshly baked cupcakes or cookies, he knew his mother had had a bad day.

Something chocolatey was now baking away, sending its fragrance throughout the house. No one had an appetite for it.

"Why, dad?" Yasmine asked, her hair was wet with her tears and stuck to her face. "Why mom?"

"Sometimes things just happen. There's no reason, and it isn't anybody's fault. It just happens," he said quietly. He felt so inadequate and unable to say the right things to make it better. It was like there was an enormous hollowness inside of him that seemed to be growing bigger and bigger as he experienced the pain all over again, through the emotions of his children. It was pure, unadulterated grief. Like a blowtorch of pain in his heart. Ten times as powerful as when he'd lost his father. Parents die. In the back of their mind, every adult child knows it's the true eventuality for their parents. But not this. This was too much.

"Is she in heaven now?" Riker asked.

"Some people believe that," Eric said. "I don't know the answer. You can believe that if you'd like."

"Ok."

They would quiet down for a moment, the tears would subside and then they would return in a wave, as one of them would suddenly be struck by the realization that their mother wasn't coming home again. They'd never get to hug her or hold her hand or watch a movie with her or make silly faces at dinner. She was just gone. Erased.

They hugged each other for what seemed like an eternity. It was Riker who finally broke from the family to use the bathroom. When he returned, he fell into his family on the couch and curled up in a ball. He wasn't little anymore, he'd started to grow. He was becoming lanky arms and legs; pointy knees and elbows.

"Why don't we get our raincoats on and take our umbrellas and go for a walk up by the lake. Sometimes being in nature helps to make sense of things," Eric said. "Like a mental detox."

"I don't want to," Yasmine replied. "I don't want to do anything."

"I know, baby," he said, kissing her on her head. "But we have to try to do something. We can drive up to the scenic parking lot and then walk around the lake for a bit. The fresh air will help."

No one moved for several minutes. They just stayed on the couch, finding, at least, a level of solace in the embrace. Finally, Riker climbed down from his father's lap and went to the hall closet to put on his boots and jacket. Yasmine followed the lead of her little brother and pulled on a knit cap as well.

"Mom," Eric called out to the kitchen to his mother. He saw the kids flinch when he said it. He didn't think about what he said. He didn't think how that very word would affect them. More quietly he said: "We're going for a walk. We'll be back in a little while."

"Ok," she called. Her voice weary from the crying as well. She had stepped out of the room after the kids had awoken. She couldn't bear to watch the children crumble when they were given the news that their mother had passed away. As was her usual, she started something baking in the oven. Then she'd busied herself with dishes. Once those were all washed and put away, she started on the laundry that was piled in the laundry room, just off the kitchen.

She heard the front door close and decided to sit down at the kitchen table with a cup of tea. She thought it was a good idea for Eric to take the kids outside and get some fresh air. Just moving, putting one foot in front of the other, would help. That's how she got through the loss of her husband not six months earlier. With this new tragedy, the pain of the day she lost her husband came flooding back.

"My dear God in heaven," she said quietly. "This family can't take any more. We just can't."

A brown, wooden sign with yellow lettering announced the scenic parking area for the Coopers Hollow reservoir. The parking area was just a gravel rectangle outlined with old telephone poles, laying on their sides. Eric guided the vehicle into the empty parking lot and brought it to a stop. He was hyper-aware of everything. The crunch of the gravel beneath the tires sounded like an industrial rock grinder to his ears. The children's breathing was uneven, punctuated with deep inhales and heavy, half-sobs. He'd kept the radio off. Music didn't seem appropriate.

There were birds calling to each other outside of the vehicle and the sound of water rushing, as it left the upper manmade lake, flowed through a spillway into the secondary lake, and then splashed and flowed its way downstream.

The un-click of the seatbelt echoed within the vehicle. To Eric, it gave him a chill, like a gun being loaded. His mind was firing in all different directions, in a mad panic. He had always been able to find a solution, a fix. When his father was killed, it was easier to rationalize that accidents happen and the man had led a full life. But now - the children lost their mother. Even if the last few years had been a struggle, she was still very good to them and they loved her immensely. He could hear his heartbeat in his ears.

"Come on, let's go for a walk," Eric said quietly, though his own voice seemed to boom in his ears. "Get some fresh air."

There was a steady pounding that was building behind his eyes.

Eric opened the door and climbed out, his shoes crunched on the gravel, and it sent a shudder up through his body. He closed his eyes and breathed deep. Once. Twice. A third time. In through the nose, hold, out through the mouth. Slow. Steady. Get control.

He was bordering on a full fledged panic attack with a migraine thrown in for good measure. He reached back into the vehicle and retrieved sunglasses off the visor. They eased the eye strain a bit, but he knew the headache was building itself into a tempest of pain.

"Come on, guys," he said quietly. "Just for a few minutes."

The children slowly complied and both came around to his side of the vehicle, each taking one of his hands.

The gravel parking lot provided access to a hiking trail that led around the entire lake. A few of the locals rode mountain bikes here, making it well worn and easy to follow. If one got adventurous, the trail broke away from the lake on the opposite side and climbed the hill through the trees. Eric used to come here, when he was a kid, to fish with his dad. They'd take a canoe out onto the reservoir and spend all morning just being together.

Deep breath.

The drizzle had abated, though the air was thick with spring moisture and felt as if it could start raining again at any moment. It was definitely jacket weather.

"Let's just walk over to the little falls there," Eric indicated with a hand which was firmly grasped by Yasmine.

The first few steps gave him an uneasy feeling. There had been several occasions in the past few years when they had gone somewhere as a family, but while he and the children were ready to explore, his wife had either elected to stay in the car, or was fast asleep from her medication.

Eric stole a glance back, but there was no one there.

The lake had initially been much smaller a hundred and fifty years earlier. And there had only been one of them. But as water power was harnessed for the mills in town, specifically the barrel mill, a steady, reliable flow was a necessity. The town built a levy with a spillway that allowed for a larger lake to form between the two steep hills. The second, much smaller lake was also built as a precaution after a flood had overtaken the village in the 1870s. As electricity removed the need for waterpower, the water wheels disappeared, and the lake and river, which was only a bit more than a stream through town, lost their importance to the village.

The cascading water made a rushing noise that reminded Eric of the static on an old-timey television set, after the channel went off the air for the night. He wondered for a moment if that was what it was like when you died. Was there anything at all, or was your body's energy lost into the universe like the static absence of a television signal?

"Look how high the water is," Riker said.

Indeed, the upper lake was filled to the brim with the remnants of winter run off. The water was overflowing the concrete channel that functioned as a runoff spillway into the lower lake. The water was nearly up to the dirt path where they were walking.

Eric tested the footing and found it extremely spongy. He looked back at his footprints and saw that they had filled ever so slightly with little pools of water.

"Kids, let's get back to the car," he said. He tried not to let panic enter his voice.

"I want to look at the waterfall," Riker said.

"No, I don't think it's safe. I think this whole levy could wash out. It's absolutely saturated with water," Eric replied. The panic he'd felt earlier intensified. He tried hard not to break into a run, but his pace was definitely quickened.

"Slow down!" Yasmine complained.

He did so when they were back into the gravel parking lot and away from the water's edge.

"We need to tell somebody," Eric said. "If a storm rolls in and we get a few more inches of rain, this whole thing is going to let loose on the town."

He winced in pain. The headache that had been building up all morning, behind his eyes, exploded.

Chapter 27

Chief McMurphy listened to Goldie, as she systematically walked through everything she knew about the shooting. Neighbors called 911 when shots were fired outside of the police station. The county dispatch first tried to contact the station house itself. When there was no answer, a full, county wide call went out for any officers in the area to respond. The first on the scene was a State Trooper who had been sitting just outside of town where the speed limit descended from fifty-five to thirty-five miles-per-hour. It wasn't quite within the village limits which would have been Jack's jurisdiction. It took the trooper less than two minutes to respond. He passed a speeding SUV, which was heading in the opposite direction, on his way to the scene. By this time a flurry of calls had come in and a neighbor was already attempting to help Agent Summers on the sidewalk. The trooper didn't pursue the fleeing SUV, rather, he called for an ambulance and any first responders when he came across the man performing CPR on Summers.

A quick check of the vital signs and a review of the wounds told him that the man was dead. But the good samaritan continued with the CPR. Before waiting for backup, the trooper drew his sidearm and vaulted up the steps into the police station. The smell of gunpowder stung his nostrils and throat, he said. He'd called out and only heard a groan of pain coming from the cell. What he found, was the bloody scene of Tricia holding her hand over Michael's wounds.

The EMTs were the next to arrive. They were informed of the victims in the police station, and rushed in with their gear. By the time they had arrived, the trooper had located the key for the lockup and aided Tricia with trying to staunch the flow of blood.

The EMTs quickly took over on Michael, plugging the holes as best they could and getting him ready for transport.

Goldie, herself, arrived maybe a minute later and helped the EMTs get Michael onto the stretcher and out to the ambulance. A helicopter was already in the air from Albany and would arrive in less than fifteen minutes at the football field behind Coopers Hollow high school.

Goldie was able to get Tricia's wounds under control by the time the second ambulance arrived. She was whisked away to the hospital in Oneonta, as her wounds were less life threatening. Only an hour later, she was transported up to Albany as well.

The FBI arrived within the hour.

They drove up from Binghamton, and immediately started locking down the scene. Goldie had started calling Jack's phone around the time Tricia was leaving in the ambulance. She didn't stop until she got him to pick up, over three hours later.

She hung around for another two hours, directing traffic off Main Street, a block away in each direction, sending all the cars over to a parallel street. After the body of the agent was removed, and the scene at street level was photographed and cleared, Goldie helped direct traffic through a one-lane bottle neck, until the FBI agents moved their vehicle and allowed the fire truck to roll back to the firehouse. By the time she pulled herself off traffic duty, it was nearly nine o'clock, and she was exhausted. She went home, showered and slept.

That was everything.

Jack had no response except for a four letter word which he uttered under his breath. Goldie echoed it.

"This is bad, Goldie. This is ten times worse than what happened last year. They came here and put down three law enforcement officers without even blinking," Jack said.

"Andrew, the trooper, he says he knows his dash-cam got the vehicle and license plate, so there's a chance we'll get them," Goldie said.

"FBI guys take it?"

"No doubt."

"Okay. I need to go talk to them. Even if this is their investigation, this is our town. Yours and mine and everybody else's that lives here. This thing is on us. It's on me," Jack said.

"The federalés are still up in the station. I peeked in the window, but they waved me away. They have some sort of tripod thingies set up all over the place. I don't know what the heck they are," she said.

"Listen, I'm going in to talk with them," Jack said. "Stick around and we can grab coffee and talk some more." He opened his door and stepped out onto the street.

"Oh, I also heard that Sylvia Owens died last night as well," Goldie said.

"Who?"

"Eric Owens' wife. Copper's daughter-in-law."

"Oh, jeez. Was she caught in the cross fire or something?" Jack asked.

"No, no, no. She died in Albany. She had a tumor and died during the procedure to remove it. Super sad. She left behind two young kids. Copper's wife called me this morning," Goldie said.

"Jeez," Jack said again. He could see through the windows of his police station, several agents milling about, with intermittent flashes from the taking of photographs.

Jack opened the front door, as he had thousands of times before, but this time he didn't go in. He was met, instead, by an FBI agent who held up both hands and practically pushed him back onto the sidewalk.

"This is a hot crime scene, sir. Please stay out here. In fact, we'd appreciate it if you'd step away from the building," the agent said.

"I'm Chief McMurphy. This is my station house, and that's the blood of my people in there. I want to talk to whoever thinks he's in charge here," Jack said.

"You're Chief McMurphy?"

"Yes."

"Chief of Police?"

"Yes!"

"Stay here," the agent said, heading back into Jack's station house. He returned in moments with another agent. This one was in a gray suit, and was maybe ten years older. He had gray seeping into his temples, and his dark skin had the signs of age wrinkles around his eyes and on his forehead. He looked like a man who scowled often. That's exactly what he was doing now.

"You're Chief McMurphy?"

"Yes, and I'd like to find out what happened in my station house."

"Where have you been for the last eighteen hours?"

"I was in Las Vegas, I caught the first flight back as soon as I heard the news."

"What were you doing in Vegas?"

"I was at a police convention. I was supposed to give a presentation today," Jack said.

"Do you go to Las Vegas often?"

"What? No. It was my first time. What's that got to do with anything?" Jack was starting to get frustrated.

"We need to talk to you," the agent said.

"Fine. That's what I thought we were doing," Jack replied.

"I mean talk, talk. We're not done in here yet. Here's my card. Go get a cup of coffee or something. Give me a call in about thirty minutes, and I'll join you for a cup and we'll talk." The card was white with blue lettering with the FBI logo in full color. The name on the card read Branson Adekoya - Special Agent. It then provided a Binghamton address and phone number along with a mobile number.

"Okay?" Agent Adekoya asked.

"Alright. I'll call you in thirty minutes." Jack turned and motioned for Goldie to follow him up the street to the Peachy Keen Diner.

They were quiet as they walked. The sky above them was gray, and had a threatening quality about it. It seemed to be perfect for Jack's mood.

"Thanks for handling things here," Jack said.

"You know me, just here to help."

As they approached the steps to the diner, Jack's phone buzzed in his pocket. It took him a moment to fish it out and slide his thumb over to answer.

"This is Chief McMurphy."

"So, how's it going, honey? You're back in town, right?" It was Paula from Vegas. Jack motioned for Goldie to go inside and that he'd follow in a moment. She pursed her lips and complied.

"It's not good. Michael was shot all to hell. Tricia is going to be okay, I think. She called me a few minutes back. They're taking Michael back into surgery. He's still in critical condition. The FBI have taken over the town, and they're giving the orders," Jack said.

"Does that surprise you?"

"Not really. They lost one of theirs here."

"So, I got the flight back today. Late cancellation, I guess. You know, it's weird. There was nothing about what happened at the theater on the news, nothing in the papers or online. They made it just go away. I need to come home and be with you," she said. A little of the tightness that had formed in his forehead eased. But only slightly.

"I could really use your support."

"I don't like being away from you, Jack. I've got it bad for you,' she said.

"Good thing I married you then, Mrs. McMurphy."

"Good thing, Mr. McMurphy."

"Listen, I've got to get some more coffee into me, then I have to talk with the FBI guys. Text me the flight you're on and I'll come up and get you at the airport," he said.

"I'll do that. I love you."

"Love you, too."

Jack hung up and went inside for his coffee. Goldie was at the counter ordering two cups from Seemo. At the far end of the counter, perched on his normal stool, was Tubby McIntyre. He was dressed in a suit and tie with a big napkin tucked into his collar. He had his head low over a big bowl of Frosted Flakes cereal.

"Hey Seemo, hey Tub-" Jack stopped himself. After nearly thirty years of calling the big man Tubby, it was tough to call him by his given name. "Hey Thaddeus."

"Hi. It's okay to call me Tubby if you want. It don't bother me no more." Tubby said.

"Okay, good to know." Jack took a seat next to Goldie at the counter and waited as Seemo poured the coffee into the ceramic mug. "I saw your thing the other night, Tubby. Paula and I came over to see you do your reading. You did a really good job."

"Thanks. I practiced a ton. I need to go, I don't want to be late for meeting," Tubby said. There was a gray bible and another book and magazine on the counter, which he grabbed before heading for the door.

"It's almost noon, Tubby. I thought your services were in the morning," Jack said.

"Well, at January the Spanish group started doing meetings at ten so I go at twelve thirty now. Which I like because I have more time in the morning to get ready," Tubby replied. "Ties are hard."

Jack saw that the knot was a bit askew, so he swiveled around on the stool at reached up to help.

"Hold up a second, Tubby." He straightened the knot and pulled it a bit tighter so it was up snug to the collar. The transition, over the last six months, of the big man standing before him was nothing short of amazing. He'd gone from an unwashed, sasquatch-like creature to a clean cut, sharply dressed man. He'd advanced from someone who could barely read to giving a public reading at his church. It was clear to Jack that the man had been mentally abused by his crazy mother for decades and, once he had gotten away from that poisonous atmosphere, he was prospering.

"Have a good day," Jack said.

"Thanks!" Tubby replied as he headed out the door, triggering the jingle bells atop the door frame, as he went.

"That's something else, isn't it?" Jack said as he turned back to his coffee.

"What, that his religion has completely brain washed him?" Goldie said as she sipped her coffee.

"What are you talking about. He was just wasting his life before, now he seems like he's happy and has a purpose," Jack countered.

"That's how they brain wash people. You know, that church tells their people to let their children die instead of taking a blood transfusion, right? And they've been caught protecting child molesters," she continued.

"What the hell are you talking about? There haven't been any reports of child molestation there? I would know," Jack said.

"Not this particular church, no. But they have these places all over the country. And their elders are told not to talk to the police about anything. They're a cult, through and through," Goldie said. "Like Jim Jones or Heaven's Gate. One day you'll get a call and they'll all have drunken the Kool-Aid."

"I don't think so. I went with Paula last week, they all seemed really nice," Jack said.

"Mind control," Goldie said, pointing to her temple.

"You need to lay off the conspiracy theory websites, Goldie," Jack said. "Stick to your porn sites."

"Dating sites for farmers, Jack," she said, only half jokingly. "Big difference."

"So, where's the girlfriend?" Seemo asked, as he came over to refill their coffee cups.

"She's flying back from Vegas today," Jack said.

"Wearing your wedding ring again?" Seemo asked, indicating Jack's hand.

"No, actually," Jack replied. "Um, well yes. Paula and I, we got married in Vegas."

"Are you serious?" Goldie nearly spit out her coffee.

"Congratulations Jack!" Seemo said, reaching over to shake his hand.

"Thanks."

"You've been dating for only, like, six months," Goldie continued. Not hiding her incredulity, and no small amount of jealousy.

"Well, it was right. It IS right," Jack said. "Don't worry, some day you'll find a nice girl to settle down with, Goldie."

"Shove it."

Jack took another sip of coffee and winced as a pain that had been growing all morning suddenly struck like lightning behind his brows.

"Hey Seemo, you got any aspirin? This headache that's been kicking up has finally gone full blown," Jack said.

"Good. It's probably the little bitty part that holds common sense getting squeezed to death in there," Goldie snarked.

"No, sorry, Chief."

"Okay, I'm going to hit the pharmacy," he said. "Goldie, get something to eat. I think your a little hangry."

"See if they have any smart pills while you're there," Goldie said.

"Love you, Goldie," Jack said, thick with sarcasm.

"Love you, too, dumbass."

Jack left a dollar for the coffee and headed out the door towards the pharmacy. It was open on Sundays now, ever since the pharmacist's wife took off on him. He didn't have anything left, except work and his spot on the town council. The pharmacy was just past the station house on the other side of the street. As he approached, he saw Tubby getting yelled at by a man with a child. As he drew closer still, he saw it was Eric Owens with his son.

"I'm sorry," Jack heard Tubby say. "I was just trying to help."

"Well no thanks!" Eric yelled. "You stay the hell away from him! You got that?"

"Hey, hey," Jack said stepping slightly in front of Eric to give Tubby a little more space. "What's going on?"

"This sonofa-" Eric looked at his son then back at Jack, calming down a little. "He was telling Riker that he was going to see his mother again. His mother died last night. She's gone. And he's telling him that she's coming back!"

"It's what the Bible says," Tubby said. He was looking down at his shoes. "I didn't mean to make anybody feel bad. He was sitting on the steps crying so I just asked him what was wrong and he said his mommy died. So I felt bad and read him the Psalms. It says, -"

"You need to keep that to yourself and leave him alone," Eric said.

"Listen, Tubby. It's not a good time for this. Why don't you head off to services and I'll talk with Mr. Owens, okay?" Jack said.

"Okay. I'm really sorry," Tubby said. "Really sorry."

"Okay, Tubby. Talk to you later," Jack said. He turned to Eric. "I'm really sorry, Eric. I heard about your loss this morning. I'm so, so sorry. Tubby, he's a little. . . special. He really was trying to help. I'll talk to him again and make sure he understands he shouldn't be talking with children about religion without their parents' consent. Okay?"

"Okay," Eric said. He was breathing hard. Trying not to break down. "I'm sorry too. I just don't want him confused. He's young. It's going to be tough enough."

"I know," Jack said. "Your family has been through a rough year. If there's anything I can do to help out, just give me a call or stop in. Okay?"

"Yeah, sure," Eric said. "There is one thing."

"Name it."

"You need to get someone out to the lake on the north of town. It looks like it's about to flood over the levy. If we get that rain we're supposed to, then it could cause some flooding," Eric said.

"Really? It looks bad?"

"Yeah. You know I'm an engineer. I do bridges and such. Levies aren't my thing, but applied physics and natural forces are. And what I saw up there this morning looks bad," Eric said.

"Okay, I'll get on it. Thanks."

Eric took Riker back to his vehicle and Jack pulled a notebook out of his pocket and made a few notes. Even though he had the voice recorder, he still couldn't give up his notebook. The headache was in full swing now, so he headed in to get some aspirin.

"Let me guess," the pharmacist said. "Headache?"

"How did you know?"

"Pressure is changing, we have a storm rolling in. Big one, too. People are more prone to headaches during atmospheric pressure changes."

"Aspirin?"

"Try some aspirin and sodium naproxen combined. It will thin the blood and help with the pain," he said. "Both are over there in the far aisle. Top shelf."

Jack retrieved a bottle of each and brought them up to the counter.

"How are Michael and your new girl? I didn't even get a chance to meet her," the pharmacist asked.

"Michael's in rough shape. I hope he pulls through, but I

just don't know. Gloria didn't want me there. Tricia Wallace is the new officer on staff. She was hit twice, but she's going to be okay, I think."

"A shame. All of it. I heard a federal agent was shot and killed too. Charlie Peters tried to give him CPR. It was no use," the pharmacist said. "Why does this stuff keep happening here?"

"I wish I knew," Jack said. He paid for the pills and turned for the door. "Talk to you later."

"Jack, just wanted to let you know, Mayor's called an emergency meeting tomorrow night. Special session of the town council. Might want to be there," he said.

"Thanks for the heads up."

As he walked back towards his office, his phone buzzed.

"Shopng thn heading 2 LV arprt. lndng @ 10. pickme up," the text read. The phone buzzed in his hand again. "Luv U!"

He thumbed a response and slid the phone back into his pocket. Federal agents were walking out of his station, carrying gear in black nylon cases.

Agent Adekoya stepped onto the sidewalk and motioned for Jack to follow him inside.

"Let's talk in your office," Adekoya said. His voice was deep and smooth. Jack nodded absently as he tried to take in as much of his station house as he could. Things were out of place, but it looked like it was due to the agents rifling through files rather than from the attack.

He tried to catch a glimpse of the holding cell, but there wasn't a clear line of sight inside, as he followed Adekoya.

Jack could see immediately that the FBI agents had gone through just about everything they could in his office. They, too, were looking for something. He made a mental note to stop by the house and get the micro memory card. It was in the tray where he left his keys every night.

A wave of guilt washed over him. Perhaps, if he had called the feds the minute he found the storage chip, he might have spared his deputies and friends from the pain they were suffering. More than likely, though, the attack would have occurred whether he'd played ball or not.

He had to believe that.

He took his customary seat, and expected Agent Adekoya to take a seat as well, but he simply shut the door and then crossed his arms.

"This thing that's happened," Adekoya began. "It is bad. People who have no reservation about gunning down cops and a federal agent are either not smart or not scared. What do you know?"

"I was in Las Vegas, I -"

"Right. At the Hilton, then getting married, then at a show where two thugs tried to take you out. Coincidence, right?"

"I didn't have anything to do with it," Jack said. "I have no idea what's going on."

"I don't believe you."

"I don't care."

"Oh, you should, Jack. If you don't play ball, if you don't spill your guts, I will bring the wrath of the entire United States Federal Government down on your head. You do not want that. I'm talking frozen assets, full investigations into every case you've ever touched, all of your dirty laundry will be aired out. We'll have a whole bunch of press conferences."

"I don't have dirty laundry."

"What about the money?"

"That belongs to my new wife, Paula. She discovered it after her building burned down. Previous owner," Jack said.

"Right. Jew gold hidden in the walls. I read the story. Totally believe it. I'm sure we could tie it up in the courts to determine true ownership and whether it's considered treasure trove or lost and belongs to the original owner's descendants, or maybe even the State of New York." Adekoya said. "You know, just to be fair."

"What's your game? What do you want from me? I've been through hell for the last few months up here, mostly because you federal boys want to play games with crooks instead of arresting them. I'm just trying to do my job here and keep the people of this town safe," Jack replied.

"You're doing a helluva job, Jack."

"It doesn't help when I'm getting agents sniffing around and mysterious phone calls and -"

"Who called you?"

"He said he was with the FDCI. You should know. Or don't you talk to each other over there? Just run around acting like Dirty Harry making threats." Jack said.

"We have thousands of agents working cases from different angles every day in this agency alone. Do you have a name?" Adekoya asked.

"Sutter. Cutter. Something like that."

"Scutter?"

"Maybe."

Adekoya was quiet for a moment. He was choosing his next words carefully, Jack observed.

"Did he give you instructions?" Adekoya asked finally.

Jack shrugged. "Just to cooperate."

"Nothing else?"

"Not that I recall. Why don't you call him yourself and ask? It was his agent out there on my sidewalk."

Adekoya didn't respond.

"Did you find everything you needed?" Jack asked, indicating the offices. "Miss going through any drawers?"

"I think we need to set up an interview with you. An official interview. In our offices in Binghamton," Adekoya said. "There are a few more questions I have, but there is a previous appointment I must honor."

"Oh, good. I was hoping I'd get to spend more time with you," Jack said.

"I think you had better take Scutter's advice and cooperate," Adekoya said. He extended a hand. "Thank you for your time, Jack."

"Chief McMurphy," Jack corrected as he stood and shook the agent's hand.

"For now," Adekoya said as he left.

Jack returned to his seat. He laid his hands flat on the desk, and he noticed his left one twitched slightly. Like a muscle spasm. He made a fist with it, but the twitching continued. He took a deep breath and tried to relax. His temples pounded.

The station house was silent. There were many times previously, when Jack was alone in the station and felt the building's silence. It seemed deeper after his father was gone. The silence was absolutely abysmal now. It was like a giant emptiness that sucked the life from him. He did all he could not to run out of the place and get in the car and just drive.

The station house was supposed to be like a castle. It was where cops went to regroup and then redeploy. It's where they'd trade jokes or stories, swap techniques or make plans for the weekend. It's where they cleaned up the day's mess with mountains of paperwork.

He knew what he should do, but he didn't want to do it. He wasn't a coward, but to look at the scene was to admit that it had really happened here. Right now it was just true in his mind's eye; only as he imagined. To see the actual cell and the blood was to give it life in the real world.

Finally, the silence of the station house was unbearable. He stood, circled the desk and exited his office. He stepped across the room, past the desks that Michael and Trisha had occupied, past the short half wall that created another barrier between the desks and the back rooms, and over to the holding cell.

Inside the holding cell, the former bank vault, there was still blood on the floor.

He looked at the blood stains for a long time.

The phone rang, breaking his quiet contemplation. He picked up the receiver from Cooke's desk.

"Coopers Hollow Police, is this an emergency?"

"Jack? Chief McMurphy?"

"Yes, who's this?"

"This is Detective Phelps, County Homicide. I didn't know if this was the office number or your cell. I had two numbers here for you," Phelps said.

"This is the office number, but it's fine." Jack said, settling into the chair. From where he was sitting, he could see out the front window and a good part of the street.

"I'm really sorry to hear about your people."

"Thanks."

"Helluva thing, huh?"

"Yeah," Jack said quietly. "Helluva thing. Anyway. You got anything on our John Doe?"

"Well, yes, actually. We have a name, Timothy Pierson. Ring any bells?"

"No. Never heard of him," Jack said.

"Well, he was a runaway, at least we think it's him. He ran away from his home in Scranton, PA. Parents figured he went to New York City. He had an argument with his father and disappeared that night. Nineteen years old. He'd been missing for three years, since he was sixteen," Phelps said. "He'd told his parents he was gay."

"Ok," Jack replied. "Think that has a bearing on this?"

"Pffft, hell if I know. Just the facts, right?"

"How certain are you that this is our body?"

"There's never a guarantee until DNA or dental records are checked, but we're about ninety-seven percent sure. Birthmark, age, height, description all check out. The parents are supposed to come up to try to identify the body. Do you want to be there when they come in? Ask any questions?" Phelps asked.

"I don't need to be there," Jack said. "It's your investigation."

"Right. Any reason why you think a runaway might be in Coopers Hollow?"

"None that I can think of. Do you know when he died? What he died of?" Jack asked.

"Blunt force trauma, more than likely from a fall. Broken neck, C3 and C4 vertebrae were crushed, broken leg and dislocated shoulder, fractured skull and multiple skin abrasions. It looks like he fell or jumped off the cliff," Phelps read from the file. "But we kind of knew that."

"What about the rope burns on the wrists and ankles. Looked like he'd been tied up," Jack said. "Think this was a gay-bash thing?"

"I don't know. We'll keep that in mind. He was definitely tied up though. Skin was freshly broken in the wrist and ankle areas, so he may have been tied up just prior to jumping."

"Or falling," Jack said. "How long ago. I mean, do you have a time of death?"

"Impossible to say. Frozen solid, so my guess is he was there for at least enough of the winter for him to have frozen and get covered by the snow. Last big snow fall was early March. So at least before that. Decomposition had begun, but the body was pretty much intact. Well, you saw it," Phelps said. He made a slurping sound, taking a sip from his coffee mug. "Any calls or anything up there early March, February?"

"I don't recall anything strange around then, but it's been a weird year. I'll ask some of the boys who ride snowmobiles on the hill. They might have seen something up there and never reported it," Jack said.

"Sure, thanks. You, uh, want to come down and compare notes, check out the homicide department sometime?" Phelps asked.

"Sure, I might drop in. Kind of busy right now, with everything, though."

"Yeah, but things change, you know," Phelps said. "Change can be a good thing, sometimes."

"Sometimes," Jack replied.

"Well whenever you want to swing in, just let me know. Might be good to have a backup plan if, you know, if things don't go your way there in Coopers Hollow," Phelps said.

"What does that mean?"

"Jack, we just met with this case and all, but I know about you. I've read the articles. The tiger -"

"I told you I didn't shoot the tiger."

"I know. What I'm trying to say is, you're a good guy, right? Sometimes bad things happen to good people. The world is unfair, Jack," Phelps said.

"I've had my share of bad things happen," Jack acknowledged as he looked around the empty police station. The conversation had taken an unexpected turn. What was Phelps driving at?

"I've heard a few things down here," Phelps continued. "After your two deputies were shot, well, the talking has gotten louder."

"What kind of talk?"

"Political talk. Wanting to put in a sheriff substation there. That kind of thing," Phelps said. "I'm only telling you because I think it's a raw deal. Just keep your eyes open, is all."

"Well, I appreciate it, Phelps. I do."

"If I get any more leads on the Pierson murder, I'll give you a shout. Should I use this number or the cell?"

"Cell phone is fine."

"Okay, take care, Chief."

"You too, Detective."

Jack hung up the phone and found his chair. He rubbed his fingers against his temples, squeezing his eyes shut as tightly as he could. The aspirin and naproxen sodium weren't even close to touching the headache.

Chapter 28

Paula McMurphy checked all their bags with the bellhop and headed towards the corridor leading from the casino to the boutiques and shops. She couldn't stay in the hotel room. Couldn't do it. There were places to shop, and she had millions in the bank. She had no plans to actually buy anything, but more than likely, shoes would find themselves on the agenda. She only had two hours before she had to be at the airport. A lot of damage could be done in two hours.

The interior and fully air-conditioned boulevard of shops were like a very upscale mall. There were still traditional touristy type shops, with casino-themed souvenirs and t-shirts. But she was interested in the higher-end boutiques. Not that she'd have anyplace she could actually wear what she bought, after returning to Coopers Hollow, but it wouldn't hurt to look.

Paula strolled under the faux blue sky ceiling and window-shopped. The front of each store was made up to look like the front of a small house or shop in an Old English village. The main corridor floor was even contoured like cobblestones, though there was a smooth path in the center for wheelchairs. The overall effect was like shopping outside, on a sunny day, in a village that hadn't really existed for a hundred and fifty years. They were even piping in birdsong over the hidden speakers.

There was a liquor store that had only the luxury brands. She stopped and had a laugh. This was too perfect.

On a display, near the entrance of the liquor store, was the artfully silhouetted figure of the singer she and Jack had tickets to see, the previous night. The performance that was cut short by a phone call and then a gunshot. Apparently Frankie Moreno had his own brand of vodka.

"Oh, I have to get this," she said, taking a bottle to the counter.

"Is that everything?" the cashier asked.

"Can you box and ship this home for me?" Paula asked.

"Absolutely, we do it all the time. Extra charge of course."

"Of course," Paula said.

"Do you want to put a little card with it? We have these," the cashier indicated a small note card that was blank on one side and had the store's logo on the other. Foote Liquors, was emblazoned over a renaissance styled ink drawing of a human foot.

"Foote Liquors?" Paula asked with a laugh.

"The owner is a former ballplayer," the cashier said. "Aiden Foote. Played major league baseball. Theres a bunch of his liquor stores out here. In California too."

"Funny."

"Every time," the cashier said, deadpan.

Paula wrote a little note with some hearts and addressed it to Jack at home. It would arrive in a couple of days and would be a sweet little surprise for him. She paid the up-charge for shipping and left the liquor store, content with her gift purchase.

She ducked in and out of more boutique shops along the way, but nothing caught her interest. She found herself wandering into a magic shop. Curiosity spurred her on. She had been fascinated with magic tricks and illusions when she was a little girl.

Paula browsed a bit before an elderly man behind the counter asked if he could help her find something. He was the living cliché of a magician; tall, white hair, black dress coat, burgundy waistcoat and matching bow tie.

"Just looking around," Paula said. There were mostly books for kids, and starter magic sets. But there were also books and DVDs on the grand masters of magic and illusion, and more advanced trick sets.

"Do you have a trick" the man asked.

"What do you mean?"

"Well, everyone should have one good trick," the man said. "You bring it out at cocktail parties, or to impress coworkers. You don't have a trick?"

"No, I guess not," Paula replied. "I spent one summer trying to learn how to juggle."

"No, no. An illusion. You'd be amazed at how powerful you become in the eyes of your cohorts when you know a trick for which they cannot decipher the solution. Here, let me show you a simple one," he said. He fished his hand into his pocket and brought it out again, opening it one finger at a time. He held a quarter and a dime in his palm.

"Now watch carefully," he said.

He closed his hand, one finger at a time, squeezed it into a fist, and then slowly opened it again, repeating the flourish with the fingers. The dime had disappeared. He held the quarter between thumb and forefinger for her to see.

"Nice," Paula said.

He closed his hand again, this time turning his fist over, then back again, and opened. The dime reappeared along with the quarter.

"How does it work?" Paula asked. "Do you slide the dime through your fingers?"

"Ah, how does it work? That's the trick. The mystery. The thing about a good illusion, is that once you know the secret, the value becomes greatly diminished. When you know a good trick, and keep the knowledge of how it is mastered to yourself, well, you are truly wealthy. But then again, knowledge does not feed the belly. So I sell my tricks. This particular illusion is valued much higher, but I shall only charge you twenty dollars, on account of your beauty. I'm a sucker for a beautiful girl. I will show you the trick and I will even give you the quarter and dime as well," he said.

"I think the real trick is you getting me to trade twenty dollars for thirty-five cents," Paula said with a laugh. He laughed as well. He took her hand and put the dime and quarter into it.

"Okay," Paula said. "It's worth it just to know."

Paula did buy shoes. They were a pair of strappy, black heels that would go perfectly with a dress that she had yet to purchase, but would in the near future. They were too cute to pass up. By the time she had the shoes, it was time to retrieve her luggage and head to the airport.

The flight from Las Vegas to Chicago was quiet. She spent most of the time typing on her laptop, or, more accurately, trying to think of something to type. Her writer's block proved too impenetrable, so she relented and closed down the laptop. There was a book on her smartphone she had started to read, but her mind was elsewhere, and she couldn't focus on it. The euphoria of completing her first book had given birth to the panic of not knowing what to write next.

The idea she continued to return to was the life and death of Tubby McIntyre's great-grandfather. She still had his notebook, the final notebook he'd used on his beat. The last note written was "campfire on hollow pointe."

The news story on his death indicated that he had been shot in an ambush by the mafia and was tossed off the cliff at Hollow Pointe. That article went into detail about his interaction with the mob, how he had put a dozen, if not more, in the ground, before they finally got him.

She had tried her hand at fiction previously, but it was not her thing. Her skill set followed along the lines of investigative reporting, and then making those stories interesting, if not compelling. Her first book seemed to write itself. If anything, there was too much story there, to try to capture into a single book. The editing process was brutal. It took longer to edit than it did to actually write the initial manuscript.

The notebook from Chief McIntyre was still in her purse.

She'd taken to carrying it, as if it was a good luck charm. There was something intriguing about the window into history offered by the leather bound notebook. Mrs. O'Neill's treed cat, an accident on Main Street between a '34 ford and a horse drawn wagon, too many drunk and disorderlies to count; they all painted a picture of Coopers Hollow decades earlier.

She'd read the thing from cover to cover multiple times, but right there, as she was waiting for the flight to descend into Chicago's Midway airport, she had to read it again.

She was still reading the notations when the flight touched down. The notebook went back into her bag, and she exited the plane, making her way to the connecting flight, across the terminal. There was a little over an hour layover, which was better, in her opinion, than trying to sprint to make the flight.

Taking a moment, Paula texted Jack that she was in Chicago and couldn't wait to see him. After a few minutes, the reply pinged her phone.

"Miss you" he said.

She had tried her best to not think about Michael and Gloria, but the closer she got to home, the more those realities were creeping in. She thought about calling Gloria to see how Michael was doing, but decided against it. Even if Gloria didn't want to see Jack, Paula might be able to give her some comfort with a visit. She made up her mind to make Jack swing by the hospital on their way back.

There was a restaurant with a bar not twenty feet from her next gate, so she stopped for a drink. It was a national chain with televisions all on sports channels, and waitresses in tight uniforms. Not her first choice for a drink, but wine was wine. It was nearly two o'clock local time, so she didn't feel the least bit conspicuous ordering a glass of wine at the bar.

"Hello there," a man said as he took the stool next to her at the bar.

"Hi," she said without really focusing on the man.

"Heading home?"

"Yes," she said, looking up, recognizing him immediately.

"Oh, it's you," Paula said.

"Well that's a nice way to say hello to the guy who saved your life," he said.

"Why did you follow us to Las Vegas?"

"I could lose my job if I told you," he said. The bartender returned with Paula's wine and Haas ordered a Coke. The bartender asked if Pepsi was okay. It was all the same to Haas, so he shrugged and said "Sure."

"You're obviously following me now," Paula said. "What do you want?" Her mind immediately went to the conversation she'd had with Jack the previous night and the micro memory card he'd described to her.

"I've got to go to Coopers Hollow too, you know," Haas replied. "My partner was killed there, remember?" The Pepsi arrived, and he sipped at it without a straw.

"I'm sorry," Paula said quietly.

"Yeah, me too. Summers was a good guy. Smart as hell. Loyal as they came. You know I told him things that I never told anyone else in my life," Haas said. There was little emotion in his voice. He sounded like he was reading a script, rather than recounting a friend.

"How long were you partners?"

"Four years. We did a lot of-" he paused. "A lot of things happened in those four years."

"So tell me, what can I do to help get the guys who did this?" Paula asked.

"Did Jack tell you anything about the El Tigre case?" Haas asked.

"He told me everything. I wrote a book on it," Paula said.

"Can't wait to read it," Haas said. He fell silent as he watched the news on the large-screen television, mounted above the bar. The news reporter was talking about the preparations for the Boston Marathon the following day.

"Has he looked at the memory card yet?" Haas asked. The question caught her by surprise, though she tried not to reveal anything. She took a sip from the glass of wine.

"What memory card?"

"Where did he find it?"

"I don't know what you're talking about."

"Did you look at it?"

"Look at what?"

"You know, he was a good agent and a good friend. It's not real yet. Won't be until the funeral, and even then, maybe not entirely. In this business, you get transferred out to someplace else in the world and you don't see the people you've worked with for years. Sometimes never again. So, it will kind of be like that. I'll just imagine that he's living the life in a better assignment someplace," Haas said. He sipped the Pepsi.

Paula was just quiet. She didn't know what to say to this. She didn't know this man, didn't have any idea what he was up to; whether she could trust him or not.

"I'm sorry," she said again.

"Let me tell you this, whatever it is that the bad guys are looking for, they're not going to stop until they have it, or they're convinced it doesn't exist. You don't even have to have what they're looking for. If they think you have it, it's the same outcome. You see how it is?" Haas asked.

"I guess so. But who is it? Who's doing this?"

"Wish I knew," Haas said. He slurped the last of his Pepsi and stood. "Good luck."

Haas walked out into the foot traffic of the concourse. In just a few seconds, Paula lost sight of him.

She waited for a few moments before she took her phone out and texted Jack.

Haas had stepped across the concourse and only walked about thirty paces away before ducking behind a pillar. He removed his black suit coat and slouched substantially. He counted to ten then slid around the pillar just enough to have a clear view of Paula at the bar. She was looking in his general direction, but she was scanning the crowd. He was as good as invisible.

For several minutes she did nothing, save for sipping at her glass of wine. Then her phone came out and her thumbs were a blur.

Haas had his phone out of his pocket.

"Scutter," he said after the line engaged.

"Scutter here."

"I think they found something," Haas said. "I dropped the memory card angle, and she bristled. She calmed when I started asking details. I think they have it, but she doesn't know what's on it."

"Back to Coopers Hollow," Scutter said.

"Flight leaves in just a few minutes."

"Be careful. Once they don't find anything in the boxes, they'll be right back there again."

"No doubt," Haas said. "I'll call back when I get to town."

He shut down the connection and continued to watch Paula. Her thumbs never stopped.

Jack was back in the office. He had run home to shower and change. He'd almost left without grabbing the little memory card. Almost. It was in his pocket now. The phone was ringing when he'd returned to the station house. They didn't stop ringing all afternoon. Paula was texting him as well. He was going in ten different directions.

There were journalists and television news people and AP reporters and bloggers, not to mention concerned citizens. The story of the shootout had made national news. It seemed to fit the current narrative that, if only guns were more controlled, things like this wouldn't happen. McMurphy didn't like the politics of the topic. There was always a hidden agenda.

He was making calls himself. He needed help. Despite the losses the department had suffered, it had to continue on. Deputy Ballard was his first call.

"Hello?"

"It's McMurphy."

"Hey, chief. How are you holding up?"

"I know you've only got a few days left with us, but is there any way I could persuade you to stay on for just a few more weeks. Even two weeks would buy me some time. Tricia will be back to work by then, and maybe I'll be able to at least hire some temporary office staff to help with the phones," McMurphy said.

The line was quiet.

"Jack, I'll help however I can," Ballard said. "Let me make a phone call and see if I can make it work."

"I really appreciate it," Jack replied.

"What happens if they say no, if they want me to start when I said I would start?"

"Just do what you can," Jack replied. "It would be a personal favor."

"Okay, Jack. I'll call you back."

The next call was to Green Temp Services, the only employment agency he could find online that was within thirty minutes.

Jack spent fifteen minutes talking with the so-called placement agent, a bright young woman, by the sound of her voice. She asked about the work he needed performed, the hours, and when he needed her to start.

"Immediately, if possible," Jack replied.

"Well I'm sure we can find someone that fits your needs," the girl on the other end of the phone said. She sounded like she was twelve, to Jack's ears. After just a few moments more, the phone call was over, and he slid back in his chair. He looked around the empty station house again and let out a primal yell that echoed off the bare brick walls. It was cleansing, cathartic.

As if remembering a conversation he'd started and left off half finished, Jack fished into his pocket and pulled out the micro memory card he'd taken from the watch.

He held it between thumb and forefinger, practically transfixed.

"What are you?" he said out loud.

The phone buzzed in his pocket. It was another text message from Paula. She'd told him about talking with Agent Haas in the airport bar. She also told him she was worried. He tried to calm her as fast as his thumbs allowed him, but he was not nearly the texter she was. He looked at his phone to read the newest message.

"On the plane in Chi. See you in just a bit. LUV U!!!!" it read.

He did some mental calculations and realized he would need to head towards the airport in Albany in the next half hour to be there in time to pick her up. If he wanted to avoid forcing her to wait for too long, that is . Of course she was bringing all of the baggage back, so that might buy him an extra ten minutes.

It was dark outside already. The phones had settled down. He found, for a moment, there was quiet. The silence of the station house, closing in on him.

The phone rang. It was like a shrill klaxon, against the silence. He actually felt his pulse elevate slightly from the shock of sudden noise.

"Coopers Hollow police department, this is Chief McMurphy."

He listened as one of the residents of the small town, Mrs. Klenotich, complained about the boys skateboarding on the side-walk too fast. She was an elderly woman, nearly ninety, and the boys were riding dangerously fast, and they were going to kill themselves or her if they weren't forced to stop. She said the word dangerous at least a half dozen times. Then she told him that she had tried to call all day, but wasn't able to get through and that she expected more from the police department. After all, didn't her tax dollars pay his salary?

"I'll talk to the boys, Mrs. Klenotich."

"You'd better," she said.

"Okay, have a nice night. Call me if you continue to have problems," he heard himself say in his father's voice. He was suddenly transported back to being ten years old, listening to his dad take a similar call. He had sat there, bored out of his mind, waiting for his dad to be able to call it a night and head home. Maybe throw the football around in the back yard.

As he hung up the phone, a stab of sadness cut him deep. His father and mother were both gone, now. His childhood was gone. So much was different. Was there anything left for him here? Jack shook off the thought, grabbed his keys and headed for Paula's Mercedes. It was an hour and a half to the airport if he took his time. If he left now and didn't take his time, he could grab a drink at the airport bar.

Chapter 29

The drive from Coopers Hollow to the Albany International Airport took about a bit more than an hour and a half, as the New York State Thruway authority had decided to leave only a single toll booth open to take cash. Neither he nor Paula had purchased an electronic square for the new Mercedes, so he was stuck waiting for fifteen vehicles, despite the relatively late hour. Even though there was no toll from Interstate 88 to this exit, without the electronic pass, you had to turn in the ticket and get the obligatory "you're all set" from the toll booth collector.

By the time he reached the airport and parked, he only had a few minutes before Paula's flight was due to arrive. Granted, it would still take time for the plane to taxi to the gate, for her to get off and then walk out of the terminal to the public area of the airport, where he could meet her, so they could then retrieve their bags. He looked at the bar, longing for a drink, but he didn't think there would be enough time to check out ESPN and sip down a Jack & Coke.

There were very few people in the airport at the moment. It was the end of the day. The digital board listing arrivals, only had a few flights remaining. The flight from Chicago-Midway was on time. His hand slid into his pocket, to the micro memory card he was carrying. He noticed one of the shops had cell phone and digital camera accessories. It carried all of the tourist items one would expect: I Heart NY t-shirts, snow globes, spoons and magnets with the state emblem, all sorts of magazines and candy, and a wall of consumer electronics items. There were earbuds and cellphone chargers, batteries and adapters.

"Can I help you, officer?" the girl behind the counter had

been thumbing her cell phone moments ago, appearing bored out of her mind. Now she was smiling at him.

"I was just seeing if you had an adapter for this," Jack said, holding up the micro memory card.

"What is that, for a camera or something?" she asked.

"I think so, yeah. It says microSD. I want to play it on my computer," he replied.

"Okay, yeah. We have that stuff over here, behind the counter," she said. As Jack walked closer, he saw her name tag said Suzie. She looked like a Suzie. Blond hair, short and curvy. She looked at the wall behind the counter and then pulled down a card with a small plastic blister on it. "See if this is the right one."

Jack looked at the packaging. It appeared to be precisely what he was looking for. A multi-use adapter that took several different kinds of media and routed them into a USB plug that would fit into his laptop.

"Yikes," he said. "Fifteen bucks?"

"I know," Suzie sighed. "You can get the same thing online for, like, two dollars. We way over charge. Oops, not supposed to say that." She smiled at him, even as she continued to chew on the bubble gum in her mouth.

"I've been trying to get one of these stupid things for a week now," Jack replied. "I'll pay the fifteen bucks just to be done with it." He fished his wallet out, and provided the department credit card to her. The transaction was done in a few moments. He didn't need to sign, as it was under twenty-five dollars.

"Go get the bad guys," she said, in a flirtatious tone. She blew a bubble and sucked it back in to make a popping sound.

"Thanks," Jack said, catching himself before he absent-mindedly said "you too."

Three-hundred, seventy-five miles away, a computer operator received a chime on his screen. One of the thousands of individuals that had been selected for special screening had just popped up, having made a purchase via credit card. The individual's name was not available for him to view, just a number. The purchase was made at an airport. That was a red flag for any person who had already been red-flagged. The computer operator selected the info and gave it an urgent status. This would cause it to pop up on another computer further up the investigative chain, for someone with a higher security clearance to review. Once reviewed, it would continue to get escalated up the chain. It took less than three minutes, from the time Jack McMurphy's credit card was swiped, until the information was on Scutter's computer screen. With just a click, he was able to pull up the transaction information: one multi-use adapter. The item number was also clickable. It sent him to a retail website where he could see the item. It adapted microSD memory cards to USB.

Scutter dialed agent Haas' number.

Paula got off the plane first, as she was sitting nearer the nose of the plane. Agent Haas received the message from Scutter, just before the plane landed. He was a federal agent, he didn't follow all of the FAA regulations for in-flight cellphone usage. What he did have to follow was the requirement of coach class tickets for domestic flights unless prior authorization was provided. He hadn't anticipated the need to sit right next to her during the flight to follow her. He knew the Albany airport was on the smaller side, as far as airports went, so the risk of losing her was minimal. So, as everyone stood to get their bags out of the overhead compartments, he saw Paula McMurphy leave the plane, twenty-five people ahead of him.

As he deplaned, he had completely lost sight of her. Agent Haas hustled to the baggage claim. He knew she had multiple bags. He'd watched her check all of them and pay more for the extra bags than the cost of her flight itself.

Paula had used the restroom a few yards away from the gate and then headed towards the security gate that released into the public area. She saw Jack waiting for her. She also saw Agent Haas. It looked like they were arguing.

"Then why don't you just show me," Agent Haas said to Jack, as Paula walked up.

"What's going on?" she asked.

"Nothing," Jack replied. "Agent Haas was just taking a walk."

"Show me what's in the bag, officer McMurphy," Haas said sternly.

"Get a warrant," Jack replied.

"You don't want this to come down on you," Haas continued. "Cooperate, and life goes back to normal. Fail to cooperate and it will get very uncomfortable."

"Wow, this is a big boy pissing contest," Paula said. "Do you boys want me to go find a ruler so you can measure each other while you're at it?"

"Might want to muzzle your girl," Haas said.

"You're a hair's breadth away from leaving here on a stretcher," Jack replied.

"Assaulting a federal officer? Could ruin your career, Jack."

"It would be worth it." They were nose to nose now. For a moment, Paula thought Jack really was going to hit him.

"Okay, sorry. Okay. I'm sorry," Paula said. "Whatever is in the bag isn't worth the trouble." She swiped the bag from Jack's hand and pulled out the contents. It was the adapter, still in its packaging.

"This is what you wanted to see?" she asked Agent Haas. "It's a stupid adapter I asked him to get for me so I could pull info off my old phone. What's wrong with you?"

"An old phone," Haas repeated.

"That's right."

"Not a micro memory card you found amongst the clothing of Agent Spaulding," Haas said. "You remember him, right? The undercover agent you murdered."

"Here's where we part ways," Jack said quietly, through clenched teeth. "Next time I see you, it had better be with a warrant or a whole bunch of friends."

"Oh, is that a threat, Jack? Come on, why are you acting this way," Haas said, trying to change tactics. "Did you forget about how I saved your life in Vegas? Twice, actually. Let's see, at the chapel and then the concert? We're on the same team."

Jack turned away from Haas and took Paula by the elbow.

"It's not going to go away, Jack," Haas yelled after him. "I'm one of the good guys. You're not going to like the bad guys."

As he watched them head towards the baggage claim, Agent Haas pulled his phone from his pocket and called Scutter.

"Haas here," he said. "Get warrants. They've got something. I want to serve them when they get out of the car back in Coopers Hollow."

"You'll have it," Scutter said on the other end. "Agent Willows is en route from NYC."

"Willows?"

"You've got a problem with Willows?" Scutter asked.

"I'll make it work," he said, closing down the connection. He headed towards the exit and to his car. He didn't have luggage.

Chapter 30

"What are you doing?" Paula almost yelled as Jack punched the accelerator out of airport parking lot, utilizing all of the Mercedes' horsepower.

"They're going to get warrants. They're going to take every electronic device we own. Cell phones, iPods, computers. Everything," Jack said.

"How does that translate to 'drive like a madman'?" she yelled.

"They will be following us. I want to see what's on this thing," he said, holding out the micro memory card. "Get out your laptop and plug it in."

He handed the small rectangle of plastic to her. She put it between her teeth as she tried to open the adapter. She pulled and attempted to tear the packaging, but just became more frustrated with it.

Jack pulled a utility knife from his belt and handed it to her.

"Thanks," she said, but it sounded more like "shanks." She opened the knife and sliced through the packaging. It was a quick process: adapter out of package, micro memory card into the adapter, adapter into the laptop, laptop into the power adapter in the car.

After a moment, she opened the folder on the tiny storage device. There were Microsoft Word documents and several video files. She clicked on one of the video files, launching the video player.

"Find a place to pull over where we can watch this," she said.

"Can you see them?"

"I have visual."

"What are they doing?"

"They've parked, and it looks like they're viewing something on her laptop," Haas said. "Can you see what she's doing on the computer?"

"We're trying," came the reply. There were three people on the conference call. Haas, sitting in his rental, Scutter sitting at an all night cafe, not too far from his office, and the surveillance tech, sitting god-knows-where.

"She must have turned off the WiFi," the tech said. Scutter had worked with him before. His name was Dimmler. He was the best. "I can't get in. If you get closer, we might be able to push through with Bluetooth."

"How close do you need me to be?" Haas asked.

"We can do it through your phone. Probably like thirty feet, at most," the tech said. "You can just be next to them and I can do everything I need to do over the Bluetooth connection."

"Can't do it," Haas replied. "They're in the middle of a parking lot. If I approach, they'll be able to see me.

"Okay, let me think of something," the tech said.

"Jack, this is bad," Paula said.

"Yeah," he replied in a whisper.

"You know who that is?"

"Yeah," he said. They continued watching.

"Okay, I've got it," the tech said. "If you roll up to them, it should only take a second or so to connect. We can send a command to switch on the WiFi via the Bluetooth connection and then we can handle it from the cell towers."

"How much time do you need me next to them," Haas asked.

"Just a few seconds. Not even that. Talk me into it. Let me know your distance."

"Okay, about a hundred feet," Haas said. He heard some typing over the line. Then silence. "Sixty, forty, twenty."

"Slow down," the tech said. More typing.

"I'm almost on them, ten feet," Haas said. "Right behind them."

"Got it!"

Haas accelerated away from them, turning towards the stores thirty yards away.

"Did they see you?" Scutter asked calmly.

"Negative," Haas said. "They are really concentrating on what they've got on screen."

"We've got their screen now," the tech said. "Sending the link over to you, Director Scutter."

"I have it," Scutter said.

"What is it?" Haas asked.

He was met with silence. The line was still open, all he could hear was a sharp intake in Scutter's breathing.

"Plutonium," Scutter said. "This is radioactive as hell."

"What do we do?" Paula asked.

"We get rid of it," Jack said. "We turn it over to the feds and we get the hell away from it."

"As a journalist, I don't know if I can do that. This is too big," Paula said. "There's another video file."

"I don't know if we want to see it," Jack said.

"We have to."

She clicked on the file and it launched another video player window.

Chapter 31

"My name is Antoine Reginald Spaulding, I'm a federal agent, and part of a classified task force for the federal government of the United States, working in conjunction with the Federal Department of Criminal Investigation." He was a dark skinned man, wearing a white t-shirt, sitting in, what looked like, a bathroom stall. He was sweating profusely. He held the camera, more than likely his phone, at arm's length, like he was taking a selfie. The image shook slightly. His hand must have been trembling.

"I've made these files so that the info and evidence I've obtained can be used to continue separate investigations into multiple, highly prominent, public figures. I've worked for the last eighteen months on operation: tiger trap. I have infiltrated the organization of one Devon Tampico, aka Devon Smith, aka Dean Smith, aka El Tigre. He's a mid-level drug dealer in the New York Metropolitan area. In the other video file, titled 'shooting.mov' you will see a meeting between Mr. Tampico, Ira Greenbau, the President of INEO Broadcasting and Gordon W. Jefferson, the well known civil rights leader. This meeting took place on October 9th, just a few days ago. I was present, serving as driver and extra security for Mr. Tampico. The other members who were present, at least those whose names I know, are listed on the Word docs also accompanying the video. I was the individual responsible for the video recording. It was done utilizing my cell phone and was done without the knowledge of any of the individuals on the video.

"I will now provide background to the accompanying video, to the best of my knowledge.

He cleared his throat and wiped the sweat from his brow with the back of his arm. He wet his lips with his tongue and began talking again.

"On October 8th, I was informed by Mr. Tampico that we would be traveling to a location in New Jersey to meet with, what he called, big-time people. He said that it would be his 'in' to hooking some big money. This was the whole point of the operation. We were trying to prop up Mr. Tampico, push him up the chain of command to nab his suppliers, and then their suppliers. But we were also trying to nab any high profile clients, as well.

"I drove Mr. Tampico and two other body guards to a home in New Jersey, near the Pennsylvania border. I've included the exact address in the accompanying Word docs. It was secluded, had a big gate with an intercom. The mailbox had the name Greenbau on it. When we arrived there were already two other vehicles there. A Bentley and Cadillac SUV. Upon entering the home, I observed a man, whom I recognized as Ira Greenbau, the president of the International News and Entertainment Organization. He was accompanied by a body guard who I did not recognize. Also present was a man I recognized as civil rights leader, Gordon W. Jefferson. Mr. Jefferson was accompanied by two men. One man I did not recognize. The other I did. He was a convicted felon by the name of Reginald Mongrove. I recognized Mr. Mongrove because he had worked as an informant for the FBI on several occasions previously. I had sat in on some of his interviews during a joint operation with the FBI. I remembered him, specifically, because I shared my middle name with his first name. I informed Mr. Tampico that I recognized Mr. Mongrove, and that he was a federal informant. I told him he had ratted out a cousin of mine. You know, something he'd believe, easy to explain. I did this because I feared that Mr. Mongrove would endanger the investigation and perhaps my life should he recognize me, or maybe inform on the operation and bring in another agency. Again, my actions were out of concern over my life and concern over jeopardizing our agency's investigation. I imagined he would be excused, fired, whatever. I recognize that my actions endangered Mr. Mongrove's life."

He closed his eyes and leaned his head back for a moment. Licked his lips again. Opened his eyes. Looked into the camera. Continued talking.

"It was at this point I began recording the meeting. Mr. Tampico informed Mr. Jefferson that Mr. Mongrove was a federal informant. Mr. Jefferson asked how he knew this. Mr. Tampico said he had sources. Mr. Jefferson then revealed a pistol, a 9mm, I believe, and held it to Mr. Mongrove's head. Mr. Jefferson asked if Mr. Tampico was certain. Mr. Tampico said yes. Mr. Jefferson pulled the trigger, killing Mr. Mongrove immediately. Mr. Jefferson then calmly returned his gun and continued the meeting.

"It was just an initial meeting. Mr. Jefferson was looking to use his connections with high ranking individuals, both in government and the private sector, to enrich himself. He wanted to setup an illegal narcotics trafficking network to the elites. He figured since he could meet with them without suspicion, he might as well take advantage of it. Mr. Jefferson said that he had been asked by more than one of these connections, on more than one occasion, if he had access to a variety of illegal narcotics. We're talking senators, congressmen, judges, as well as CEOs and other business people."

He wiped his mouth with his hand.

"Mr. Jefferson even had access to the White House from time to time, as an adviser on civil rights matters."

He cleared his throat again.

"Mr. Jefferson and Mr. Greenbau were apparently friends, and Mr. Greenbau was a client of Mr. Tampico's. It was Mr. Greenbau who set up the meeting. The entire thing lasted only a few minutes. There was an exchange of phone numbers for future discussions. That was it. I don't know what became of Mr. Mongrove's remains."

"I have included a sworn statement with these files."

Agent Spaulding took a deep breath. The video ended with the image of a gravely concerned man, frozen on the screen. It was the man that Jack had shot in Gloria Graves' driveway, nearly six months ago.

Chapter 32

"This will never see the light of day, Paula," Jack said. "There are too many powerful people who can make this go away."

"We've got to try," Paula said. "What if we uploaded it right now? I could post it to any number of websites. It would get noticed. And once it's out, they can't make it go away. Toothpaste out of the tube."

"They will hunt us down and kill us, baby. Even if we turn it over now, they will probably still come after us. The only thing we can do is turn it over to the FBI or FDCI or whoever, and swear to secrecy. Maybe even go into witness protection," Jack said. "All bets are off with this. We need to get as far away from it as possible."

"How can you say that? You're an officer of the law! You've sworn to uphold the law, Jack. Did you forget that?" Paula said.

"I can say it, because I'm not stupid."

"Oh, so that makes me stupid?"

"I didn't say that. Listen, I'm thinking about you, right now. You're my priority. This is a systemic problem, two people aren't going to change it," Jack said.

"So we just look the other way?" Paula asked, her voice tinged with disgust.

"What other option do we have?"

"Are you getting everything?" the tech asked.

"I am," Scutter said. "You're recording what you're receiving from the laptop's audio and video feeds?"

"Of course," the tech said.

"Something's going on," Haas said, still connected to the conference call. The tech had hacked audio and video from Paula's computer, by remotely switching on the microphone and camera. It gave everyone on the call both eyes and ears inside the McMurphy's vehicle. Haas watched on his cellphone, while Scutter viewed and listened on his tablet. He was sipping coffee at the cafe, near his office. He had to leave his family in Hawaii and head home. He hadn't actually been home yet.

"What's happening?" Scutter asked.

"Looks like they're getting picked up," Haas said.

"By who?"

"FBI," Agent Haas replied.

"Step out of the vehicle with your hands in the air," a voice boomed from the external speaker mounted in the grille of the unmarked vehicle. It was one of a half dozen cars that sped in to surround Jack and Paula's Mercedes.

Slowly they opened the doors to the car, keeping their hands in the air.

"I'm an officer of the law, I'm carrying a side arm," Jack hollered to them.

"Get down on your knees, both of you," came the order.

"What if I don't want to get my pants dirty?" Jack hollered back.

"I will shoot you without even a second thought," came the response.

"I think we'd better listen," Jack said to Paula, who was already on her knees.

"You think?" she said.

"Interlock your fingers on your head." With jaw flexing, he complied.

Three agents rushed Jack, while two handled Paula. Two of the agents secured Jack's hands behind his back, while the third removed Jack's pistol from his belt.

"Wow, how many agents does it take to screw in a lightbulb?" Jack said.

"Okay, smart guy, you are hereby detained by the FBI, pending further investigation," said Special Agent Adekoya. "You should have played ball, Jack."

Jack and Paula were transported in separate vehicles to the FBI field office on McCarty Street, in downtown Albany. All of their personal effects were removed, watches, wallets, everything in their pockets. They were taken to separate interview rooms, given a seat and provided a bottle of water each. They were then left to sit there, in silence and solitude, for two hours. Finally, Special Agent Adekoya entered to speak with Jack, another agent in tow.

"Do you know why you're here, Mr. McMurphy," he asked.

"Chief McMurphy," Jack corrected.

"For now," Adekoya said. "Do you know why we've brought you here, you and your wife?"

"You said we needed to have an interview. I didn't think it would be in the middle of the night on a Sunday. Or make that Monday," he said.

"Drop the act, Chief," Adekoya said. "We know you have more information than you're sharing. We're going through your laptop now. Make it easy on yourself and tell me what you've got."

"Where's Agent Haas?"

"Who?"

"You want me to believe you don't know?" Jack asked. "Agent Haas. His partner was Summers, the guy that got shot outside my station house in Coopers Hollow. Agent Haas, the guy who followed us to Las Vegas and took a couple of ex-FBI agents into custody. Surely, you know about them. The guy who tailed us through the airport when we got back."

"I don't know an Agent Haas," Adekoya said.

"Then I suggest you call his boss, Scutter," Jack said. "Get your side all straightened out and then come back and talk to me."

"Why are you being so difficult, Chief? We're on the same team," Adekoya replied.

"Are we? You're the second person to say that to me today. I'm not sure who's on who's team right now."

"If you're on the side of the law, if you want to find out who shot up your station house, then yes, we're on the same team," Adekoya said.

Jack was quiet for a moment. He hadn't gotten an update on Cooke. He didn't know if he'd made it through surgery.

"Here's what I know: six months ago a couple of drug dealers come to town looking for some punk kid. One of those drug dealers kills my father. Then they try to kill my girlfriend, and a couple of other women in town. My friend, Michael Cooke and I stopped them. Then, a few days ago, a couple of guys who say they're federal agents with FDCI come around looking for some of the evidence from the case. But they don't want to sign off on anything. They just want to take it. A couple days after that, I get invited out to Las Vegas. Completely out of the blue. My wife and I get jumped, not once, but twice. And my friend Michael, he and my new deputy get gunned down in my station house. Oh, and surprise, surprise, the evidence is stolen. Then you show up asking why I'm being so difficult?" He spoke in an even tone. "Somebody is turning the screws on this whole thing. It's big."

"Why don't you tell me how big?" Agent Adekoya asked.

"Because, right now, I have no idea who I can trust and who I can't," Jack replied. "And until I know for sure, neither I or Paula are saying a word."

"Well," Adekoya said. "I guess I'll go see if she feels the same way."

The flight from DC to Albany took just over two hours. Scutter's flight landed with a priority clearance at Albany International Airport, right around the time Adekoya was walking out of McMurphy's interview room. Agent Haas was on the tarmac, with a car ready to go.

"This is a complete charlie-foxtrot," Scutter said. "Somebody at the bureau is pulling strings on this. We've got to watch our backs. Has Willows made contact with you yet?"

"No, sir," Haas said. "Not a word."

"Let's go get this thing done," Scutter said.

Haas steered away from the jet and pointed the nose of the car towards the airport security gates. It was a seven minute ride to the Albany FBI field office. Haas did it in five. It wasn't difficult at one o'clock in the morning.

"Thank you for waiting," Special Agent Adekoya said, extending a hand. They were standing in the lobby of the Albany FBI field office. Adekoya was annoyed for getting called out of his interrogations with the McMurphys. Who ever it was that was demanding to see him had some explaining to do.

"That took two minutes too long," Scutter said, looking at his watch, and not shaking hands. "I'm Special Director Scutter, FDCI."

"You're Scutter?" Adekoya cleared his throat. "I see. How can I help you?"

"I really don't want to be here in the middle of the night talking to you. I want to be home. But you have gone and stumbled into something way above your pay grade. You have two people in your custody right now that belong to me," Scutter said. "I have a car sitting out front right now. I don't want to keep the driver waiting another two minutes. Round them up and I'd like you to escort them out yourself." He turned toward the door.

"What gives you the clearance?" Adekoya asked. "We are pursuing an investigation here."

Scutter reached into his jacket and removed a business card. He held the card up without turning, waiting for Adekoya to step forward and take it. Adekoya looked at the card. There was a single phone number in the middle on one side, and nothing on the reverse.

"What's this?"

"Call that number. Ask who I am," Scutter said, without turning. "My driver and I will be waiting."

Scutter walked out of the FBI office and down to the car, a waiting Agent Haas behind the wheel.

"Well?" Haas asked.

Scutter didn't say a word. He looked at his watch. It took just over a minute and a half. Adekoya was leading Paula and Jack McMurphy down the steps towards the car. They carried their belongings in tear-proof envelopes. Adekoya opened the rear door, and the two slid in.

Adekoya stepped to the passenger window and tapped it with his knuckle. Scutter rolled the window down.

"Here," Adekoya said, quietly, handing back the business card. "Director Gibbons gives his regards."

"Thank you," Scutter said. He turned to Haas. "Drive."

Haas obeyed, and they left Adekoya standing on the sidewalk, looking both confused and annoyed.

"Where's the computer?" Scutter asked without turning around.

"We don't know what you're talking about," Paula said. Jack put his hand on her leg and gave her a pat.

"It was in the car," Jack said. "But he said they were going through it."

"Where's the memory card?"

"In the computer."

"Did you make a copy?"

"I'm pretty sure you know we didn't," Jack replied. "Where are we going?"

"To get your car," Scutter said. "So you can go home. Been a long couple of days, wouldn't you say?"

"Why is it I don't quite believe you?" Jack retorted.

"I'm not sure. If there's anyone who's been untruthful through this whole thing, it's you. Maybe you're, what's the term? Maybe you're projecting, Chief," Scutter said.

"So what happens to us?" Paula interjected.

"What do you want to have happen? Would you like to go into witness protection, or are you willing to keep your mouth shut and pretend like you didn't see what you saw?" Scutter asked.

"We'd have to do that either way, it seems," Paula said quietly. She was brooding, with arms crossed.

"Well you can tell the world about it if you'd like," Scutter said. "First, no one would believe you. Second, you'd probably have trouble staying alive. We are dealing with the type of D.C. career people who have found their way onto the other side of the law. Of course, once that happens, they start corrupting the very system they've been claiming to fight for. Bending it to their own devices. And then the corruption spreads. Like a disease. A cancer."

"So what are you going to do about it?" Jack asked.

"What do you normally do with cancer?"

"Cut it out."

"When it's practical to do so, we will. There are other treatments as well. Some involve pressure, some involve manipulation to achieve other goals. Depends on what we really need and when we need it," Scutter said.

"So that's it then? We go our separate ways? What's to prevent the bad guys coming back to my town and causing more trouble?" Jack asked.

"At this point, nothing. We can get word to the appropriate

parties that we have the info, the video, and that they need to back off and play ball. But there's always that chance that the message doesn't get down to the players at ground level for a few days. In which case, I would suggest disappearing for a week or two. Then contemplating relocation," Scutter said. "Maybe taking a new job." Scutter turned in his seat and looked at Jack. "Maybe a job from a new friend."

"What? You mean like a job working for you?" Paula scoffed.

"Maybe. You're a college graduate, with law enforcement experience. You've been in a fire fight, you've seen some action. There's always room for a seasoned individual like yourself," Scutter said. "Still young enough to sign on too. Could be a great career move."

"I don't think I'm the right fit for you," Jack said.

"You're not," Paula said. "He's not."

Scutter scowled at Paula, then turned back to face front. They were pulling into an underground parking garage. This caused the hair on the back of Jack's neck to stand up.

"Where are we going?"

"I told you, to get your car. Send you home," Scutter said.

Haas showed his badge to the security guard. The guard called on his radio, and then hit the button to lift the gate.

They drove down one level, then two. As they rounded the bend, they saw Paula's Mercedes.

"Keys are in the ignition. You're not getting the computer back," Scutter said. "I'll be in touch, Jack. Consider the offer. Small town police gigs don't last forever."

"I'll take it under advisement," Jack replied. "Let's go, Paula."

They climbed out of the back of the car and headed towards the silver SUV. Haas and Scutter drove away, leaving the McMurphy's standing in the quiet, concrete parking garage. They could hear the car's tires squeal in the distance as it rounded the corners exiting the garage. Then it was quiet, except for a low frequency hum, coming from the building or the city itself. It was as quiet as a tomb.

"Do you think they did something to it?" Paula asked. Her hushed voice still echoing slightly.

"Like in the movies? Turn the key and we go kaboom?"

"Yeah, just like that," Paula said. There was no mistaking the trepidation in her voice. "They wouldn't just let us go, would they?"

"I think so. They are looking for bad guys like in the video. Not us. We're small time, baby. Giving us a hassle for discovering a clue for a bigger case isn't going to advance any of their careers," Jack said. "I think we're fine. I'm more worried about the thugs working for that Jefferson joker. I think they're the ones that hurt Tricia and Cooke. They have to be."

"What if they try again?"

"Scutter said he'd put word out. I just hope the message makes it down the line," Jack said. "If not, I've got to be ready for them."

"Like Rambo?"

"I was thinking more like John McClane from the *Die Hard* movies," Jack said.

"Ugh, I hated those movies," Paula said. "When he was jumping on the back of that jet, I mean, come on."

"That was," Jack started. He sighed. "The first one, that was *Die Hard*. The rest were like, just Hollywood."

"What do you even mean? Hollywood made the first one too," Paula said.

"Never mind. I don't want to argue about the movie. Get in the car," he said.

Jack was behind the wheel, even though it was Paula's vehicle. And even though he hadn't read her book yet. He pressed the engine start/stop button and the car roared to life. Both of them let out a sigh of relief.

"High tech," he said. The backup camera clicked on when he put the car in reverse. "Very high tech. I like it."

"Only the best."

He steered the SUV to the security gate, which opened before they reached it. They drove out into the rainy night and headed home. They didn't say much as they drove. It wasn't until they were on Interstate 88 that Jack broke the silence. Paula had been dozing off.

"If things do go bad again, I want us to be ready. Both of us," Jack said. "I want to teach you how to shoot a gun."

"Okay," she replied, with a yawn.

"Okay?"

"Yeah, I'd like to learn. I think it would be a good thing for me to learn," she said. She sat up a bit and rubbed her eyes.

"Where are we?"

"Coming up on the Duanesburg exit," he said.

"Okay, I can sleep for a bit before home." She leaned the seat back and rolled onto her shoulder, facing away from her husband.

"I have a .22 pistol that you can practice with. We'll have you put some rounds down range and get you used to general firearm safety. Get you a permit, then we can go and pick out something a little more powerful for you. Something that you'll like," Jack said.

"Sounds good," she replied. Jack looked at her with a level of skepticism. She looked over her shoulder at him and scowled. "What?"

"You've never liked guns before," he said.

"So, things are different now, right?"

"Yes, they are."

"So a girl can change her mind, can't she," Paula said.

"Yes she can."

"You were expecting a fight?"

"Maybe," he said. "At least some resistance to the idea."

"Well I think you're right. I think I should know how to shoot," she said. "I humbly yield to my husband's superior wisdom."

"You goofball," he said, giving her a shove.

"I have to tell you something," Paula said. She straightened up in the seat. "I have a little confession to make."

"Uh oh."

"Promise you won't be mad," she said.

"What is it?"

"Promise first."

"I can't promise I won't be mad about something if I don't know what it is," he said.

"Then I'm not telling you."

"You're so difficult sometimes," Jack said.

"I am."

"Stubborn."

"Like a mule. Promise you won't be mad."

"Okay," he sighed. "I promise I won't be mad."

"So when I was in Vegas, after you left, I did some walking around. You know, I was just walking around. Shopping. I got some shoes. And I got something else. There was this little magic shop in one of the casinos."

"Okay."

"So what they did at this magic shop was sell tricks. You could buy trick decks of cards, trick quarters, that kind of thing," she said. "Did I ever tell you when I was a little girl I wanted to be a magician?"

"No. Never told me that."

"Well, when I was a little girl, I wanted to be a magician. Well, I thought it would be cool, at least. Anyway, in Vegas I went into the magic shop. They had this trick. I was going to use it on you.

The guy there, he showed me how to use it," she said. "It was a trick quarter."

"I'm afraid I'm not following," Jack said, stealing a glance at her as he drove.

"Just listen. This magic quarter. It has a small opening on the side that lets you slide a dime in. Or something else, if it fit. It's so you can have two coins in your hand, close your hand, squeeze them together and, presto-change-o, only the quarter. I still had it in my pocket when we were arrested," Paula said. "I slid something inside."

"What?"

She slid the quarter from the tear-proof envelope, and thumbed the nub on the edge that triggered the side to open. She pulled something out of the quarter and held it up for Jack to see.

It was the micro memory card.

"What?!"

"I'm sorry, Jack. You promised you wouldn't be mad."

Chapter 33

"Look out!" he screamed. His voice was hoarse, and instead of a scream and words that were well articulated, what emanated from his lips was a low, guttural moan. Then he coughed as his throat closed up from the dryness.

The room was dark. He tried to move, but his body didn't respond. He had the sensation that he was a puppet, a marionette doll suspended by strings, unable to control his own limbs. Was he dreaming? Was he awake? Was he dead?

"Tricia," he croaked.

"Oh my God, Michael!" It was Gloria. She was beside him, leaning over him, kissing him.

"Gloria," he mouthed the words, but his voice was completely gone. "Water."

"Yes, water," she said, retrieving a cup from the bedside table with a large plastic straw extending out of it. She held it to his lips and he slowly drew in the refreshing liquid. It hurt at first. Then it soothed his throat.

"What happened? Where am I," Michael asked in a raspy voice.

"You're in the hospital in Albany," Gloria said. "You were shot. Some men shot you."

"Tricia?" He felt panic wash over him. His stomach tied into a knot and he felt like he was going to vomit. The low beeps on the machine, next to his bed, increased in frequency. His heart rate was up.

"She's okay," Gloria said. "You saved her. You shielded her with your body. Oh my God, Michael. You came back to me." She was sobbing as she gingerly hugged him, mindful of his wounds.

"Of course I did," Michael said. "I'll always be there for you."

"Promise?" she whispered.

"Promise."

Chapter 34

It was Monday morning. The village of Coopers Hollow was still and quiet, shrouded in a dense fog that had settled over the valley, overnight. The sun had yet to break over the mountains to the east, so the valley was dark, though the sky above the fog was brightening.

Eric Owens laid in his bed, staring at the ceiling. He'd been awake since three in the morning. After taking a pill at midnight, he had drifted off to sleep. It was anything but restful. He dreamed of his wife, before the depression. When she was full of life, laughing and pushing their daughter on the swing. Then there was a thick smoke that moved across the playground. It was the playground right here in Coopers Hollow, and he was a teenager again. And she was a teenager too. Though they hadn't met until they were both adults, it made sense. He had the understanding that it was just a dream, so it was okay. Both kids were there, too. And there was that thick smoke, like an immense tsunami or one of those sandstorms in a post-apocalyptic movie.

"Run," he was yelling. "Run!" But she just turned to face the thick smoke, which was now a rushing wave of muddy water. She just stood there as it washed over her.

He awoke with a shudder, words still on his lips. He rolled to look at the clock and it said three-oh-nine. His heart was beating hard in his chest, his breathing was coming in great heaves.

"Dad?" he heard footsteps in the hall, and his door opened. It was Riker.

"Dad, was that you?" Riker asked, eyes still closed, head leaning to one side, Batman pajamas too tight, shirt sliding up to reveal his belly.

"Come here, buddy," Eric whispered. Riker climbed up into bed next to his father and snuggled in. At seven, he could still be snuggly, but he was longer and more elbows than snuggles.

"I love you, little man."

"I love you too, dad."

All was quiet for a moment, as Riker's breathing became deeper and heavier. It shortened for a moment.

"Was it mom?"

"What's that?"

"Did you have a dream about mom?"

"Yeah, but it's okay. Go back to sleep."

"Okay. It will get better, dad."

"I know."

"I miss her, too."

"I know, go to sleep. We can talk in the morning."

"I'm glad I'll see her again in paradise," Riker said.

Eric clenched his jaw. Riker must have been talking to that big, bible-thumping oaf again. He felt his face flush and nostrils flare. The guy was filling his son's head with crazy ideas, pipe dreams that would never come true. He had to keep his head in reality, not escape it. For the next three hours Eric laid in bed, wide awake. He resolved to go talk to Chief McMurphy as soon as he was in his office and end this thing once and for all.

Even if it meant getting a restraining order.

Chapter 35

John Anakausuen couldn't sleep, either. He'd rolled over to look at the green numbers on the bedside alarm clock, at least two dozen times over the previous four hours. It was to be the biggest day of his life and it was looking increasingly more likely that it would be run on copious amounts of caffeine and adrenaline.

He was sixty miles to the east of Coopers Hollow, in a hotel room in Kingston. The drive up from the city the night before was meant to give him plenty of time for rest and a head start in the morning to meet with the TV and newspaper people. Give them an in-person heads-up about why they needed to be in Coopers Hollow that evening to cover the town council meeting. Press releases just got stacked in the pile with the others. In-person meetings explaining things got attention.

He'd gotten wind of the special session from Pearl Hoffman, one of the town council members. She served as secretary, and was responsible for sending out the notices. She was in her fifties, a widow. She deserved to have a nice diamond bracelet, John had told her three weeks earlier. John knew a guy, he'd said. He always got great deals in the city, he'd elaborated. She had smiled and told him she couldn't afford such a thing. When the package came in the mail, she was thrilled. The note had just said that he hoped she could keep him informed of any upcoming meetings. He was interested in making Coopers Hollow his permanent home, he said. She called him on Thursday to tell him about Monday's special session. He asked if the public would be allowed to speak and whether it would be just on the topics listed on the pre-arranged agenda, or if new business could be introduced. She told him that the bylaws allowed for new business during a special town council session. That was the very purpose of such a session. After he got off the phone with her, he booked his room in Kingston for Sunday night.

Though his room had a little coffee maker, he preferred the properly brewed stuff in the dining room just off the lobby. So at five minutes before five, after giving up on any attempt at sleep, he made his way down to get the good stuff and read the morning paper, if it had arrived.

First he'd visit the television station. There was a reporter there, Kylie was her name, he liked her. Then the newspaper. By the time he was done, he knew that State Assemblywoman Carson Pendergast would be in her office in Albany. He knew she'd take his call. His donation to her campaign had been the maximum allowable, during the last election cycle. As had the donations of twenty-seven other members of the Mahican Tribe. In a private meeting, two weeks previous, he had revealed his proposal to her. She pledged her support, and yes, her daughter was enjoying her new Lexus while at college, in Fairport.

The final call of the day he had to make before driving to Coopers Hollow was to Senator Bucky Schooner. The long-time Senator from New York State was currently in Washington, but was also in full support of Anakausuen's proposal. Schooner was the leading proponent of Native American issues in the United States Senate.

All the big guns were in place. They were all on his side of this thing. In a small town like Coopers Hollow, the local politicians would be easy to push around. There were seven town council members including the Mayor. Anakausuen had hired a private investigation firm out of Albany to perform background checks on each of the individuals so he knew what he was up against.

The report on each member was concise. It didn't tell him much, but he didn't need that much. Pearl was the easiest for him. Widowed three years previous, and the beneficiary of a substantial life insurance policy, Pearl liked the video poker machines at the casino, just off the New York Thruway, east of Utica. She was easy, wouldn't be a problem.

Mayor Elliot Patterson had his own agenda for Coopers Hollow. He was tough to read. At times he seemed completely self-serving, and at other times he seemed to truly have the best interests of the town at heart. Whether he would cause trouble and be an obstacle, or go along with the proceedings was a variable in Anakausuen's equation. But even with a worst-case-scenario, the Mayor's term was almost up. Swaying a local election would not be difficult. Heck, Pearl Hoffman might suddenly get the urge to run for the office.

The other council members were Dennis Ponder, the town pharmacist, Jude Elkland, co-owner of Elkland Brothers Farm Equipment, Heddy McDougal, owner of McDougal Realty, Perry Ponce, who owned a construction company, and Richard Street, owner of the flower shop and storage units in town.

Ponce was a sure thing, as he was guaranteed to get a contract out of the operation. McDougal was a solid sure thing as well, since the operation was certain to bring more people to town and up the value of all the real estate. Ponder and Elkland were variables. Like the Mayor, they could go either way. Street was an old timer, the most likely candidate of the lot to stomp his foot and declare "not in my back yard." But he was old, and Anakausuen doubted he had the energy for the type of fight that would be necessary to stop the plans.

The law and the big-gun politicians were on his side. Sure they could run off and file a lawsuit and get a temporary injunction, but eventually he would win out. He had the will, the support of the right people, and the money to back him up.

The other advantage he had, was he wasn't an outsider, an interloper. This was not a story about a big company or a group of outsiders coming in and changing the small town. It was the story of a local boy returning home after making it big, bearing gifts. That was the narrative. The news people already liked the story. Everything was stacked in his favor.

This was as close to a sure thing as one would ever find. It's why he was able to get the backers to support him with their investments.

He pressed the button for the elevator, newspaper under arm, coffee cup in hand. In the elevator foyer, there was a mirror. Anakausuen caught a glimpse of himself and smiled.

"They're not going to know what hit them," he said to his reflection.

Chapter 36

Jack awoke while it was yet dark outside. Like Eric across town, he did not have a restful sleep, it was filled with stress-dreams and angst. He contemplated rolling over and getting another half-hour of shut-eye, but his mind was racing with all that had happened over the last several days. Sleep became completely unachievable. Instead he reached over for Paula, but his hand dropped onto crumpled bed sheets. She was already up.

Jack made a pitstop at the bathroom before padding, barefoot, out to the living room, where he found Paula typing away at the wireless keyboard, linked to her computer tablet.

"Hey, babe. Whatcha doin?" Jack asked through a yawn. There was a pot of coffee already half drained, so he steered towards the kitchen.

"Writing my next book," Paula said.

"What's it about?"

"When I was writing the first book, I had little bits of research about the first chief of police. You know, Tubby's great-grandfather. Anyway, he was like a total bad-ass gunslinger. Did you know that?" Paula asked, pausing from the keyboard.

"Well, kind of," Jack said. "Dad talked about him a couple of times. About how he pissed off the mob somehow and they came up here from the city, hunting him. Dad used it as a way to talk about always being ready. For anything," Jack said, taking a sip from the mug with the Superman logo on it. "Mmm, coffee's good."

"Well, it's been eating at me. The story. It won't let go," she said. "When I finish this one, maybe I'll do an expose on the video."

"I still haven't decided what to do about that," Jack said. "They'll be back for it, you know."

"Who? The FBI or FDCI or whatever they were?"

"Or worse. You heard Scutter."

"The cat is out of the bag now. The bad guys know, now. They don't need to worry about us anymore," Paula said. "It's going to be subpoenas and arrests, right? We let it blow over, then I can write my next book. Maybe in a few years."

"Can't put the toothpaste back into the tube," Jack said. "You said that."

"Exactly. Can you give me a few more minutes of quiet time. I need to write a couple more pages before I can quit. I'm rolling."

"Sure," he said, sitting in his chair.

The television was on the twenty-four hour news channel, with volume muted. Jack watched the news-crawl at the bottom of the screen with the day's headlines. There was a big storm coming up from the Gulf of Mexico, bringing with it an enormous amount of rain. A few weeks earlier, and it would have been a Nor'easter of biblical proportions. Now there was a good chance they would get some serious rain out of the spring storm. There was a chance of snow in the higher elevations. When they said "higher elevations" they meant places like Coopers Hollow.

"Looks like bad weather ahead," Jack said.

"Shhh," was the reply.

He kept the television muted, but switched it over to ESPN. He thumbed on the closed captioning and continued to sip at his coffee as the previous night's games were recapped.

They stayed like that for nearly a half hour, Jack silently watching the muted television, Paula typing away at the keyboard. He stole glances at her from time to time, but remained silent. Finally, as Sportscenter was about to start a new hour, Jack took his mug to the kitchen and headed back towards a the bathroom to shower and then dress for the day. He paused and looked back at Paula.

He felt something he'd never felt before: contentment.

Less than an hour later he was sliding the key into the lock of the station house. It was another dreary day, it was still very foggy. The forecast predicted the storm could start off as snow, and then change over as the temperatures came up during the day. Or it might all just be rain. It depended on only a few degrees difference. There was a razors edge between inches of rain and feet of snow, this time of year.

He started the coffee maker, an old stainless steel monstrosity which required fifteen minutes to really get rolling. It was a comforting, familiar aroma that swept through the station house, in just a few minutes. It reminded him of better days. Of his father. Of being a boy growing up and thinking that all he ever wanted in life was to be a cop like his dad and his granddad before him.

He forced himself to go and look at the holding cell again. To focus on why he was here and what was on the line every day. He was lost in thought when the front door opened. He spun to face the visitor, trying not to show he'd been caught off guard. But there was no hiding his surprise.

"What are you doing here?" he asked, as he walked towards her.

"Where else am I going to be, boss?" Tricia Wallace walked slowly into the station house. There was a smaller bandage on her head now. Her arm was still in a sling.

"Um, home, resting," Jack said. He walked over and gave her a hug. She hugged him back with her good arm. "You shouldn't be here."

"I can be in pain at home or I can be here with you, trying to find out who did this," she said. "They call that a no-brainer. No?"

"You gave descriptions to the FBI, they're handling this case. We don't really have much say in it," Jack said. He knew who was responsible, at least in a round about way. It was such a convoluted mess that, thinking on it fresh, on a new day, made it seem not only implausible, but down right idiotic.

"Sit down," Jack said pulling out a chair. "Do you want anything? Coffee? Did you get breakfast?"

"I'm fine, boss," she said. "I got a call this morning, I couldn't stay in bed. I had to come talk to you."

"Who called?"

"Gloria."

Jack's heart sank. He bit his bottom lip, unable to ask if Michael was improving, or if he'd passed on.

"He's going to be okay, boss," Tricia said.

"Really?!"

"He woke up, he's talking. He's hurting, but the doctors told Gloria they think he's going to pull through. He's through the toughest part. He's tough as hammers, that one."

"Tough as nails," Jack corrected with a laugh. "He's awake? When did he wake up?"

"Last night. He was awake all night, Gloria told me. He didn't want to sleep. Said he'd done enough sleeping. He wanted to call you, but Gloria wouldn't let him. She said she didn't want him getting worked up or trying to solve this thing while he's still recovering," Tricia said. She was smiling ear to ear, her bright teeth contrasting against her dark skin.

Jack couldn't contain himself. He bent and gave her another hug, careful not to squeeze her injured arm.

"I need to go see him," Jack said.

"Maybe you should give him a day or two with Gloria," Tricia replied. "I don't tell you what to do, chief, but Gloria is still angry at you. Give her some time to be happy that she has him back, and she'll forgive you. I know it."

"You know her that well?"

"She came and sat with me a lot. To talk."

"Well, Paula should go up and make sure they don't need

anything. Butter her up for me," Jack said. He fished his phone from his pocket and dialed Paula. She picked up on the second ring.

"Michael's awake and talking," Jack said.

"Really? Are we going up to visit?"

"Tricia's here, she said Gloria's still angry. Can you drive up and sooth her a bit? I'll go up this evening," Jack said.

"You can't go up tonight, the special council is tonight," Paula said. "I'll go up this morning and make sure Gloria loves you again and we can go back up tomorrow."

"Okay, babe. I love you."

"Love you, too."

Jack went and poured himself a mug of coffee. He poured a second cup for Tricia.

"Cream or sugar in the coffee?"

"Nothing. Thank you, chief."

"Okay, you're going to have to drop the chief thing," Jack said, as he brought the coffee over. "I'm just Jack."

"I can't make any promises," she said.

The door opened again, and Dennis Ponder walked in. He was the round-faced pharmacist whom everyone called Den. He always wore his white pharmacy coat on a work day. This morning he had it on under a long wool coat. It peeked out at the bottom, so Jack knew he was heading in to the pharmacy.

"Morning, Den," Jack said.

"You're in a good mood," Den said in a flat tone. It was delivered as a clinical observation.

"Yeah, we just heard Michael Cooke is awake and the doctors think he's going to pull through," Jack said. "So, yes, I'm in a pretty good mood. That's the best news I've had in awhile."

"Yeah, well, Jack. That's good. That's real good. I wanted to talk to you. Off the record," Den said. He stole a glance out the front windows.

"Off the record? Um, okay Den. Let's go into my office."

"Morning," Den said to Tricia, nodding as he did so. "Good to see you up and about."

"Good morning to you, too," Tricia said. "Thank you."

Jack held his arm up, directing Den into the office. He closed the door behind them and walked over to his desk, to take a seat.

"Den, what's on your mind?"

"It's the special council tonight," Den said. "I got wind what it's all about. I wanted to tell you."

"Okay."

"Jack. Your dad and I, we were friends. I think we were friends. He was there for me when my wife left. He let me talk to him. Anyway. I liked your dad. I trusted him. Liked your grandfather too. Both good guys. So I want to tell you what's going on. They're going to vote you out, Jack. They're going to fire you tonight."

"What?"

"They called the special council to get rid of you and put in the Mayor's brother from the sheriff's department," Den said. "I'm sorry."

"Well they need a unanimous vote for that, Den," Jack said. He let the words hang in the air for several seconds before he spoke again.

"Are they going to have a unanimous vote, Den?"

Den looked at his shoes. His lips quivered, and his hands were shaking.

"I think so, Jack. I'm sorry."

"But you're on the town council, Den. Are you going to go along with this?"

"I - I think so, Jack," he said, quietly. "I'm sorry." It was barely a whisper, but the words punched Jack in the gut, with the force of a freight train. "When the called the meeting last week, I would never have thought I could. But Saturday, watching that man die in the street. It's too much. You understand?"

"Yeah, I understand." Jack McMurphy, Chief of Police of Coopers Hollow, had nothing else to say. His jaw was clenched and his fingers dug into the arms of his chair.

"I've got to go open the pharmacy," Den told him. "I'm sorry, Jack."

Den walked out of his office, and Jack heard him give Tricia a parting greeting.

Jack stared at the wall outside his office door. He saw a crack that he had never noticed before. It traveled down the wall to the chair moulding, which gave way to wainscoting. He was sure the crack had never been there before.

"Boss, um, chief?" Tricia called. "You okay?"

Jack didn't reply. He swallowed hard, fixated on the crack in the painted plaster. The squeak of her shoes on the tiled floors grew louder, until she was blocking his line of sight to the newly discovered imperfection in the wall.

"Chief, what is it? Everything okay?"

"Um, Tricia, I think you can forget about calling me chief any more," Jack said.

"What's that supposed to mean?"

"There's a special town council tonight. Den's one of the council members. He just informed me that the purpose of the special session is to hold a vote to terminate me and bring in Aaron Patterson, the Mayor's brother," Jack said.

"What? Can they do that?"

"Oh, yeah. They can absolutely do it. The vote has to be unanimous to carry, but they can do it."

"And he is voting with them on this?"

"It would appear so," Jack said. "I've known him all my life. Didn't think it could happen."

"But why?"

"I guess people need to feel safe. That's why they move here. It's why they stay here. They want to stay safe. I can't say I blame any of them. Between what happened last fall and the other night, heck, I don't feel safe. It's no wonder they don't," Jack sighed.

"That's just stupid. It doesn't make sense to make a change after a thing like that. I'm going to go and tell them it's a bad idea," she said.

"Don't," he told her. "Don't make trouble for yourself. You've still got a job here for the time being. If I don't put up a fuss and play nice with Patterson, I can maybe make sure he keeps you on, you know?"

"I don't want to stay if you're not the chief, Chief."

"Don't say that. You hardly know me. Patterson's probably a good guy."

She looked him in the eyes. She locked on, and he could see the fire behind them.

"I know you. I'm going to say my piece."

"We'll talk about it some more in a minute. I've got to call Paula."

Paula came straight over as soon as she heard the news. She was still in her pajamas and her hair was up in a nest of a bun. She didn't say a word, just walked up and hugged her man. He squeezed her right back. She kissed him on the mouth.

"I'm proud of you," she said. "More than you'll ever know."

"Thanks, babe."

"Tricia!" Paula exclaimed as she put eyes on the deputy. She rushed over and went in for a hug, but slowed when she saw the arm. "Can I hug you?"

"Just be gentle."

They embraced for a moment, and then Paula stood to address them both.

"Are we going to let this happen?"

"There's nothing we can do," Jack said. "Of all the people I would think would break up the unanimous vote, I would have counted on Den. Street and Elkland will go along with whatever the mayor wants, so as not to rock the boat. McDougal never liked me. She never liked dad either. I never understood it. And who's left? Ponce? He might side with me on this. I've helped him out more than once. Even when dad was around. We caught those kids who kept spray painting the side of those shipping containers on his lot. It's worth a shot there. I'm guessing, though, that if Den came in to tell me what he did this morning, it's a done deal and we won't be able to count on Ponce either."

"The vote hasn't happened yet," Tricia said.

"That's right," Paula said. "I can call each of them and ask for comment. Ask them how they could do this to you. Tell them I'm doing a follow up article on the shootings in the fall. Ask them how they could betray the man who stood between the town and the bad guys, willing to risk his neck-"

"Babe, relax," Jack said. He reached over and pulled her to him. She fought his grip at first, but then settled into his embrace.

"It's not fair," she said.

"I know."

"They're not just turning their backs on you, they're betraying all that your father did for this town," she said. "All your grandfather did. Your entire family kept this town safe for years."

"Things change," Jack said, more for himself. "We'll just deal with it."

"Screw this town," Paula said. "If they take this job, they can have it. You and me, we don't need this job. We can travel. We can go anywhere we want."

"You're right."

"This could be good for us."

"We'll just take it one step at a time," Jack said.

"Okay. I'm going home to get cleaned up. I'm going to go up and see Michael and Gloria. I'm going to tell them," she said.

"Don't get them upset. He's just woken up. He doesn't need the extra stress," Jack told her.

"If we tell him after the fact, he'll shoot you," she said. "And he doesn't miss."

"Just don't get him worked up, okay? Promise me?" Jack asked her, holding her in his arms.

"Okay. I promise I won't purposely get them worked up. Fair enough?"

"Fair enough," Jack agreed. "Please let them know I'll come see them as soon as I can. Maybe you should call ahead to see if Gloria needs anything from the house."

"Okay, I will." Paula went on tiptoes to give him a kiss. Then headed for the door. "Love you, husband."

"Love you too, wife."

Tricia looked at Jack with wide eyes at the revelation.

"You got married?"

"Yeah."

"You went to Las Vegas and got married?"

"That's right."

She just shook her head and sipped at her coffee, not saying another word.

Chapter 37

Agent Haas was playing the part of messenger boy today. Scutter wanted the whole thing done, tight and quiet. This meant Haas was showing his ID to the security detail in the foyer of INEO Broadcasting in Manhattan. Moments later he rode an elevator to the top floor.

The receptionist had an earpiece with mic hooked over her ear. She was typing furiously at a keyboard behind the raised counter. She didn't look up as Haas approached.

"Do you have an appointment?" she asked, not looking at him. He didn't reply. It didn't really sound like a question. It was robotic and monotone.

She stopped typing, let out a sigh and looked up at him.

"Do you have an appointment?"

"No. But Mr. Greenbau is going to see me. Special Agent Haas. I need to speak with him." He showed her his badge and then slid a card across the elevated counter. She reached up and took the card.

"Mr. Greenbau is unavailable," she said. "You'll need to make an appointment."

"Oh, I'll just wait. Please let him know that I'm out here. Also, let him know I'd like to talk about a story the network will be running soon about Jefferson and the tiger," Haas said. "I think he'll want to talk to me."

The receptionist didn't call anyone. She simply returned to her typing. She paused for a moment, then rose from her chair.

"Come with me, Mr. Haas," she said. "Mr. Greenbau has a few moments for you."

"Agent Haas," he corrected.

Haas tried to crane his neck to see her screen as he walked past the desk, following her through the door, but she had a privacy shield blocking the view from his angle.

"This way," she said. Haas didn't mind following her, she was quite shapely. Her hair was pulled up into a severely tight bun, perched atop her small head. She probably looked stunning with it down, he guessed.

They came to a large door at the end of the hallway, and she rapped a knuckle softly on it before opening it and moving aside to let Haas step in.

She closed the door behind him.

"What do you want?" Mr. Greenbau sat in a tall backed chair, with all of Manhattan on display behind him, through the floor-to-ceiling windows. "I'm extremely busy, so get to your point."

"I'd like to talk about Mr. Jefferson and a man called El Tigre and a poor sap named Mongrove. You know the first two people, I'm sure of it. You might not know the third guy by name. He was the sucker who was shot by Jefferson while you looked on, not even blinking," Haas said. "To the point enough for you?"

Greenbau didn't say anything. He tented his fingers under his chin and swiveled his chair to the left, allowing him to look out over the city.

"What do you want? What's your price? I assume you're not here to arrest me, or else there would be a few more agents with you, and probably my rivals' cameras as well."

"I'm here on behalf of the US government, Mr. Greenbau. We just want to make sure that when we ask a favor of you in the future, you want to help us, that's all," Haas said.

"I like being helpful," Greenbau said.

"Very helpful," Haas insisted.

"I like being very helpful," Greenbau said.

"Okay. That's what I needed to hear," Haas said. "I'll pass it along."

"That's it?"

"That's it. Have a nice day, Mr. Greenbau," Agent Haas said. "I'll show myself out."

Scutter sat in a booth at a diner, an hour west of Washington D.C. on Interstate 86. He sipped a cup of coffee as the sun rose in the sky. He looked at his watch, though he knew that it was just five minutes later than the last time he'd looked. In three hours Agent Haas would walk into INEO Broadcasting headquarters in New York City and fire a shot across the bow of Ira Greenbau. The first shot across a bow was happening here, in the rolling hills of Virginia.

Scutter was in the process of creating his ticket back into the big game. Greenbau would be an asset to achieving that goal. Another asset was getting out of the black Cadillac Escalade, in the parking lot, just outside.

Gordon W. Jefferson, voice of the little man, the Great Equalizer, dressed in a pinstriped suit, with bright pink necktie and matching breast pocket kerchief, stepped towards the diner. He opened the door and stood at the threshold, surveying the nearly empty interior. Besides Scutter, there were two truckers on stools at the counter, the lone waitress, and the cook, who could be heard but not seen, in the kitchen. Jefferson sucked in his lips in an immense frown. He was a large man, filling the entire doorway. His physically imposing stature was supplemented with a deep baritone voice.

"Scutter?" Jefferson barked from the doorway. The truckers at the counter turned to see who was making the commotion. Jefferson stared them down until they turned back to their breakfasts.

"Have a seat," Scutter said quietly, indicating the bench across from him. Jefferson marched to the booth, but instead took a chair from one of the tables that sat in the center of the diner, separating the lunch counter and the booths at the windows. Jefferson pulled the chair up to Scutter, seat facing out, effectively trapping Scutter in the bench seat. Jefferson put a leg on each side of the chair and folded his large arms across the chair back as he sat down.

"Speak," Jefferson said. "Why am I here?"

"Because you've been naughty," Scutter said. "And I have a video proving it."

"What is this, a shakedown? Videos can be doctored and edited. Photoshopped. Whatever it is, I didn't do it, and you'll never be able to prove it. Right-wing fanatics will do anything to besmirch my name," he said. "Did you see that video where they made the Greek finance minister flip the bird to the audience? Everyone thought it was real, until that gag TV show, over there in Germany, admitted they'd doctored the thing. Whatever you've got on that video, whatever you think I've done, it's all propaganda. Don't believe everything you see. Anything else?"

"Humor me," Scutter said. "I need to know that you'll play ball with us. We're not here to break up your enterprise. We both need friends."

The men stared at each other for an eternity. Neither flinched.

"Would you like to see the video in question? I can play it for you," Scutter said finally. "Might be educational."

"How many people know about it?" Jefferson asked in a low, barely audible voice, his hand over his mouth, as if he were itching his nose.

"Myself, a few other agents. A technician," Scutter said. "They're not going to say anything. They've got careers. They like their jobs."

"What about any people who might say something?" Large hand, still obscuring his words for anyone more than three feet away. "I have a public reputation to protect. Even from lies and propaganda."

Scutter studied Jefferson for a moment. The dark eyes were intense, and bottomless. It was like looking into an abyss of heartlessness. What Jefferson was asking for, without actually asking for it, was permission to take out the loose ends in exchange for agreeing to work with Scutter, going forward. It was a tough bargain for Scutter. It was hardball. The hardest. High and inside.

"There are two variables. As far as we know, that's it," Scutter said quietly.

"The same two variables that were in Vegas?" Jefferson asked.

Scutter nodded.

"The same two that are back in upstate New York?"

There was a long silence between the men. The ticket Scutter was buying was being paid for in blood. It wasn't the first time.

"The same," he said, finally.

"I'm down several good people on this. I know you've had your losses as well. I'm going to write a phone number on that napkin it's for you, and you alone. You need something from me, and I will see what I can do. Don't abuse that privilege. I never want to hear about some doctored video ever again. Because that's what it is. If you're unclear about who really holds the advantage in this little discussion, please call my friend, the President. I'm sure he would let you know his opinion about this kind of harassment," Jefferson said. He glared at Scutter.

"I don't work for him," Scutter countered.

Jefferson took a pen from the inside breast pocket of his jacket and wrote something on the napkin. He folded it in half and in half again. He tossed it onto the table. Scutter looked at the napkin for a moment. To reach out and take it was to sign the death warrant for two people who had done nothing wrong. They were just in the wrong place at the wrong time. But then again, if they hadn't stuck their noses in, things might be different. But probably not.

This deal needed to be sealed in blood.

Scutter used two fingers to retrieve it.

"We have an understanding?" Jefferson asked.

"We have an understanding," Scutter said.

Jefferson didn't speak another word. He stood and, with one hand, lifted the chair and replaced it at the table. He straightened his tie and smoothed his jacket before marching out the front door, never looking back at Scutter.

Scutter unfolded the napkin and looked at the number. He memorized the digits, then retrieved his lighter. He lit the corner of the napkin and set it on the edge of his plate.

"You can't smoke in here," the waitress called out.

Scutter ignored her until the number had been burned into oblivion. Then he poured a little coffee onto the ashes, effectively extinguishing it.

It might take a month, it might take a year. Whatever the case, he now had his lever and fulcrum. His retirement just got a little bit more comfortable.

Chapter 38

"How is he?" Paula asked as she approached Gloria in the hospital hallway.

"He's raring to go," Gloria said with a tired smile. Paula gave her a big hug, and Gloria reciprocated.

"Can I go see him?"

"They're changing his bandages. I didn't want to see it," Gloria said. "It will take a few more minutes."

"Want to join me for a cup of coffee?"

"I have to grab my purse."

"No, I'm buying."

"You don't have to."

"Stop," Paula said. "It's the least I can do. You've been through hell."

"I'm surviving."

"That's what they need, you know. We need to be strong for them, when they can't be. Without us, they'd crack up," Paula smiled as she took Gloria by the arm and they walked down the hallway towards the elevator.

A short ride to the bottom floor, a few turns, and they were in the cafeteria. It was very nice, for a hospital. It reminded Paula of a Panera Bread, the way it was decorated. A far cry from the institutionalized cafeterias she had experienced at other hospitals.

Even the coffee was good. It looked as if they had it brought in from one of the name brand coffee shops in town.

"We can sit for a bit, before we go up," Paula said.

"Anything new in town?"

"Well, yes. We got some crazy news today," Paula looked out the large windows that opened onto the parking lot. It was beginning to rain.

"Are you going to tell me, or do I have to guess?" Gloria pressed.

"Well, there's a town council meeting tonight. We just found out that the main thing on the agenda is firing Jack as chief of police," Paula said.

"What?!"

"The mayor, his brother works at the sheriff's department. The council is asking for Jack's resignation, and they're going to hire the mayor's brother," Paula explained.

"That's a, well it's got to be a conflict of interest somehow, doesn't it?"

"If the vote is unanimous, there's nothing that can be done."

"When would it take effect?"

"Immediately," Paula said, looking at her coffee. She stirred it, absent-mindedly, just to do something.

"I guess Michael won't feel bad about telling Jack he's not coming back to work, then," Gloria said. Paula let out a laugh.

"I should hope not," Paula said. "You know, Jack is heartbroken over what happened. If he could have, he would have taken those bullets instead of Michael."

"I know, everybody behind the badge is a hero," Gloria said. "You know when it first happened, I wished it was Jack instead of my Michael. I'm sorry."

"It's okay, that's normal."

"But now that he's awake, and they think he's going to pull through, I don't know, it seems like it was meant to be. He saved that girl's life. He saved my life, too," Gloria said. "It's what he does, I guess. To ask him to be anything else would be asking him to not be true to himself."

Paula nodded and sipped her coffee.

"When he goes home, we're going to do everything we can to make your life easier," Paula said. "We've got money. We can help out. Whatever the insurance doesn't cover, we will."

"Thank you," Gloria said. "I think we should go back up. They should be finished now."

They retraced their steps back to Michael's room. The doctor was in, checking the bandages that the nurses had changed. He nodded to the women as they walked in.

"Hey sweetheart," Michael said, his voice still a bit weak. "Hi, Paula."

"Mrs. McMurphy," Paula said, holding up the ring on her finger.

"Are you serious? Congratulations!" Michael said.

"You didn't tell me!" Gloria gushed. "Let me see the ring."

"Well, I guess that clinches it," Michael said. "Now we have to get married."

"What?" Gloria exclaimed, spinning to look at Michael.

"Well I'm not going to let him one up me like that," Cooke smiled.

"Is that the reason?"

"No, that's not the reason," Michael said. "It's because I love you and I can't imagine living another moment without you by my side."

Gloria rushed to his bed to embrace him.

"Take it easy, take it easy," the doctor said. "Don't squeeze him too hard, he might leak."

Gloria kissed Cooke on the mouth, ignoring the breathing tube feeding his nostrils.

"Yes, I'll marry you," she said.

"Okay, good. Everyone's happy," the doctor said. "Sutures look good, bandages look good. We want you to stay a bit longer, maybe another few days, maybe a week. We don't want any clots forming and taking you out. Okay?"

"Okay, doc," Cooke said.

"Any questions?"

"No, sir."

"Okay, enjoy your engagement, you crazy kids," the doctor said, as he walked out of the room. He was probably half Michael's age.

"Well, I just stopped in to see you for a minute," Paula said. "I brought your change of clothes, Gloria. I have it in the car, I forgot to bring it in."

"Okay, I can walk out with you and get it," Gloria said, kissing Michael again. "I'll be right back."

"I'll be here," he said. As the girls walked out the door he called after them, "Make sure you say hello to Jack."

"I will," Paula said.

"It wasn't his fault," Michael continued. "Tell him."

"I will."

The women walked to the elevator again. This time they took it down to the third floor, where the pedestrian bridge to the parking garage was located.

They had to walk up the stairs one level in the garage to get to Paula's car. As they walked out onto the level, Paula noticed that her Mercedes' door was open, and a man was in the driver's seat.

"Excuse me," Paula said.

"Paula. Wait," Gloria said, grabbing at her arm. Paula pulled away and marched towards the car.

"Excuse me, what do you think you're doing?" The man was looking at something around the steering wheel.

"What?" the man said to her. He was dressed in a suit, his tie was loosened. He looked like he was exhausted.

"What are you doing in my car?" Paula demanded.

"Oh, I'm sorry," the man said. "I thought this was mine. They all look the same." He climbed out and straightened his coat.

"Like hell," Paula said.

"I'm sorry," the man repeated. "Listen, my father just died in there. We were in a car accident a few days ago." He indicated his arm in the sling.

"I was kind of on auto pilot," he continued. "I hit the button and the lights blinked, and I thought it was mine." He held up the key fob and pushed the button. The doors locked and the horn honked on Paula's car.

"Oh," Paula said. "That's weird."

"It looks just like mine," he continued. "I couldn't figure out why the button wouldn't start it. I'm an idiot. I'm sorry."

"No, no. I'm sorry," Paula said. "It's been a crazy week. My nerves are a bit frazzled."

"Mine too," the man said. "Again, I'm sorry to have scared you. Mine must be on the next level. Have a good night."

"You too," Paula called after him as he walked up the ramp, looking for his car.

"That was weird," Gloria said.

"I didn't think car alarms could get confused like that any-more," Paula said. "I thought they were paired, or something."

"Well, maybe it's just a one in a million chance," Gloria said.

Paula looked at the steering wheel and down under the dash, to see if she could see anything, but it looked fine to her. She didn't even know what she was looking for.

"Let me get your clothes," Paula said. She reached across to the passenger seat and retrieved the small bag she'd taken from Gloria's house.

"Thank you," Gloria said, hugging her.

"Anything, and I mean anything you need at all, don't think twice about calling. You call me."

"Okay."

"Promise me, Gloria."

"I promise."

"Now go back and get some lovin' from your fianceé."

"Drive safe," Gloria said. She stood and watched as Paula pulled out and drove down the ramp towards the exit. Then she turned and headed back to the pedestrian bridge.

"That was too close," the man said, as he climbed into the van that was parked one level above. He winced as he settled into seat. His arm still hurt from where he'd been shot. It was a through and through, in the meaty part of his right shoulder. It carved a nice groove out of the flesh and bled a river, but missed the bone.

"Way to think on your feet," the other man said. Once upon a time they had introduced themselves as Parks and Parsons to Michael Cooke, in the Coopers Hollow Police Department. The other conspirator, Eaton, hadn't survived the shot through his chest. They'd buried him off a side road as they drove back to New York City, that night. Parsons had some training as a medic, so he tended to Parks' wound as he drove. The bullet that had hit Parsons in the back had impacted his Kevlar vest. He had a nasty bruise, but it was already fading.

"Did you get it in?" Parsons asked.

"Yes," Parks said. "We just have to be within fifty yards to make it work."

"So now what," Parsons asked.

"Now we wait until both of them are in the car together," Parks said.

"So back to the Catskills?"

"Guess so," Parks said. "You drive. I want to sleep." He took a couple of pills from his pocket, tossed them in his mouth and took a drink from a bottle of whiskey. "Don't get pulled over."

"Roger that."

Chapter 39

"You're wearing your blues?"

"Of course," Jack said. He was putting on a clean t-shirt first, his button-up uniform shirt was already pressed and hanging on the door handle. He thought about his Kevlar vest, but decided against it.

"It's going to be rough," Paula said.

"What do you want me to do, run away from it? If this is how it goes down, this is how it goes," he said. "It's part of being a big boy."

"But it's not fair, what they're doing to you."

"Life's not fair. We'll figure something out. Frankly I could use some time off. I feel like I've been going non-stop for the last year. You can work on your next book, I can work on the car. We'll be fine."

She slid into his arms, still half undressed.

"We have some time, right?" she asked, using her seductive voice.

"Not really," he said. "Later. Promise." He bent and kissed her on the mouth. She grabbed his head and held him longer than he intended. He found himself getting lost in the kiss. Then it was too long.

"I gotta go," he said, pulling away. "Later. I promise."

It felt warmer outside than it had the last few days. It was still raining, but it was a warmer rain than previously. The precipitation didn't start as snow, and it didn't look like it was going to change to snow, either. That was fine by him. The winter had been long enough.

He drove through town, crossed the bridge over the headwaters of the Delaware River and parked in front of the police station. As he climbed out of the patrol SUV, he had a notion to walk a block and a half back to the Peachy Keen Diner and get a slice of pie and ice cream or something. He looked down at his midsection, patted his stomach and decided to just brew up some coffee and save the calories for later.

It took a few minutes to brew, but the coffee tasted good and familiar. He put it into his travel mug so he could take it with him to the town hall. As he approached, sipping at the stainless steel mug, he noticed two television vans parked across the street.

He opened the door to the town hall and was hit by the sounds of a dozen conversations, going on all at the same time. It wasn't arguing, it was just talking, loudly.

The council chamber was down the main hallway of the town hall, through a set of double doors to the left. It was basically a medium sized conference room with several tables at one end and about thirty chairs in five rows of six. All around the back of the room, people were standing and talking; either to each other or on cell phones. There were four cameras setup. Not the cheap local news cameras, but the high-dollar, HD cameras that he'd seen the larger news channels bring out, during the shootings, back in the fall. He recognized one of the reporters. She had covered the story on the tiger, back when he'd done the news conference. She was from Binghamton, he thought he remembered. She saw him looking at her, as she spoke on her mobile phone. He nodded a greeting, and she nodded back.

Several of the chairs were already taken by people from around the village. Mrs. Avery attended just about every town meeting. She was quite the busy-body. She used to play piano at the church before they'd switched over to recorded music. Jack walked over to say hello.

"Mrs. Avery, how are you this evening," he said.

"I've been better," she answered. "This weather is killing my arthritis. Is your girlfriend coming?" The way she said girlfriend, it was clear that she either had disdain for Paula or for the relationship itself.

"She should be," Jack said. "And she's my wife. We got married over the weekend."

"Really? I hadn't heard that. Did you have a ceremony here? I usually hear about these things. Was it at the church?"

"No. We decided to elope. We got married in Las Vegas. Neither of us have family still around, so it just seemed right," Jack said.

"Oh, Las Vegas?" The disdain had returned. "Well, I guess people do that," she said.

"They do," Jack answered. "Have a good evening."

"Thank you," she said.

Jack shook hands with a few others in the room. The loan officer from the bank, Ira Gimble, wouldn't look him in the eye, when they spoke. There was a definite tension in the room.

Then John Anakausuen walked in, along with two other men, all dressed in suits. Immediately the news people pulled away from their conversations and headed over to John.

They were asking him a flurry of questions. He just repeated that he'd talk with them after the council meeting. Jack watched the scene with curiosity. He was sure that the special council meeting was about letting him go and hiring a new chief of police. Why else would Den Ponder come talk to him? What John Anakausuen was doing here and why the news people were so interested in him, was a mystery.

"Hey John," Jack said, extending his hand.

"Chief McMurphy. Jack. How are you?"

"Could be better."

"Yeah, well, get ready for tonight, partner," Anakausuen said. "It's going to knock your socks off."

"What are you up to?" Jack asked.

Anakausuen looked at his watch.

"You'll know in about twenty minutes," he said.

Paula came in just as the council members started taking their seats at the front of the room. Several others filed in as well, completely filling the thirty seats, and leaving many to stand.

Jude Elkland adjusted the small microphone in front of him, and looked out at the crowd.

"Packed house tonight," he said. "Let's call the meeting to order and open with the Pledge of Allegiance."

Those who were sitting, stood and recited the same pledge they had all said since grade school. Jack noticed that John Anakausuen stood, but didn't say a word.

"Okay," Elkland said. "As chairman of this council, I called this emergency meeting, to address a pressing issue. Over the last few months, we've had some problems, here in town. I'm sure you'll all recall the loss of both our Chief of Police and the Fire Chief within a week of each other, back in October. Additionally we had drug dealers decide they were going to try to burn the town down and hurt some people while they were at it. Just on Saturday, after we decided to call this meeting, in fact, we've had some of the same people, causing trouble again. Most of us moved here or stayed here in Coopers Hollow for a simple reason: it's a safe place to raise a family. At least it has been. With what's gone on here the last several months, a great many people in town have voiced their concerns to this body over safety.

"I've spoken to each member of the council in private to discuss what our best options are. And we felt that it was necessary to call a meeting to discuss the replacement of Jack McMurphy as our Chief of Police."

The words hung in the air. The room was as silent as it could be, packed with nearly fifty people. Jack began to perspire. He felt it at his neck and under his arms. His hands went cold and clammy, while his ears burned. He knew they had to be a shade of crimson. Paula reached over and squeezed his hand and he squeezed back.

"Though we don't want to make any rash decisions," Elkland continued. "We think a move is necessary. But this is not a dictatorship, this is a closely knit town. We're family here. So we would like to open up this topic to anyone who would like to comment. We would take those comments into consideration as we make our decision. Are there any comments at this time?"

At first, no one said anything. No hands went up. The audience looked around to see if any of the others were going to say anything. Finally, a hand raised.

"Mr. Everett," Elkland said. "You would like to make a comment?"

"Yeah, I have something to say," William Everett stood up, using his cane to help in the maneuver. He had just celebrated his eightieth birthday, and was still very spry for his age. He walked with a cane, but more than one person wondered if he needed it, or if he carried it as more of a weapon. There was more than a few kids, over the years, who had been rapped on the head with that cane. Old man Everett drove a large Lincoln Town Car in the summer, and a Toyota Forerunner in the winter. He still did his own shopping and banking, and even showed up at the Peachy Keen every now and then. He was seemingly as old as the town itself.

"I've been in this town since the first chief of police was appointed. I've seen every one of 'em. Chief McIntyre. I remember him. Long time ago. Back then, we had gangsters coming up here. Rolled up from the big city, or New Jersey. Some of the boys from New Jersey were the worst. Tough guys. They were just as rough and violent as any of these other punks we've seen around here lately. Worse, sometimes. They weren't happy until they got their revenge. Weren't happy until he was dead and in the ground. They dumped him off the pointe. Then they finally went away. When he was dead. The way I see it, young Jack here did something to get them all riled up, and they're not going to quit coming back until he's not here. Dead or otherwise. It's probably for the best, both for him and our town, if he's done as chief. It's just the way of the world. Nobody's fault but the bad guys, just like back then. So, if it's up to you all, putting in a new chief will not only save the town, but maybe Jack. That's all I got to say." He slowly settled back into the metal folding chair, resting both hands on the cane in front of him. Jack looked at him, but the old man wouldn't return his stare.

"Thank you, Mr. Everett," Elkland said. "Any other comments?"

Paula raised her hand. Jack tried to stop her, but she pushed his hand away.

"Okay, uh, Paula. You have something to say?" Elkland said, reluctantly.

"I do. I think you're all forgetting what Jack has lost as well. His father was killed on these streets. Jack could have left, could have given up. But he didn't. He stepped between you and the bad guys. He laid his life on the line to do what's right. If it hadn't been for dumb luck, it could have been Jack in the hospital in Albany, instead of Michael Cooke. You can't blame the good men for the things bad men do. It makes no sense. If anything, we need to give Jack our support, not pull the rug out from under him. I think this decision to make a change, now of all times, is ridiculous. I think it's underhanded, and you should be ashamed of yourselves," Paula said. "His father, and his grandfather both sacrificed their blood, sweat and tears for this town. And Jack has done nothing short of the same. He saved my life. We owe it to him to stand with him."

"Is that all?" Elkland said. He squirmed a bit in his seat, seeming to be at a loss of words for a moment. Finally: "Thank you, Paula, for your comment."

"I'd like to say something," Heddy McDougal said. She was sitting just to the right of Elkland, at the council members' table.

"Go ahead," Elkland said.

"Jack, I want to speak directly to you. This may, very much, seem like we're not thankful for what you and your father and grandfather have done for this town over the years. But nothing could be further from the truth. We know the sacrifice your family has made. And I would like to extend our thanks," she said.

Jack tried to swallow but his mouth was like the Sahara. He wanted to say something, but didn't want his voice to crack. Didn't want to let them see him get emotional about what was going on. So he stayed silent.

"I agree," Mayor Patterson said.

"Me too," Richard Street, the owner of the town flower shop said.

"We just think that with the pressures and challenges that we're now facing," Heddy continued. "It would be better if we had someone in the position of chief of police who had experience at the next level. I think all of us are in agreement that we want you to remain as part of the police force. Of course that would be at the discretion of the new chief, but each of us is prepared to sign a letter of recommendation to have you stay on the force."

"Very well put," Perry Ponce said.

"Thank you, Heddy. Are there any further comments," Elkland asked. No one raised a hand or spoke. "Okay. Let's move on then. It is the recommendation of this council that we ask for the resignation of Jack McMurphy, chief of police, and hire, Aaron Patterson, who is currently serving with the Delaware County Sheriff's Department. I'll need someone to make a motion."

"I move to accept the recommendation of the council," Perry Ponce said.

"Can I have a second?"

"I second the motion," Heddy McDougal said.

"All in favor?" All the council members, except for the Mayor raised their hands.

"Any opposed?" No hands went up.

"I'd like it noted that I abstained from the vote," Mayor Patterson said. "To avoid a conflict of interest."

"We'll make that note," Elkland said. "Okay, I guess that's it. It's six for, none against, and one abstaining vote. That carries as unanimous. Therefore, it is the decision of this council to ask for Chief Jack McMurphy's resignation, effective immediately. Thank you all for coming this evening. I know it's not an easy thing, but -"

Paula clung to Jack's arm. Tears were rolling down her cheeks, and she buried her head in his shoulder. Jack was emotionless. He stared at the council. He wanted to hate them for what they'd done, but he couldn't. He felt heat at his neck, and his ears were ringing slightly. There was a burning of unspent adrenaline in his stomach. He realized he was clenching and unclenching his jaw, and forced himself to stop. He was about to stand and walk out when another voice spoke.

"Excuse me." It was John Anakausuen. "I was told that we would have an opportunity to address other topics this evening."

"Um. Yes. According to the bylaws, we can allow for new business to be addressed to the council," Elkland said. "Could you please state your name for us?"

"John Anakausuen. No middle name. My father and grandfather both lived in this town. Both grew up here. And, as many of you know, I grew up here as well. I'm one of the last living members of the Mahican Indian Tribe, who once called this valley and the surrounding mountains home. When the settlers arrived, my ancestors did not make war. We worked with them, and welcomed them to the land. Ours is not a story of conflict with the white man, but one of cooperation. Over the years, the tribe dwindled, as we were assimilated into the white culture. But nearly two hundred forty years ago, a promise was made. It was a promise to the Mahican tribe by a man who helped settle this area for the white man. His name was Zadock Pratt. He was given the deed to the land just to the south of town, including what we now call Mount Pratt and Hollow Pointe. It was deeded to him by the State of New York. It was taken from the Mahican people by the State of New York without permission. Zadock knew this.

"He was a fair man. He told my ancestors that they were welcome to use his land for whatever purpose they would like. Farming, hunting, even selling craftwork. That tradition continued on for many generations. Some of you old timers may remember my grandfather using the small hut, by the fire tower, up on Mount Pratt, to sell goods to tourists years ago.

"But getting back to Zadock Pratt. When he passed away, his land was left to his descendants, and then to their descendants. Until the family line ended. The land was then given back to the village of Coopers Hollow, and some of the parcels were sold off to private individuals. To the credit of the village, they retained the majority of Mount Pratt and the surrounding area and preserved it. They built a nice picnic area atop the peak and maintained the road up to it. Granted, they also licensed cell phone towers to be placed atop the mountain, and most recently have been talking about putting in a wind farm. That's all well and good, but there is an element of Zadock Pratt's will that needs to be addressed. I have a copy here, and have made copies for each council member," Anakuasuen motioned to one of the men who was with him. The man jumped up and passed copies of the will to each of the council members, as instructed.

Jack looked at Paula who was drying her eyes and trying to take in what was going on.

"What's this about?" she whispered to him.

"No idea," he whispered back.

"I want you to look at section three. Towards the bottom, where it says 'land ownership'," Anakuasen continued. "Do you see it there? Let me read it to you: Should there come a time at some future date, whereupon the lineage of Zadock Pratt should be entirely extinguished, and there be no further descendants who can rightfully trace heritage back to me, be it my will that any and all lands held aside, as described in the attached notation, shall return back to those noble people, the Mahican Indian tribe, who have been a friend to the white man since our arrival, and to the

Pratt family since our settling in this beautiful verdant valley."

A murmur grew in the crowd, and amongst the council members. Phrases like "is this for real" and "is he kidding" popped up more than once.

"In the transactions controlling the land, as described in the notation attached to the will, which transpired over two-plus centuries, a good portion remained as a single parcel and that parcel is now currently under the control of the village of Coopers Hollow. But that control is not ownership. Rather, the language that was used to give the village control over the property was a legal escrow. Should another descendant ever be able to lay claim to the land, the village would surrender its rights to the property to that descendant. What the village was unaware of, was the condition in Zadock Pratt's original will that returned the land to the Mahican tribe, should there be no descendants. That said, I hereby notify the village of Coopers Hollow of my intent to reclaim the area known as Mount Pratt and Hollow Pointe, as well as surrounding acreage for the Mahican tribe and our descendants."

There was silence for a moment. Then everyone in the crowded room began talking at once.

Jack and Paula slipped out the door, no longer the focus of everyone's attention.

"Let's get out of here," Paula said. "Let's drive somewhere. Disappear. Let's go to New York and shack up in a thousand dollar a night hotel room and get drunk on champagne and forget it all. We don't need them. We've got money."

"I still have a duty to turn over the office to the new chief. I'm going to do this the right way," Jack said. "For dad."

"Okay. We give it a few days, then we take off. It doesn't have to be New York. We could go to Disney World," Paula said. "Or a cruise. Anywhere."

"Let's just go home," Jack said. "Have a few drinks and mess around."

"I can do that," she said. "We drove two cars. Should we just leave the department car here? Take the Mercedes home together?"

Officially the SUV he'd purchased belonged to the department. He and Paula had made the donation and had a thank you note for tax purposes. He'd have to turn the keys over in the morning. It was an eventuality.

"I'm going to drive it home. For tonight, I'm still the chief until they swear in the new one. So it's still my vehicle to use. And I'm driving it. If they don't like it, they can come tow it out of the driveway. I'll see you at the house," Jack said. He kissed Paula on the lips and headed up the sidewalk towards the station house.

"This is it," he said, as they sat in the car, watching Jack and Paula standing and talking next to her Mercedes.

"Five dollars says he takes the patrol car," the other said.

"It's an SUV."

"Whatever."

"Five bucks?"

"Yup."

"Okay. Another five says we get them tonight."

They watched as the couple talked. Then Jack kissed Paula and walked toward his police SUV.

"Ha. Ten bucks. Pay up."

"The night's not over yet."

"Make it look like an accident. That's what we were told to do. Now if you want to win your five bucks, we can go cap them in their bed while they sleep, or we can wait until they're both in the car and we can use the device."

Silence fell over the car as they watched the tail lights, of both the SUV and Mercedes, disappear into the distance.

A bill was peeled from a wad and handed across the car. It was accompanied by cursing.

"Let's call it a night."

They started the car and drove out of town towards their hotel in Oneonta.

Jack and Paula were oblivious to the wagering men in the car. They drove the route they'd taken hundreds of times before, almost on autopilot. It was one of those trips where at the end, sitting in his driveway, Jack didn't even remember how he got there.

A misting rain speckled the windshield. It was enough of a drizzle that his view of Paula walking into the house was blurry. He sighed heavily and looked at himself in the rearview. He had tired eyes. For a split second, he swore they belonged to his father.

After a moment's pause, he started gathering all of his personal items out of the vehicle. There wasn't much, really. A few pens, some loose change, a few receipts that weren't department related, a snow brush, a flash light in the console, and a couple of music CDs. It took about fifteen minutes to pull everything together. He could wait to grab his winter boots out of the rear of the vehicle in the morning. He didn't have enough hands at the moment.

Paula had left the front door open a crack for him, so he was able to nudge it all the way open with his knee. Jack dumped the car items on the small table by the door, where he traditionally left his keys. He kicked off his shoes and headed towards the bedroom to strip off his clothes and then take a quick shower before bed. He had just about soaked through his uniform with sweat.

Paula was already in the bedroom, with a bottle of wine and two glasses. She joined her husband in the shower and then in bed. They wore each other out, and slept soundly as the rain grew heavier outside.

Chapter 40

The phone rang at 3 a.m. It startled Jack awake, but he was used to such calls throughout his life; an accident, a domestic dispute, a drunk who was being unruly and wouldn't leave the tavern, or the concerned parents of a teenager who was still out, way past curfew. In a town as small as Coopers Hollow, the phone still rang at three in the morning.

"This is McMurphy," he said. Paula stirred beside him, but remained asleep. He moved from the bedroom into the hallway and eventually the kitchen.

"Jack, this is Ed Gable with the National Weather Service in Albany. Based on the rain in your area, there's a threat of flash flooding. I'm calling you personally, because some depth alarms on a couple of streams have started pinging us here. And, well, you should probably check on them and call me back."

"Um, yeah," Jack said. It was a barrage of words to strike his ear so early, but after a moment of forcing himself to focus on what he'd just heard, the concept was clear. He needed coffee.

"Okay," Jack said, buying himself a moment.

"Sorry again, that it's so early, but well, nature doesn't sleep," Gable said on the line.

"Right. Can you let me know where the pings are, so I can check them out?"

"Well, I can send you the GPS coordinates, want me to text them to you or maybe send you an email?"

"Text them to me, I guess. I'll punch them in on the car GPS," Jack said. The filter was in the machine, the coffee was scooped into place, and the glass pot was poised to accept the water from the faucet.

"Okay," Gable said. "I'll send them now. Get back to us right away. We are poised to go from a watch to a warning here, and we've still got another inch of rain yet to come in the next twenty-four hours. Thanks again."

Jack said goodbye and finished the process of starting the coffee maker. In less than five minutes he was dressed, had splashed cold water on his face to wake up a bit, brushed his teeth, and filled his travel mug with coffee. He kissed Paula on the head, but she didn't move. When she drank more than one glass of wine, he had learned, she slept like the dead.

It was raining steadily outside. In the Catskill Mountains the rain could be nothing more than a mist not much thicker than fog, just enough to make you clean your glasses, or it could be a torrential downpour soaking you in a matter of moments. Right now it was closer to the latter than the former. Big fat raindrops were saturation-bombing the landscape. Even with his rain jacket on, McMurphy felt drenched, in the short run out to the patrol SUV. The wipers were on full speed, but they still had trouble keeping up with the rain. He punched in the first GPS coordinate and hit the button that would give him the closest driving directions. It was less than a mile away from his house, a creek that ran parallel to Brickhouse Road and fed into the headwaters of the Delaware River.

He backed out of the driveway, and headed towards Brickhouse Road. The clouds made it a desperately dark night, and the rain seemed to swallow up any illumination from his headlights. It made just staying on the road a tricky task. He sipped his coffee as he drove at a moderate speed. The noise from the heavy rain on top of the vehicle was borderline deafening. After about three minutes he was as close to the GPS location as a road would take him. Looking out through the rain, he could neither see the stream bank, nor the depth sensor. It was a plastic white box mounted on a stake with two leads heading down into the water. He turned his collar up and exited the SUV, leaving it running with the heater on.

He walked through the flattened grass, that was just now starting to resurrect from the heavy winter snow. Most of the snow was now melted away after the consecutive days of on-again-off-again rain. The temperature was hovering around forty, according to the reading on the console, back in the SUV. The weather report from yesterday had said rain all day, with a high temperature in the mid-forties. Warmer temperatures then they had experienced through the cold winter, but still bone-chillingly cold with the soaking rain and driving wind.

About ten yards from the road, the grass sloped down to the water's edge. The top of the white box with the computer equipment that measured the water pressure, calculated the depth, and fired off a report to the National Weather Service was barely visible above the water's surface. Jack fished his small, but powerful, flashlight from his pocket and spotlighted the box. The water was brown and foaming with ferocity. He shined the beam across the water's surface. Another foot or two and it would be over the banks and causing trouble on the road. He traced the water's edge downstream, about thirty yards, where the main road passed over it. The bridge was still about four feet above the water's surface, but it usually cleared the water by a good eight feet.

It was going to be a long day.

Flash flooding in the mountains was not uncommon. During the melting season, if accompanied by heavy rains, the small streams would often overflow their banks, over-taking some of the roads throughout the area. There were three problem locations around town that were more susceptible. This creek, another like it, but on the other side of the Delaware up stream, and then the very Delaware River itself near where it came out of the man made lake on the north end of town. On two occasions, that he could remember, the lake burped up over its levy and caused a roaring torrent of water to blast down the river. And to call it a river was really a great embellishment. It wasn't much more than a stream itself, but it was the northern-most traceable point of that which would become the great Delaware River. The same one that General Washington had crossed far down stream, centuries earlier. Here, it was usually only a few feet deep, and perhaps twenty feet wide.

He returned to the SUV and thumbed over to Ed Gable's number from his earlier call. After two rings, the line picked up.

"Gable? Chief McMurphy here."

"Flooding?"

"Your box is almost underwater. Flooding the banks is imminent. We may have to shut down some roads in town, if we're really going to get the rain you're predicting."

"Yeah, I think you'll need to. This storm, it's a beast. Bringing up the entire Gulf of Mexico with it, practically. If it was just a few degrees colder, this would have been one of those late season blizzards like back in ninety-three," he said.

"Okay. Well, put out your warnings, we'll get things taken care of here. Thanks for the call," Jack said. The coffee was starting to work, and the brisk walk in the rain was definitely a waker-upper.

"Thanks. And sorry again about the early hour," Gable said. "Nature never sleeps."

There were two more locations to check, but he was hungry, and it still wasn't even three-thirty yet. He figured he could drive home, cook up an egg and some toast and be back out the door in less than a half an hour. Not even the farmers in the community were up milking the cows yet, so the danger to anyone was limited.

He retraced his path on the road, and nosed the SUV back into the driveway. It didn't seem possible, but the rain actually intensified for a moment as he sat there. He thought maybe if he waited for a few seconds it would let up a bit, but seconds stretched into minutes, and he finally gave up the wait and dashed out into the rain, slamming the door behind him.

On the front porch he shook off the water, and caused a nice trail of it to slick back off his head and run right down his neck, past the collar of his shirt to just between his shoulder blades. It gave him a chill and he shuddered. He was inside, jacket and boots stripped off and into the kitchen in a mere moment. The coffee was still hot, and he drained half of the remaining pot into a big mug.

As quietly as he knew how, he retrieved a frying pan and all the elements he would need to create scrambled eggs for himself. Before the first egg was cracked, Paula was up, wrapped in her big robe, her hair a maniacal tangle upon her head. Her eyes weren't really open, as she zombie-walked to the coffee maker.

"What are you doing up?" she asked, in a whisper.

"Got a call from the weather service, flash floods," he said, giving her a peck on the cheek. "They wanted me to go out and confirm."

"So you're going?"

"I already went. I have to get in to the office and start making some more phone calls to the fire department. We may have to setup some road blocks in a few places where the water goes over the road. DOT road crews will need to help too. They're probably already heading this way."

"What? Why? You don't work there anymore," she said.

"I haven't turned in my badge yet," Jack said quietly. "There's a duty that goes with the badge."

"That is such a crock! They turned on you, Jack. You stood up for them, and they stabbed you in the back for it. These people, they don't care about you anymore. Why do you care about them?" She wasn't quite yelling. Not quite. But in the quiet of four in the morning, it sure sounded like yelling.

"You don't understand the responsibility that comes along with this job," Jack said.

"But it's not your job anymore."

"I know."

"Then what are you doing? Let the new guy do it. Let him go out and set up the roadblocks and check for flooding and -"

"There's still a civic responsibility," he responded. "I don't want to fight about this." The eggs were nearly done, so he got a plate, then paused.

"Do you want some?" he asked.

"I'm not hungry," she said. "I'm going back to bed."

"Okay," he took just one plate over to the stove and scooped the eggs onto it with the spatula. Paula exhaled in frustration and stalked back to bed. With the kitchen returned to silence, Jack dug into his eggs.

Ten minutes later, after another cup of coffee, he moved towards the door. He stopped in the living room and looked down the hallway, at the bedroom door. He shifted his weight on his feet, deciding which way to go.

"She's probably already asleep," he said to himself, under his breath. He pulled on his boots, slipped on his overcoat and headed back out into the rain.

She heard the door shut, and was more awake than she had been in days. She was awake and ready for a fight. It frustrated her to no end that he would keep working for people who had rejected him outright. It was foolish, and she hated him looking like a fool. She was angry at him and angry for him at the same time. And it all left her with such a rage of frustration, that she felt like breaking something.

Paula laid in bed and looked at the ceiling. It would still be dark for a few hours, yet. The heavy rain clouds only extended the darkness of the night. It was going to be a miserable, wet and dreary day. The type of day she loved for writing. After brooding for a few more moments, she hopped out of bed, turned on the light and retrieved her laptop bag. Within the bag was the diary of the first chief of police of Coopers Hollow, James McIntyre.

She opened it and began to read it for the hundredth time. After reading for fifteen minutes, she retrieved her own notebook and a pencil and scribbled down some story notes. Though the diary gave an insight into those first years of police work in Coopers Hollow, there were so many gaps, so many jumps in the action, that she really needed someone to help her fill in the white spaces. The only good thing that seemed to come out of the previous night's town hall meeting, was the fact that she now knew someone who was alive during that time and could thresh out some of the stories that she found in the diary.

Today she would go visit William Everett at his house on the mountain, overlooking Coopers Hollow.

Chapter 41

After leaving the house, Jack headed in to the police station. He checked his email notices and the fax machine. There were several warnings that came through from the National Weather Service. Flash flood watches. A notice was rolling off the fax machine as he came in the door, and it upgraded the watch to a warning. That meant flooding was imminent.

There was a map of the town of Coopers Hollow on the wall, with a few hand drawn roads that had been added after the map's publication. There were blue pushpins on several roads where flooding could occur regularly. There was something nagging him in the back of his mind, something pertinent to what was going on with the flooding, but he couldn't remember.

The clock said it was approaching five in the morning, which meant that most of the town wouldn't be up for another hour or so, and traffic wouldn't really pick up for about two more hours, as people headed out for their jobs. There wasn't really a rush hour in Coopers Hollow. Just a few cars deeper at the traffic light a few times a day. The big furniture mill, in the center of town, expected workers to punch in by seven. Then there was a company that made components and handsets for radios in the railroad and oil industries. They wanted their workers there at eight. The banks, pharmacies and other stores in town would open around nine. It meant steady, but not heavy traffic, from about a quarter-to-seven, until ten or so. Then it died down until just after eleven when the mill would let out for lunch. The lunch hour was busy in town, as people ran out to the restaurants, or the grocery store, or the Stewart's Shop convenience store, on the corner by the light. Then it died down around two o'clock again and wouldn't pick back up until three-thirty, when workers started heading home.

All of that meant, he had some time to get out and check the problem areas for flooding, before there would be traffic snarls. He contemplated calling Aaron Patterson, the new chief. The thought just made him angry. He called fire chief, Goldie Bristol, instead.

"Hello?" the voice was tired.

"Goldie? It's Jack."

"Oh, hey beautiful," she said, dryly. "How are you holding up? I wasn't there, but one of the guys filled me in. It sucks."

"Yeah, I'm doing okay," he said. "It is what it is, right?"

"I guess," she said. "Says more about this town than it does about you, Jack. You know that, right?"

"Sure," he said. "Listen, we've got a flood warning for the county. I was wondering if you or some of the fire department could check a few areas to make sure there's no water going across the road."

"Yeah, I can," she said. "Let me get out of bed and get going. Want to know what I'm wearing?"

"Maybe I'll yell sexual harassment and sue the town," Jack said with a laugh.

"If I'm going to get in trouble for harassment, I better make it worth my while," she said.

"Easy, Goldie."

"Okay, where do you need me to go?" She asked. He gave her three locations that flooded regularly, and she confirmed their locations.

"I'll go check on them," she said. "Getting dressed and heading out." Jack heard the flush of a toilet in the background.

"Were you going to the bathroom with me on the phone?"

"A girl has to get her thrills somehow," she said. "Talk to you in an hour or so."

She ended the call before he could respond. He imagined that the flirting was harmless. It felt nice to have someone flirt a bit, even when she knew that he was a married man. He would never cheat on his Paula, not with Goldie, not with anyone. He wasn't that kind of guy. It didn't mean that he didn't have a bit more color in his cheeks from the conversation.

He next called Patrolman Ballard. He'd agreed to stay on for a bit longer, but it didn't mean he would be happy to get a phone call at just after five in the morning.

"Hank? It's Jack."

"Hey Chief. What's up?"

"We have a flood warning in town. Are you at your apartment, or are you south?" Jack heard Ballard say something to someone in the background, and then some rustling of blankets.

"Okay, Chief, uh, I'm south of town a bit," Ballard said quietly. "It will take me about forty-five minutes, but I'm on my way."

"Thanks, Ballard," Jack said.

"Listen, this whole thing with the town," Ballard said. "It sucks."

"You're the second person to tell me that this morning. I appreciate that," Jack said.

"I'm kind of glad I won't be there for the new guy," Ballard said. "I don't know if I'm up for training another chief, all over again."

Jack laughed and said, "See you soon."

The next phone call was to Tricia Wallace.

"Good morning, it's Jack."

"Hi, Chief," she said. She didn't sound tired at all. She sounded as if she'd been awake for hours.

"Did I wake you?"

"No, I couldn't sleep. I don't know if I want to work in Coopers Hollow any more," she said.

"Why?"

"You're a good man. A good chief. They are just throwing you away," she said. Then she was quiet. Jack could sense that something was on her mind.

"What is it?" he asked.

"Do you think it's because you hired me?" she asked. "Because I'm black?"

"No, I don't think so," he said. But realistically, he hadn't even thought about that. He'd grown up in a family that didn't have a tendency toward racism. In fact, his father had preached often about the equality of all men. But the small town had its pockets of racists. Mostly they were the uneducated and poorer families in town, who used racism as a way to put themselves above someone else in society.

"Okay. I'd just hate it if it was my fault," she said.

"No, this whole thing has been going on since before my father passed away," Jack said. "It's small town politics. The mayor is the brother of the new chief. Dad warned me about it."

"Oh, I see," she said. "So why are you calling my phone at five in the morning?"

"We have a flood warning this morning," he said. "Do you feel up to doing a few drive-bys and checking on some of the roads in town? I already have Goldie from the fire department taking a look. Ballard will be up in about an hour. But if you're available, well, I could use the help."

"This your last day?"

"As chief? I think officially yesterday was. But Patterson hasn't shown up yet, so until all of that happens, I guess I'm still chief. Who knows if he'll keep me on or not."

"Okay, chief. I'll slip into uniform and see you in fifteen minutes," Tricia said.

"Thanks, I really appreciate it," Jack said.

"Anything for you, Chief."

With that, there wasn't much else for him to do, except clean out his desk and get ready to turn over his keys to the new chief. He went down into the basement and retrieved a couple of the flat cardboard file boxes they used to store documents. There was a whole stack of them, so he figured no one would miss a few if he used them to clean out his personal effects from his desk. He had been on the fence about staying on as maybe deputy chief, but the conversation with Paula, that morning, had pushed him away from the idea. As he gazed around the office, he realized that today was going to be his last day as a police officer. There was a measure of satisfaction and sadness accompanying the thought. Bittersweet.

The front door opened, and Jack saw Aaron Patterson shaking off the rain from his overcoat. Patterson locked eyes with Jack and gave him a nod.

"McMurphy," he said. No good morning, no other form of pleasantry. Just an acknowledgement of existence. The few times that he had interacted with Patterson in the past, he hadn't liked the man. He liked him even less now that he was taking his job.

"Patterson," Jack acknowledged. "Just cleaning out the desk."

This elicited a grunt from Patterson, as he stripped off his coat and hung it on the old rack by the door. He didn't have a hair on his head longer than a quarter inch. He thought it took away from the fact that he was balding. The "Bruce Willis" look, Patterson called it. He had a little bit more weight to his face than the actor, and it made him look thicker through the jowls. Without hair, the top of his head looked like an eraser, bright and pink.

Patterson was about Jack's height, but out-weighed him by at least seventy-five pounds, if not a clean hundred. Everything about the man was thick. His head, his neck, his chest, his gut, his hands, even his fingers. They looked like thick, pink cigars jutting out from large hamburger patties. He smelled of cigarettes as well. How the town could possibly think that Patterson was a more fit candidate for chief of police than he, boggled the mind.

"You going to stay on?" Patterson asked as he moved towards the back of the station house.

"Not sure yet," Jack said. Patterson grunted again.

"Is the can back here?"

"End of the hall, on the right," Jack said.

"Too much coffee," Patterson said, as if an explanation was needed as to why he had to urinate as soon as he got in the door.

Jack set down the first box and then the second, on the desk that Michael Cooke had occupied, during his short stint with the Coopers Hollow Police Department. After a few minutes Patterson returned to the main office area.

"So, you cleaned out?"

"Yeah. It's all yours," Jack said.

"Flash flood warning this morning," Patterson stated.

"Yeah. I've got Ballard coming up for the morning to help out," Jack said. "Tricia Wallace, the new patrolman is coming in as well. I already called up Goldie Bristol over at the fire department. They're going to go out and check on a few problem areas. I have them marked on the map here."

"Okay, thanks," Patterson said. "I guess that's it, then. You staying on or going?"

Jack hesitated for a moment. He thought about Paula, he thought about his father and grandfather. He imagined his life working for this buffoon and then the one that he could hardly imagine, traveling around the country or the world with Paula.

"Going," Jack said. He dropped the keys on the desk.

Chapter 42

Paula went about her morning routine. The ingredients for a perfect day involved a shower, lotion, fixing her hair, applying a little makeup, mixing in some coffee, yogurt and fruit. Before long, she was ready to face the world. It was half-past eight when she headed out the door. Nearly four and a half hours since Jack had left.

She had her notebook as well as the diary from Old Chief MacIntyre. It would be a guide for Mr. Everett, helping him with specific dates. A blueprint, if you will, that would help guide the conversation. In her past experiences with interviewing someone in their golden years, she found they often remembered four decades ago more clearly than four days ago. She hoped that was the case here. Maybe it was too early to call on William Everett, maybe it wasn't. She knew some older folks got up at the crack of dawn and were already well on their way with the day, by eight in the morning. This was, after all, a community of farmers. Life started early in rural towns. Nothing to keep people out late at night in a small town like Coopers Hollow. And the cows needed milking early in the morning. Old habits die hard.

The rain was heavy, it didn't let up any less than a steady downpour. She prepared for it with her boots, her long, waterproof jacket, her brimmed hat, and an umbrella. She zipped her notebooks securely into her satchel, and folded over the large flap, protecting the contents from the elements. She took her phone and considered texting Jack, then decided no. Then she thought about driving through town to find him, but realized she was still mad at him for being so naive.

When nobody wants you, and they make that fact abundantly

clear, you just appear like a fool, if you tried to stick around. Like the kid at a junior high dance, that nobody wanted there.

As she backed out of the driveway she thought about it more. The unwanted kid in her junior high dance had ended up going on to make some pretty big money. Did that sense of rejection push a person harder? She wasn't the most popular kid in her school, but on the scale of popularity, she was at the top end, rather than the bottom. There were the gaggle of girls who were very exclusionary and who had all ended up going to college and getting rich husbands almost twice their age, none of whom probably loved them. The smart kids with the social skills seemed to be the real leaders of her class, and she fit in with them. They were involved in drama club, worked on the yearbook, wrote for the school paper, which eventually became the school website, and participated in some of the sports like basketball or volleyball, but steered clear of the baseball, football and softball teams.

It helped that she was one of the wealthier students. She didn't have to deal with the stigma of being a couldn't-afford. If there was a school dance, she had the new dress, if there was a school excursion, she had the money and the new backpack or skis or sunglasses and cute bikini. Upon a moment's reflection, she had to admit, she had led a privileged childhood and adolescence. When she'd driven up to this small town on a whim, with her, then, boyfriend, had spotted the old hotel, she thought she knew exactly how life was going to go. At eighteen years old she figured she was one of the smart few who would forego college and go right into making money. The next newspaper mogul. Then her boyfriend spent all the dot com start up money on frivolous things, including drugs, and her mom decided that taking a bottle of pills with a bottle of wine was far better than enduring the shame of having to work every day, again. The family fortune had been gobbled up by a Ponzi scheme that ensnared some of the more notable rich and famous in the New York City area.

Paula made her own way. The paper thrived for several years, and then she found herself ousted by a bad business deal, one that gave control of the paper over to the outfit in Kingston, NY.

That was a hard pill to swallow. And then she had fallen in love with Jack McMurphy. The small town cop who got himself in way over his head with criminals from the big city, but managed to survive nonetheless. The man who was dedicated, who cared about people, who would never give up. Never.

She wouldn't stay mad at him. How could she stay angry with him for displaying the very nature that had attracted her to him, in the first place?

Before she realized it, she was pulling into the long driveway that snaked up the mountain to William Everett's home. The rain had made it a muddy affair, but the crushed stone provided plenty of traction. Her new Mercedes, with the all-wheel-drive, climbed the hill with little effort, the eight cylinders easily mustering the horsepower. As she drove up to the house, which was situated upon a relatively flat area, not quite on the mountain's peak, everything looked quiet and lifeless. There were no cars present, but the two-stall garage, more than likely, contained Mr. Everett's vehicles. Maybe eight-thirty was too early after all.

Paula parked the car and waited for a moment to see if the rain would subside a bit. It didn't. She grabbed her satchel and dashed for the door, which was under cover, fortunately.

The house wasn't extravagant, though it was obvious that someone with money lived there. It was a large ranch style home, of the popular design from the late sixties and seventies, in upstate New York. It had large picture windows in the front, a recessed front porch with stone facia and patio. The garage was a single-doored two-stall affair, with about ten feet of concrete leading in from the stone driveway. The stone facia of the front porch gave way to vinyl siding that looked newly installed. The roof looked new as well. Mr. Everett had money. Old money, as people in town would say. He owned quite a bit of the land around town.

He had bought and sold property over the years, buying low and selling high. He had no offspring and had never been married, so whatever wealth he'd accumulated, he'd kept. The front door was solid wood, painted red. There was no doorbell, so she knocked hard on the wooden door and then let the storm door hiss shut on its pneumatic closer.

At first there was nothing. No answer, no movement, no life at all.

"Well, I guess I'm either too early, or too late," Paula said to herself. She thought about going over to the garage and looking in the window to see if there was a vehicle. She turned to walk down the steps when the door opened.

"Can I help you?" It was a young man, maybe in his early twenties.

"Um, yeah, I hope so," Paula said. She wasn't expecting a young man who wasn't wearing a shirt and looked like he'd just thrown on his blue jeans. He was fairly good looking, a bit on the skinny side.

"If it's religion stuff, we're not interested," he said.

"Oh, no. Nothing like that," she said. "My name is Paula Sch- McMurphy. Paula McMurphy. I'm a writer, and I'm working on a book about the first Chief of Police here in Coopers Hollow. Last night Mr. Everett talked about remembering some stuff about the him. Um, he said so, at least, when he was at the town council meeting. The old chief's name was MacIntyre. Anyway, I was wondering if Mr. Everett was available to talk with me. There isn't much info on the chief from back then. He might be the only person that can help me connect some of the dots."

The young man seemed like he had no idea what to do. He looked over his shoulder, then back at Paula and just let out an "uhhhh."

"Maybe I could step in for a moment and if Mr. Everett has another time that's better, I could come back," she said. "Can I come in?"

She knew that it was much harder to say no to a person who was already inside, rather than someone who was on the doorstep.

"Okay," the young man said. "I'll have to go check on him.

See if he's up and stuff." He opened the wooden door further and let her in. The living room and library stretched from the front of the house to the back, with a fireplace in the corner. Hardwood floors ran throughout, polished to a shine. There was a wall of shelved books that ran all the way to the rear of the house, and a hallway which cut through the wall of books. Off to the right was the enormous kitchen, which probably had a door out into the garage. Many of these ranch style houses had similar floorpans. The bedrooms and bathrooms were down the hallway to the left, the kitchen to the right, the main living space conveniently in the middle. But this house was larger than it looked from the outside. The back side of the kitchen had been extended, and the ceilings in the living room and library were vaulted, making the rooms feel cavernous.

The young, shirtless man, padded barefoot on the hardwood floor, towards the hallway.

"I guess, make yourself comfortable," he said. "I'll check on Billy, um, Mr. Everett."

"Okay, thanks." She looked at the leather chairs and couch with the area rug in the center of the living room. A soft blanket and a t-shirt were on the couch. The big screen television had the volume on mute and the closed captioning was on.

She heard the young man's voice, not his words, just the fact that he was talking with someone in the back rooms of the house. She had a sudden, uneasy feeling about being there. She continued to look around the room. There were bronze sculptures of cowboys on horseback that stood nearly three feet high. Similar sculptures accented the bookshelf.

The enormous shelving was filled with hardcover and paperback books from numerous authors. Then there was a section of books that looked like they were not mainstream, but maybe something expensive. They were leather-bound, with a metal label holder on each spine. There were maybe twenty or thirty of them. Each had a small slip of paper slid into the holder. Some had names, others just letters from the alphabet. She slid out the M volume. It was heavy, nearly two inches thick. It was more the size of a photo album than a regular book.

She gently opened the pages, and was surprised to see that it had been a blank book once upon a time, but had been filled with freehand writing. Was old man Everett a writer?

Paula started reading a random page, and didn't quite understand what she was looking at. She flipped over a few pages and read some more. And the feeling of uneasiness changed into one of cold, abject horror.

She heard footsteps returning down the hall. She quickly shoved the book back in place just before the young man came back into the room.

"I'm sorry," he said. He had the sense that she was suddenly nervous, and he looked over at the bookshelf, and she knew he saw the book that was pushed in slightly more than the others. "Mr. Everett isn't able to talk with you today." His demeanor changed from pleasant to suspicious.

"What was it you said you wanted again?" he asked, moving towards her. He was tall and thin. His eyes, now that she really looked at them, seemed hollow and unkind. He'd gone from being a good looking young man to having a menacing aura in a moment. He reminded her of an evil scarecrow, disheveled hair, hollow eyes, narrow frame with pants too big for him. He clutched at his jeans with one hand, preventing them from sliding down too far. She saw he had a tattoo on his left forearm, but couldn't tell what it was.

"I'm doing a story on old Chief MacIntyre, that's all. Is there another day that would be better?"

"I don't think so," he said.

"Maybe I can get your number so I can call ahead next time."

"I don't think Mr. Everett wants to talk to you about anything," he said. "He asked me to show you out."

"Okay, and what was your name again?"

"Barry," he said.

"And what do you do for Mr. Everett?"

"Gardner," he said. "Anything else?"

"I guess not," Paula said. She backed towards the door. "Thanks for your help."

He didn't say another word, just watched her open the door to leave, and then closed it firmly behind her. She realized her hands were shaking when she got back behind the wheel of the car.

She had to talk to Jack right now.

Chapter 43

In his dream, she was still alive, and young, and healthy, like when they had first gotten married. There, she was amazing. Laughing. Happy. Perfect. She was the love of his life.

And then he awoke to the empty bedroom, and reality sank in. There, in the darkness, before the kids were awake and getting ready for school, he felt horribly, hopelessly empty and alone.

One day at a time, one hour at a time, one minute at a time. Just breathe. He looked at his alarm clock and tried to count the seconds in the minute. He got to about sixty-five before the clock ticked to the next minute. That's how it felt. Every minute took longer to live. Every moment seemed an eternity and a struggle.

At five o'clock, he decided to get out of bed and make some coffee and cook breakfast for the kids. He found that, with Sylvia falling ill for awhile, he had been unwittingly prepared for life as the single dad. He was now responsible for all the meals, unless they went to eat at his mother's house. It had only been a few days, but it already felt like an eternity.

Eric Owens kicked off the covers and pulled his knees up to his chest, stretching his back. He hated this bed. It was far too soft for his liking, and made his back hurt in the morning. The closest mattress store was in Oneonta, so it was going to cost an extra seventy-five dollars for delivery. With the money they had from Sylvia's life insurance, he had plenty, but it irked him to pay extra for delivery. The bed had been for Sylvia, she liked it soft. Now that she was gone it didn't matter. He'd get something he liked. Whether it would be a queen or king or maybe just a full size, he wasn't sure yet. Maybe it would be one of those adjustable beds that he could prop up, so as to watch the late baseball games in bed, or turn on the massage.

After a few more stretches on his feet, he dropped to the floor and did ten push-ups. His shoulders burned a bit, but it made him feel alive. Sleep had been elusive since Sylvia had died. The doctor prescribed a sleeping pill, but he hated how he felt groggy in the morning, so he just tried to get to bed a bit earlier. He'd put the kids to bed, then retire himself. Sometimes with a book, sometimes to watch television. The doctor had also suggested more physical activity. He was contemplating building a garden in the back yard in the spring. It would be one of those activities he could do with the kids. He remembered helping his own mother in the garden when he was very young, and now he cherished those memories.

He found himself trying to think of ways to not hurt inside. Distractions, projects, baseball games, whatever. He would do okay during the day, but at night was a different story. And it had only been a few days.

The house was chilly, so he pulled on his robe and headed down stairs in his bare feet to start breakfast. It was approaching six o'clock now. He'd snoozed in bed for longer than he'd thought. The kids had to be in school by seven-fifty, so they had some time to sleep yet. As he put his foot on the second to last step, his foot just slipped on the carpet and shot out in front of him. His hand was on the railing, but he didn't have a strong enough grip to prevent himself from crashing down onto his tailbone. The impact shook the house and he let out a howl of pain.

His other foot had remained on the step and bent awkwardly, twisting and inevitably spraining his ankle. His momentum carried him down to the bottom of the steps and deposited him in a pile on the landing. He groaned loudly, and slowly began moving his body to see if anything was truly broken. His ankle hurt, but he could still move it. His tailbone definitely felt broken. It had sounded like someone cracking their knuckles when he hit the edge of the step, and it brought on a quick waive of nausea.

After a few breaths, he stood up, treating his right ankle gingerly. Riker was at the top of the steps.

"Are you okay, dad?" he asked as he rubbed his eyes. He was

now seven, nearly eight. He still looked young, though, the shortest in his class. His pediatrician had blamed it on the fact that he had pretty much stopped eating for three months after his sister, Yasmine, had tried to kill herself. His appetite had eventually returned, but by that time his body had already adjusted. He was never going to be as tall as Eric was.

"I slipped and fell down the steps," Eric said, through clenched teeth, still stretching to make sure there weren't any other injuries besides his ankle and tailbone.

"Did you get hurt?"

"I twisted my ankle and I think I hurt my tailbone," Eric said. He took a step on his hurt ankle, and red hot pain shot through it. He braced one hand against the wall, then the back of the chair. He made it to the couch, and lowered himself down, gently. When his rump hit the cushion, he let out another gasp of pain. His tailbone screamed in agony when his full weight rested on it.

Riker came down the stairs, skipping the last two with a jump. He came over and sat on the couch next to his father.

"Can we watch cartoons?" Riker asked.

"Sure."

His son was back up on his feet, retrieving the remote from the coffee table that Sylvia just had to have, but that Eric had hated from the moment he saw it. When Eric was a kid, you got cartoons on Saturday mornings and sometimes after school. These days, they were on twenty-four-seven. It also seemed that they were the most obnoxious and noisy creations ever made. No more Bugs Bunny or Mickey Mouse. Now they were jabbering squirrels and boys with magical dogs. And there were always vampires. Eric leaned his head back and closed his eyes, trying to wish away the pain.

"Can you go get an ice pack and a paper towel out of the kitchen, buddy? I need to ice my ankle."

Riker was up and in the kitchen and back with the items in less than thirty seconds. Eric lifted his foot and put it on the coffee table and then balanced the ice pack on his ankle with the paper towel between them to take the bite away from the cold. They sat like that for nearly an hour.

"Crap. We need to get you guys to school," Eric said. "Go wake up your sister, then get some breakfast. I was going to cook, but I can hardly walk now."

Riker jetted off the couch and Eric could hear him head to his sister's room. He heard Yasmine yell at him. She was not a morning person. Her wrath knew no bounds, if you were the one who woke her. The yelling followed Riker as he ran back down the stairs, through the living room and into the kitchen. The sounds of drawers and cupboards and spoons hitting bowls and cereal going into bowls echoed from the other room. Eric stood, but it seemed that his ankle hurt even worse than when he'd first put the ice on it. It was swollen, but wasn't purple. He didn't think it was broken, just badly sprained. He had bandages upstairs in the bathroom, but getting up the stairs, wrapping the ankle, getting dressed and then driving the kids to school seemed like it was a Herculean task.

Jasmine came down the stairs, hair hanging down in her face, a blanket around her shoulders. She flopped onto the couch and curled up under the blanket.

"You need to get ready for school," Eric said. "I meant to get you up earlier, but I fell down the stairs and hurt my ankle."

"I heard," Yasmine said. She said it with a level of disgust, as if he had fallen down the stairs just to wake her up and annoy her. "I'm not going to school today."

"Why not?" Eric asked.

"I started my period. I'm cramping." She said it with such authority, it was as if he had no say in the matter. "Besides, I have to look after you." Her demeanor softened as she looked at his swollen ankle.

"I still have to take Riker," Eric said.

"I can ride my bike!" Riker called from the kitchen.

"It's raining outside," Eric said.

"I can wear my poncho," Riker said. "I like the rain."

"You'll be soaked all day," Eric argued. "I'll drive you."

"Dad, you need to rest up," Riker was standing in the entryway to the kitchen, leaning against the wall. He sounded like he was really concerned, not just trying to get away with riding his bike in the rain. "It will take me like three minutes to get to school on my bike. I'll be fine. You should go back to bed and put your ankle up. Remember when I hurt my ankle, I had to stay in bed all day with it up on the pillows? Mom made me do it. Well mom's not here to tell you to do it, so we have to."

Eric wanted to reply, but he couldn't. His throat closed up, and his eyes began to water. He didn't want to cry, he didn't want to sob like a baby in front of the kids, so he didn't say anything. He willed the tears to suck back into his eyeballs. The bright colors of the cartoons seemed to help. There was some vampire girl shooting rainbows out of her hands at the boy and his stretchy dog. Finally, Eric let out a cleansing sigh.

"Okay, you can ride your bike," he said. "And you can stay home, but you have to help me get back upstairs to bed."

"Okay!" the kids said in unison.

"And you have to make me lunch, Yasmine," he added.

"I will. I'll make you a good lunch and bring it up on a tray, like mom used to do when we were sick," she said.

Riker ran through the living room and up the stairs. He hurriedly got dressed, brushed his teeth, and ran a comb through his hair, though it did little good. His hair had grown quite unruly over the last year or so. Sylvia didn't want to cut it. She said she liked how he looked with it a bit longer. It was yet another thing that Eric had just not had the energy to argue about, at least not towards the end.

"Did you eat breakfast?" Yasmine asked.

"I never made it to the kitchen," Eric replied, stretching for the remote, but wincing in pain from his tailbone. Yasmine grabbed it, turned it to ESPN, then handed it to him.

"I'll make you breakfast," she said. Her grumpy attitude had miraculously disappeared as soon as she knew she didn't have to go to school. Eric was going to say something, but decided to just let it go. It was kind of nice to get attention from the kids like this.

"Bye dad!" Riker said as he headed towards the door.

"Wait a second! Come give me a hug," Eric called. Riker came in with his backpack, on under the big, yellow, plastic rain poncho they'd gotten at Disney World the year before. He looked like the Hunchback of Notre Dame, and Eric told him so. They had a laugh over it, and Riker hugged his father. He looked at the clock. It was a quarter to eight.

Riker was out the door with a bang. Eric could see his son ride out the driveway to the road, poncho tucked under his bottom so the back tire wouldn't spray up his back.

The house was quiet for a few minutes, save for the hosts on ESPN talking about the upcoming NFL draft. Who would be the top picks this year? They argued the topic as if their lives depended on it.

A few minutes later, Jasmine brought a plate with bacon and eggs. She carried a glass of juice and a fork in the other hand. She set them on the coffee table.

"I got some of the shell in the eggs. I think I got it all out, but be careful," she said. "Sorry."

"It's okay, sweetie. Thank you."

He leaned forward to take a bite of the eggs. As he brought them to his mouth, there was an enormous rumbling noise coming from somewhere outside. He could feel it in his hurt ankle and in his tailbone. The house was vibrating and the rumble was growing.

"What is that?" Yasmine asked. At first Eric didn't know. A garbage truck with a full load? A huge explosion? It didn't match up.

Then he realized. His brain put all the data together, and his stomach dropped.

"Oh my God," he said.

Chapter 44

Jack handed over his badge, and left his gun belt on the desk. He also removed, from his keyring, the keys to the front door and to the SUV parked out front. He handed them to Patterson, who snatched them away and tossed them into the top desk drawer.

"I'm going to leave the boxes and my gun here for now," Jack said. "I'm going to go get some coffee at the Peachy Keen, then come back with Paula to pick it up."

"Fine by me," Patterson said. "I may call you if I need help with anything. I hope that's okay." Jack wasn't okay with it. He wanted to watch Patterson twist in the wind, while hanging by the neck, until he was dead, dead, dead. But he wasn't going to say that.

"Fine by me," Jack echoed as he headed out the door, pulling his collar up against the rain. Then he paused.

Patterson didn't say anything, he just nodded and grunted. Always nice when people make a tough situation even tougher.

The Peachy Keen was only a few blocks across town, but in the rain, it seemed like an eternity. The walk took him across the bridge over the headwaters of the Delaware River. He looked down at the churning brown waters that were just a few feet from cresting the banks. It looked like it wasn't done rising. If the rain didn't stop, there might be some serious flooding right through town.

A few minutes later, Jack was inside the restaurant, removing his wet jacket. He ran his hand through his wet hair, wiping the wetness on his pant leg. Seemo was behind the counter, back to the door, arms crossed, watching the small flat screen television, that was attached to the wall. He cast a look over his shoulder then returned to watching the TV.

"What you like, chief? Eggs? Bacon?" Seemo said.

"Just coffee to start," Jack replied. "And you'll have to start calling me Jack, I guess."

"You guess? Why you guess?" Seemo asked.

"I'm not the chief anymore. They voted last night."

"Then who's the chief?" Seemo turned to look at Jack, hands now resting on the counter.

"They voted in the mayor's brother. He was with the sheriff's department. Aaron Patterson is now the new Chief of Police for Coopers Hollow," Jack had a catch in his throat, but he played it off as a cough. "How about that coffee?"

"Coming right up, chief."

"Seemo, come on."

"Listen, when the President is done being President, they still call him Mister President, no? So just because you're not chief, doesn't mean I stop calling you chief," he said as he poured steaming blackness into a mug. "And today, the chief eats breakfast on me. So order already."

Jack smiled and sipped his coffee.

"Alright, French Toast with bacon and two eggs."

"Yikes! Maybe I should just shut my big mouth and call you Jack, huh?"

Jack laughed.

"Okay! French Toast, bacon and two eggs, coming up! Scrambled or what?"

"Yeah, scrambled is fine," Jack replied. Seemo headed off to the kitchen, leaving Jack with his coffee and the news. He grew bored and found himself gazing back out the front door watching the rain come down. It seemed to lighten in intensity a bit, though it remained gray and dreary. The cars splashed by, with headlights on and wipers slapping at the raindrops. It was as if someone was playing with the saturation of the color outside. Even through his limited view out the front windows and door, the greenery of the bushes and grass that had finally shed the snow cover, seemed to grow even greener before his very eyes. He contemplated that for a moment. It brightened his disposition a bit. Spring and summer were coming. There was nothing like summer in the Catskills.

Then he looked at the larger piles of snow, which the plows had mounded at the edge of the roads and parking lots throughout town. They were now almost black. As the snow piles melted, the gravel, which had been spread on the roads all winter long, was far more concentrated. Black mounds of grit that would need to be shoveled up and removed when spring finally sprung, in full.

As Seemo brought out Jack's breakfast, the door chimes jingled, and Tubby McIntyre came in, dressed in a trench coat and wide brimmed hat, with a shirt and tie and dress slacks. He had a satchel with a shoulder strap across his body.

"Mornin' Mr. Seemo. Mornin', Chief," he said as he took his usual seat at the counter, with a straight-line view of the television.

"Frosted Flakes coming up," Seemo said.

"Thank you." He set the hat on the swivel stool next to him and rested his chin on the meat of his enormous hands.

"So what are you all dressed up for?" Jack asked, as he sprinkled some pepper onto his eggs. "Preaching again? On a day like this?"

"Yup." As he spoke, his jaw remained on his hands and the rest of his head moved instead. It was like watching an enormous eight-year-old boy. Gone were the beard and long hair that had been Tubby's trademark look since he was a middle teenager. He was now clean cut and clean shaved. His clothes weren't exactly put together, but it was an amazing transition from the ratty flannel he'd grown accustomed to wearing for a decade and a half. Though he acted like an eight-year-old boy on occasion, he looked like a nice gentleman.

"I can't let some rain stop me from helping people," Tubby said. "That wouldn't be right."

"No," Jack said. "I guess it wouldn't be right. Did I tell you we, uh, Paula and I got to see your reading? Did I tell you how good a job you did?"

"Yeah," Tubby said. "Miss Paula did too."

"Well you did," Jack said. He was a little frustrated. He was forgetting things. Forgetting conversations. There was just too much going on in his head, and he was slipping. Maybe the town was right to get rid of him. Maybe he was a liability.

They didn't say much else, as the television was updating the news about a kid in a hoodie who was gunned down on the street in Florida a few weeks back. Though it wasn't a white cop who did the shooting, the media did everything they could to make it sound like it was part of a larger epidemic. If it was just some poor kid that got himself murdered, it was horrible. If it turned out he was high on something or provoking a fight, well, that's what that type of lifestyle got you. It always had and it always would. Didn't mean the media wasn't going to sensationalize the story for ratings.

Maybe it was the right time to stop being a cop.

Tubby closed his eyes and bowed his head when the Frosted Flakes arrived, and Jack watched quietly. The last time he had said grace before a meal, he was probably twelve, and it was probably a Thanksgiving dinner, and his father had probably forced him to do it for the whole family. The memory brought a dull ache to his chest. Jack turned away as Tubby raised his head to start eating his cold cereal.

McMurphy picked through his French Toast and bacon and eggs leisurely. He didn't really have anywhere to be, and would have to wait on Paula to give him a ride home. Once home, he could go out and continue working on his car in the garage. If he focused on it, over the next few weeks, he could probably have it done and ready for inspection before the last of the gravel-adulterated snow piles had melted away.

Eventually the news gave way to sports and whether the New York Yankees were going to be the contenders everyone thought they would be. Jeter was in his prime, and the pitching and extra bats they were bringing in looked like it would be the right formula to win the pennant.

Jack finished his breakfast and got a refill on the coffee. Yesterday's New York Times and Wall Street Journal were stacked at the end of the counter. He reached down and took most of the stack and set it next to his mug. For the next hour, he lost himself in the world's news, as the rain continued outside, and Tubby continued reigning down terror on his bowl, make that bowls, of Frosted Flakes.

Tubby pulled out money from his pocket and put it next to his fourth empty bowl. He thanked Seemo and said goodbye to Jack. He carried a book bag with a strap that he put over his head, so the strap went across his body and held the bag against his hip. On a normal person, the bag would have looked just fine, but on Tubby, it looked more like a small satchel or ladies' purse. After putting on his hat, Tubby ventured out into the rain, jingling the door chimes as he went.

"You know," Seemo said, watching the television but talking to Jack. "He goes through seven boxes of Frosted Flakes every week."

"That can't be healthy," Jack mumbled.

"One box a day," Seemo said. "That's more than the super-market sells every week. You know that? I get the delivery truck to stop and bring me my boxes every other week. I have to buy them by the dozen. They come in a big cardboard box. I always have an extra carton. One time I ran out. He already eat two bowls, but wanted more, and I run out! And I swear to you, I think he gonna cry. Big man, all beardy. Well that was before. Now he's using manners. Pleases and thank yous. Get him away from his crazy mama and he's okay, no?"

"I guess so," Jack said. "I'm glad he fell in with some good people. Looks like they're taking good care of him. Can't argue with the results."

"No. Can't argue."

A few more patrons came through the door, but sat at tables rather than the counter. Jack felt like they were burning holes in his back, staring at him. He stood to go use the restroom, and stole a glance at their table. They weren't paying any attention to Jack at all, they were noses down, consuming their menus. He was back at his perch at the counter, ready to finish off the Wall Street Journal, when John Anakausuen came through the door.

"Chief Jack McMurphy," Anakausuen said as he spotted Jack at the counter. "Mind if I join you?"

"Not at all, have a seat," Jack said. "Though it's just Jack now."

"Right. Last night. Big night all around. From what I heard, sounded like you got a raw deal," John said. "As a Native American, I can certainly empathize with someone getting a raw deal."

McMurphy didn't know how you were supposed to respond to such a statement.

"I'm just messing around with you. It's a joke," John said. "You and I, we go back, right?"

"Sure."

"I mean, I remember you in school. You were what, three years younger?"

"I think so," Jack said.

"Did you know, your dad caught me smoking a joint once? Did he ever tell you about that?"

"No, never heard that story," Jack replied. He turned to look at Anakausuen. "You know he's dead, right?"

"I do, and I'm sorry. I read the article in the fall. I was following all the news about this town online. Got a little dicey here for a bit. Then again over the last few weeks, I guess," Anakausuen said. "But you did your job, didn't you? Did what had to be done. Your buddy, Cooke. He did too. It's a shame about what happened to him, too."

"Yeah, no kidding. My fault. I should have been here."

Anakausuen ignored the comment. "So your dad, he catches me behind the school with a joint. I take a hit, turn around, and boom, there's your pop. I just freeze, man. Caught red handed. Indian. Red handed. No? Anyway, you know what he did?"

"No. What did he do?"

"Nothing. Well, not just nothing. He said to me 'Johnny, don't do this. You're a smart kid. You want to break your father's heart. Don't get mixed up with these chuckleheads in town. You're going places. You got the wits and the work ethic to be anything you want to be. Don't flush it all away because you want to get high. Don't disappoint your father like that.' That's what he said to me."

"Wow," Jack said in a whisper. Anakausuen said it, but Jack heard it in his father's voice.

"He was a good man, your dad. I never touched the stuff after that. He said what I needed to hear."

Jack took a sip of coffee, so he wouldn't have to respond and so his voice wouldn't crack when he did.

"You're a good man, too, Jack," John said. "I need a good man. Somebody that knows the area, knows the people, knows the mountain."

"What do you need a good man for?"

"Security. The announcement last night was just the first shot in a battle that will probably take a decade to solve. In the meantime, until a court order forces us to stop, my company is going to start claiming Mount Pratt. We'll begin surveying immediately. Well, truth be told, we've already started a little. Just getting some rough estimates, mind you," Anakausuen said.

"First we'll plan to widen the road to the peak. Then we'll put in a hotel up on top. A couple hundred rooms. Heated pool, sauna, day spa, the works. Very high end. Then, we'll start the fight for the casino. Did you know there are twenty casinos in New York State?"

"No, I didn't know that."

"Did you know that eleven of them are Native American owned?"

"No, but I could have guessed," Jack said.

"Well, you would think that they would not want additional competition, right? But here's the thing. New York State wants to allow another half dozen casinos across the state. They want them non-Native American owned. They want to choke out our business so they can line their own pockets. They want to cheat our people again. But this time it's different. This time we have money. And wherever we can, we're going to put a casino. We're going to make them so nice, so beautiful, so amazing, that nobody will want to go up against them. We're going to give our people good jobs that will pay them enough to give their kids and their grandkids, and their grandkids' grandkids full educations. And then, we'll use those educated kids to continue the fight. And people aren't going to like it."

"I could guess they wouldn't," Jack said. "But fair is fair."

"That's right. Fair is fair. So here's what I think. I think I bring you on as head of security. It will be a cushy job at first. You'll just have to patrol the mountain from time to time. Make sure nobody is up there messing around with the gear when we start bringing it in. We'll set up an office right here in town for you. Give you a computer, a truck, a good paycheck. Then when things start rocking and rolling, you'll start hiring a security team. By the time the casino goes in, you'll be overseeing the entire security operation. Nice gig," Anakausuen said. "What do you say?"

"Well," Jack said. He followed it with a long pause. He took a few more sips from his coffee. John didn't say a word. He just waited. It was a solid tactic. Jack remembered reading about it in a sales book he'd picked up once. Lay down the proposal and force a response. "I guess I'd have to talk it over with my wife," he said finally.

"Okay," Anakausuen replied with a smile. "Okay I can work with that. Slow yes is better than a fast no." That had been in the book as well.

"Can I buy you breakfast?"

"I've already eaten," Jack said. "Seemo picked up the tab, on account of my getting canned from the police department."

"Well, I hope you don't mind if I order and eat, then" John said.

Jack thought about texting Paula, but he was still smarting a bit from their little, early-morning argument. He'd give it another half-hour.

Chapter 45

"Tubby!" Riker was riding his bike along the sidewalk when he saw the big man up ahead. He pulled his bike alongside Tubby and pushed his hood back slightly so he could look up at him.

"Hi, Riker," Tubby said. "I'm not 'sposedta talk to you no more."

"Why not?" Riker asked. He genuinely like the big man. He was nice and talked about how Riker's mom could come alive again. And that made Riker very happy inside. And it didn't make any sense why somebody, like his dad, didn't want him to be happy inside.

"Sometimes grow'dups have their reasons, and they don't make sense," Tubby said. "My mama used to have reasons for things, but I didn't alway understand them. But maybe that's not a good way to say it. Because my mama wasn't right about a lot of stuff. And sometimes she was just mean to me. So maybe grow'dups are just sometimes mean, and that's the only reason."

"Yeah," Riker said. "You have a way of explaining things so they make sense. I guess that's why I like talking to you."

"Thanks, Riker," he said. "You should prolly get off to school now. Can't be late. Maybe your daddy will change his mind and we can talk sometime."

"I hope so," Riker said. He leaned his chin down onto his arms, which were folded across the handlebars. He watched the raindrops make rings in the puddle on the sidewalk. "Why are you all dressed up?"

"I'm preaching to people. But nobody's out right now. So I'm just waiting for people so I can preach to them," Tubby said.

"That's cool," Riker said. "I don't think my dad believes in God. I think that's why he doesn't want me talking to you. I think he wants me to believe just like him."

"Maybe."

"But how did the Earth get here? How did everything end up just right for us? Like I was eating a banana, right? And it's like, food, but with packaging. Like it was just made for us that way. Mom used to tell me bedtime stories about how God watches over us. Especially when Yasmine was in the hospital. Mom would say that God would protect our family. I don't think dad knew she would tell me that stuff. Anyway, I don't care if dad doesn't believe in God, I do. And I want to see my mom again," Riker said. "Can you get me a Bible and show me where it says my mom will come back to life?"

Tubby bit his bottom lip and looked around. He didn't see anybody at all. Just a few cars going by, but nobody he recognized.

"You can have mine," Tubby said. He took his Bible out of his bag and handed it to Riker. "I don't know where everything is, but there's a thing in the back that helps you find stuff. You just have to know how to spell the words. Can you spell the words right?"

"Yes! I can totally do that!" Riker said. "But if you give me yours, what will you use?"

"I'll get another one."

"Okay! Can you put it in my backpack?" Riker asked. Tubby complied, lifting up the back of the yellow poncho, unzipping the bag, depositing the book, and zipping it closed again.

"I gotta go," Riker said, starting off on his bike. "Don't worry, I won't tell anybody!"

Chapter 46

Paula didn't notice the car parked across the street from the police station, when she pulled up. Didn't recognize that it was the same car from the previous night, with the same two men sitting in the front seats. She didn't notice much of anything during the drive from William Everett's house and her encounter with his gardner, Barry. She felt light-headed and sick to her stomach. When she arrived at the police station, she took a few deep breaths to compose herself.

She waited for a few cars to pass by, then she opened her door and darted across the road, past Jack's SUV and up the steps to the police station.

"Jack?" She walked toward his office, and was met in the doorway by Aaron Patterson.

"Can I help you?" he said.

"I'm looking for Jack."

"Well, he's not here."

"Do you know where he is? His truck's out front."

"Not his truck anymore. He gave me the keys. He left some boxes and his gun belt on that desk. Thought it was him coming in to get them," Patterson said. He leaned against the door frame and crossed his arms. Paula wanted to punch him.

"No idea where he went?" Paula asked.

"Maybe to the diner to get breakfast. He was on foot, so he couldn't have wandered off to far," he said. "You're that gal that was with him last night. Needed to say a few words, right? Get them off your chest." He emphasized the word chest in a way that made her pull her coat closed.

"Thanks for your help," she said. Paula walked out the front door, closing it somewhere between normal and a slam. She waited for a car to pass before she ran back to her Mercedes and climbed behind the wheel. She didn't notice that a second car was now parked across from the police station, behind the one with the two men in the front seat. This one had just a driver.

Jack contemplated his phone, he hated text messaging. It was something he hadn't done until he started dating Paula. It seemed to be her primary form of communication. He did not have a smart phone, so he had to thumb through the letters according to the old phone keypad. "Where are you?" took an extra minute.

"Across from the station. Where are you?"

"Pechy kedn," he misspelled.

"Be right there."

She performed a U-turn in the street and headed back towards the diner. There was water flowing across the road where the bridge crossed the headwaters of the Delaware River.

"Jack, the bridge is flooding."

Jack got the message and threw a few dollars onto the counter for tip. Seemo was in the kitchen, so he couldn't argue about it. Jack grabbed his coat and dashed out the door. He could hear the roar of the water even over the sound of the driving rain. And the rain had intensified. He saw the water lapping over it's banks and up over the bridge. It was a torrent. He saw Paula on the other side of the twisting, foaming brown deluge. Her wipers were slapping at the water on the windshield, but not keeping up. Water poured off Jack's uncovered head and down his neck. It had grown darker. As dark as night. The headlights of Paula's Mercedes sent out bright illuminated cones of rain, falling on the quickly moving waters of the Delaware River as it overtook the small bridge.

Jack pulled out his phone and dialed.

"Stay there, don't try to cross," Jack said into the phone when Paula picked up.

"I'm not stupid," she said.

"I know. This is bad," he replied. "I think the levy above town is going to go. Copper's kid, Eric, warned me about it." Jack cursed. He'd been warned, and he didn't do anything about it. It had completely slipped his mind. With everything going on, he'd just forgotten.

Jack was standing by the flowing water, trying to look up stream. He thought about calling Patterson, but paused a beat. He started to dial Goldie's number.

The two men in the car saw the scene unfold in front of them. They pulled a U-turn after Paula had. They drove past the grocery store, three car lengths behind Paula's car. Then she stopped in the street. They saw the flowing water as well. They backed up and pulled into the parking lot of the grocery store, turning around to face the street with Paula's car on one side of the flood waters, Jack standing on the other side. The flooding was now splashing over the river bank and into the parking lot as well, pooling several inches around some parked cars.

"I think this is it," the driver said.

"Really? What would you like me to do?" the passenger asked.

"Drive it into the water. He'll chase after her."

"What will that accomplish?"

"See how fast that water is going? It will push the car right off the bridge. He goes after her, we have our accident."

The passenger opened the laptop. It had an antenna plugged into the USB port. The software had been developed by the CIA. The two men in the car had it because they had both been on a job in Libya, and needed to wreck a car. A Mercedes, in fact. The

CIA obliged with the software. After all, the car wreck had been a direct request from the CIA. They'd paid for the operation. The CIA guys never asked for the software back, so they never gave it back. They'd used it twice since.

The hardware was very simple. A module was plugged into the car's port under the steering wheel. They had taken care of that in the hospital parking lot, several days earlier. Then it had just been a waiting game. All it took was activating it and then taking control of the vehicle. It was usually most effective at highway speeds. Driving the car off the road into a bridge column, or into the trees. It was also effective at traffic lights, sending the car through a red light into speeding traffic. The software didn't work on every car. In fact, it didn't work on most cars.

Most cars were still controlled mechanically, that is, turning the steering wheel actually turned gears, with power steering assistance, and those gears turned the wheel mechanisms. Brakes were applied and they mechanically forced a lever which activated the power brake system which pumped more pressure into the brake line and activated the brake calipers which clamped down on the rotors and braked the car's momentum. The transmission selector physically moved mechanical gears which put the car in drive, reverse or park. Most cars were still mechanical.

But some cars had moved to a drive-by-wire system, or had computer controlled elements in place that could instruct the transmission to select reverse, or tell the power steering to turn the wheels left, or provide the accelerator with the instruction to increase acceleration, and perhaps even disconnect the brake switch from sending the information to the master cylinder brake system. The cars with parking assist were most susceptible.

So in that respect, they had lucked out when Paula bought the brand new Mercedes. It was the same model used in Libya. The big V8 version, top of the line. The Mercedes in Libya had gold-plated wheel covers, however.

"What are you doing?" Jack yelled into the phone and at the car as he watch the Mercedes accelerate into the flood waters. It nosed in and the water lapped up past the rocker panels on the doors. It then stopped dead.

"I didn't do it!" she yelled. "My foot was on the brake the whole time!"

"Okay, carefully put the car in reverse and back it up," Jack said, trying to be calm.

"It's not working," Paula cried. "Nothing's working. It won't go backwards it won't go forwards."

"Okay, open your door, carefully, you're going to have to climb out onto the hood and jump for me. You're right in the middle of it. You can clear at least five feet of it. It's not that deep over here," he said. He waded carefully into the water. It was past his ankles, and just half a step forward, it was to his shins. It was pulling at him with such force as he'd never experienced. The water in the center of the torrent was deeper, even though the ground beneath it didn't descend. The water was just taller in the center, where it was raging faster. Jack saw the water start to rise up the doors of the car. More water was coming.

"It won't open! The doors won't unlock, the windows won't go down. Jack! I'm stuck!"

"You can do that?" the driver asked.

"Right here," the passenger said. "I can disable the locking system and the window system. It's all computer controlled, so I just send a command to disable and it won't work. Bip, boop."

"Nice."

He looked at the height of the water, and if he didn't act now, it would be too late. He took a step back, and ran towards the water. It was eight feet from the edge of the water to the front of her SUV. A step in ankle deep water and a leap, and he was onto the hood of the car on his belly. The rain made him feel like he was five hundred pounds. His jacket was soaked, his boots were soaked. The hood was slippery with rain, on it's well waxed surface.

Jack didn't have his glass breaking hammer with him, it was on his gun belt, back at the station. He did have his keys, however. He gripped the largest key in his hand, leaving about a half inch of the steel tip protruding from the bottom of his clenched fist. He climbed up onto the windshield, and brought his fist down on the sunroof. It bounced off.

"What do you think, does he do it?" the driver asked.

"Twenty bucks says he breaks it and gets her out," the passenger said.

"Can you do anything about that?"

"Sure."

The car lurched backward, the wheels turned hard, and it almost backed clear of the water. Jack had closed down his phone, so he yelled through the sealed sunroof.

"What are you doing?"

"I'm not doing anything! The car's doing it!" came the muffled reply.

The Mercedes lurched forward, and Jack nearly lost his footing and his grip. It forced him to get low on the surface of the windshield and roof, locking his toes under the wipers, which were still going, fighting him the entire way. The car pushed forward hard and slammed into the bridge railing.

"Get your foot off the gas!" he yelled at her.

"It's not on the gas!"

"Put on the emergency brake!" he screamed.

"Well, can't do anything about that," the passenger said.

"What?"

"She put on the emergency brake."

"Can't you override it?"

"No, that's still a completely mechanical thing. Pulling on the brake pulls a cable, which clamps down the brakes. It also sends a kill message to the computer, won't let the transmission engage."

The driver swore.

"I know."

The car stopped moving, it's nose hard against the bridge railing. The water flow was increasing, it was now up over the tires. It was enough to float the back end of the car around and push the entire side of the car up against the bridge railing. In the distance, the fire horn wailed, and Jack knew that help was on the way.

He climbed back into position, and brought his fist with the keys down again, smashing it against the sunroof. It shattered into a million pieces. It was still held together with plastic, though. It was safety glass. He put his keys back in his pocket and brought down his fist, knuckles first into the glass. He punched a hole through. The glass shards rained down on Paula.

"Hurry!" she yelled.

He punched and punched, his hand gashed and dripping with blood. After the first penetration, the others took far less force. He reached down his bloodied hand to Paula.

"Let's get you out of here," he said. He pulled her through the sun roof, and got her out, so both of them were sitting atop the roof of the car, legs down over the windshield, feet braced against the hood.

"What the hell?" he said. He kissed her on her mouth, and she kissed him back.

"The car, it like, malfunctioned. The computer must have shorted out. It just went crazy," she said.

"Well, we just have to sit tight, fire department will be here with a ladder to get us. We step into that water, and we're gone," he said. As if on cue, a firetruck came roaring down the street towards them. First responder vehicles, with their blue, dash-mounted lights followed. Goldie was the first out of the truck, she walked quickly but didn't run.

"Jack," Paula said. "Old Man Everett. I have to tell you. It's awful."

"What is?"

"He had all these books -"

"Looks like you guys have gotten yourselves into quite the mess," Goldie called out to them.

"Looks like," Jack yelled.

"I'm going to toss you each a rope to tie off. Then we're going to put a ladder across to you. This is a new bridge, it will hold," Goldie said.

New was a relative term. It was ten years since it had been completed, which made it one of the newest bridges in the county. The ropes were tossed over, with life jackets. Jack helped Paula get secured before securing his own. The car was lurching against the bridge railing now, as the water was actually forcing the car up off the road's surface, effectively floating it. Depending on the vehicle's center of gravity, it could get rolled from the force of the water, or crash right through the railing.

Six firefighters slid a ladder above the water's surface, extending it hand over hand, until Jack was able to grab a rung and pull it further up onto the hood of the car. They braced it right up against the bridge's railing. It was just inches above the water's surface, but if they hurried, it would only take moments to get across.

In those times, when the adrenaline is pumping, it's as if time slows down. The senses are heightened. Colors seem brighter, sounds are more crisp. It's the body's natural defense mechanism. Time slows down because the brain records more information in times of emergency. More memory of a moment makes it feel as if the moment lasted longer, though it may have just been a split second.

In that moment, as they were preparing to climb across the ladder, Jack looked back toward the grocery store parking lot. Everything seemed to be moving in slow motion. He saw a kid in a bright yellow parka, on his bike. He was only a few feet from the growing pool of water that was close to floating some of the parked cars away. It was just a natural reaction to the danger he saw. Jack waved to the kid, waved him away from the water. The kid seemed to nod, but didn't move. Paula was starting out onto the ladder, Jack turned his attention back to her, steadying the ladder for her, as she climbed out on her hands and knees.

They all heard the rumble. It was like distant thunder, but the way the ground shook, the way the windows rattled in the buildings, it felt more like an earthquake. From his vantage point, he could look straight upstream, and what he saw was a wall of foaming, brown water bearing down on them.

"Go! Go!" he yelled. Paula paused and looked upstream. She saw the wall of water too, and froze.

"Go!" he yelled again.

It hit them with such force that it pushed the car right through the bridge railing and off into the water. The big SUV rolled, and Jack went straight down beneath it. The car floated for a bit, even as it pushed him down into the roiling torrent. He had managed a deep breath just before impact. He felt the life jacket at his waist go taut against the rope, then it felt as if he were being beaten. He was tossed back and forth, violently. It felt like someone was raining down punches into his head and chest. The life jacket pulled up against his arms, the strap around his waist tightening, squeezing out some of the air in his lungs. He tried to lock his arms at his side to hang onto it. He kicked as best he could, trying for the surface, but the speed of the water above, was forcing him down. He immediately knew that there was no way they were going to be able to pull him out against the current. He fumbled for the release at his stomach. He popped the plastic latch and went limp, putting his arms above his head, letting the life vest and rope slip up and over his arms.

Chapter 47

The force of the water ripped up trees, and blasted homes off their foundations. It all channeled down the river's path, but it came with such force, that it enveloped the houses on both sides. Goldie saw the water hit them. She saw Jack get launched over, with the car rolling on top of him. She saw Paula get knocked from the ladder and go over the railing, which bent and buckled and went below the surface.

"Pull them up! Pull! Pull!" she yelled. The force of the water was dragging the firefighters toward the water's edge, stubbornly holding tight to Jack and Paula. One of the first responders took the end of the rope and looped it around the winch assembly on the front of his truck, anchoring it. He then jumped behind the wheel and began backing up. The rope gave, and an empty life vest shot out of the water.

"Do the other one!" Goldie yelled, her voice barely audible over the raging waters. They repeated the maneuver. But the rope was taut. It wouldn't give.

"It's caught on something! Tie me off," she yelled, donning a life jacket.

"No! You can't," one of the other firefighters yelled. "You'll drown too!"

She did a split second appraisal of the situation and knew he was right. There was no way to battle the kind of forces at play here.

"The rope is caught on the bridge railing," she yelled. "Give out some more slack, we'll let him float down stream a bit. Do it!"

They gave out the slack, hoping that it would dislodge from the railing. Goldie saw the car and the ladder floating down stream, which made a hard angle to the left behind the grocery store. The water was blasting up into the air against the rock embankment, opposite the grocery store, and was pushing right up against the store wall. It was all getting funneled into the narrow gap. The car lodged there for a moment, then part of the brick wall of the store gave way and the SUV floated further down stream and out of sight.

They tried to whip the rope up and over where they believed the bridge railing was under the water's surface. They tried to pull again, but it pulled taut again and would budge.

"Get down river," she yelled. "We've got to cut them loose. The life vest will pull him to the surface." Goldie had no idea who was still attached to the end of the line and who had slipped out of their vest. But it was their only hope for saving one of them. A utility knife was produced, and the rope was cut.

Jack tumbled through the water, his lungs burning. He had no idea which way was up, where the surface even was. Then it felt like the force of the water slackened just a bit. It wasn't quite so violent. He wondered if he was dying. Then he hit something hard, and stuck.

The water was bitterly cold, and he was already going numb. His cut and bleeding hand wasn't helping. But when he hit the tree, he could tell what it was. And it was holding on against the water. He wrapped his arms around it, and kicked with his legs, trying desperately to shimmy up above the water's surface. It was then that it seemed like the water helped him. It ripped off his boots, and that made him feel about a hundred pounds lighter. He pulled with all his might against the trunk, and found a branch with his hand. He gripped it and pulled, heaving himself upwards. His head broke through the surface, and he gasped in a lung-full of air.

He felt a wave of fatigue wash over him, even as the frigid water continued to pound him against the trunk of the tree. He gripped the next branch up and hauled himself up. Then the next, then the next. He was up in the tree, above the water's surface by about three feet. Debris of all sorts was crashing through the water, parts of houses, tires, a lawn tractor rolled over and smashed against the shore, then went under the surface.

Hypothermia was already starting to set in. He shivered in his perch, with numb fingers and frozen toes. His socks had been washed away along with his boots. His jacket was soaked through, so he shed it, figuring that the water was keeping him colder and draining his already diminishing body heat. He looked around at his surroundings to see if he could tell where he was.

From Coopers Hollow, the normally small stream, that made up the headwaters of the Delaware River, winded south, along the base of the hills, bordering a wide swath of farmland. It eventually came to the small town of Hobart. There, it met with several dams, as it channeled through the middle of the town. Jack was in a tree which would normally have been about twenty feet away from the stream's edge, in what was once a grazing field. He looked across the water, saw the embankment, followed it up the hill about thirty feet, and could see, through the bare trees, the guardrail on Route 10. If they were looking for him, they would find him. He just needed to hold on.

Paula felt the punch of water as it knocked her off the ladder. She felt something hard hit her in the head. It was the most pain she'd ever felt in her life.

She saw stars and then blackness.

Chapter 48

One of the first responders saw Jack clinging to the tree about a mile south of Coopers Hollow, just off Route 10. The water here was not nearly as violent, as it had the room to flood out into the field that stretched across the valley. It didn't make the extraction and rescue of Jack any easier. They first attempted a rescue with a rubber raft that sported a big powerful motor, but the speed of the water was too much. They couldn't risk trying to anchor against the tree for fear of flipping the raft and loosing the rescuer along with Jack.

They opted for a helicopter rescue. The closest responding helicopter rescue unit was out of Albany, which was nearly sixty miles away, by air. It was going to take nearly forty-five minutes just to get them on site. And then they would only have about an hour in the air before they'd have to find a place to refuel. Word went out, and a fuel truck was dispatched from Stewart Airport, over on the Hudson River. It would take it an hour and a half to get on site. They planned to drive to the high-school ball field and be prepared for a refuel if necessary.

Jack clung to the tree, hoping they had pulled Paula out. She was closer to safety than he was, when he'd last seen her. He'd nearly been killed by the car, but she was closer, only a few feet away. She was pulled to safety, he was sure of it.

A crowd had gathered on the road above the water's edge. The flashing lights of the rescue vehicles sprayed the falling rain with red and blue. His arms and legs were growing stiff. He knew it was the cold, so he tried to move them, keep the blood flowing as best he could, without losing grip. When the rescue helicopter arrived, he'd need all his strength to grab on and hold on.

It took around thirty-five minutes for the helicopter to arrive. As it hovered overhead, the rescuers called down over a loudspeaker.

"Do you think you can grab onto the basket and climb in? Wave one arm above your head for yes," the voice called down to him.

He moved his arm above his head and waved it. He wasn't sure if his body would respond, but it was the only option. Dangling a rescuer down to help him would endanger yet another life, and he wasn't going to do that.

Suddenly he was transported in his mind to football practice, ninth grade. Coach Ellison, was barking at him. He was down in the mud, unable to breath. He'd just been blindsided during a drill. It was raining. The mud had gotten in his face. He wanted to cry. He wanted to quit and go home.

"Get up! I know your body is telling you to lie there in the mud, but don't listen to it. Listen to me! Listen to my voice. I'm telling you that your body doesn't know crap about nuthin! It doesn't know what you're capable of. Only your heart knows. Only your heart can get you up out of that mud. When we're down by seven, with a minute left in the game, and your body tells you that it's got nothing else to give, it's your heart that's going to say 'Bullcrap!' Now get up and show me some heart, Jack McMurphy! Show me!"

Jack grabbed onto the basket as it swung towards the tree. His legs felt like lead weights, but he swung them up and got his heel wrapped around one of the basket supports. He wasn't in the basket so much as he was clinging, like a spider-monkey, to the bottom of it. The helicopter swept him up above the water, and moved north. It was a sixty second ride to the school's field, where he was gently set down. Rescue personnel rushed to him, getting him onto a stretcher, and covering him with heated blankets. He was in the back of an ambulance before he really could comprehend what was happening. He saw a familiar face next to him. It was Goldie. She touched his face. He was shivering, fiercely. He thought he said something, but he didn't remember, as the cold overtook him, and his world went dark.

"It was a horrifying scene here in Coopers Hollow earlier today, as floodwaters ripped through this small Catskill Mountain town," the reporter's voice played over scenes of rushing brown water, as it ripped through the town. "Former police chief Jack McMurphy was rescued from a cluster of trees south of town, having been washed away after a rescue attempt in town. Just take a look at this incredible footage of the rescue."

The reporter went silent as the video switched to Jack practically leaping from the tree and grabbing onto the rescue basket. He looped his legs up and around and clung tightly as the helicopter swept away from the camera's view.

"Just, incredible footage there," the reporter said, the camera now on her. She was standing with a microphone in one hand and an umbrella in the other, the brown water of the Delaware still raging behind her. "Now it seems that the flooding was caused not only by the enormous amount of rain we've received here in the area over the last week or so, which was in addition to the winter run off, but also because of the failure of a dam north of town. The dam created a manmade lake and had been in place since the nineteen-thirties. It was past due for repairs. As of right now, the State Engineers aren't making any comments on the tragedy."

"Two people are still missing," the reporter continued. "Paula Schumann, a local reporter who was, we have confirmed, the individual former police chief McMurphy was attempting to rescue. Also missing is eight year old Riker Owens. He was last seen riding his bike to school in a yellow parka. Search teams are still hoping for a miracle.

"Suzanne, back to you."

Chapter 49

He suddenly felt hot, like he was burning up. He tried to push the covers off his body, but his hand and arm stung, and any movement made it worse. He was sweating, and it ran into his eyes. They burned as he opened them. The room was dimly lit. He could see shadows of people, who moved towards him.

"Jack," the voice was soft and female.

"Paula?" he croaked, his throat dry.

"No, it's Goldie," she said. "Here's some water."

He took a sip from a straw. His throat burned too, but the water made it better.

"You gave us a scare. Your body temp dropped to about eighty degrees, partner. I thought we were losing you," she said. She put her hand on his head.

"Where's Paula?"

Goldie was quiet. She sighed heavily.

"We haven't found her yet, Jack. I'm so, so sorry." Goldie began to cry. She wiped the tears away.

"Maybe she was in a tree, like me. You've got to go back out," Jack said.

"We're looking. It's been two days and we're still looking, Jack."

"You're not looking! You're standing here, talking to me! You need to get out there and find her! She's freezing, and she's scared!" he yelled at her, his words ripping at his throat. "You need to find her, dammit! You need to find her!"

"Okay," Goldie said to him softly. "We'll find her."

She left the room. Ballard was there, leaning against the wall, looking out the window. Unable to look at Jack.

"Ballard," Jack said. Tears were streaming down his face.

"Yeah, boss?" he replied quietly.

"Is she gone?"

"I think so, Jack. It's been too long. You barely survived the water. It was like liquid ice," he said.

"What happened? She was in front of me. She was almost safe. What happened?"

"The rope got caught on the railing. They couldn't pull her free. She was stuck. The only hope was to cut her loose and hope she was able to grab onto something like you did," Ballard said. "She was still wearing her life jacket. She had a good chance. It was the right move."

"And they haven't found her?"

"No."

"Oh my God," Jack cried. "What am I supposed to do now? What am I supposed to do now?" He weeped. Ballard had to step out of the room, leaving Jack all alone.

"Get up! Your body doesn't know crap!"

"Coach, I can't!" He was in the mud, rain was pouring down on him. Coach was standing over him. He was sinking in the mud too. It was up over his white gym shoes. It was nearly to the red stripes on his white socks.

"You can too! Don't listen to your body, listen to your heart! Your body will say no. Your mind will say no. It's your heart you gotta listen to, Jack! Get up!"

"I can't, coach!" They were both sinking in the mud. Jack couldn't move.

"Why not?"

"My heart's broken, coach. It don't work no more."

When he awoke on the third day, Goldie was there again. She smiled at him in the way that people do in hospitals. A smile, with the edges of her mouth turned down. More of a weak grimace than a smile.

"Did you find her?" Jack whispered.

Goldie just nodded. She came to his bed side and took his hand. The one that wasn't bandaged up from having slammed his fist through the sunroof.

"I'm sorry, Jack. We found her at the dams in Hobart. I'm so sorry," she said. She squeezed his hand.

"It's definitely her?"

"I identified her. It wasn't nice."

"Ballard said you did everything you could to give her a chance."

"Yeah," the tears were back. Goldie heaved with each word. "We gave her a fighting chance. We gave her the best chance we could give her."

"Thank you," he whispered. He reached up, and pulled her in for a hug.

She sobbed on his shoulder and repeated over and over, "I'm so sorry. I'm so sorry, Jack."

On the fourth day, he wanted out. His vital signs were all back to normal. Even his hand was mending. They were concerned about infection in the hand, but so far, it was scabbing up and beginning the healing process. He was in Albany, in the same hospital as Michael Cooke.

Jack had been moved from intensive care on the second day to a regular room. By the third day they wanted him up and walking. Every muscle in his body ached. His toes absolutely burned. They kept checking his toes and fingers for frostbite, but he had managed to avoid it. He hadn't been so cold as to have damaged anything permanently. When he'd hit the tree, he'd cracked three ribs. When he'd grabbed onto the rescue basket, he'd wrenched his shoulder. The adrenaline didn't let him feel it then, but he felt it now.

By the morning on the fourth day, he was ready to go. He was able to walk around as much as he needed, though they still wanted the IV in his hand. They let him walk around with his monitor if he wanted.

Jack rode the elevator to the next floor and walked into Michael Cooke's room.

"Jeez, look what the cat dragged in," Michael said.

"Hey partner," Jack said. "Mind if I sit for a minute?"

"Feel free. Gloria ran out to get some real lunch. If you're not dead when they bring you in here, they try their darnedest to kill you with the food," he said.

"You heard?"

"Yeah, we heard," Michael said. "I'm sorry."

"Me too. I did everything I could," Jack said. "It just wasn't enough."

"Sometimes it's not. Sometimes, there's nothing that can be done," Michael said. "You know, when I left the Marine Corps, I joined up with the NYPD. I was their sharp shooter for awhile, you know? Of course you know. Anyway, I'd sometimes head out and talk with some of the VA groups, you know, do my part to help. Help some of the guys who saw the thick stuff over seas. I didn't see much action in Gulf War One. But the boys coming back from Iraq and Afghanistan after 9/11, they saw some of the most brutal action the military has ever seen in the history of this country.

"I was talking to this boy who lost both legs in an IED explosion. He was the lucky one. He was in the back. Three of the other guys in the vehicle were shredded. The thing was, he was supposed to drive. But this new kid had just been assigned to their unit. Nineteen years old. Kid wanted to drive the Humvee. So he said okay. Two miles out, boom. Everybody's dead, and he looses his legs," Michael said. "The point is, he was beating himself up over it. Saying maybe the kid would still be alive if he had done something differently. You know? Blaming himself. Survivor's remorse. But sometimes, there's nothing that could have been done. Just completely random. That's all life is, just a series of random events, sometimes."

"I guess," Jack said quietly. "It just seemed like something was working against us, you know? From the beginning."

"Sometimes it can feel that way."

They were quiet for a few moments.

"I'm glad I married her," Jack said. "I'm glad we did that."

"She was too. Gloria told me how happy she was. That's what you have to focus on. You made that girl the happiest she ever could have been, even if it was just for a short time."

"Thanks," Jack said. "For everything. And I'm sorry."

"About what?"

"About everything."

Goldie wanted to drive him home, but Jack asked Ballard to do it. He drove him first to Oneonta, which was the most convenient location for a rental car, even if it meant adding an extra forty minutes of driving. Then Jack drove the rental the rest of the way home. The rental place had wanted to give him a Taurus, but he decided to go with the smaller Fusion instead. He pulled into the driveway, and there were a pile of flowers left at the door. He opened the door and stepped over them. He thought about just leaving them there, but then decided that he would bring them in, even if he planned to just throw them all away. Fourteen flower arrangements in total. All of them with sympathy cards.

It was three o'clock in the afternoon, and he needed a drink.

As Jack drove through town, in his rental car, he was overwhelmed by the damage. Though centralized along the banks of the Delaware River, the swath of destruction ran right through the heart of town.

It had been five days since the flood, but the damage was still apparent throughout town. The bridge had stood against the flood waters, even if the ground on both sides had washed out. The bridge was closed and traffic diverted south of town to Hobart. There were two bridges there. Then the detour looped up on the eastern side of the river, up through the mountains, over the saddle between Hollow Pointe and Mount Pratt and back into the village of Coopers Hollow. Trucks were being warned to find an alternate route completely, as the grade was extremely steep both going up and coming down from the saddle ridge.

The village of Coopers Hollow would have a difficult time recovering. The flood had gutted the town, right down the middle. The fronts of gingerbread Victorian home were ripped off, the porches washed down stream. As the water subsided, it revealed orphaned tires, lawn tractors, toys, plywood, sheds and multiple cars. Debris and mud was everywhere. The grocery store had water forced in through the wall, where Paula's Mercedes had smashed away concrete blocks, on it's way downstream. Six inches of water filled the Grand American grocery store, rendering the food throughout as unsellable. The parking lot was layered with inches of mud and scattered fragments of wreckage.

The road that ran along the river's western side, as it came into town from the north, was completely washed out. This made access to the school next to impossible, even though the school itself remained undamaged. It was a miracle that more kids weren't swept away in the flood. Fortunately, as the flood water rose, the teachers and other school personnel corralled the kids away from the road and up into the school building. Had the dam given way, even ten minutes earlier, dozens of children, or more, may have been lost.

The entire community was in shock. All they could do was pick up and try to continue on. The Governor promised help, in front of all the cameras, an upturned four-wheeler and a pile of debris behind him, as he spoke. Chief Patterson was right next to him, on all of the television screens, across America.

Jack had watched the press conference from a distance, and then driven along the detour, back to his house.

He had numerous visitors on the fifth day, after the flood. Goldie stopped by, as did Ballard. To his credit, Mayor Patterson stopped by as well, though his brother, the new chief of police didn't. He was busy with everything, the mayor said.

Flowers and sympathy cards continued to arrive. By five o'clock on the fifth day, Jack was ready to start drinking again.

The sixth day after the flood was a Monday. There was a knock at his door at nine-thirty in the morning. His head was pounding from the alcohol the previous night. He didn't remember going to bed at all. When he came out to answer the door, he saw two whiskey bottles on the table, both empty.

He opened the door and saw a man in a suit, with a women dressed like she was going to church.

"Can I help you?"

"Mr. McMurphy, I'm Ken Crandall, we met at the Kingdom Hall a few weeks back when Thaddeus MacIntyre did his Bible reading," the man said. He had silver hair and wore glasses.

"Oh yeah, I remember. I hope you'll forgive me, I'm not feeling so well," Jack said. "Would you like to come in?"

"Well, we won't take much of your time," he said. "This is my wife, Sandy."

"Nice to meet you," Jack said, shaking her hand. If the two of them noticed the empty whiskey bottles, they didn't say anything about them.

"So, what can I do for you?"

"Well, first of all, we understand that Ms. Paula, well, that you two were married and all and, well, we're just really sorry about it all. Just heart broken for you," he said. "To lose your wife. It's just awful. We really feel for you."

"I appreciate you saying so," Jack replied. He sat in his chair, while the Crandalls sat across from him on the couch.

"We know that you and her, well, you kind of looked after Thaddeus a bit. Well, at least Thaddeus thinks the world of both of you. Anyway, I wanted to stop by and tell you that, they came and arrested him last night," Crandall said.

"What? Why? For what?"

"Apparently Thaddeus was talking to a boy the day the flood happened. The Owens boy, who's still missing. Anyway, Thaddeus told us that he was told not to talk to the boy anymore, but that he did that day. And now the Owens boy's father is saying that he didn't drown in the flood, but that Thaddeus did something to him," Crandall said.

"That's ridiculous," Jack said.

"We know. But they arrested him anyway. He's in the jail right now. We wanted to go talk to him, you know. Show him some support. But the Chief of Police there said we weren't family, so we weren't allowed to see him. Now, I'm an elder in the congregation, so I should have the right to go and talk with him, but the Chief, well, he's being difficult. I don't know if there's anything you can do about it, probably not. And I'm sorry for even asking, but anyway, I am asking," Crandall said.

"He's just a big boy," Sandy said. "He's probably scared."

"I'll see what I can do," Jack replied. "Thanks for letting me know."

"Well, thank you for seeing us," Crandall said. "If there's anything at all we can do for you. Please let us know."

"Thank you," Jack said.

"I'm making some chicken parmesan for dinner. If you'd like we could bring some by," Sandy said. "Or you could join us for dinner."

"I really appreciate the offer," Jack said. "But I'm okay."

"Alright, well if you change your mind, here's our number," Sandy said. She handed a little slip of paper to Jack.

He showed them out and after they pulled out of the driveway, he punched a hole in the wall. The scabs on his hand bled a bit, but not much.

Chapter 50

"Hey, Patterson," Jack was standing in the doorway of, what used to be, his old office. Chief Aaron Patterson was leaning back in the chair, feet on the desk, phone to his ear. He was talking baseball with someone.

"What do you want?" Patterson asked, holding his hand over the phone.

"I want to talk about Tubby," Jack said.

"Not your business, Jack. Let it go," Patterson said. He went back to his phone call. It sounded like he was getting the opening lines of the different baseball games. He looked back up. "You still here?"

"Yeah, I am," Jack said. "I'm not leaving until you tell me what's up."

"I'll call you back," Patterson said. Then he stood, pulled up his pants a bit by the belt and marched over swiftly to face Jack. They were about the same height, just a hair or two over six feet tall. But Patterson had at least another hundred pounds over Jack. That said, if he thought the aggressive move was intimidating, Jack didn't flinch.

"I told you, not your business. End of story," Patterson said.

"I think not. I saw the kid. The Owens kid. I saw him by the water's edge. I saw him just before I went into the water. Just before I lost Paula. Thanks, by the way, for stopping by to see how I was," Jack said.

"You saw the kid," Patterson said. "You swear it was him?"

"On a bike, in a yellow parka. I waved him back from the edge. He nodded like he understood."

"Then what did he do," Patterson asked.

"I don't know," Jack said. "I was too busy trying not to drown."

"Well that doesn't prove anything," Patterson said. "Tubby could have grabbed him after you saw him. In fact, it just proves that he didn't go into the water at all."

"Where was Tubby after the flood. Which side of the river?"

"He was in the Peachy Keen," Patterson said. "Went back there when he couldn't get over to his church, because of the flooding. If you must know."

"The Owens kid, I saw him in the grocery store parking lot. Opposite side of the river. How was Tubby supposed to get over there to do anything to that kid?"

"He could have driven down to Hobart. That bridge wasn't affected. It was higher up. He could have seen the kid, saw his chance," Patterson said. "And if he did, I'll get it out of him."

"Tubby doesn't drive. He never has. He walks everywhere," Jack said.

"What about that whole thing with his dad's corpse? That guy is a whack job. He's crazy," Patterson said. "I read up on him."

"He's harmless. He was just confused about that whole thing," Jack said. "He's like an eight-year-old himself. If anything, though, since that whole thing, he's gotten better. He found Jesus or something. He's preaching and stuff."

"You know those cults and how they view kids. They abuse them all the time and cover it all up," Patterson said.

"You know, you're a real jackass," McMurphy said. He was nearly nose to nose with the man when he said it.

"You best watch yourself, Jackie," Patterson said slowly. "You better really watch yourself."

"I'm getting a lawyer for him, and we're going to go after you for wrongful arrest and incarceration," Jack said. "Watch me."

"Oh, I'll be watching you," Patterson said. "You just struck out. One. Two. Three. Nobody comes into my office and threatens me, buddy boy."

"My office," Jack said. He turned and marched out the front door, slamming it as hard as he could, hoping that he'd break the glass. It rattled, but didn't break.

"Hey, John, it's Jack McMurphy. Well, I appreciate that, thank you. I'm sorry too. I have a favor to ask of you. I have a friend who's being held on trumped up charges, I need a lawyer for him. Somebody big time. No, I've got money. Okay. Got it. I'll tell them you recommended them. Thanks," Jack said to John Anakausuen over the phone. "And John, I won't forget this. Thank you."

It took the lawyer five hours for things to start in motion. The lawyer from New York City sent up a paralegal to get the ball rolling. Jack wrote out a twenty-thousand dollar check as retainer. The lawyer, Reese P. Montgomery, got on the phone with the Delaware County prosecutor, while the paralegal went to the lockup at the station house to inform Patterson that Thaddeus MacIntyre was now under their legal care. Despite the big guns coming in, the prosecutor would not force Patterson to release MacIntyre until he had a chance to review all of the evidence. Which wouldn't be for another twenty-four hours.

Montgomery made every threat imaginable, and promised Jack that he was going to follow through with them, even after they got Tubby cleared of everything. Tubby was a diminished capacity individual, and as such, should have been given far more assistance than had been afforded him. Montgomery said it could cost Patterson his job.

Jack liked the sound of that.

For a Tuesday evening, Taylor's Taproom was fairly busy. Jack had never been one to frequent the establishment, as he preferred to do his drinking at home. But he didn't want to be home alone. Not the night before Paula's funeral.

Not with a gun in the house.

He knew what everyone was thinking, even if they didn't want to say it. He knew why people kept stopping by, unannounced. He knew the statistics, like everyone else. Some called it blue suicide. Cops, when they retired or were fired, and didn't have anything else in their life, could grow despondent. More than a number had put the barrel of their gun in their mouth and ended it all. All departments were well aware of the issue. They try their best with therapy and support. But sometimes the hurt is too deep.

Since her death, since losing his job, since back when he lost his father, the thought had been there. If it ever got too much, there was a way out. Right there, on his gun belt. Click, boom. Done.

He pushed the thought from his mind even as he pushed open the door to Taylor's Taproom. Behind the bar, Gregor, the owner, was retrieving bottles for a couple of the guys sitting on stools at the bar. Jack recognized most of the people there. They were locals who were here on a Tuesday night because they didn't have anywhere else to be. Add to it that Taylor's Taproom had extended happy hour on Tuesdays, from four until seven, with two for one drinks, and it wasn't too bad of a crowd at all.

In the corner was Spike. He had thick glasses, and the right side of his face drooped. He'd had a few strokes over the years. He'd hold his beer with his left hand, and sip it through a straw. His right arm hung almost useless to his side. A couple others were familiar to Jack as well.

Joe Branch, a skinny, gray-headed and gray-bearded fellow sat at the bar, with his buddy Gary "Kraky" Krawkoski. Branch was the silent type, unless he was discussing world politics, and Kraky was the town loudmouth. Bobby G. was playing the video Keno game, and a couple of gals were laughing and carrying on at one of the tables against the wall. Bill Granger was throwing darts with John Kronk.

Darlene, a barfly if there ever was one, was sipping a fruity cocktail of some sort through a straw. She smiled as Jack came in and sat down, giving him a wave. He'd let her pay for some makeup she'd tried to take from the grocery store instead of charging her with theft. The manager had allowed her to pay, at Jack's behest, even if it was begrudgingly. She claimed she'd forgotten about putting it into her pocket, that her brain was on autopilot, that was all. She would have lost her job in the office at the stool and chair factory if she'd been arrested for theft, she had told Jack. She managed payroll and a few other things for them, and there was no way they'd trust her with anything if she was arrested for stealing. So she liked Jack.

"Hey there," Gregor said. "Good to see you out and about. Whatever you're having, the first one's on me."

"Thanks, how about a pint of Guinness," he said. "To start off."

"Ah, staying true to your ancestors," Gregor said, in his best Irish accent. "One pint o' Guinness for ol' McMurphy, coming up, and it's on the house."

"Hey, what about us?" Kraky said from down the bar. "We drop more money in here than he ever does, where's our free Guinness?"

"The only thing I'll give you for free is my boot up your backside, Kraky," Gregor said.

"What's he ever done," Kraky continued to his buddy, Branch. Making sure he was loud enough for both Gregor and McMurphy to hear. "I mean, all he's ever done was screw things up. Tell me I'm wrong. Takes the job when his poor old daddy dies. Boo-frickin-hoo. Then gets the town all shot up and burned down. Then what? Get's another cop shot up, brings in a Negro cop, and oh yeah, drowns his girlfriend. But he deserves a free beer, right?"

"Hey, I'll tell you once, Krakowski. You start trouble and I'm tossing you outta here for a week," Gregor said.

"Probably the best week of my life," Kraky muttered. He drank his beer empty, then tapped the empty bottle on the counter, looking for another.

Jack took his Guinness and sipped at it. He knew that Krakowski was the typical, empty-headed loud mouth, but it didn't mean that the guy hadn't managed to piss him off in less than thirty seconds. Jack watched the television and tried to let the anger subside. He gulped down the beer and watched the Buffalo Sabers skating against the Islanders. Before he realized, the glass was empty.

"Another?" Gregor asked. Jack nodded. It arrived. He drank. There was an anger building inside of him. It was a rage. Like an insatiable fire. His mind drifted across everything Kraky had said. Lost his dad, lost his job, got Cooke shot up, lost Paula. He really was a royal screw up. It made him angry at himself for knowing it to be true. It made him even more angry that a loser like Krakowski knew it too.

"Another?" Gregor asked as Jack drained his second.

"Yeah," Jack said. "And a shot of your best whiskey too."

"Boilermaker, coming up," Gregor said. Then as he served it, he said quietly, "Drinks are on me tonight, okay, Jack. You'll get through this thing."

"Seriously?" Krakowski bellowed. Jack gulped down the shot of whiskey and chased it with three gulps of Guinness. He felt warm. He felt angry.

"You got something to say?" Jack asked.

"Come on, Jack," Gregor said. "You know he's just being a jerk. I'll kick him out for ya. Just relax and enjoy your drink." Gregor moved down the bar and talked to Kraky. "Why don't you take off, Kraky."

"No way I'm going," he bellowed again. He looked like a big toad, perched atop the stool. He was maybe five and a half feet tall, and at least three hundred pounds. He worked over the hill to the north, just outside of town, at a big junkyard his dad had left him. "He's nothing. He ain't no cop no more, he ain't nothing. If he wants me to shut up, let him say it."

Jack gulped down the rest of his beer, stood up and walked over to Krakowski. He didn't say a word. He kicked the stool out from under the chubby man and brought his hand forward against the back of his head, effectively smashing the man's face into the bar as he fell. Kraky shut up. He crumpled onto the floor, unconscious.

"That was a real crap thing to do, man," Bunch said, jumping down from his own stool to have a look at his friend. "Real cowardly, man."

"Aw, jeez, Jack," Gregor said, peering over the counter. Blood was starting to flow out of Kraky's nose. He was out cold for a few minutes. Jack stood over him, the anger slowly fading away. He'd stopped himself from pounding the man's face in with his fists, as well. A few long minutes passed, and Kraky started to come around, though very groggily.

"What are you doing, man," Branch said. "Somebody call the cops. That's assault, man."

"I'm not calling the cops," Gregor said. "He had it coming."

"You know, that's kind of funny," Jack said. His head was spinning a bit. "You slag us cops all the time, then the first sign of trouble and all you want are cops there to protect you. You're nothing but a hypocrite."

"If you ain't gonna do it, then I am, man. This cannot stand," Branch said. "Give me the phone. This is just wrong, man."

Gregor looked at Jack, and then handed the phone over to Branch. Jack went back to his stool and asked for another boilermaker.

"Maybe you should just go," Gregor said.

"Give me another drink," Jack said. "I bury my wife tomorrow. My wife of less than a week. You get that? Some fat toad decides he's going to talk junk about her, he'll end up on the floor in his own fluids. Give me another drink."

"Jeez," Gregor said. He poured the drink and served it. "You're going to lose a lot of this town's goodwill you act this way."

"What's this town done for me?" Jack asked. It was about that time that Aaron Patterson walked through the door.

Chapter 51

"Well I'll be damned," Patterson said as he strode into the Taproom. "Jack McMurphy, as I live and breathe. Want to tell me what happened here?"

"Ask him," Jack indicated Krakowski on the floor. He was getting helped into a sitting position by Branch.

"He just knocked him off his stool," Branch said. "Smashed his face into the bar. Knocked him out."

"That true?"

"I was going to go over and shoot some darts with the boys and tripped on his stool. You know how it is. Just tried to catch my balance is all," Jack said. "Just got clumsy all of a sudden."

"Oh yeah? Clumsy, huh?" Patterson looked at Krakowski. "Is he okay? Does he need an ambulance?"

"Naw. I don't need an ambulance," Kraky said. His mouth started working before the rest of his brain was in gear. "Nice cheap shot. You want a fair fight, just ask. None of your cheap shot garbage. I'll take you on any day of the week."

"Okay, well, Jack. Looks like you're spending the night in jail, partner. Put your hands behind your back," Patterson said.

"And if I don't?"

"Oh, God, I was hoping you were going to say that," Patterson said. He pulled his cell phone out of his pocket and hit a number. "This is Chief Patterson in Coopers Hollow. Can I get some backup at Taylor's Taproom on Main Street? I've got a drunk and disorderly Jack McMurphy here. I'm trying to take him in on assault charges. Need some backup." Patterson put the phone away.

"Coward," Jack said.

"I told you I'd get you," Patterson said.

Jack didn't say anything. He thought about that gun, at home, in the gun belt, by his bed. He wondered what the metal tasted like.

In less than ten minutes, two sheriff's deputies arrived. Jack knew both of them by sight, but not by name. They were young, new to the department. He'd been hoping Ballard would come, now that he had switched over full time to the sheriff's department, but he was probably in the southern part of the county this time of night.

Patterson explained the situation to the deputies, who he obviously knew well, having worked with them.

"So, are we going to have a problem?" His name tag said Brewhauser on it.

Jack didn't say anything.

"Right now, we've got you on drunk and disorderly. Maybe assault if he wants to lawyer up and press charges. Maybe the prosecutor lets it all go away. You decide you want to take a pop at us, I can guarantee you it's not going away," Brewhauser said. "Come along with me, I'll take you over to the lockup."

"No cuffs," Jack said. "No cuffs and I'll go. Just let me finish my drink."

Brewhauser looked at Patterson, who just rolled his eyes and shrugged.

They stood there and let him take the last swallow of his beer before they put hands on him and marched him out the door. Brewhauser put him in the back of his car for the three block ride to the station house. Patterson and the other sheriff's deputy followed.

They prodded him up the front steps, then through the desks and back to the old bank vault which had been converted into a jail cell. They shoved him through the door, because he made them. Then they locked the door behind him.

"Hi, Jack. What are you doing here?" Tubby asked.

He took a deep breath and sat down on the bunk opposite Tubby's. There was a toilet, straight back, attached to the wall. Stainless steel, with a wash basin built into the top of it. About thirty inches separated the two bunks, which were only about six feet long. Tubby had to bend his knees to fit into the space. He was still dressed in his shirt and slacks. They had taken his belt and tie. They let him keep his shoes, as they were slip ons.

"Tubby," Jack said. "Jeez, Tubby. I screwed up."

"Me too, I guess," Tubby said. "But thanks for the lawyer you got me. The guy came in and talked to me. Told me I'd probably be out tomorrow. Did you come to spend the night?"

"Looks like," Jack said. He laid back on the bunk, the thin mattress offering very little comfort. No pillow, no blanket.

"They say I took Riker and hid him," Tubby said. He leaned up, to look at Jack. "But the lawyer guy said that he died in the flood. Did Riker really die in the flood?"

"I don't know," Jack said. "They haven't found him yet."

"Oh," Tubby said. He laid back down.

Jack didn't remember falling asleep. But he did remember getting woken up by Tubby, who was shaking him like a rag doll.

"Chief! Are you awake? Jack!"

"Jeez, what is it? What time is it?"

"I don't know, I had a bad dream," Tubby said.

"Oh, cripes," Jack said.

"No, listen," Tubby continued. "I was really sad. So I did what Mister Anton always tells me to do when I'm sad, I prayed."

"And that gave you a nightmare?"

"I don't know. But I remembered something. Something from when I was a little kid."

"When were you ever little?"

"I remember a bad man coming after me. Doing bad things to me," Tubby said. He was shaking, sweating. "He said he'd kill me if I told anybody. So I didn't. Then I remember mama yelling and screaming. She said 'you're not touching him no more' and she shot the man."

"Jeez, Tubby. You remember the night he got shot?" Jack asked. "Your mama, she shot him and stuffed him in the freezer, remember?"

"I know. But that wasn't the man," Tubby said. "It was somebody else. Because I remember the man saying to me that if I told anybody, I'd disappear just like my dad did. I remember it."

"Do you remember who it was? Who the man was who said it?"

"No. In my dream, it was just a shadow." Tubby was calming down, no longer heaving with fright.

Jack leaned up to look at him. The alcohol was really hitting him. If he'd tried to stand, he would have fallen over. What Tubby said to him seemed like a dream. Like a joke. Jack told Tubby to go back to bed. Then he turned towards the wall and tried to go back to sleep.

He dreamed he was being chased by old man Everett and his cane.

"Do you think he knows?"

"How could he?"

"I don't know, I'm asking you."

"No way he knows."

"We should have just done him at his house. Made it look like a suicide. Nobody would have questioned it. Not after everything he's been through," the driver said.

"Wouldn't make sense until after the funeral."

"You got it all figured out, huh?"

"I almost feel sorry for the guy," the passenger said.

"You feel sorry for him? You killed his wife and tried to kill him."

"Naw, the water did that," the passenger said. "I'm innocent."

"So what now?"

"We wait until they let him out. And we take care of him. We don't get paid unless he's dead too."

"Call it a night?"

"Yeah, he's not going anywhere."

Jack continued to dream, that night. He relived the flood, over and over. He saw Riker in his yellow parka. Instead of turning around and getting away from the water, he was getting closer and closer. Jack yelled for him to stop, but he kept getting closer. Then Paula was on the ladder, Jack tried to reach out to her, to help her. He turned back to look at Riker, but the boy was gone. Nowhere. When he turned back to Paula, she was gone too.

"Wakey, wakey," Patterson said. "Did you ladies sleep okay? Never mind, I don't care. Tubby, looks like all your lawyering paid off. You're free to go."

"What about Jack?" Tubby asked.

"What about him? He's here for something else, he is not free to go."

"Well, I want to stay with him," Tubby said.

"What? Why?"

"Because he needs a friend," Tubby said, looking sorrowfully at Jack, who was still laying on the bunk, eyes open to just slits.

"Tubby, get out of here," Jack said. "I'm fine. When I get out, we'll go over to the Peachy Keen and get some breakfast."

"Promise?"

"I promise," Jack said.

"Okay."

Patterson opened the door and let the big man out. Tubby had to duck his head to get out of the cell. Jack sat up and watched Patterson walk him to the door. There were two other officers at the desks. Neither was Tricia Wallace. Apparently Patterson had already done some hiring. The new chief of police headed back to his office.

"Hey, Patterson!" Jack called. "Tell me what happened. Did you find the kid?"

"What's it to you?"

"I paid for his lawyer," Jack said. "And I may have been the last to see the kid. Did you find him?"

"No, but we found his bike," Patterson said. "It was downstream. Only a matter of time before we find him. Wasn't Tubby at all. The father's in rough shape."

"He lost his wife too, you know," Jack said. "Brain tumor not but a week or so ago."

"Jeez," Patterson said. That's all he said as he went back into his office. Jack heard the door close.

By eleven o'clock, Patterson was back at the cell.

"Okay, Jack," Patterson said. "Your lucky day. Prosecutor thinks a night in jail will do. He's not going to pursue charges against you."

"What about Kraky?"

"You tripped over his stool, remember? Can't charge a guy for being clumsy, right?" Patterson said. "This is literally your one get-out-of-jail-free card. Now get out of here and go get cleaned up for Paula's funeral."

Jack climbed to his feet and walked out of the cell. Patterson handed him the keys to his rental car.

"No more second chances, Jack."

McMurphy didn't say another word. He left the station house, walked the three blocks to his rental car, and drove it home. He showered, shaved, and dressed in his suit. The only suit he had. The one he'd worn with Paula in Vegas.

"What do you think? Do it now, looks like a suicide, right? Couldn't take going to the funeral?"

"Or we wait until after," the driver said. "If we do it now, people will come looking for him. We wait until after, and they won't miss him for a few days, right? We'll be outta here, no muss, no fuss."

"I think we do it now," the passenger said. "I don't want to be here any longer than I have to."

"Flip on it?"

"Heads we do it now, tails we wait until after the funeral."

"Alright, but I flip."

The funeral was held at the only funeral home in town. There were news vans outside. Jack shook hands with everyone, even if his hand still hurt from the sunroof. Most people he knew, some he didn't. Paula's old staff from the paper came to pay their respects. It was a surreal, three hour affair. He felt like he was in a fog, a daze. Like his head was floating above his shoulders, and he wasn't really there. That none of it was real.

When the calling hours concluded, he shook hands with the funeral director, thanking him.

"I have her things," the director said. "I was going to have Goldie bring them to you. Well, she offered at least. Anyway, if you'd like them, I have them in my office."

"Okay," Jack said. A moment later, and he was handed an envelope that contained the items that were found on Paula's body. He thanked the director once again and headed out to his car.

"Jack!"

He was about to get into the rental car when he heard his name called. He turned and saw Eric Owens crossing the parking lot toward him.

"Eric, how are you holding up?"

"Not well," Eric said. "Not well at all. I wanted to come. Pay my respects. I just -"

"It's okay, I understand. You've been through so much more," Jack said.

"It's just tough. There's no closure. Until we can lay him to rest, there's just no closure," Eric said. "I knew Tubby didn't have anything to do with it. I just hoped that maybe-"

"I understand, and Tubby does too," Jack said.

"Anyway," Eric straightened up and cleared his throat. "I'm sorry for your loss."

Jack almost said "you too," but he caught himself, and just said, "Thank you."

"Can I ask a favor of you," Owens asked.

"Sure."

"I'm going to walk along the river banks again tomorrow, looking for Riker. Would you come with me? I don't know who else to ask," Owens said.

Jack was quiet for a moment. In his life, he'd been on two drownings. He wasn't up close and personal with the bodies, once they were found. But he was close enough, and it wasn't pretty. One had been in the very lake, north of town, that had overflowed its banks and destroyed the town. Seven years old. Fell out of his canoe and sank like a rock. Jack was there when the divers pulled him out.

He looked Eric in the eyes. Saw the depth of his pain.

"What time?"

"Tomorrow morning," Eric said. "It's getting too dark now."

"Okay," Jack said. "I'll do it. Call me when you're ready."

Eric extended his hand and Jack shook it.

Eric Owens turned and walked back across the parking lot. Jack watched his shoulders drop, and he could tell by the way they convulsed slightly, that the man was crying. A lump formed in his throat.

He sat in the rental car and started the motor. He put the envelope on the seat next to him.

There was the thought again. He wondered what it tasted like, the steel barrel of his gun.

Chapter 52

He pulled the car into his driveway to find a vehicle already there. He didn't recognize it. He stepped from the rental, not knowing what to expect. The doors opened to the other vehicle, and Mr. and Mrs. Crandall stepped out. She was carrying a covered dish.

"Mr. McMurphy, I hope you don't mind," Sandy said. "I just couldn't live with myself thinking that you might not have a good meal. I just brought this by. I hope you don't mind."

"No, not at all," Jack said. "It's very sweet of you."

"Are you hungry now? I could reheat it and get it ready?"

"Actually, I am hungry. Come on in," Jack led the way.

He showed Sandy to the kitchen, then cleared the empty bottles off the table and offered Ken a seat.

"How are you doing?" Ken asked him, with true concern on his face.

"It's tough, but I'll manage," Jack said.

"Well, you don't have to do it alone. I know we don't know you very well, but if you just need somebody to talk to, I'm more than happy to listen," Ken said.

"Well, I appreciate that, I really do," Jack said. They fell quiet for a moment. "I'm sorry, would you like some coffee or something?"

"We're fine," Ken said.

"Yes, you just sit and relax," Sandy said. "I'll have this heated up and ready to go and then we'll get out of your hair."

"How's Tubby?" Jack asked.

"Oh, he's fine. Sometimes I think he's better equipped to deal with disappointment than any of us," Ken said. "He's been through a lot already."

Jack's house phone rang, and he checked the number. It was Detective Phelps from the sheriff's department. He reminded himself that he had to go to Oneonta and get a new cellphone.

"Excuse me, I need to take this," Jack said, standing and moving into the living room, with the cordless handset. "Detective," he continued.

"Jack, good to talk to you. How you holding up?"

"Day by day, minute by minute, you know."

"Well, I was wondering if we could get together and compares some notes on the Pierson death," Phelps said. "Parents ID'd the body, so we know for certain who he was. Now we just have to figure out why he was where he was."

"Well, you know, I'm not on the force anymore," Jack said.

"Don't matter to me if it don't matter to you? I'm alone on this thing. I could use a, what do you call it? An independent consultant on this," Phelps said. "What do you say?"

"What time?"

"Heading your way. Thirty minutes?"

"Let's make it forty-five, I've got a few guests. Let's meet at the Peachy Keen for coffee."

"Sounds good, see you in a few," Phelps said.

Jack returned to the dining room and took a seat across from Ken Crandall.

"Sorry about that," Jack said.

"No problem at all. It's good to stay busy," Crandall said.

They made chit-chat as the meal heated. True to their word, Sandy plated and served the meal, and then they took their leave to allow Jack to eat in quiet. In a way, he wished they had stayed.

They were a nice, older couple, and Ken's silver-gray hair reminded him a bit of his father.

It took him less than ten minutes to finish off the meal, and put the dishes in the sink. He washed the plate and the fork and knife and put them in the drying rack because Paula hated dirty dishes left in the sink -

He caught himself on the edge of the sink, his knees buckling suddenly. It was like getting punched in the chest. He found it difficult to breathe for a moment, and the room started to spin. He saw his glass, still on the countertop by the sink. He suddenly wanted it smashed into a million pieces. He grabbed it and hurled it into the stainless steel sink. The crash was like a lightning strike of noise, sudden, intense and spine tingling. The sound of the crash echoed in his ears as he regained his calm.

In through the nose, out through the mouth. Slow steady. One breath at a time, one step at a time.

On the table were the envelope with Paula's items and his belt with gun holster. He looked at them both. He decided to leave Paula's envelope for later. He took the gun and holster off the belt and slid it into the back of his pants.

"Now?"

"Give it a minute."

"Listen, let's just do this guy and get out of here. The longer we're in town, the better chance he's going to recognize seeing us."

"You're in such a rush. You've got to savor these moments. This is like a work of art. We want this so perfect, nobody ever suspects. We rush in there, and he puts up a struggle, we run the risk of ruining everything. We botch it, we don't get paid. And I don't know about you, but I like getting paid."

"Okay, okay. We wait a minute."

Jack was out the door and into the rental car, carrying a notebook and pen. He knew that there wasn't anything Phelps needed help with. He knew the guy was just being a good cop and trying to give him something to keep his mind off Paula. Jack didn't care if it was all play-acting, or if he would be a legitimate asset to the investigation. He couldn't stay cooped up in the house.

The sun was starting to come out, the clouds of the last few days were giving way to blue skies. There was a measure of solace in that. He put the car in reverse and saw a vehicle roll by the end of his driveway, then speed away.

"Here he comes."

"He's getting in the car, he's leaving."

"Do we do it now, in the car? Shot to the head, plant the gun?"

"Nope. Nope. He sees us, we're rolling."

"We should have just done it the first night."

"I told you. I've studied this stuff. Too quick. A day or two more isn't going to kill you, is it? For forty grand? Just relax."

Jack drove the mile or so into town. He followed the route he had traveled thousands of times previously. He'd bought the house when he'd married his first wife. When she left, he understood. It hadn't exactly been a match from the beginning, even though they'd tried to make it work. The last time he'd talked to her, she was in Florida someplace. She'd called to see if she had left behind something in a box in the attic. He'd looked, and she had. He packaged it up and mailed it to her without hesitation. He couldn't recall if he'd kept the address or not. Surely he had it someplace.

He found himself sitting in the car in front of the Peachy Keen. It had been spared by the flooding, if by only a matter of feet. The building right next door was shifted off its foundation.

The one closer to the river from that, was being torn down today.

As he sat in the car, trying to will himself into going inside, he decided to go over all the details of the Pierson kid's death. Naked kid, off the edge of Wedding Rock, maybe some rope burns on wrists and ankles, run away because of his sexuality. No connection to anyone in town. According to the autopsy, it was the fall that killed him, so he wasn't dumped there. The focus helped. He breathed out and exited the car. One step at a time.

Detective Phelps wasn't there yet, but John Anakausuen was sitting at a table, eating a mid afternoon lunch. He smiled when he saw Jack walk into the diner.

"Jack! Come join me," Anakausuen said.

"I'm actually meeting someone else here," Jack said. "But maybe for a minute. Thank you for your help with Tubby."

"My pleasure," Anakausuen said. "I like helping my friends, when I can."

"Well, thank you again."

"Have you considered my offer? I know it's probably not a good time. Actually, forget I said anything. Let me give you my card and you call me when you're ready. I'm ready when you're ready," Anakausuen said.

"I haven't made a decision yet."

"Okay, okay. I know." He took his iPad and slid it across to Jack. "You want to see something cool? I've marked our boundaries, according to the old maps. Of course, the survey team will give us really precise measurements. But there it is."

The computer tablet had a satellite image of Mount Pratt and Hollow Point. Lines were superimposed over the map, marking out the boundaries of Anakausuen's claim. It contained most of both mountains.

"What then?"

Anakausen took the tablet back and hit and swiped and hit

again and handed it back to Jack. Now it showed buildings and parking areas and improved roads on top of the satellite image.

"Then we start construction. We've got to clear trees here and here. I've got an offer in on this property over here," Bill slid his finger across the map and moved it to focus on the satellite image of a farmhouse with a barn and large area of farmland.

"The Brunswick farm? What do you need that for?"

"Parking. Land on top of the mountain is a premium. We want buildings and hotels and eventually the casino up there. So the game plan is to have parking off mountain, with a shuttle to bring guests up and back. Shuttles will leave every ten minutes during the day, and then every half hour overnight." Jack looked at the map on the iPad as Anakausuen spoke.

"John," Jack started, he sighed heavily. "John, this is my home. I grew up here. It's kind of hard for me to think about a project of this, uh, magnitude happening here."

"I know," Anakausuen said. "It's tough for me too. I'm just like you. We grew up here. This is our home. But look around. How many more shops have to close. If the factory closes up, which it could at any minute, then what happens. Coopers Hollow dies. Sure a few people with money might stick around. The rest will be on the government dole. We're too far away from any other jobs to make it worthwhile for people to live here and drive to their job. Then what, we try to lure some hipsters up from the city? No thank you. You see. I'm not just doing this for me and my ancestors, I'm doing this to help make sure Coopers Hollow survives for the next fifty or a hundred years."

"You're a heck of a salesman, John," Jack said. He nodded to Seemo behind the counter who immediately brought over the pot of coffee and poured it into one of the mugs already at Anakausuen's table. "Thanks, Seemo."

"Here's the thing, John. I don't know what I want to do. I mean, with Paula, we were ready to leave. We were going to travel or something. Now, I just don't know what to do," Jack said. He quickly sipped the coffee, masking the catch in his throat from talking about his dead wife.

"I understand," Anakausuen said. "Listen, for right now, I just need somebody to drive up every once in awhile, you know, maybe a few times a day, and just look everything over. You know, just make sure nobody is messing around with our equipment or that kind of thing. Somebody to put up posted notices around the property. It will give you something to do. I'm no expert on these things, but from what I hear, keeping busy is really important in the healing process."

"I'll think it over," Jack said. "I'll let you know this week, deal?"

"Okay, I appreciate it," Anakausuen said, extending his hand. Jack shook it. "One more thing."

"Sure."

"This house right here," Anakausuen said. "You know who lives there? The tax records say it's W. Everett. Is that still old man Everett?"

"Yeah. The old dude is still alive and kicking," Jack said. "In fact, that was him at the town council meeting."

"Wow. He was old when we were kids. I don't know about you, but he wasn't exactly nice to me. Called me and my sisters half-breeds. It used to make me so angry. We were pure-bloods, you know. My father always warned my sisters and I about playing near his house, said he was a crazy old man," John said.

"Yeah, I think his bark was worse than his bite," Jack replied. Something itched in the back of his brain as he looked at the map. He and his friends from school had climbed all over Mount Pratt and Hollow Pointe. They knew enough to stay away from old man Everett's well manicured yard. Jack knew that his father received calls regularly from the curmudgeon with complaints about trespassers.

"Do you think he's ready to sell, move to Florida?" Anakausuen asked.

"I don't think so. I think he's one of those guys that's going to stay until the day he dies, or is carted out to a home," Jack said. "Even then, he probably wouldn't sell, just out of spite."

"Do you have any pull with him? Think you could talk him into it?"

"Why? Why do you want that land too?" Jack asked.

Anakausuen sighed. He took the iPad and stroked his fingers across the screen a few times. Then he showed it to Jack.

"If we get his land too, it means we can use these plans instead."

Jack looked it over. Pretty much the only difference was another building located where Everett's home was now.

"What's this building?"

"That will be a high end Spa. Like the kind they have in California. Four-hundred dollars a day and you're pampered head to toe. Massage, mud baths, saunas, mineral pools, the works. You see here, it connects to the main hotel. We'd put in a glass covered escalator that would go up and down the mountain. Won't be another one like it in the world. So you come, stay at the hotel, gamble a bit in the casino here, then go get pampered in the Spa. See, it just works better if we can get his land too," Anakausuen said.

"I guess I never realized just how close his house was to the top of the mountain. You have to get to it from this road over here and the driveway comes up the back side to get to the house," Jack said. He studied the map a bit more.

"Well, if you're interested in coming onboard with me, maybe we can go talk with him, see if he's interested in selling. He may not want to talk to the half-breed," Anakausuen joked.

"I don't think I'll be any help," Jack said. "You heard him at the meeting. He wasn't exactly a fan of mine, I guess. Or my dad's."

"Okay, okay. I'll regroup. I'll do some more digging. First pitch has to be good to somebody like him. Otherwise he'll shut down negotiations. I've seen it before," Anakausuen said.

"You may be right."

The door chimes jingled as Detective Phelps entered the diner. He walked over to Jack, toting a soft leather bag on a shoulder strap.

"Jack, how's it going?"

"It's going," Jack said. "Detective Phelps, this is John Anakausuen. Maybe you've heard about his project."

"Oh, yeah. You're the trouble maker," Phelps said, extending his hand. Anakausuen shook, even as he sized up the detective.

"I like to think of myself as the rainmaker, you know making it rain cash. Coopers Hollow is going to erect statues of me when I'm done. I'm going to put this place on the map," Anakausuen said. "And put a bunch of money in people's pockets while I'm at it."

"Rainmaker, that's funny," Phelps said. There was an uncomfortable pause. "I mean, what I meant to say-"

"I'll do a rain dance first," Anakausuen said. "Appease my ancestors." No smile on his face. Deadpan.

"Listen, I didn't mean anything by it," Phelps said.

"I'm just yanking your chain," Anakausuen said, with a big smile. He gave Phelps a soft knock on the arm with his fist. "Very nice to meet you detective."

"Uh, John, this is my appointment. So I'm going to go have coffee with him," Jack said.

"Go. Go. Thanks for giving me a few minutes," Anakausuen extended his hand.

"I'll let you know this week," Jack said, shaking hands again. "Promise."

"Thanks, Jack."

McMurphy and Phelps found a table in the front window where they could look out onto the street and watch the traffic. Though, with the bridge out because of the flood, there wasn't much traffic. It was all being rerouted south of town. All told, it was an extra seventeen miles. All for one bridge being out.

"How are you holding up, Jack?"

"I'm numb right now. It's not real yet," Jack said. "You know, I was married before."

"I guess I didn't know that."

"She left me after about two years. I was working all the time. Just trying to prove to my old man I was as good a cop as him. Took all the overtime, you know. Took the crap assignments. When she left, she stuck a note to the fridge. I didn't see it for two days. Didn't even know she was gone," Jack said.

"You sure you don't want to be on the detective payroll? We can use those types of skills," Phelps said.

"You know, it never hurt. I never felt it inside. Actually, I felt like she was completely justified and I kind of had this, almost relieved feeling. Like she was free and I was happy for her," Jack said.

"Yeah," Phelps said. "I've been married twice. First one, well, it lasted three months. She didn't want me signing up for the army. I did it anyway. She divorced me. Second wife, well, that one was my fault. I was less than faithful."

"That will do it," Jack said.

"Every time."

"With Paula, it's different. I really could see myself being with her forever. So now there's an emptiness inside. It's like I've been hollowed out. You know those scoops they use on watermelon in the summer to make those perfect little balls? It's like someone took a big one of those and just gutted me. I'm just a husk, a shell. But it's like my brain hasn't figured it out yet," Jack said.

"I'm sorry, buddy. You should talk to somebody. Your priest or something. If you want, I can get you the number of the department shrink. Might help," Phelps said.

"Yeah, maybe."

"Let's get your mind off it. I want to go over the investigation I got going on the Pierson thing. You game?"

"Absolutely."

"Want to order something to eat? Might take some time."

"I just ate," Jack said. "I'm good with the coffee."

"Alright. Let's do this."

Chapter 53

Across the continent, in Las Vegas, five men emerged from the Clark County Detention Center. One was a lawyer, the other four were not. The lawyer worked for a firm that worked as a liaison for a firm that had a single client, Gordon Jefferson, civil rights advocate. The day was not yet hot, but it was certainly dry. It could have been a hundred degrees, or twenty below, it didn't matter. It was fresh air.

"Well, gentlemen," the lawyer said as he climbed behind the wheel of the rented SUV. "Where to?"

Denver had a cast on his arm from where Jack McMurphy had broken it in the steel door. His partner that night, Rook, sat next to him, while Brinkman, and his partner from the botched Chapel O' Love kidnapping, Hammond, occupied the front and third row seats.

"What's the boss say?" Denver asked.

"He said, and I quote, 'those two dumbasses in the Catskills are busy playing paddy-cake with the cop. Tell the boys if they want a bonus they can go take care of him' end quote," the lawyer said. "I'm sure I have no idea what any of that means."

"Pay?" Brinkman asked.

"Double, the big man said," the lawyer replied.

"I'd do it for free," Denver said. "He broke my arm."

"I'll take your portion," Hammond said. "I'm in."

"Me too," said Brinkman.

"Not me," Rook said. "I'm on a plane outta this country. You jokers can chase after the small time. I'm going to get me some big money and some sweet *chicas* in Brazil. Got it all set up. Drop me at the airport, Jeeves."

"Oh, I'm in," Denver said. "And nobody's taking my portion."

"Need anything before we go to the airport? Stop at hotels for luggage or the like?" the lawyer asked. He received head shakes. "Okay, to the airport."

Agent Haas' phone rang in his pocket. He was sitting behind the wheel of an agency car in Houston, Texas. Beside him was Agent Willows, a lanky guy who popped his jaw and his knuckles constantly. It was one of those idiosyncrasies that drove Haas crazy. Silence, pop, silence, pop, pop. Constantly. And if Haas complained about it, Willows did it more.

"This is Agent Haas," he said into the phone. Pop, pop. He covered the phone and turned to Willows. "I swear to God, if you don't stop I'm going to put a bullet in your head and dump your body in the desert."

Pop.

"Yeah, what's up?" Haas spoke again into the phone. He listened to his friend from the Las Vegas field office explain that, the four hoodlums he'd help round up, were now free. Their lawyer got the DA to drop the charges for lack of evidence. The casino surveillance went missing and the DA decided it wasn't worth his effort to get the guys in front of a judge, for what would equate to, a slap on the wrist. The four of them had spent a total of eight days in jail.

Agent Haas thanked his friend and closed the connection. He dialed another number. His boss picked up on the first ring.

Haas explained the situation.

"And what do you want me to do about it?" Scutter asked.

"Well, I'm not a gambling man, but I'd bet my pension they're heading to the Catskills to finish off McMurphy," Haas said.

"We're done with that case," Scutter said. "It came to an acceptable resolution. Focus on the assignment in Houston. Was that it?"

"Yeah."

Scutter didn't say anything, just closed the connection. Haas swore.

He sat for a moment contemplating whether he should call Jack McMurphy or let it go. Whether he should interfere, or let nature take its course.

"That's our guy," Willows said, indicating a lone man walking out of the strip club. "Let's go, partner."

Haas put the phone in his pocket and followed his partner to intercept their target.

Chapter 54

"We've got some results back from the lab," Phelps started. "I think it can help us piece together this thing a bit better."

"Go ahead," Jack said. He finished his cup of coffee and looked over to the counter. Seemo was already brewing another pot.

"Just a minute or two, chief," Seemo said. Jack let it go. Once you had a nickname from Seemo, it didn't change. Just ask Tubby.

"The thing I was most interested in, was his feet," Phelps said.

"If he was barefoot and ran for any length of time, his feet would be cut up and there would be items embedded. If he was dragged and dumped off the pointe, then they would be free of cuts," Jack said. "Maybe abrasions on the heels."

"Absolutely," Phelps agreed. "So the initial examination showed that he had been walking or running through rough ground prior to his going off the cliff. We found gashes, dirt, pine needles and leaves on and embedded in his feet, just like you said. Everything tested as local. Soil samples were a match to the surrounding area, as were the pine needles and leaves."

"So he was brought up to the mountain, and escaped and ran off the cliff in the dark," Jack posited. "Or was he on something?"

"Possibly. But I'll get to that. The other thing we checked were additional injuries to his body. He had small scrapes on his arms and legs, his abdomen and face and neck. This corresponds to injuries sustained running through the forest," Phelps said. "The path from the top of the mountain where the picnic area is, and where the cliff is doesn't have many branches like we're looking at. He was going through enough forest to scratch up his legs pretty substantially."

"So he was running naked, through the woods?"

"Yeah. And also, he had been sexually assaulted," Phelps said, in a more hushed tone, so other patrons wouldn't hear him.

"Really?"

"Yeah. We recovered additional DNA not belonging to him. Lastly, there was a sedative in his system," Phelps said. "Commonly used for date rape. A black out drug. Flu, uh, flu something. I can't pronounce it." He pointed to the word on the report.

"So he's picked up and roofied, and tied up and assaulted and he escapes and falls off the cliff?" Jack said.

"That's what I'm thinking," Phelps replied. "Got any local pervs who might do something like this?"

"None come to mind," Jack replied. "But you never know. Did he have gravel in his feet, like from the walking path or the parking lot at the entrance of the hiking trail?"

"Um," Phelps looked at the report again. "No. No gravel. Soil, pine needles, leaves and lichen. No hard gravel."

"Ran through the woods to get there," Jack said.

"Probably."

"There's nothin up there," Jack said. "I was just looking at a map. Hang on a second." He stood and walked over to Anakausuen. He spoke with him for a moment, then returned with the iPad. "Take a look at this."

Jack showed the satellite image map to Phelps. "Here's where we found the body, and the cliff, here's the Brunswick farm and here's Mr. Everett's house. That's it over there. You'd have to run through some thick forest from both places, but it's not too far a run."

Phelps looked at the map for a moment.

"How do you pull back, zoom out?" Phelps asked. Jack was

not computer savvy, but he'd worked with Paula's iPad in the past. He touched the screen with two fingers and pinched them together slowly. The image zoomed out, showing even more of the terrain in the satellite image.

"Closest houses to the scene by a long shot," Phelps said.

"Yeah. I didn't interview Mr. Everett or the Brunswicks. Did your team?"

"No, we did not," Phelps said. "I have to admit, I didn't look at a map like this. We interviewed all of the home owners along this road leading up to the entrance. But this is on the back side of the mountain."

"Well, maybe we should go up and have a look," Jack said. "If you don't mind a ride along." He went quiet and sipped at his coffee as soon as Seemo poured it. He tried to drown the sharp stabbing pain in his stomach with more of the dark, caffeinated beverage.

"Let's go for a ride," Phelps agreed.

"He's got the cop with him now."

"What do you think he's up to?"

"Just normal buddy-cop stuff. You were in the army, you know how these things go. You bump into a guy you worked with, and you get coffee or a drink."

"Not me. Dishonorably discharged. You get that when you use too many rag heads for target practice."

"Let's follow them. Maybe we get in some more target practice."

Phelps and McMurphy drove to Old Man Everett's house first. They rolled to a stop outside the ranch-style home. It seemed quiet, like nobody was home.

"Whatcha think?" Phelps asked.

"He's old. Maybe he's taking nap."

"Let's wake him up."

McMurphy and Phelps climbed out of the car and walked up to the red door. Phelps pounded his fist against the door a dozen times, then went quiet to listen for any movement inside. There was nothing.

"Go check the garage to see if any cars are here," Phelps said. Jack walked off the porch and over to the garage. He looked in and saw a Lincoln Town Car and a Toyota Forerunner.

"Two cars in the garage," Jack called out.

"Mr. Everett?" Phelps called out, banging on the door again.

They waited for a few moments, but there was no motion inside.

"What do you think?" Phelps asked.

"Well, let's take a walk around the house, see if we can see anything in any of the windows. Maybe he fell and broke a hip," Jack said.

They moved in opposite directions around the property. The windows were high enough off the ground, that they couldn't peer into them. Most of them. On the back of the house, they met up and looked in through the sliding glass doors that led out to the sprawling deck. They could see the library and kitchen. Both were dark.

Jack looked at all the books on the shelf. He thought about Paula and the day he lost her. She'd said something about books and being awful. He figured she was talking about him speaking up at the town council meeting or something. There was an idea trying to bubble up in his brain, but it wasn't forming. He'd been trying to kill thoughts and ideas over the last week with lots and lots of alcohol.

"Well, looks dead," Phelps said. "Let's go have a look at the Burdick place."

"Brunswick," Jack said.

"Right."

"What are they doing?" the driver asked as he watched them pull out of Mr. Everett's driveway and head down the road.

"They know something's up," the passenger said. "McMurphy called in a friend to help him investigate it. Maybe they had tracking on the Mercedes. Maybe they knew she was here. Maybe they're retracing her steps."

"That doesn't make any sense," the driver said. "My guess is, it's something else completely. This is a small town. Only so many players. Maybe they were just checking to see if the guy was okay."

"So what now?"

"We ease off," the driver said.

"Really? Again? Why don't we just buy a house and settle down, while we're at it? Raise some kids and a few dogs?"

"Okay, fine," the driver said. "By the end of the day tomorrow. Whether it has to be messy or not. Then we're out of here. Okay?"

"Okay."

"You are such a baby."

Phelps and McMurphy drove to the Brunswick farm and talked with Mr. And Mrs. Brunswick and their two boys. They hadn't seen anything at all that might indicate that there was a kidnapping, or somebody running through the woods on or around their property. The boys were ages three and five, and it looked like Mrs. Brunswick had her hands full. Mr. Brunswick had inherited the family farm and was making a go of it. They baled hay and had fifty cows that they milked. They also grew corn, but only sold it locally.

"What about the truck driver for the milk truck?" McMurphy asked. "Is it the same guy or different?"

"Earl? He's been running this route for a couple years now. It's not easy to back the truck in next to the milking barn, so there aren't many substitute drivers. I think there was one or two this winter though. He had the flu. I can ask him for their names," Mr. Brunswick said.

"If you have the number of the company, we can follow up," Phelps said.

"And this is about that boy that was found off Hollow Pointe?" Mr. Brunswick asked.

"Yes, sir," Phelps replied. "We'd like to find out what happened. How he got up there."

"We thought it was a camper that got lost or something," Mrs. Brunswick said.

"Could be," Phelps replied. Mr. Brunswick handed him a business card for the milk trucking company. "Thanks for your help."

Phelps and McMurphy headed back out to the car and sat for a moment.

"Well?" Phelps asked.

"They didn't do it. The milk trucker is a possibility. Maybe he had him and he got out of the truck," Jack said. "But there would have been gravel or rocks in his feet. Look at this driveway."

"Well, it was winter," Phelps said. "Maybe it was all iced over. Snow can get deep around here."

"I've got a funny feeling about Mr. Everett's place," Jack said. "Listen, I've got some errands to run. I need to go get a new cellphone in Oneonta. Then in the morning I promised Eric Owens I'd walk with him along the river banks to help look for his son."

"Jeez."

"I know. But I told him I'd do it," Jack said.

"Well, listen," Phelps sighed. "Let's get together tomorrow afternoon and see if we can go and rattle old Mr. Everett out of his slumber. See what he has to say."

"Sounds good."

Phelps drove them back to town. They had to take the long way around, because of the bridge being out. They headed down the backside of the saddle, through Hobart and back up route 10.

Jack said goodbye and got into his rental and steered towards Oneonta, twenty-five miles away. He drove a bit faster than he normally would, he didn't want the cellphone store to be closed, and he wasn't sure if it closed at eight or nine.

A car came up behind him. It rode uncomfortably close. Jack pushed the accelerator down to the floor a bit more, and watched the speedometer needle climb to seventy. The car stayed on his tail.

"What does this jerk want?" Jack adjusted the rearview mirror. For whatever reason, adjusting the mirror when someone is tailgating, had an effect. It was a message like, yeah, I see you there. Back off.

This car didn't back off.

The speed limit dropped to thirty-five through the small town of Davenport. Jack eased off the throttle and thought they were going to trade paint with him for sure.

Then, behind the trailing car, another set of lights. They were accompanied by bright red and blue strobes from a light bar on top of a police cruiser. The car behind him backed way off and pulled over. The police cruiser pulled in behind it, and Jack left them both behind as he continued on towards Oneonta.

"Following a little close, wouldn't you say?" the officer asked.

"Guy was going slow, I was looking to pass," the driver said.

"This is a no passing zone."

"I know, before that. Before the town. Then when we got to town, he slammed on his brakes," the driver said. "We could have had an accident."

"I need to see your license and registration on the vehicle."

The driver calmly fished out the documents and handed them

over. They were fakes, but he had memorized the info. He was Paul Parks. He was from Connecticut. They were on business. Just passing through. This was a rental. Everything looked legit.

The officer wrote him a ticket for following too closely and handed it to him along with his license and the vehicle registration and rental agreement.

"You look familiar," the officer said. "You come through this way often?"

"First time," Parks said.

"What'd you do to your arm?"

"Broke it skiing a few weeks ago. Thought I'd get a few more runs in at Windham Mountain. Kind of icy. It's almost better," Parks said.

"Okay. Have a nice evening, and don't tailgate," the officer said.

Parks rolled up the window and pulled away from the side of the road. He let out string of profanities.

The man who carried a license and fake FBI ID with the name Parsons on it, rode quietly in the passenger seat. He was growing tired of this little operation.

Jack made it to the cellphone store before it closed, and got his first smart phone. The clerk explained how everything worked, but he didn't think he'd use a fraction of the apps or functions. Still, at least he was embracing the future. Paula would be proud.

As he climbed into the rental car, he thought about the close to forty minute drive ahead of him, and the empty house that awaited. It didn't appeal to him at all. There was a hotel with a bar only a half a mile away. He decided he'd get a few drinks and crash in a room for the night.

Just because.

First, he decided to drive past the new and used truck dealer in town. He was thinking a nice big pickup truck. Maybe something that would accommodate a truck-bed camper. There was a RV lot outside of town as well. He could get the room tonight, then swing by the RV lot in the morning on his way back to meet with Eric Owens.

Parks and Parsons drove back and forth through the mall parking lot, then headed towards downtown. The problem with the car that McMurphy was driving, was that it looked like twenty percent of all the other cars on the road.

After nearly two hours, they weighed their options. He had more than likely headed back to his house by now. Even if he'd stopped off for a late dinner, or had gone to the movies. So they circled around and headed back to Coopers Hollow. It took them forty-five minutes, as they did not want to get another ticket.

They arrived at his house, and he was nowhere to be found.

They traded profanities as they headed back to Oneonta to their hotel.

He liked the Ford F-250 King Ranch. Steep price, but it looked like you'd be riding everywhere in the comfort of your sofa at home. The big engine, and the large cabin space would make it perfect, if he decided to get the camper. And he even liked the color.

Jack got back in the rental, and it suddenly seemed completely inadequate. He drove from the Ford dealership over to the hotel. He checked into a room first, and then headed to the bar. They had a ballgame on. Giants versus the Dodgers. He watched for awhile and drank for awhile.

After he drank a few beers, he decided that he had to get up in the morning and walk with Eric Owens, so he had better not overdo it. So he only drank a few more beers.

The hotel room key was a plastic card that pressed up against the handle to unlock it. He was glad. He would have had trouble using an old metal room key. He had trouble finding the right room, let alone sliding a key into a lock. He closed the door behind him and stumbled to the bed in the dark.

He fell asleep with his clothes on.

About the time his head hit the pillow, Parks and Parsons pulled up outside. They too visited the bar for a few drinks before heading to their respective rooms.

They didn't notice the black Ford Fusion parked in the lot.

Chapter 55

Jack was awake and showered and checked out by seven the next morning. He hadn't brought a razor or a change of clothes, so he wanted to stop by his house before he met Eric Owens in Coopers Hollow. He climbed into the rental car, covered in a heavy dew. It was cold enough that he could see his breath, and there was fog all through the valleys in the region. It hadn't been cold enough for a frost, so he didn't have to spend time scraping the windshield. He was able to just turn on the wipers and drive off.

Parks and Parsons missed him by five minutes. They opted for breakfast in the opposite direction before they started their day. They talked about their bad luck from the previous night over pancakes, sausage and eggs. They discussed how this was it. This was the last day they were going to fool around with this assignment.

Jack McMurphy was going to be dead by the end of the day.

Eric Owens dropped Yasmine off at his mother's house. The school was closed for the week as the town tried to recover from the flooding. There was a good chance it would need to remain closed for another week, as part of the road that lead to the school had been washed away in the deluge.

Yasmine was struggling with the situation. Losing both her mother and her brother within a week was too much for anyone to handle. But for her, she felt like if she hadn't tried to kill herself, then they never would have moved from New Jersey. And even if Sylvia had still passed away during surgery, at least Riker wouldn't have died in the flood. They would have been safer staying in New Jersey.

Eric couldn't help but think about his pilot friend, and the string of incidents that led to every air traffic disaster. Eric thought that by moving, he'd halt the catastrophe. Instead, it may have initiated it.

Eric didn't know how to respond to his daughter. He could only tell her that none of it was her fault. That it was just bad luck. That they had to stick together now and they would find a way to pull through.

When she climbed out of the car to go to her grandmother's house, she stopped and looked back at her dad.

"It's not your fault either, dad," she said. "You know that, right?"

"Yeah," he said. It was barely audible. He cleared his throat. "I love you."

"I love you too, dad."

He watched his remaining child walk to the door of the house that had been a safe haven for him, ever since he was born. His mother and father had done such a good job of protecting him when he was growing up. Sure he got into a scrape now and again, but he'd lived. All he could think of was how horrible a job he had done in comparison.

Eric drove to the Peachy Keen diner and waited for Jack. Since the grocery store parking lot was the last place anyone had seen Riker, they were going to start on the river bank there. They could trace the river out of town. It was more of a stream, now that the flooding had subsided. Teams had already combed the area, but nothing had been found. They didn't believe Riker had gone over the dams in Hobart, as his bike was found there. Anything was certainly possible, but the fire chief said that she believed he would be found someplace between Coopers Hollow and Hobart. More than likely, his body had become entangled underwater in a tree or some other debris, and he would be found once the water receded.

Eric didn't want to be the one to find his son's dead body. But he also didn't want anyone else to be the one either. So he would go out every day until his son was found. Until he could find closure.

Jack arrived, drank down a mug of coffee at the Peachy Keen and then accompanied Eric down to the river bank. They walked in silence. The ground was still very damp and muddy along the bank, despite the waters receding several days previously. Eric walked with a walking stick, his tailbone and ankle still giving him pain.

They walked nearly a half a mile before Eric spoke.

"When we find him, after we bury him next to his mother," Eric said. "I'm leaving. I'm taking the family away from here."

"I don't blame you," Jack replied.

"There's a job in Louisiana. An opening for head engineer for the Lake Ponchartrain Causeway outside of New Orleans. It's the country's longest bridge over water. Nearly twenty-four miles long," Owens said.

"I think I've heard of it."

"It will be good for Yasmine. Good for me. Probably good for mom, too." He stepped awkwardly on a rock and tweaked his ankle. He let out a grunt, but kept walking. They were scanning the water as well as surrounding land where the water had flooded. Riker had last been seen in a bright yellow poncho. If he were still under water, they might yet be able to see the yellow plastic.

"How is she doing, your daughter?"

"It's not easy. We've been through so much. Before we moved up here, she had trouble, you know," Owens said.

"I didn't know that."

"She was getting bullied. It wasn't good. She tried to hurt herself. Riker, he found her. He saved-" he stopped mid sentence. It was a few moments before he spoke again. "She blames herself."

"It was nobody's fault," Jack said. He was thinking about Paula.

The wind shifted, and the smell hit their nostrils. It was the smell of death. Both of them recognized it, but neither said anything. Jack checked the wind by wetting a finger. He started walking into the wind. The smell grew stronger and more foul as they went.

Ahead, there was a cluster of trees right on the river bank. Jack could see the water had left silt almost ten feet up the tree trunks. The smell was coming from that direction.

"Why don't you rest your ankle for a minute," Jack said. He walked forward towards the odor. It was strong and unmistakably that of decaying flesh. He pulled up his t-shirt over his nose and mouth, but it didn't help. As he approached the cluster of trees, he saw something jammed between the tree trunks. Flies were buzzing all around it. This area had been underwater even twenty-four hours ago.

He stepped closer, and then let out a sigh.

He hurried away from the stench to get to fresh air. He almost gagged a few times.

"It was a dead cow," Jack said. "Must have been out here grazing when the flood hit."

Eric started sobbing. He held his head in his hands, dropping the walking stick. He stood like that for several minutes, unable to compose himself. Jack turned his back and walked along the river bank, giving the man some privacy.

After a few minutes, Eric caught up with Jack.

"I'm sorry," he said.

"It's okay. Nothing to be sorry about," Jack said.

"I thought I could do this, but I can't. Somebody else needs to find my boy. I want to go back," he said.

"Okay," Jack replied. "We can go back."

They turned around and started to back track on the nearly two miles, they had already covered. They were both quiet.

"Jack," Eric said. "I need to ask you something."

"Go ahead."

"When I told you, that morning, about the dam. About it not being safe, and that you should get somebody to look at it. Did you call anybody?"

The question hung in the air. It was worse than the stench of the rotting cow. Jack didn't answer for several paces.

"I told someone," Jack said. Though factually accurate, he felt like he was lying. Knew he was lying. He was stricken with guilt. What Eric was really asking, was whether Jack had followed up with an engineer or the State of New York, or somebody higher up, and whether they had dropped the ball. What he was asking was, who was really to blame. Jack stopped and looked at Eric.

"I told someone, but it wasn't nearly soon enough," Jack said. "I never went to look at it for myself. I didn't know how bad it was. It's my fault. All of it."

Eric nodded. He walked past McMurphy and continued hiking back into town on his own.

When they finally arrived back in Coopers Hollow, Eric climbed into his SUV without looking at Jack again. He put the big vehicle in gear and squealed the tires, as he sped away.

Chapter 56

"Afternoon," Phelps said as he walked into the diner and spotted Jack at the counter.

"Afternoon," Jack responded.

"Ready to go up and see what's what with Mr. Everett?"

"Ready when you are," Jack said.

They used Phelps' car, and drove down through Hobart again and then back up the southern side of Hollow Pointe to the steep, gravely driveway of William Everett's house.

Jack had remained silent the whole trip. Phelps steered the car up the winding, gravel driveway, stealing a glance at Jack, as they rolled to a stop. They still weren't within sight of the house.

"What is it?"

"That day when Paula died, she said something about Old Man Everett and awful books. She was really upset," Jack said.

Phelps was quiet. The car idled as they sat in the driveway.

"Do you think she was out here?"

"Maybe. I thought at first she meant about what he'd said at the town council meeting the night before. But we saw all those books on the shelves through the back windows the other day. I don't know if it means anything or not," Jack said.

"You carrying?" Phelps asked.

"Yeah, I am."

"Good."

"Hope for the best, plan for the worst, right?" Jack said.

"Yeah."

"They're back here? They're piecing it together. They know. They're retracing her steps," Parsons said. They'd come into town and immediately picked up Jack and Eric leaving the diner to walk along the river's edge. Both of their cars were parked by the diner, so they didn't bother following them. They just waited for them to return. Then Jack had lunch and left almost immediately with the detective.

"Shut up. They don't know anything. It probably has nothing to do with her," Parks said.

"This was the last place she was at just before."

"Shut up."

"We should do it here. Right now. Take them out and get the hell out of here."

"Shut. Up. We wait," Parks said. His phone vibrated with a text message.

Phelps and Jack both surveyed the house. A large ranch home. Two stall garage. Recessed porch. The lawn was starting to green up. There was maybe fifty feet of lawn on all sides of the house, with a thick ring of trees beyond.

"So, I've been thinking this over since yesterday. Our victim is trapped here, right? Then gets free and runs. If he goes out the back door, he makes it into the trees and just keeps going," Phelps said.

"And if you go straight back from the house, you get to the top of Hollow Pointe in just a couple hundred yards," Jack agreed.

"Straight shot on the map," Phelps said.

"Let's go talk to Mr. Everett."

The skies were gray, blocking out the sun. At this elevation, there were the barest wisps of clouds moving over the mountain. It wasn't exactly fog, but it also wasn't exactly clear visibility either. It felt like a misty rain was in the air.

Jack walked behind Phelps by a few steps, trying to take in as much as he could of the house and surroundings. Everything was quiet, just as it had been the day before.

Phelps was up on the doorstep, knocking hard on the door. His hand rested on the gun at his hip, but was obscured by his sport coat.

Jack had his hand behind his back, fingers tucked into the waist of his pants, curving around the handle of his pistol. Phelps was about to knock again when the door opened.

"Yeah?" It was a young man in blue jeans and a faded t-shirt.

"I'm Detective Phelps with the Delaware County Sheriff's department. You are?"

"Uh, Barry."

"Got a last name, Barry?"

"Diggard. Barry Diggard."

"Mr. Diggard. Is Mr. Everett here?"

"Uh," Barry looked over his shoulder, then tried to step out and shut the door behind him. Phelps didn't step back. So barefoot Barry was just inches from the detective. "He's sleeping. Taking a nap."

"I'm sorry, you're going to need to wake him up. We need to talk to him about a murder investigation. It's pretty important, Barry. If you don't mind, we'd like to step inside. It's damp out here," Phelps looked the young man in the eyes, but the contact didn't last. Barry looked away and then stepped back into the house.

"Don't you need a warrant?" Barry asked.

"Why would we need a warrant, Barry? We just want to ask Mr. Everett a few questions about something that happened up behind his house. Just to see if he saw or heard anything. It's just a formality, really," Phelps said. He flashed a wide smile. They stood there, for a moment, Barry dithering by the door, Phelps smiling, Jack still touching the handle of his gun behind his back. "Why don't we come in."

"Okay, fine. I'll go wake him up," Barry said. "But he won't be happy."

"We'll take our chances," Phelps said. He stepped through the door, with Jack right behind him. Barry shut the door and then padded, barefoot, down the hallway and closed another door. They could hear him talking, but not his words.

"Look at that," Jack said, indicating the bookshelf. "Think Mr. Everett would mind if I admired his books?"

"You're just a private citizen," Phelps said. "With an admiration for books."

Jack walked over and ran his hands along the books. One was pushed in further than the rest. It was large, maybe fourteen inches tall and two inches thick. It had a leather binding with a metal bracket on the spine. The letter M was hand written on a piece of paper that was slid into the metal bracket.

"Were you here?" Jack whispered to himself. "Did you find something, Paula?"

Jack lifted the book off the shelf and opened the pages. It was hand written. He read a page. A lump grew in his throat.

"Phelps. Look at this." Jack called Phelps over. He pointed to a passage on the page that described, in first-person, explicit detail, the sexual assault of a young boy. On the next page was a photo, secured with little black corners, like an old fashioned photo album.

Barry walked quickly back down the hallway and out into the living room. He froze when he saw what they were looking at.

"What are you doing?" Barry asked.

"Come here," Phelps said. "Do you know what's in this book?"

"I don't know," Barry stammered. "Mr. Everett, he's a writer. He writes stuff."

"And what about you? Are you his photographer?" Phelps asked.

"I just - I'm the gardner."

"Barry the gardner," Phelps said. "Where is Mr. Everett?"

"He's in the back, getting dressed. He just woke up, he -"

"Jack, can you please cover Barry the gardner?"

Jack put the book back on the shelf and drew his gun. Phelps had his out as well. He was also thumbing a few buttons on his phone.

"Yeah, this is Detective Phelps. Can you send some back up to 117 Woodward Lane in Coopers Hollow?" Phelps said into the phone. "How long?" Phelps swore and closed down the phone. "Twenty minutes."

"We got this," Jack said. "Mr. Diggard, please come out into the living room and take a seat. Keep your hands where I can see them."

"I don't know what any of this is about. I'm just the gardner. He just pays me to look after the landscaping. And I help him out. He lets me live here," Barry said.

"Never looked in these books, then?" Jack asked.

"I'm not much of a reader," Barry replied.

"Mr. Everett?" Phelps called. "Mr. Everett, I'm with the Delaware County Sheriff's department. I'd like you to step out of the room slowly, with your hands where I can see them."

There was some noise in the room, something fell and hit the ground. It was a hollow thump, like a box had dropped to the ground.

"Mr. Everett," Phelps called out. He was about to open the door, when it exploded outward in a mass of splinters. He felt the impact before he heard the shot. It registered to his ears a moment later as he fell to the ground. There was extreme, shooting pain across his entire abdomen.

"Crap," Parks said. He showed his phone to Parsons. The message said: Sending backup. Stay out of their way.

"I told you!"

"We finish it now, and go collect the money," Parks said.

"It won't look like an accident."

"What other choice do we have? I'm not letting someone else get our money."

"Did you hear that?" Parsons asked. They both went quiet for a moment. It was an unmistakeable sound.

"Yeah. Gunshot," Parks replied.

"No doubt about it."

"Somebody's shooting up there."

"Let's go. This could be our lucky day."

"Phelps!" Jack called, his ears ringing from the shotgun blast. Barry stood up from the couch.

"Get back down! On the ground, now!" Jack yelled at him. "Get on the ground and put your hands behind your head!" Barry hesitated, then got on the ground.

"Phelps! You okay?"

A groan emanated from the hallway. Jack swore and started down the hallway. "You move," he said to Barry. "And I'll put a bullet in you. Got it?"

Barry didn't say a word.

"Tell me you understand, Barry."

"I understand," Barry yelled, with voice quivering.

"Phelps!" Jack saw the man on the floor, trying to crawl back down the hallway. He was trailing blood behind him.

One arm wasn't working. The other was doing all of the pulling.

"He hit me," Phelps said. He coughed and wheezed. He drew in a ragged breath.

"How bad?" Jack was beside him, gun still pointed at the door that was now a shredded hole.

"Can't move my arm. Hit my vest, mostly. Not sure how bad I am," Phelps said. Jack put his gun back into his holster in the back of his pants and rolled Phelps over. He was bleeding from numerous places in his neck, arm and legs. His shirt was blasted wide open, revealing his vest with hundreds of small holes in it.

"Bird shot," Jack said. "Hang on, partner." McMurphy grabbed Phelps under the arms and dragged him back into the living room, where Barry was still lying with hands laced behind his head.

"Jeez, Phelps, you're a bleeder," Jack said.

"Shut up," Phelps replied. Jack ripped open Phelps' sleeve and saw his arm was peppered with bloody holes where the shot had hit him.

"You're not gushing," Jack said. "Looks like you're going to live to fight another day. Can you call out?"

"Yeah, I got this," Phelps grumbled. He pulled his phone out of his pocket and punched in 9-1-1. He held the phone to his ear and requested back up and an ambulance.

Jack drew his weapon again and started down the hall.

"Jack, just wait for backup."

He walked along the wall, careful not to step in the trail of blood. He saw Phelps' gun on the ground. He kicked it down the hallway with enough force to get it just a few feet from Phelps, who was now sitting up and coughing. Phelps was regaining his breath. He was injured, but not badly.

"Put the gun down right now," Jack called out. "We can still talk about this. I'm sure it was just an accident."

Jack reached over and kicked in the rest of the door. It broke away from the lock and fell open. There was still smoke in the air from the shotgun blast. The gun was on the floor. The spent cartridge was jammed halfway out its bottom. It looked like a Remington pump action 12 gauge.

He trained his weapon around the room. It was a large, master bedroom. A bed, dressers, a closet and a bathroom. There was no

Mr. Everett. Jack stepped over the jammed shotgun and ducked into the bathroom. He moved quickly, checking the towel closet and behind the shower curtain. Nothing.

He carefully walked back into the room and checked the closet. It was a large, walk-in closet. He pushed the clothes aside, but there was no one there. Back in the bedroom, he went to the windows. They were locked. He was about to exit back into the hallway, when he noticed one of the area rugs with a corner up. The floors were hardwood, all going in one direction. But there was a break in the hardwood, revealed by the peeled back carpet.

He kicked aside the carpet and revealed a panel with a recessed handle.

"Phelps! There's a trapdoor in the floor," he called.

"Jack, wait for back up!"

"Twenty minutes? Can't do it."

"Jack, wait!"

He trained his gun on the trapdoor and reached for the handle.

"It's quiet."

"Yeah."

"Who do you think shot the gun?"

"Don't know."

"We go in, shoot our guy, drop the guns and walk away. Not our problem."

"Okay."

They both climbed out of the car, but were careful not to shut them. They left the motor running. They ran up to the door, tried the knob and pushed it open.

Chapter 57

Jack opened the trapdoor and stepped back. It was a three foot by three foot door and gave way to steep steps, with a railing.

"There's a passage into the basement," Jack called out to Phelps. "I'm going down."

He lowered himself down and tried to see what was beyond the base of the steps. It was dimly lit, with plywood walls and a concrete floor. It looked like a room or hallway leading back down the length of the house. It was about an eight foot drop to the basement floor. Rather than climb down the ladder-like stairs, Jack squatted, put his free hand on the edge of the opening, and jumped down, crouching low to the ground as he landed. The impact jarred his ribs and his shoulder and he let out a gasp of pain.

There was a long corridor with plywood walls lining both sides. The hallway ran the entire length of the house. There were several heavy metal doors with padlocks on each side. About four total. It looked like maybe four separate rooms.

"What is this place?" Jack whispered to himself. The hairs on the back of his neck stood up as he slowly made his way down the corridor. There was a strong smell of bleach in the air. Beneath the bleach, there was another smell. It reminded Jack of a hospital or morgue. It was the smell of death, masked by bleach. He shivered.

"Mr. Everett!" Jack called. His voice did not carry far. He glanced at the ceiling, and saw it was heavily insulated, sound-proofed. He called out again, but there was no answer.

Instead, about halfway up the plywood corridor, there was a thumping noise. Like someone pounding on one of the doors with a flat palm. It was frantic.

Jack cautiously walked forward, until he was next to the pad-locked door with the thumping. He rapped his knuckles against the door.

"Hello?"

A muffled voice came from behind the door. It sounded like a woman's voice. It sounded like she was yelling "Help!"

"Stand back!" Jack yelled. He pointed his gun at the padlock and fired. The lock broke open. He ripped the lock off and threw back the latch to open the door. It was dark inside. There was a light switch outside the room mounted to the plywood wall. He flipped the switch and a single overhead bulb came on in the room.

"Oh my God."

Phelps was facing away from the door when they came in. It hurt to turn his head, so he swiveled slowly.

"That was faster than I thought," Phelps said.

He never heard the gunshot.

"No! Wait!" Barry yelled. Two more shots rang out. He laid motionless on the floor.

"Where is he?" Parsons asked.

"Check the back," Parks said.

Riker Owens was lying on a mattress in the small room. His hands were cuffed, with a chain leading from the handcuffs back to the painted concrete wall. The chain was connected to an eyelet mounted right in the concrete cellar wall. Riker was stretched out as far as he could across the mattress. His hands were above his head, straining to a bright pink against the cuffs and pulling the chain taught. He was just barely able to slap his foot against the door.

Jack rushed over and tried to loose the restraints.

"It's okay. You're safe now," Jack said. Riker started crying.

Jack pulled him up into a sitting position and put his arm around him. He was wearing, what looked like, a nightshirt, or maybe just an oversized shirt. His legs were bare. "You're okay buddy. I'm taking you home."

Just then, gunshots sounded from above. They were muffled from all the sound-proofing, but Jack still recognized them for what they were. He had Riker stand up. Jack ripped the mattress off the floor and covered Riker with it as best as possible. There was a steel eyelet, cemented into place, that held the chain to Riker's cuffs. Jack fired at it, blasting away some of the concrete. The room filled with concrete dust and the smoke from the gunpowder. The steel eyelet loosened, but didn't come free. He fired again. It loosened more. He grabbed the chain and worked the eyelet back and forth. It gave a little. He put his foot against the wall and ripped at it with all of his strength. His ribs shot lightning bolts of pain through his body, and his shoulder felt like it was going to rip clean off. It was nearly eight inches long, and still had chunks of concrete attached, when it pulled free.

Jack looked at the handcuffs. They looked like standard cuffs, but he didn't have a key. Phelps might.

"We're going to have to wait to get these off. Can you carry the chain for now?"

Riker nodded.

"Can you walk?"

Another nod.

"Okay, stay behind me. We're getting you out of here."

Riker looped the chain up and over his shoulder so it wouldn't drag and make noise.

Parks and Parsons heard the shots shortly after their own. It caused them to freeze for a moment. The gunshots were muffled and came from below. They spread out in the house, carefully avoiding the bloody trail in the hallway. They saw the splintered bedroom door. Saw the open trapdoor in the bedroom floor. Saw the shotgun on the floor with the jammed cartridge.

"What's going on?" Parsons asked.

"I don't know. Let's find him, kill him, and get the hell out of here," Parks said.

"Okay," Jack said, he stuck his head out of the room and checked both directions. He moved out with his back to the stairs, aiming his pistol down the corridor he had yet to explore. "It's clear. Up the stairs, quickly."

Riker hustled as best he could, while carrying the chain. He moved down the hallway but stopped short at the base of the steps. He looked up and froze. He backed away.

Jack motioned for him to go up the steps. Riker shook his head.

"What's wrong?" Jack mouthed.

"There's someone up there," Riker said in a whisper. "They have guns."

Jack pushed Riker back and craned his neck to look up into the bedroom. A shadow fell across the opening. He moved back into the corridor. If it was his back up, they'd be calling out. Whoever it was, they weren't calling out, they were trying to be quiet, they were hunting. He had a sick feeling in his stomach.

"Go," he whispered to Riker, indicating he move back down the corridor. Maybe Barry had overtaken Phelps and stolen his gun. Maybe Everett had circled back around and Phelps got him. Or maybe Everett got Phelps. If that was the case, it meant there was another exit. There was no more sound coming from above them. He feared the worst for Phelps.

At the end of the plywood corridor, there was a left turn. Jack carefully took the corner, gun out ahead of him. Another ten feet of corridor and there were stairs up to another trapped door. It was open.

They heard a motor start in the garage and the garage door opening. They both ran down the hallway, tracking through the blood as they lost all level of caution. Parks slipped in the blood and crashed to the floor, yelping in pain as he hit his damaged arm.

They bolted through the dining room and then the kitchen. A door led from the kitchen out to the garage. They ripped it open and saw the car backing out of the garage even as the door was still going up. They opened fire on the car. Unloading their handguns on it. The windshield exploded in spiderwebs of shattered glass. Bullets ripped into the hood and grill and headlights. The car continued rolling out of the garage, but lazily, as if it were just idling. It rolled backwards into the detective's car.

Both were about to reload with another clip when they heard him from behind.

"Freeze!" Jack yelled. "Drop the guns now!"

He was slowly climbing the stairs, his gun leveled at them. He didn't recognize who they were, but they obviously were not cops. Not the way they were dressed. Not the way they opened fire on Everett's car like that without yelling a warning.

"Drop them, now!"

They looked at each other, then ran in opposite directions. One back through the kitchen door, the other straight out through the open garage. Jack fired. Two quick shots caught the guy heading out the garage square in the back and dropped him to the ground. Jack kept his gun on him, but he didn't move again.

"Stay here," Jack said to Riker. He then paused a moment and fished his phone out from his pocket. "Call 9-1-1. Tell them everything."

Jack left Riker on the steps in the garage and cautiously walked into the house. He mentally took note of how many cartridges he had remaining in his pistol. Two downstairs to free Riker.

No, three total. There was the first one on the lock to get into Riker's cell. Then two to drop the bad guy. That was five spent rounds from his 9mm Glock 19. It was his conceal carry weapon. He'd grabbed it because it was small and fit well in the holster on the back of his pants. Sixteen minus five was eleven. He hadn't bothered to grab a backup clip. If he was still in uniform, he'd have one on his belt. Instead, he had only eleven rounds. Under normal circumstances that would have been plenty, but these were not normal circumstances.

There were bloody footprints leading back through the kitchen, through the living room, over Phelps' body, and out the front door. Jack stopped to check on Phelps. There was no pulse. He used every foul word he knew.

Jack followed the tracks out the front door to see the perpetrator throw his car in reverse and back onto the lawn. He spun his tires, ripping up grass and mud, as he sped towards the driveway. Jack emptied his pistol into the back of the car, all eleven rounds. But it continued down the driveway. He could hear the squeal of tires as the car made it out onto the road and raced away.

He ran back into the garage from the front lawn and found Riker on the garage steps, talking to the 911 operator. He took the phone from Riker.

"This is Jack McMurphy, uh, former chief of Coopers Hollow. We have an officer down and at least three other casualties on location." He gave the operator the address.

She repeated all of the information back to him. She asked him to stay on the line, but he told her he had to make a call.

Eric was sitting on the couch, with the television on. He had a beer in his hand. On the couch next to him was a picture album. Yasmine was at his mother's house. He wanted some time alone.

The phone rang. He looked at the number. It was Jack. He

thought about not answering. Thought about letting it go to voicemail. It rang two more times before he pressed his thumb on the green button, to answer.

"Hello?" he said. His voice beleaguered.

"Dad?"

Chapter 58

Jack took Riker out to Detective Phelps' car. He sat him in the back and left him with the phone. Already, the sounds of sirens from the fire department and ambulance were echoing up the hill from the valley. Jack ran into the house to Phelps. There was no helping him. He'd taken a shot to the back of the head. He was gone. The kid, Barry, had been shot twice, but was somehow still breathing. Jack ran to the bathroom and grabbed a towel and put it on the wounds, applying pressure to help stem the bleeding.

"Can you hear me kid?"

Barry just groaned and blood dribbled from his lips.

Jack heard the sirens getting closer, and the tires on the gravel driveway.

"Hold tight," he said. "Don't go dying."

He ran out into the front lawn and motioned for the ambulance crew.

"Gunshot victim inside!" he yelled. "He's still breathing, but he needs assistance now!"

The ambulance team grabbed their bags and hustled inside.

"Oh my god," one of them exclaimed.

Jack followed them in. They pulled the towel off Barry and used some clotting powder to help stop the bleeding.

Jack knelt beside Phelps and placed his hand on the man.

"I'm sorry, buddy," he said. He took a moment to fish through Phelps' pocket and retrieve his keys. There was a handcuff key on the ring.

"You guys okay?" Jack asked.

"Yeah, we need to get him mobile quickly," one of the EMTs said. "He's going to bleed out on us."

Jack walked back out the front door, as two more first responders pulled up. He directed them onto the lawn, so as not to block the ambulance. They rushed inside with their bags.

Jack walked over to Phelps' car and opened the back door. Riker was still on the phone, and was crying.

"I'm sorry I had to leave you, buddy. Let me see those hands." Jack unlocked the cuffs and tossed them to the floor. He rubbed Riker's wrists gently. "Let me see if I can get you and ice pack for them."

He got one out of the back of the ambulance, just as the first responders came out to grab the stretcher. They rushed past him back into the house. Jack took the icepack to Riker, and then went to check on the Lincoln Town Car that was still running, sitting tail to nose against Phelps' car.

Inside, William Everett was slumped over in the seat. He had several wounds to his head and chest. He was obviously dead. There was a pistol on the seat beside him.

Jack reached in and put the car in park and turned off the engine. He left the keys in the ignition. He then walked over to the man laying on the driveway.

The man was half on the concrete pad, leading into the garage, and half on the gravel. He'd dropped his gun when Jack had shot him, and it lay a few feet from his body. Jack bent down and checked for a pulse, but there wasn't one. He'd hit the guy square in the back. One in the spine, one through the heart. He was as good as dead before he hit the ground.

Jack went through his pockets for a wallet, and found the FBI ID. He swallowed hard, wondering if he'd just shot another agent. He looked at the name. Parks.

That was the name of one of the guys who had shot Tricia

and Michael. He was sure of it.

New chief of police, Patterson roared onto the scene in Jack's old SUV. He came out of the vehicle with his gun drawn.

"Take it easy, Patterson," Jack said. "The shooting is over."

"What is going on here?"

"To tell you the truth, I'm trying to piece it together myself," Jack said. "Detective Phelps and I were investigating the body that was found a few weeks back, up on Hollow Pointe. We came here to question Mr. Everett when all hell broke loose. Phelps was killed." He sighed heavily. His hands were shaking. He was in shock.

"Why were you investigating anything?" Patterson asked. "You're done."

"Phelps asked for my assistance."

"And now he's dead," Patterson said. "Where is he?"

"Inside." Jack leaned against the front fender of Phelps' car.

Just then, the ambulance team brought Barry the gardner out on the stretcher, rushing him to the back doors of their vehicle. They pushed the stretcher in and locked it into place. Then they closed up and headed down the driveway, with sirens blaring.

"My God, Jack. Is there anything you haven't screwed up?" Patterson said as he went inside the house.

Chapter 59

There were three of them in the rental vehicle. They had stopped off at a contact, south of Albany. The contact was a firearms dealer, located just to the west of Catskill, NY, in the mountains. He had a legitimate retail location along with a firing range. He also had a hidden armory beneath his garage, where he kept the weapons for a more exclusive clientele.

After they loaded up on weapons, they took Route 23 into Coopers Hollow. As they rolled into town, they realized the hit was not going to happen that day.

Denver was in the passenger seat, Hammond was behind the wheel. Brinkman was in the back seat. The guns were in the trunk. All of them were suddenly jealous of Rook, who had split for Brazil.

"I don't like this," Hammond said.

"Just drive slowly, don't get pulled over," Denver said. His arm was still in a cast, after Jack had broken it against the steel door, in Vegas. "What is this, a cop convention?"

"The other team," Brinkman said. "They must have screwed up. Either caught in the act, or didn't leave it like an accident."

"Idiots," Denver spat.

"What now?" Hammond asked. Three New York State Trooper vehicles were parked along the street in front of the Coopers Hollow Police Department.

"We get a hotel and wait it out."

"Where?"

"Closest town with a hotel. Doesn't matter. Just make sure it has a bar," Denver said. Brinkman was on his smart phone in the back seat. He was thumbing through their options.

"Head east on twenty-three," he said. "Best choice is in Oneonta."

"How is he?"

"I don't know if he'll ever be okay," Jack said. He was sitting in the hospital with Michael Cooke. Gloria was out of the room for the moment. She said she didn't want to hear about what had happened, so she excused herself.

"Poor kid," Michael said. "Lost his mom and then this."

"I know," Jack said. "I talked to his dad. He wanted to know if I killed the guy that did it. Doesn't matter. One's dead, the other is in ICU. May not make it out. They got what they deserved."

"Jack, you're one lucky SOB. You know that right?"

"How come I don't feel that way?" he replied.

Michael nodded. The television was showing sports highlights for the third time that morning. But for the moment, it held the attention of both of them.

"What now?" Michael asked.

"I don't know," Jack sighed. "I don't think they're ever going to stop. What Paula found, what we saw, there's no way to un-see it. I don't think they're going to stop, until I'm dead. Those two guys, they came back. Came back to finish the job. There will be more."

"Maybe," Michael said. "Or maybe its done now."

"I don't think so. I don't think it will ever be done. Not until I'm dead," Jack said.

"You could leave. Disappear. Nothing keeping you here any-more, is there?" Michael asked, growing quiet. He looked at Jack, who was staring absently at the television.

"I'd miss you, though," Michael said.

"What do the doctors say, about, you know?" Jack indicated Michael's legs, trying to change the subject.

"I can move them okay, they just go numb on me," Michael said. He moved his legs under the blankets, but winced as he did so. "My back still hurts like a mother, though."

"When do you start physical therapy?"

"Next week. They want to make sure there are no clots and all. I'm on these blood thinners, besides the pain killers. The sweet, sweet pain killers," Michael said, with a laugh.

They watched the highlights until they started repeating for a fourth time. Then Jack excused himself from the room.

"Rest up," Jack said.

"Okay, see you soon," Michael said. "And Jack."

"Yeah?"

"Don't do anything stupid, partner."

"No promises. Get better."

He met Gloria as she was coming out of the elevator with a cup of coffee, from the cafe downstairs.

"Jack," she started. She wanted to say something else, but no words came out.

"I know," Jack said. He put his hand on her arm as he stepped into the elevator. "I'm sorry too."

He was walking out of the hospital lobby, when he stopped and did a double take. He'd just seen someone he knew. He turned and looked back at the elevators and caught a glimpse of a man in shades and a ball cap. His fatigued mind raced through the catalog of names and faces in his memory. It didn't take long.

It was Eric Owens. He had a bouquet of flowers in his hands.

"That's strange," Jack said. Owens had walked right past him and didn't say a word. If anything, he'd tried not to be noticed.

Jack walked back towards the elevators and watched the numbers on the panel, above the doors, count up to three and then stop. He looked at the list of floors beside the elevator to see what was on the third floor.

Intensive Care Unit.

Jack didn't wait for the elevators, he bolted through the door to the left that led to the stairs. He launched himself up the stairs two at a time. Three floors in only a few seconds. His heart was pounding in his chest and sweat was breaking out across his brow.

He burst through the third floor door and looked both ways. No Eric Owens. The sign on the wall indicated ICU was to the left. He ran down the hallway and saw the man in the ball cap with the flowers.

"Eric!" he yelled.

A nurse who was walking by shushed him.

Eric Owens froze and looked back down the hallway. He looked like he wanted to run, but he didn't. He stood there and waited for Jack to run up to him.

"Go away, Jack."

"What are you doing here?"

"Go away," he repeated.

"Let's go get a coffee downstairs and talk," Jack said, gasping for air. Eric was dressed in an oversized flannel shirt. It was untucked, with tails falling below his crotch. There was a bulge at his waistband.

"You know," Jack said, quietly. "Just carrying that thing in here can get you arrested."

"What they did to my little boy," Eric said. "They don't deserve to live." He was sweating profusely. Jack couldn't be sure, because of the sunglasses, but some of the sweat may have been tears streaming down.

"It's not how things are done," Jack said. "Listen to me. You do this, and you may go away for a long time. Riker doesn't need that. He needs you. You're taking that job in New Orleans and you're leaving this place behind, along with all the memories."

"I want him dead," Eric said. "He deserves it."

"I can't disagree with you. But Riker needs his dad more than he needs that piece of garbage in there dead and in the ground," Jack said. He reached out and put his hand on Eric's arm. "Let's go."

Eric resisted for a moment, and then relented. He let Jack steer him back towards the bank of elevators.

Chapter 60

Mr. William Everett was killed behind the wheel of his car, by two career criminals, who had ties to drug dealers out of New York City. The FBI handled the investigation. They found it to be a planned attack against Jack, in an attempt to get even for the death of El Tigre from the previous fall. At least that's what they claimed. They also pinned Detective Phelps' and Barry Diggard's deaths on them as well. Barry had died in the hospital, later in the afternoon, after Jack had talked Eric out of shooting him. It may not have felt the same to Eric, but dead was dead.

After their interview with Jack and the autopsy they found that Phelps would have survived the shotgun hit, but the bullet to the back of his head killed him. Special Agent Adekoya made sure he told Jack that detail. He seemed to take a perverse pleasure in turning the screws on McMurphy at every opportunity.

Those were the official findings. There was no mention of a video or civil rights leader Gordon Jefferson. Jack didn't bring it up, and neither did anyone else.

What was mentioned was the massive collection of self-penned books and photos that outlined Mr. Everett's evil. He had chronicled his exploitation of at least seventy young men and boys over the course of four decades. Many of the passages described a number of bodies buried in the forest around his home. He even had a map.

The investigators tended to believe what they read in the journals, as the last entries mentioned the young runaway from Scranton, PA. There was a detailed description of how Mr. Everett and his garnder, Barry, had trolled New York City, looking for a victim. They'd picked up Timothy Pierson, promising him a fun weekend, in exchange for drugs and money. There were drugs, alright. They drugged him and kept him in the plywood cell, under the house, for two weeks. The journal went into great detail about those two weeks. It also described how Pierson had escaped, slipping from his restraints, somehow, and bursting out of the door when Barry had brought him his dinner. Notably, at the end of Pierson's entry, Everett had written: "I think I may be in trouble with this one."

Because of the scope of the case, and the fact that some of the individuals in the books were from across state lines, the FBI took over the entire investigation, as well. Two concurrent investigations took place in Coopers Hollow, over the course of three weeks.

One of the first things they did in the Everett investigation, was acquire a court order putting a halt to any of John Anakausuen's construction. This ensured that the area around Everett's house would remain untouched until fully investigated. It also meant that the top of Hollow Pointe was closed to any visitors as well. They broadened their scope to include Mount Pratt as well, just to be safe. The whole mountain ridge was a crime scene, as far as the FBI was concerned.

The investigations stretched on until the first days of May. The flowers and trees were in full bloom, and the town was putting itself back together. True to his word, the Governor released disaster funds to help with the reconstruction. Things slowly began to return to normal. But they would never actually, ever be normal again.

The enormity of the evil that was William Everett left a cloud over the town. It was a blight that couldn't be shaken. For decades, parents had been wary of the man, warning their children away. There were rumors over the years, but no one followed up. Nobody paid attention to the wickedness that resided right there amongst them.

The entire McMurphy family had failed the town.

Jack sank deeper.

Chapter 61

They spent three weeks in the same hotel that Parks and Parsons had stayed in, while they were stalking Jack McMurphy and his wife. There was one moment of panic, when the FBI came to the hotel to investigate the rooms that Parks and Parsons had rented. Apparently, a hotel key card was found in Parks' pocket. Denver, with his broken arm in a sling, went down to the lobby and casually asked the girl at the front desk what was going on. She told him what the FBI agents told her. He returned to his room and filled in the other two conspirators.

Parsons was found on the side of the road twenty miles to the west, dead behind the wheel. Two of Jack's shots had hit him, as he sped away from the crime scene, at William Everett's house. He must have lost consciousness and eventually bled out, as the car came to a stop against the guardrail, still in gear.

The three of them didn't shed a tear. It was part of the risks that came with the job. They continued to lay low, waiting for an opportunity.

They ventured out into the city of Oneonta, to pass the time. Sometimes together, sometimes on their own. The hotel was only a few hundred yards from a bowling alley, but Denver wasn't going bowling with his arm, and the other two had no interest. The city had two colleges, so there were plenty of bars, but they weren't any better than the one right there in the hotel. The city also had a small mall, with a theater and a bookstore and all the other mall-related shops. There were multiple restaurants, and even a strip club. But the distractions weren't enough. Three weeks seemed like an eternity.

About every other day, Denver would drive the twenty-plus

miles to Coopers Hollow to check on the heat in town. For three weeks it was too hot.

And then it wasn't.

"We're going tomorrow," Denver said. They were sitting in the hotel bar. It was karaoke night. Several drunk college students were on stage belting out an N'Sync song. They thought themselves hilariously ironic.

"You sure?" Hammond asked.

"You want to stay here another night?"

"If it means doing it right."

"We'll do it right."

"Things have calmed down?" Hammond asked, sitting back in his chair and turning his attention to the stage as another group of college students took their turn with the microphone. He sipped at a beer.

"It's back to normal," Denver said.

"Why wait until tomorrow?" Hammond asked.

"No reason," Denver replied.

"Why not tonight?" Brinkman asked.

"Well, boys, I'm game if you are," Denver said, finishing the last swallow of his beer. "We go tonight."

"It has to look like an accident or suicide," Brinkman reminded. "What's your plan?"

"We go up, knock on his door, invite ourselves in, then beat him to within an inch of his life."

"Sounds like an accident or suicide to me," Brinkman said.

"Then we dump him off that cliff in town," Denver said. "But I'm breaking both of his arms before we do."

Chapter 62

Jack sat at his dining room table with two bottles of alcohol a Bible and a gun.

He had to laugh. It sounded like the start of a bad joke. It was more like the end of a bad joke. Everything he knew and loved had been taken away from him. He lost his father, his wife, his job and his town. Gone. No getting them back. And why? Because he'd tried to do the right thing.

The icing on the cake was when a somber Special Agent Adekoya came knocking earlier in the day. He held in his hand a small plastic plug. He had asked Jack if he knew what it was. He didn't.

"This was found plugged into your wife's Mercedes, under the dashboard," he said. "It's a remote transmitter. It is paired with a computer and software found in a car a few miles to the west of here, a day after the shoot out at William Everett's house. It was with the man who fled."

"I don't understand," Jack had said.

"We think the two men who tried to kill you, controlled the Mercedes remotely. We believe they drove it into the water. We believe they were trying to stage a deadly accident," Adekoya said, quietly. "They were only partially successful. I'm sorry."

That revelation had made Jack's world spin. He'd replayed those last moments over and over again. He couldn't figure out how Paula had accidentally driven into the water. It didn't make sense, how the vehicle could possibly malfunction right at that moment. He'd believed that she must have made a mistake, she must have done something wrong. He felt horrible for believing it, even for a short time.

Knowing the truth didn't make anything better. Yes he'd killed the men who had been responsible for Paula's death. But he didn't know that at the time. And it didn't bring her back. It just left him more empty than ever.

He ran his hand over the gun on the table. It was different than the Glock 19 he had used at the Everett house. That gun was now in the possession of the FBI. He'd never see it again. This was his father's revolver. A good, old, Smith & Wesson .38 Special. It would do what it had to, tonight.

It was late. Maybe midnight. He had lost track of time. The only light on in the house, came from the hood lamp, over the stove. Heavy shadows played across the table. The shadow of the gun stretched nearly ten inches. It made it seem far more ominous. The shadow from the bottle of whiskey fell off the table. He opened it, but didn't pour any into the glass. He tipped it over, and watched the conents drain off the table, and onto the floor.

Also on the table was another bottle of alcohol. It had arrived by mail from Las Vegas, two days after Paula had died in the flood. It was a bottle of Frankie Moreno vodka, purchased by Paula before she had flown back to New York. She'd written a note and strung it around the bottleneck.

"Oh, what could have been," she wrote. "Maybe next time. Love you, my husband."

He knew that she had been talking about their prematurely shortened trip to Vegas. But it felt like her words were reaching out to him, from beyond the grave. They stabbed at his heart.

He picked up the gun and hefted it in his hand. This would be the last night he would hold a gun.

The Bible on the table had been a gift from Tubby. The big man had grabbed him and given him a big bear hug when he had come to his house, along with Mr. Crandall, to see how Jack was doing. It caught Jack off guard. Then they talked. Tubby gave him the Bible and told him not to give up. Jack told him he wouldn't. But even though he was holding the Bible at the time, he was lying.

They had talked for a while and Jack informed him that his great-grandfather had been murdered by Mr. Everett, decades earlier. Tubby didn't say much about that. He was very happy, however, to find out that he would be allowed to talk with Riker again. Eric Owens had decided that if Riker wanted to be friends with Tubby, it was okay with him. Eric figured they were only going to be in town for a short time anyway. With all that the poor kid had been through, his father might as well make him at least a little happy.

Tubby repeated that Jack not give up.

Jack lied again.

He had already given up.

He knew what he was up against. He knew that they would never stop. He also knew that the FBI, or any other government agency, for that matter, didn't seem in too much of a rush to stop Gordon Jefferson. And as long as that man was around, and as long as he thought Jack was alive, it would never end.

History had a way of repeating itself. Tubby's great-grandfather had gone through the same thing. Jack found old Chief McIntyre's notebook in Paula's bag, recovered from the Mercedes. It had been zipped in, and was relatively protected from the floodwaters. He knew what it was, as soon as he'd found it. He let it dry for a couple of days before attempting to leaf through it. He understood why Paula was so fascinated. The notations about the attacks. Their relentless nature. Had it not been for the revelation from William Everett's own writings, the world would have always believed that the mafia had finally gotten old Chief McIntyre.

Jack wasn't sure if he liked knowing the sordid truth.

He did know that if he didn't do something, the same thing would happen to him and the town all over again. They wouldn't stop coming after him. An endless loop of violence. Inside, he felt empty, hollow, and numb. He'd reached the point where there was nothing left for him here. Nothing.

The Bible was open to Psalm 34. It was a passage Mr. Crandall had shared with him when he and Tubby had visited. Jack read it one more time, then put his hand on the Bible and said a prayer. He hoped God would forgive him for everything that had happened and all that he was about to do.

As they drove closer to the house, they realized something wasn't right. Thick smoke was rising from the structure, and they could see the flames inside, through the windows.

"Did somebody beat us to it?" Brinkman asked.

"I think," Denver said, with uncertainty. "He went ahead and killed himself."

"You kidding me?" Holland said from the back seat of the car.

All three of them stared out the windshield with incredulity.

"Maybe he faked it," Brinkman said.

Denver let out a sigh. He knew what Brinkman meant. They had to wait, to make sure McMurphy was really dead, before they could call the job done. He put the car in reverse, performed a three-point-turn in the road, and headed back the way they came. They drove to Oneonta to rebook their rooms at the hotel with the bar.

McMurphy's closest neighbor was a half mile away. If it wasn't for their dogs barking, they wouldn't have gotten up to see the orange sky over the trees, in the middle of the night. They called the fire department immediately.

By the time the firetrucks arrived, it was too late to save the structure. The flames were fifty feet in the air. All they could do was try to contain the fire by dousing the trees and brush around the house. It took almost three hours for the fire to be reduced to a smoldering heap. They could see that a car was still in the garage, and a rental was in the driveway, the front end scorched from the heat of the flames.

Goldie Bristol knew that the two cars were the only ones Jack owned. She also knew what they were going to find. It took two days for the structure to cool enough to let the investigators start digging.

Jack's remains were found in, what had been, the dining room. There was a broken bottle of whiskey and one of vodka and Jack's father's revolver. The revolver was loaded, except for one spent round. The fire had burned so hot that the revolver barrel warped substantially. There was nothing left of Jack's body. No bones, just his watch and ring, which Goldie identified.

She fought the state investigators over the cause of the blaze, trying to get them to declare it an accident. But in the end, they declared it arson, and part of Jack's suicide. There was never a note that anyone knew of. But one wasn't really necessary. Everybody knew why he'd done it. And nobody blamed him.

The day of his funeral, police officers from the State Troopers and the Sheriff's department, as well as the Coopers Hollow police department all came to pay their respects. There were at least fifty officers at the service.

Agent Haas was in the back during the service. He'd driven up from D.C. for the day. It was his vacation, he'd spend it how he wanted to. Three other individuals were there too. Haas recognized them all. He walked over and talked with Chief Patterson, who, in turn, spoke with the State Troopers and Sheriff.

Before the conclusion of the service, a dozen officers surrounded Denver, Brinkman and Hammond and escorted them out to waiting patrol cars. Each of them was carrying a gun. Since the service was being held in the Coopers Hollow High School gymnasium, and since it was illegal to carry a firearm onto school property in the State of New York, each of them would be going to jail for awhile. There was no way a local judge would let them walk. Not after what the town had been through. Not after Agent Haas made sure that the information about the charges in Las Vegas made its way to the county prosecutor.

They'd go away for the maximum penalty of four years, for the Class E Felony. Not long enough in Haas' estimation, but you took what you could get.

Days later, in an office building, back in Washington D.C., Scutter sat at his desk, reading a file. Agent Haas was sitting on the other side of the desk, waiting for his boss to finish. After a moment more of reading, Scutter closed the file and set it on the desk.

"What's your conclusion?" Scutter asked.

"I think he faked his death," Haas said. "I think he knew it was the only way out. They weren't going to stop until he was dead. Eventually his luck was going to run out. Heck, I think the three guys we picked up at the funeral were heading his way. He beat them to it."

"What evidence makes you say that?"

"Fire was too hot. Too concentrated on where the body supposedly was. The bottles, the gun, the watch, the ring. All conveniently placed. It looked staged. I've seen enough staged suicides in my time. I'm not even sure if there was a body. But the report is the report, and there's what's official and there's what my instincts tell me," Haas said.

"So you think he's still alive?"

"I'm not putting that in the report."

"Do you think, based on what you know about him, that he'll make the video public?" Scutter asked.

"I don't think so. I think he knows that if he does that, they'll know he's still alive," Haas said. "If I had to guess, I'd say he's headed south. Or maybe out of the country. Someplace completely different from the Catskills, if I had to put money on it. Of course I could be wrong. He could have swallowed some whiskey, lit the house on fire and swallowed a bullet as a chaser. It could be his ashes they scooped up and buried after all."

There was silence for a moment. Scutter looked out the window. The sun was falling in the sky. It was well after five, so traffic was insane on the beltway and beyond. He would be working for another few hours before heading home to his family. Then he'd have his customary dinner and drink, watch some television and go to sleep. He never lost sleep over people like McMurphy, or Phelps or any of the other small time people who lost their lives on any given day. He was worried about the big picture. The investigation into the Secretary of State was moving along, based on intel from his new friend. The next time he needed information on a big name, he knew he could count on Gordon Jefferson, once again, to spill his guts, or the video would get leaked, ruining his multi-million dollar operation.

Scutter was back in the game. Mr. Shadow was alive and well.

"There's one thing I'm not sure about," Haas said. "How did Jefferson know about the video? Who tipped him off?"

"I had a freelancer I used from time to time. Guy by the name of Dimmler. He was in email contact with Agent Spaulding a few times. Spaulding had uploaded the data and sent him a link. Told him to forward it on, should anything ever happen to him. Dimmler watched it and decided to try to make himself some money by contacting Jefferson's people. Didn't exactly think it all the way through," Scutter said.

"Where's Dimmler now?" Haas asked, his jaw clenched.

"Uh, I believe he was in a car accident last week," Scutter said. "Traffic is brutal in D.C."

"What now?"

"Well, Agent Haas, this investigation is officially closed. Take the rest of the day off and report back tomorrow, for a new assignment," Scutter said. "Thanks for your work on this. And good job in Houston, too. A bit easier that one."

"That's it? What about Gordon Jefferson?"

"I said it's closed."

The truck drove slowly along the paved path, between the gravestones. It was easy to see which plot belonged to Jack McMurphy. There were more flowers on it than any other. Gloria put the truck in park.

"Do you want your chair?"

"I think I can manage with the crutches," Michael Cooke said. He opened the door, and lowered himself onto his legs, which had grown numb during the drive. He braced his arms against the crutches and slowly walked his way through the dew-moistened grass, to Jack's grave. It took him several minutes, but he walked it. He didn't have anyone push him around in a chair, like an invalid.

The message on the grave marker had the usual information of birth and death. It also read "Beloved Husband." Gloria had some influence on that. Beneath that were the words "To Serve and Protect."

"Goodbye, buddy," Michael said. "Until we meet again."

He stood for a long time looking at the grave. Next to Jack's grave, was Paula's. On the other side, were Jack's parents.

Michael hadn't brought flowers. He always thought it was a stupid tradition. Who was going to enjoy them? He'd wait and buy flowers for Gloria, instead.

Then he'd have a drink in honor of his friend, wherever he was.

Acknowledgments

There are people, along the way, who have encouraged me and my desire to continue writing professionally. Those kind words spur me on, each and every time. But none are as motivating as those from my wife, Belinda. There is no possible way I could complete a single manuscript page, without her support. During the writing of this novel, I lost both of my grandmothers, Josephine and Lillian. I wish both of them could be alive now to read this latest work, as each were so encouraging in their own ways, as I began my writing career.

About the Author

Adam Cornell was born in upstate New York but spent some of his life in Louisiana, which he considers his second home. He has written several books, including thrillers, middle-grade adventures, picture books and comics. Adam has worked on the air as a radio personality utilizing the name Adam Speed while in Baton Rouge and New Orleans, LA as well as Elmira, NY. He has also made a career in the field of graphic design, working at several ad agencies and companies in the printing, housewares and automotive industries. Adam currently lives with his wife and three children in Watertown, NY, where he hosts the morning radio show on Tunes 92.5.

Follow Adam on Twitter: @AdamintheAM

THE
CATSKILLS
FEATURES A PREVIEW OF THE SEQUEL *HOLLOW POINTE!*

ADAM CORNELL
REVISED EDITION WITH AUTHOR'S SKETCHES
PREVIOUSLY RELEASED UNDER THE PEN NAME ADAM SPEED

Also Available from
Jade, Hudson & Steele Publishing

www.ingramcontent.com/pod-product-compliance
Lightning Source LLC
Chambersburg PA
CBHW060240030726
47493CB00024B/1437